# DEATH'S DETECTIVE

## THE MALYKANT MYSTERIES

### VOLUME I

# CHARLOTTE E. ENGLISH

# CONTENTS

# THE
# ROSTIKOV
# LEGACY

# 1

The Bone Forest at night is a dangerous place to be. The ground is marshy, spread with silent pools of water waiting to catch the steps of the unwary. A permanent fog shrouds the air in the colder months; in winter little can be seen of the landscape save the twisted trees looming out of the dark, their branches reaching into the sky like stripped bones.

Once in a while, though, the moon shines briefly from between layers of heavy black cloud and the mists gleam bone-white in response. And even more rarely, a flicker of ghostly white near the black earthen ground begs to catch the eye: a glimpse of a marsh spectre, so easy to miss.

The marsh spectre is not, as might be inferred, a spirit but in fact a flower. It grows in only the wettest of marshes; were its delicate petals to dry out it would crumble and fade into the wind like a wraith.

It crouches low to the ground, its foliage ash-grey veined with silver. It is rare. The conditions for its growth are specific; a particular temperature, a significant degree of moisture, not too much light. Without these it will never thrive and its coveted blossoms - only one per plant - will never appear.

On one particular frosty night, few souls were abroad to witness the delicate white glow of the marsh spectre as it unfurled its petals. Coveted as it was, few could brave the dangers of the night-shrouded Bone Forest with impunity. Konrad Savast was one such, and as he navigated with care through the dripping fog a bright glow caught his eye, blazing briefly but powerfully in the grey forests that ringed the city of Ekamet. It was a light he recognised, for he had set out on this cold, wet night in search of this very blossom.

Swirling his long, dark coat out of the way of his legs, he was on his knees in an instant, heedless of the ice-touched, waterlogged mud staining the thick fabric of his trousers.

But he was not the first. He swore at finding himself too late; too late to prevent this most virulent of poisons from being harvested, processed, sold and above all, used. The centre of the flower was gone; only a few petals remained.

Konrad sat back on his heels, disturbed. Whoever had harvested this particular specimen was not a professional poison master; the drooping, bruised state of the few surviving petals spoke of the rough lack of care with which the valuable parts of the flower had been removed.

When amateurs played at poison craft, the results were never good.

He closed his eyes and let his consciousness shift into the spirit-world. In his mind's eye the landscape drained further of colour, becoming a faded tableau in hazy white. He could see the wind streaming through the trees, feel the faint traces left by the passage of wraiths through the aether.

'Eetapi,' he murmured. 'Ootapi.'

An answering whisper touched his thoughts, and then a second close behind. Twin phantoms twined through his senses like a persistent cold wind, making him shiver.

*Yes, Malykant,* they both said together.

*Search the aether,* he told them silently. *Bring me news of the unquiet.*

His companions caught the ribbons of the wind and sailed away. He opened his eyes and watched them go, their long serpentine bodies fading into the mist. They had been brightly coloured in life, their beaded hides advertising their venomous natures in vivid purple and red. In death they were moon-pale, insubstantial and cold as winter.

Abandoning the broken marsh spectre, Konrad straightened and continued on, picking his way expertly through the sluggish pools of water that saturated the forest. He threaded through the hillocks of drier land that dotted the landscape, ignoring the steady trickle of dampness that ran off the brim of his hat and flowed down the waxed cloth of his coat. After some minutes his workshop materialised out of the fog, a wooden structure raised on stilts high above the stagnant water. A rope ladder served as the only means of entrance; he climbed up it to his trapdoor entrance and let himself in.

The pockets of his coat were stuffed with folded cloth packets. He drew these out one at a time, storing the fruits of his ramblings in the jars and boxes that crowded the shelves in his one room. Dark purple inkwort he had found in plentiful quantity, and sunbane and weak orange pepperroot. He'd even discovered a pocket of ashleaf sheltering on the lee side of one of the taller hillocks, hidden behind a mess of tall, prickly grass. Were it not for the loss of the marsh spectre, he would have considered it a fruitful day's work.

Harvest stored, Konrad shrugged out of his coat, stepped out of his tall boots and removed his hat. He flopped gratefully onto the rude and untidy bed, yawning. He had been walking all night and most of the day, covering many miles of the marsh in his search for the materials of his trade.

But he would not sleep yet. Not until the serpents brought him the news from the spirit lands.

He sensed their return as he framed this thought. They came billowing through his open door, bringing a renewed chill with them. He sensed agitation, some manner of disturbance in the normally placid minds of his familiars.

'Peace, Eetapi,' he said to soothe them. 'Ootapi. What have you discovered?'

*An unclean death*, a hissing voice replied. *One of your kind, Malykant.* He recognised the melodic tones of Eetapi, her voice like the tolling of funeral bells.

*We sense the displeasure of The Malykt*, added Ootapi, in a voice like splintering ice.

Konrad tensed. The Malykt was the spirit Overlord who presided over the transition from life to death, and incidentally he was also Konrad's master. Years ago now, The Malykt had made Konrad His chief servant, granting him the serpent-seers as his aides. As the Malykant, head of the Order of Death, Konrad's duties were clear.

That the Overlord was displeased by this particular death did not bode well. It meant that it was time for Konrad to go to work.

*Show me*, he instructed, and the serpents complied, seizing his mind and carrying it away, back out into the marsh. Along the aether

3

they sped, weaving through the ghostly trees, their essence mingling with the mist.

Less than a mile from Konrad's workshop a wide hillock rose out of the fog like a barrow, and here they stopped. The patch of ground was dry and largely bare of trees, clothed in short, half-frozen grass. Atop it lay the corpse, shreds of its soul still lingering at the scene of death. Konrad sensed the Malykt: the Spirit Lord had been here, drawn by the dank and acrid aura of defilement that polluted the air.

An unclean death indeed. Konrad felt The Malykt's anger and shuddered under it.

As he took note of these details Konrad was distantly aware that his body followed where his mind had already gone, drawn inexorably through the trees until consciousness and physical form merged at the splayed feet of the corpse. He stood motionless for a moment as his mind and body merged once more, waiting until the dizziness faded away. When he felt stable, he opened his eyes.

The corpse was a woman, and a young one, perhaps in her twenties. Her dark hair was decorated with jewels and she wore a fine gown. A knife was buried in her torso, a small weapon with a plain handle. But her blue tongue and blackened face told him that the stab wound had not killed her.

Poison, he judged, and he could guess which: marsh spectre. A blade coated in that sticky substance would have killed her within five, maybe ten minutes. That was far too long a time to suffer the vicious pain that this type of poison inflicted.

Konrad frowned and crouched by the woman's side. Agony had distorted her features, but he recognised her. She had been a prominent figure in the city of Ekamet, owning a fine house in the centre and much property besides. She had also been a popular society hostess.

His frown deepened. What had Lady Navdina Rostikova been doing out in the Bones? Wearing her finery, no less, and as far as he could tell not a jewel was missing.

'Eetapi,' he whispered. 'Ootapi. Bind her.'

They did as he ordered, collecting the flickering shreds of her spirit and binding them together. There was not much of her soul left; most had already fled into the Deathlands. He would be lucky to get anything out of her at all.

The Serpent Seers dived into the corpse, dragging the sundered and shredded soul with them. The corpse choked, racked with violent shivers. Then Lady Rostikova's eyes opened and stared blankly at the sky.

'Speak,' he commanded.

'Rostikova,' the corpse gasped. 'I am Lady Rostikova.'

'I am aware of your name. Who killed you?'

'Rostikova,' the corpse repeated. '*I* am Lady Rostikova.'

'That has been established. I ask the name of your killer.'

The corpse shuddered and said nothing.

'Very well. Why were you here?'

'I was meeting…' The dead eyes blinked. 'Rostikova,' it said again. 'I am Lady Rostikova.'

Konrad said nothing further. He was too late; her distressed spirit had already fled too far. She was too confused and disorientated to be of use.

'It *hurts*,' the corpse gasped, shivering more violently than ever.

'Release her,' he ordered. The serpent-shades streamed out of her and the corpse collapsed back into inanimate silence, its borrowed breath escaping in a long sigh. Lady Rostikova's spirit frayed into ribbons and melted away.

Recognising his duty, Konrad bowed his head.

'I am in the service of The Malykt,' he said to the wind. 'I do his bidding with respect and honour for the dead.' He clasped his bone talisman as he spoke, protecting himself from the malignant influence of unquiet souls.

Then he drew a long and wickedly sharp knife from his boot. Kneeling by the side of the corpse, he laid his blade to her torso and cut down. Layers of clothing parted and fell away, revealing her dead white skin. This too he carved through, cutting with strength and efficiency until he could see the wet gleam of her bones.

Another few moments were all he required. With practiced movements he extracted one of the largest of her rib bones, wrapped it in cloth and stored it in his coat. Later he would clean it and sharpen its ragged edges. Until he had found Lady Rostikova's killer, this piece of her body would remain with him at all times.

'For The Malykt's Justice,' he said to the still night air. A gust of wind howled in response, brief and unnatural and very, very cold.

2

Konrad went back to the city. He returned to his house discreetly, entering through a rear door that nobody else was permitted to use. He went straight to his dressing room and began the transformation from the Malykant, unkempt and smelling of the marsh, back into Konrad Savast, gentleman of Ekamet.

He bathed, taking care to scrub all of the blood and mud from his olive skin. He washed and styled his black hair, and anointed it with scent. He donned a fine linen shirt, a dark green silk waistcoat and black trousers. His best black coat went over the top, and lastly he covered his head with a tall top hat.

When his carriage came round to his door, no sign remained that Mr Konrad Savast had done anything with his day save enjoy the privileges of the wealthy.

A servant handed him his favourite silver-headed cane as he left the house. He found that it gave him an air of refinement and authority, and so he carried it with him everywhere, at least when he was in the city. Nobody had ever asked why the top was wrought into the shape of a serpent's head.

'To Rostikov House,' he directed his coachman as he got in.

The carriage drew up a short time later in front of a large, detached mansion, somewhat over decorated according to Konrad's taste, but he knew it was the fashion at present. As he had hoped, the house appeared quiet. Nobody yet knew of its mistress's fate. He stepped up to the front door and rapped smartly on it with his silver-headed cane.

'Her Ladyship is not at home,' said the butler on opening the door.

'That's all right,' he replied gravely. 'I'll wait.'

'Her Ladyship left strict instructions that no callers are to be admitted.' The butler started to close the door, but Konrad inserted his cane into the opening.

'I said I'll wait,' he repeated, and he allowed a little of the chill of the Bone Forest to enter his voice. He pushed his way into the house, shed his coat and handed it to the manservant.

'If you'd please to follow me, sir, I'll conduct you to the drawing-room,' said the butler, his tone frigid with disapproval.

'I prefer the study.' Konrad made his way there without awaiting a response. He'd attended enough parties at the Rostikov House to be able to find it himself.

'Shall you require any refreshment, sir?'

Konrad waved a hand in dismissal. 'Nothing, thank you. Just peace and quiet.'

The butler withdrew, his back stiff with offence. Konrad stood in the centre of the room and surveyed Navdina Rostikova's private study.

He knew that her husband had been a reading man, but apparently Navdina didn't share that interest, for very few books graced the shelves. Instead they were crammed with ornaments and trinkets, many of them expensive but most in poor taste. It was a wasted room, all space given over to the frivolous and vulgar instead of intellectual pursuits or business.

The desk, though, that was a more interesting prospect. The top was well-dusted and completely empty, but what of the contents? Konrad claimed the chair that sat before it and began opening drawers, quietly so as not to attract the notice of the servants whose footsteps he occasionally heard passing the door. Most contained nothing of interest: bills for household goods and invitations to parties. In one he found a stack of personal correspondence, and he devoted some minutes to perusing these, but found them useless; most were mere vapid notes discussing gossip and fashion and new gowns.

The bottom drawer was locked. Unconcerned, he touched icy fingers to the keyhole. Metal twisted and turned and the lock slid open. In a matter of seconds he had the drawer open and was browsing the contents.

In it lay a single note, worked in handwriting that matched none of the other letters he had found.

*There is but one way to settle this matter to my satisfaction. On new moon night, meet me at the South Gate at the tenth hour of the night. Do not think to bring an escort, for you will not need one.*

Konrad turned the note about in his hands, thinking. It bore no address or direction, so presumably it had been delivered by hand. Had Navdina been the intended recipient, or had she intercepted this note and entangled herself in someone else's business? Either possibility may have led to her demise.

He pocketed the note, closed the drawer and stood up. A search of the rest of the room revealed nothing of any further interest, only more tasteless, gilded ornaments. He waited until the hallway outside the study was quiet, then slipped out of the room.

His coat hung on the coat rack near the front door. He retrieved it, shrugged it on and left the house, quietly closing the front door behind him.

'Home, Aktso,' he said to his driver.

Once there, he went straight to his desk and composed a note of his own. He used plain block letters rather than his own handwriting, and he did not sign it. He wrote a single name on the front: Nuritov.

This note was marked URGENT and dispatched with all due haste to Ekamet's police office.

Konrad received the day's papers in bed the next morning, as was his custom. He read them at a leisurely pace, revelling in the comfort and luxury of a real bed after his three days and nights out in the Bone Forest. With his head cushioned by several pillows and a tray of hot chocolate and pastries at his elbow, he perused the primary headline of the day with considerable interest.

*A Mysterious Death*

*The popular society hostess Lady Rostikova was found dead last night. Her body was discovered more than a mile from the south gate, inside the treacherous marsh-ground of the Bone Forest. It is not known why her ladyship so far departed from her usual habits as to travel out into the Bones, a place wisely avoided by most good citizens of Ekamet.*

*The cause of death is reported to be a knife wound in her ladyship's torso. Her torso was also split open and a bone taken, a known sign that the mysterious figure known only as the Malykant has already attended the scene. The murderer or murderers had better look to themselves, for the justice of The Malykt is swift and absolute…*

Konrad was not surprised that the police investigation had missed the signs of poisoning, or missed their significance. But it was this element that most interested him. Properly positioned, the knife alone would have been sufficient to kill the victim; why use poison as well? And why choose such an agonising one? The method had been chosen to inflict a slower, painful death upon the Lady Rostikova. And that suggested that the crime was personal in nature.

But had Navdina been the intended victim, or had she taken the poison meant for someone else? He needed more information.

He glanced regretfully at his breakfast, only partially finished. He would like to enjoy his morning a little more thoroughly before he went out again, but The Malykt was an impatient master. *Swift and absolute,* indeed. Konrad would certainly ensure that the murderer's punishment was absolute, but the swiftness required a little more effort.

With a sigh, he folded up the paper, laid it aside, and threw back the covers.

3

What Konrad needed was informants. He hadn't known Navdina
well himself; he couldn't hazard any guesses as to her close associates.
But she had family. A second branch of Rostikovs resided within the
city of Ekamet: Amrav Rostikov was cousin to Navdina, and quite
newly married. Since the dead woman had no children, this cousin
would now inherit the title.

Konrad's analytical brain lost no time in noting that point as a
possible motive for the killing.

Amrav Rostikov was not a secretive man, and Konrad had no
difficulty gleaning all the relatively sparse information that was
available about him. The new lord had already been wealthy before
inheriting the Rostikov estate; that alone was interesting. If he had
been involved in his cousin's death, then, it had not been about
money. Was he the sort to value the title itself highly enough to kill
for it?

Even if he was, that did not explain the peculiar note found in
Navdina's desk. Konrad frowned as he stepped from his carriage into
the street outside the lesser Rostikov house, where Amrav still
resided until after his cousin's funeral. The matter was already too
complex; a simple explanation would not suffice.

He rapped on the door with his silver-headed cane. It was
answered by a manservant, somewhat less grand than the Rostikov
butler but hardly less exalted in attitude.

'*Lord* Rostikov is not at home,' the man informed him.

Konrad sighed inwardly, disliking the sensation of repetition.

'Where has his lordship gone?' he enquired.

'I am not at liberty to reveal that information,' came the reply. 'If you'd like to leave your card?'

Irksome, but very well. Konrad handed his visiting card to the officious manservant and walked away. At the end of the street he paused and closed his eyes.

'Eetapi,' he murmured. 'Ootapi.'

On twin gusts of wind they came, leaving a pattern of frost on his skin as they twined about him.

Yes, *Malykant.*

*The new Lord Rostikov*, he said to them silently. *Find him.*

He opened his eyes. The serpents, so vivid in his mind's eye, were barely discernible in the light of the weak winter sun. Mere puffs of smoke they seemed as they streamed away, scattering themselves on the wind. He waited, drawing his coat closer around himself to keep the cold out. It would not take them long to locate their quarry.

A summons wormed its way into his thoughts. Ootapi called him.

He followed it on foot, ignoring the people he passed. His companions drew him to a small park a few streets away from the house, where several families were strolling the ornamental gardens or sitting on ironwork benches under the trees.

Eetapi guided his consciousness to the right group: a tall man wearing a tall top hat, walking arm-in-arm with a woman expensively dressed in wide, impractical skirts. Konrad stood back for a moment, watching as the man tilted his head to listen to something his pretty wife was saying.

Konrad approached slowly, swinging his cane, ostensibly taking a stroll himself. When he collided with the lady, it was of course an accident.

'My apologies,' he said with a low bow, picking up the gloves the lady had dropped. She and her husband were both pale and dark-haired. She wore a fur coat and matching hat; very expensive, he noted. They certainly had not been short of money.

Konrad looked for a moment at the gentleman, then affected a double-take.

'Mr Rostikov, is it not?' He bowed. 'Ah - pardon me, I do of course mean *Lord* Rostikov.'

The lady smiled at this amendment, but Rostikov's face registered confusion. 'Have we met?'

11

'Oh, once or twice I believe, at some gathering or other. Not for some time. My name is Konrad Savast.' He bowed again.

And waited, while understanding dawned in their eyes and their manner became suddenly more welcoming.

'Naturally we know of *you*, Mr Savast,' said the newly-elevated lord; and even though he was a lord, he bowed rather low to Konrad in return.

Konrad flashed a brief smile. He was no social leader, but he had a reputation for riches far greater than he really deserved. The Order of The Malykt had seen to that. The only social advantage greater than aristocratic blood was obscene wealth, and his certainly opened doors for him.

'May I condole with you on your loss?' Konrad said politely.

'Thank you, Mr Savast.' Rostikov glanced down at his clothes uncomfortably. Konrad understood: they were not wearing mourning clothes. But then, they must have received the news only yesterday; there had not yet been time to assemble a wardrobe of suitably fashionable mourning attire.

'And also I congratulate you on your good fortune,' Konrad continued.

The lady looked uncomfortable at this allusion, but her husband smiled. 'Never thought it quite right, a woman holding the title like that. Not speaking ill of the dead, of course,' he amended as his wife frowned at him.

'Of course not,' Konrad said blandly, watching the reactions of both. He often wished that the serpents were as sensitive to the thoughts of others as they were to his. It would never be possible, of course; his mind had been bound to those of his companions by The Malykt Himself, and he had been a consenting party to the business. He could hardly expect the Overlord to perform this task on request, upon any individual whom Konrad suspected of foul play.

But it would make his task so much easier.

Teeth nipped at his ankle, distracting him. He looked down to find a small but very pugnacious dog attached to his foot.

'Oh, Pikat,' sighed the lady, and bent gracefully to pick up the dog. It was an utterly repugnant creature but she petted it as if it was a thing of extraordinary beauty.

'I am sorry,' she remembered to add.

Konrad fixed the dog with a cold stare, not gracing its mistress's perfunctory apology with a reply. 'Excuse me,' he bowed as the dog began to whine. He left the park at a quick pace, his purpose accomplished. He had seen Amrav Rostikov and his wife; he had shown himself to them in friendship. When their next meeting came, he intended that it should be at their invitation.

Konrad waited until the sun had set, and then he ventured out into the city on foot. He walked without hurry, his coat buttoned high on his throat against the chill of the night. Snowflakes drifted down out of the darkened skies, glowing eerily in the light of the gas lamps that illuminated the streets.

Eetapi and Ootapi streamed along behind him, catching snowflakes in their insubstantial mouths and absorbing the frigid water.

He was approaching the south gate, beyond which the Bone Forest spread. Lady Rostikova had met someone here, not three days ago, and that someone had lured her out into the heart of the wetlands. This element of the mystery intrigued him: why had it been necessary, or desirable, to conduct the killing so far outside the city? But now was not the time to investigate the killer's probable path. He bypassed the city gate and directed his steps instead towards a small shop that nestled beneath the city wall in the south-east sector. The position of this establishment was no accident: its owner was an apothecary, a poison master and, on occasion, an alchemist. Like Konrad, she spent much of her time out in the wetlands.

The shop was closed up at this hour, but Konrad was unfazed. He slipped around to the rear of the building and tapped on the door with his serpent-headed cane.

No answer, but he could hear the apothecary muttering inside.

He unlatched the door and went in. He took care to make at least a little noise, but still he remained unobserved; Irinanda was working. She stood over a workbench that rested in the centre of the floor, her clothes covered by a grubby coat and her exquisite pale blonde hair tied into a loose bun.

'Snake blood powder,' she muttered, and a chittering patch of golden fur streaked away to the shelves that lined the walls. It leaped again, back to the tall bench that dominated the room. The monkey offered a small glass jar to the apothecary, who grabbed it, wrenched off the lid and shook a quantity of dark red powder into a bubbling pot.

She set the jar down and the tiny monkey picked it up, replaced the lid, and leapt energetically back to the shelves.

'Ashleaf,' she said next, and the monkey brought her a phial containing the pale white dust of the ashleaf plant.

'Quiet now,' said the apothecary, and the monkey sat down on the bench, tucking its long tail around itself.

Irinanda took a small measuring spoon from a pocket and dipped it into the neck of the phial.

'One,' she counted, dumping in a spoonful. 'Two.' With each spoonful of dust the liquid in her mixing pot bubbled higher and harder, threatening to explode out of its confines. 'Three.'

Konrad blinked. *Three* measures of ashleaf? This would be a volatile potion.

'Fou...' Irinanda's head suddenly whipped round to stare at Konrad, who stood as still as he could in the shadow of the door.

'Four,' she repeated, returning her attention to the pot.

'That's five,' Konrad corrected. 'You added four already.'

He could hear the frown in Irinanda's reply even though the apothecary stood with her back to him. '*Four,*' she insisted, adding the fifth spoonful. She capped the phial and handed it off to the monkey.

'Inkwort,' she instructed.

The pot bubbled and foamed and began to spit.

Konrad waited.

The apothecary swore.

'*Down, Weveroth!*'

The monkey instantly leapt off the bench and took refuge beneath it. The apothecary was not so fortunate. The pot exploded and the contents spilled over the surface of her workstation and onto her coat.

'Sorry,' Konrad said. 'I did try.'

Irinanda muttered something. She spent several minutes cleaning up the bench and the pot and the floor. Then she left the room. When she finally returned, she was wearing a clean coat and most of the annoyance had gone from her face.

'You're a liability, Konrad,' she muttered.

'Marsh spectre,' he replied without preamble.

Irinanda fixed her glorious but cold blue eyes on him. Her face was expressionless but he didn't miss the gleam of avarice in her eyes.

'Where?' was all she said.

'Already harvested,' Konrad added.

'Damn you.'

Konrad leaned his cane against the door and took off his hat. 'Not by me, more is the pity. I think that an amateur was involved.' He described the condition of the blossom, watching Irinanda's reactions as he spoke. She hardly moved.

'It wasn't me,' she said when Konrad had finished.

'Of course it wasn't you,' Konrad replied coolly. 'What I want to know is whether you've heard anything. Any new poisoners in the city? Any customers with too much interest in marsh spectre poison?'

Irinanda turned from him and began roaming around the room, briskly setting things to rights. 'Not recently,' she said.

'Recently meaning?'

'Not in the last few weeks.' She collected a bowl of nuts from a cupboard and began feeding them to the monkey.

'All right,' Konrad said, taking a seat on one of her uncomfortable high stools. 'How about before that?'

'There was one man,' Irinanda said, watching with rapt attention as the monkey devoured a walnut. 'Six months ago or so. Turned up after hours asking for my inventory of virulent poisons. He wanted "the painful sort".'

Konrad lifted his brows. 'Did he mention marsh spectre?'

'No. I did. I told him it was the most suitable type for his requirements.'

'Did he buy some?'

'Would have if I'd had any at the time.'

'Maybe he went elsewhere.'

Irinanda shrugged. 'He might have, but I doubt he would've had any better luck. Wrong season. And I doubt he had the right paperwork.'

Konrad nodded. Nanda's business was legal, but she couldn't sell virulent poisons to anyone without a permit to trade in them. 'Did you tell him that?'

'Of course.'

'And you haven't seen him since.'

'No. I wondered if he might come back when winter started, but he didn't.'

So he'd either found someone else to supply him with the poison,

15

or he had gone in search of it himself. Konrad suspected the latter. A few months was plenty of time for him to learn about marsh spectre - how to find it, how to identify it and how to harvest it.

'You didn't get a name, I suppose?'

Irinanda snorted. 'He as good as told me he was planning to kill someone. You think he'd leave a name?'

Konrad grunted. 'True. Damn him. Describe him for me.'

She turned back to Konrad at last and looked him full in the face. 'Gypsy stock,' she said. 'Black hair and eyes, dark skin. A lot like you, in fact.'

Konrad mulled that over. His colouring wasn't that rare; a number of people in Ekamet had a little bit of gypsy blood somewhere in their family tree. But it helped to narrow it down.

'Any other unusual sorts coming in for marsh spectre?'

Irinanda shook her head. 'I've some regulars but they know what time of year to call.'

Regulars. He knew the sorts of people she spoke of: he dealt with them himself on occasion. Most of them were traders, taking the poisons to far countries where the symptoms wouldn't be so easily recognised, identified and traced back to the source. Using marsh spectre on a prominent target within Ekamet's own wetlands was unwise: not something a professional was likely to do.

He'd be willing to bet that this mysterious customer of Irinanda's had something to do with the death of Lady Rostikova.

'Thank you,' he said, standing up and collecting his hat. He drew a pouch from the inside pocket of his coat and tossed it to the poison master by way of payment.

Irinanda sniffed it and her eyes widened.

'Ijgaroot,' she murmured. 'Generous.' She tucked the pouch away quickly, as if fearing that he would change his mind.

But when Konrad turned to leave, she spoke again.

'Is this about the dead aristocrat?'

Konrad turned around again slowly, pondering his response. Why would she expect him to be investigating a murder? He'd wondered before whether Irinanda had guessed about his other identity. It wasn't the first time that he had tapped her for information, and she was an intelligent woman.

'Yes,' he said simply, searching her face.

She nodded. 'Do you think it's true? That the Malykant is after the killer?'

Konrad thought of the rib bone that rested inside his coat, cleaned and sharpened and ready for use. 'It must be,' he said slowly. 'Unless someone else in this city has a penchant for collecting ribs.'

Irinanda looked him over, as if wondering where he kept the bones. Konrad stood still, enduring her scrutiny without expression.

But all she said was, 'Have you got any sunbane? I'm running low and I have an order to fill.'

'I can spare a little.' He had some in his coat pocket, in fact; he always carried it when he had a case to solve. It would make things much easier when he found the killer. But he allowed Irinanda to take the little packet from him and empty out a little of the powder.

When she handed back the packet, her fingers brushed his. It was the merest feather-light touch, but it felt, in a strange way, profound. Irinanda's eyes closed for an instant; when she opened them again her gaze had become speculative.

'Thanks,' she said.

Konrad blinked. Was that it? He'd expected something different, though he wasn't sure what.

Irinanda's white teeth flashed in a sudden grin. Lifting a hand in farewell, she wandered out of the workroom. Her voice came floating back after she had passed beyond his sight.

'Lock up, will you? I don't want any more visitors tonight.'

Konrad left without replying, his mind busy. He had no notion what had just happened, but that Irinanda knew or suspected a few uncomfortable things about him was indubitable. That was an alarming thought, but then again this was Irinanda: his friend, or so he hoped. Would it be such a bad thing for her to know?

The answer to that, he supposed, depended on what she planned to do with the information.


Navdina's funeral took place the next day. Konrad attended, placing himself at the rear of the temple where he could watch the behaviour of the other guests.

The new Lord Rostikov and his lady sat in the first tier of seats. They were the only family Navdina had, but they did not choose to participate in the ceremony. Instead Navdina Rostikova was given into the hands of The Malykt by priests, their faces hidden behind the traditional spirit masks. Konrad bowed his head, murmuring the familiar words of devotion along with the congregation as Navdina's pyre was lit. The smell of smoke mingled with the thick fragrance of incense, the combination quickly turning acrid. He lifted his eyes to the open roof, watching as the smoke sailed into the sky.

The service passed without interruption. There was no sign of the dark-skinned man that Irinanda had mentioned; all those he saw with such colouring were people he recognised, people Irinanda would probably recognise too. Only one guest caught his attention: an elderly woman, her grey hair disordered and her dark mourning clothes hastily assembled. She showed far more emotion than anybody else in that gathering, stifling soft sobs in her handkerchief throughout the proceedings. He did not recognise her.

He lingered afterwards as the surviving Rostikovs stationed themselves outside the temple doors. They received the condolences and thanks of the funeral guests with the utmost graciousness. Konrad shook the hands of his and her ladyship in his turn, watching their faces. They were both pale but composed, and perfectly courteous.

His duty thus discharged, he retreated into the shadows cast by the setting winter sun. Concealed within the portico of the building opposite to The Malykt's temple, he watched until every funeral guest had offered their condolences and departed.

The grey-haired woman was not among them. That confirmed one of his suppositions: her shabby clothes proclaimed her to be a servant and this omission offered further evidence of her station. She did not emerge at all, in fact, and he guessed that she had been obliged to use the lesser entrance at the rear of the temple.

It was unusual for servants to be permitted at the funeral of so high-ranking a person. Why had she been present? And who was she?

Only when the Rostikovs had also departed did he move from his hiding place. He crossed to the now deserted temple and sat in the tall tiers at the back.

He fixed his gaze on the faintly smouldering remains of Navdina's pyre. He spent most of the night there, savouring the chilling presence of his master, The Malykt, and thinking.

# 4

The new Lady Rostikova had been quick to furnish herself with visiting cards. A fresh one lay on his hall table when he returned the following morning. It was a prim little rectangle of card, printed with her new title and her address in gilded lettering. The address in question was Rostikov House, already given into new hands.

The lady had left a note for him along with the card, and an elegant invitation scribed in gold ink. She was returning his visit, she said, and would he do them the honour of attending their little gathering on the thirteenth?

The invitation was no surprise; he'd known it would come, as soon as he had introduced himself to them at the park. His acquaintance was worth having to a newly aristocratic couple, anxious to establish themselves in their new position.

And in keeping with that wish, the opulence of the invitation told him this event would be no "little gathering". They were flaunting their new status, proving their suitability for the highest echelon of Ekamet society.

He knew that few people would blame them for it.

They weren't wasting any time, either. The thirteenth was just two days away. They were gambling on their terrific rise in status to bring guests at such short notice. It was a gambit that would probably work.

Konrad wrote his reply immediately and handed it to a servant to deliver.

In one respect, this news was disconcerting. If Rostikov House had already been claimed by its new owners, they would have stripped it out. No further clues as to its former mistress's fate were likely to be found there. But his most promising leads were people: the poison-seeking man whom Irinanda had described, and the old woman at the funeral.

It seemed indubitable that the woman was connected to Navdina in some way; closely connected, given her distress. It was quite possible that she herself still resided at Rostikov House, at least for the present, and the upcoming party would give him the perfect opportunity to look for her.

He rang the bell. Within moments, footsteps approached and Mrs Orista, his housekeeper, bustled in and bobbed a curtsey.

'I'm expecting someone,' he told her. 'Make sure he is shown into the parlour as soon as he arrives. Without delay, please. And send someone in with tea, and something edible.'

'Of course, sir.' She smiled - the woman was always beaming - and left in the direction of the kitchen.

Nuritov arrived as the clock struck eleven. He was always punctual, thought Konrad approvingly as he rose to greet him.

'Ten minutes only,' the man said to Konrad as they shook hands. He perched on the edge of a chair, not even pausing to remove his coat and hat. 'Baris has me jumping this morning.'

Baris was Artoni Baris, chief of Ekamet's police, and Nuritov was one of his inspectors. Konrad paid him to share findings with him. Sometimes he paid in money, and sometimes he paid in information. Nuritov knew him only as a somewhat eccentric amateur sleuth.

'Rostikov case, I'm guessing?' Nuritov accepted a cup of tea and drank half of it down in one gulp.

Konrad lifted a brow.

'It's the big one at the moment,' Nuritov explained. 'Everyone's talking about it. Thought it would be up your street.'

'Do you have anything for me?' Konrad selected a cake and began delicately pulling it to pieces.

Nuritov nodded emphatically. 'The victim's servants have been talking. Said Navdina went all to pieces a few weeks ago. Cancelled most of her social engagements and started spending all her time locked up in the house.'

Konrad leaned forward. 'Does anyone know why?'

Nuritov produced a piece of paper from a pocket and thrust it at Konrad. It was a transcript of the note he had already seen.

'We think there were more,' Nuritov said as Konrad pretended to read the page. 'Footman says he saw the lady throw a note into the fire once. She was upset. And the butler told us she used to tremble whenever the post was delivered.'

Konrad frowned. The destroyed notes doubtless contained the missing information, such as what precisely she had been accused of. Why had she destroyed those and kept this one?

'This meeting,' he said, tapping one of the notes. 'At the South Gate. Did she go?'

Nuritov refilled his tea cup and drank that down too. 'Apparently not. Instead she locked everything up, barricaded herself inside the house. But a maid heard voices in her room around midnight: her mistress's and someone else's. Another woman, she thinks. There was no sign of how she got into the house.'

A woman? Konrad would have expected it to be Irinanda's unidentified customer, if anyone.

So now he had two people involved.

'Did anyone see this mysterious visitor?'

'No. Everything was quiet again at one when the maid went to bed.'

'Nobody was surprised to find her absent in the morning?'

'They were, but they assumed she'd gone out. The front door was unbarred on the inside.'

So nobody had wondered where she was; no one had raised the alarm, not even under such unusual circumstances as these. Poor Navdina.

'Anything else?' he asked Nuritov.

The inspector shook his head, hastily swallowing a mouthful of cake. 'That's it. May be more later.'

Konrad nodded and stood up. 'Thank you,' he said. 'You'd better go. But I've a tip for you before you do.' He gave the inspector Irinanda's name and the address of her shop. He wasn't afraid of the consequences: her poisons trade was perfectly legal.

'Ask her about marsh spectre,' he finished.

Nuritov's brows rose. 'Is she involved?'

'Doubtful. But she has information that may be relevant.'

Nuritov grinned. 'You should join the force. I know you don't need the work, but we could use you.'

Konrad shook his head. 'I prefer to work alone.'

When Konrad returned to Rostikov House for the party, he hardly recognised it. Gone were Navdina's collections of ornaments, the gilded trinkets and the clutter. In their places stood expensive antiques and pieces of new art; and books, books of the sort to be looked at rather than read. The effect was much more tasteful, though it lacked character to Konrad's eye. He could have walked into the home of any aristocrat in Ekamet and seen examples of the same kinds of things.

The affair was, of course, splendid. Everything about the party dripped money, from the clothes of his hosts and fellow guests to the food laid out in the dining room. Lord Rostikov and his lady sparkled with pleasure and affability as they greeted their guests, but he paid them only the briefest of courtesies before moving on. It was not the hosts he was interested in speaking to this evening.

He was looking for the shabbily-dressed servant, the one who had wept so hard at Navdina's funeral. She wouldn't be among the party guests; her prim black drabness and grey hair would not fit among the sparkling birds of paradise that flocked through Navdina's hall, dining room and ballroom. But perhaps she was somewhere else in the house.

He paused a moment longer where he was, watching the revelry. He kept his disgust hidden behind his mask of stone indifference, the face that nobody knew how to read. They had no respect for the dead, these preening gentry. They swarmed over her house, dripping in silks and jewels, laughing and courting one another's favour, their faces smiling but their eyes calculating and hard. They would have danced on Navdina's own grave with as much abandon.

Konrad endured the fawning attention of his hosts with cool indifference. He was obliged to endure still more, as every one of the Rostikovs' friends was brought forward to be introduced. When at last they let him alone, repelled and puzzled by his blank countenance and bland manner, he allowed himself to meld into the milling crowd and made his slow way towards the stairs.

He slipped up one flight, and then two, welcoming the gradual cessation of the brittle chatter and laughter of the party. He paused briefly on the second storey, thinking again about the weeping woman. It was likely that she had been Navdina's servant, inherited along with the house. The new mistress would have brought all her own staff with her when she moved in; where might she have placed an unwanted extra?

Further up, he decided. The attic.

He climbed to the top storey and began opening doors. They were all empty, their owners busy serving at - or cooking for - the party that proceeded at a busy hum some way below.

At the back of the house he found a small, mean room, smaller than all the others. It was barely more than a cupboard. On the narrow, hard bed sat the woman he sought, so still that Konrad wondered if she was asleep. Then, slowly, her head turned and her eyes focused on him.

He stared at her for a moment, contemplating her features. She was younger than he had thought: her hair was grey but her face was relatively unlined and there was no frailty about her figure. Konrad guessed her to be in her fifties.

'I saw you at the funeral,' he said. 'I wanted to speak to you.'

A faint flicker of interest registered in her blue eyes. 'Who are you?'

'A friend of Navdina Rostikova.'

He watched in silence as her face crumpled and she began to sob.

'And that's why I want to speak to you,' he added. 'Because of the way you cried at her funeral.' A single, hard chair rested next to the bed. He took it, passing her his handkerchief as he did so.

'It's as though she was never here,' said the woman at last. 'They dance and dance in her house, drinking and carousing like they were... they've already forgotten her.' She began twisting his handkerchief in her hands, binding it into a tight knot. 'Every little piece of her life has been stripped out of this house. Thrown away, like it was rubbish. *She* did that, the minute she set foot in here.'

'Who are you?' Konrad asked.

The woman sighed deeply. 'Etraya Marodeva. I was Navvy's nurse. I knew her from the day she was born.'

'You were very attached to her.'

'She was a sweet child,' Etraya said with a wobbly smile, 'and she grew up to be a fine lady. Not stuck-up, like some of those others you meet.' Her lips quivered again. 'I should have done better for her, protected her somehow.'

'From what?' Konrad kept his voice low and his posture still. He wanted her to forget he was there, to keep on talking.

'I was almost a mother to her,' said Etraya tearfully, without answering his question. 'It's a mother's job to protect her child.'

'What of her own mother?'

'Died,' she said. 'She was never well after the birth; only a few weeks after Navvy was born, she was gone.'

'And you've been part of her household ever since?'

She nodded, eyes glittering. 'She said she couldn't part with me. I was to be nurse to her own children, whenever she married.'

'And now?'

'I've been given notice.' Twist, twist went her hands with the handkerchief. 'She needn't have bothered. I'd no intention of staying.'

'I take it by *she* you mean Lady Rostikova.'

Etraya pulled a face of disgust. 'They didn't get on,' she said. 'It doesn't seem right that she's here, taking over Navvy's space after... well, after...'

After someone had stabbed her to the heart with a poisoned blade and left her to die alone in the middle of the Bone Forest. Well, indeed.

Konrad watched her, thinking. She had so much to say about the Rostikov family, but she'd skirted the topic of the murder. She was obviously heartbroken by Navdina's death, but in like circumstances most people asked questions. Why her? Why us? Why did this have to happen?

Etraya hadn't asked any of those things.

'Ms Marodeva,' he said slowly. 'Do you know why Navdina was murdered?'

Etraya's tears stopped. She looked back at him, and he detected a trace of fear in her cool blue eyes.

Fear, and something like guilt.

'Of course not,' she said. Now she looked at him with suspicion. 'Who are you really? Why do you ask these questions of me?'

Her defensiveness was interesting. He made a note of it.

'Just a friend,' he said, standing. 'Thank you, Ms Marodeva.'

He left the room, quietly closing the door behind him.

Several things about her manner interested him, but the most pressing question in his mind was the reason for the nurse's tears.

Was it grief that had made her weep so at the funeral? Or was it remorse?

5

*I want to see you.*

The note said nothing else, and it was not signed, but Konrad knew who had sent it.

The fog still hadn't lifted, and the trees were dripping wet when he stepped beyond the city gates into the marshlands. Beads of dew twinkled on the branches, and half-frozen water sloshed and splintered underfoot, eerily loud in the hush. He strode through the hazy atmosphere, sure of his path, unconcerned by the fact that he could see only a few hand spans in front of him.

The serpents glided into position on either side of him, coalescing out of the mist like puffs of steam.

*Be gone,* he told them silently. *I go where you must not follow.*

*You go to meet the apothecary,* said Eetapi.

*You think she does not know?* Said Ootapi.

*She might guess,* he conceded. *But I do not wish for her suspicions to be confirmed.*

Eetapi flicked her tail derisively and vanished. But Ootapi lay around his neck like a scarf, and would not be moved until Konrad had almost reached the house-on-stilts in the woods.

*Go,* he urged, and Ootapi melded back into the fog.

Irinanda was already inside when he emerged through the trapdoor in the floor. She was cleaning, dusting and organising the bottles and jars on his shelves. She knew he had arrived; he read it in the way she turned her body to avoid appearing to notice him. He smiled inwardly and sat down on his makeshift bed, waiting for her to finish.

'This place could be so pleasant,' she said at last, still without looking at him.

He shrugged. 'Why should I keep it tidier? The mice and the birds and the insects will still find their way in to put all my preparations in disarray. And this space is not intended for entertaining.'

She sniffed. 'I dislike your city house. I dislike you when you are in the city. You become an insufferable prig.'

He smiled openly. 'Because I wear a nice coat and a top hat? You like me better in these things, perhaps.' He glanced down at the waxed great-coat he wore, the tall boots splashed with mud, the trousers and shirt of thick, unpretending cotton.

'Yes,' she said firmly. 'You're more real.'

'Are you saying that Mr Konrad Savast of Bakar House is fake?'

'Quite fake,' she said, turning a severe gaze upon him. 'You've better things to do than hobnob with the social butterflies.'

'Some of them are quite amusing.'

She frowned at that and turned away again, removing an imaginary speck of dust from a nearby jar with the cuff of her coat sleeve.

'I tease, Nanda. I assure you, the social butterflies are as much in my poor graces as they are in yours today.'

'He came back,' she said, abruptly spinning around.

He sat up, alert. 'Who?'

'The poison man. The one looking for marsh spectre.'

He patted the seat beside him. 'Come here, and tell me everything.'

Irinanda folded her arms and remained where she was. 'He came in yesterday. He tried to *flirt* with me.'

Her indignation made him want to laugh. He stifled it. She didn't like to be laughed at.

'I suppose he liked you,' he said mildly. 'It's not impossible that people might, once in a while.'

She narrowed her eyes. 'If he hasn't already committed murder he's planning to. He makes me sick.'

Konrad sighed inwardly. He agreed with her about this person, but she tended to say similar things about everyone. No matter how minor their crime.

'Just tell me what happened.'

'I thought he'd come back for the marsh spectre, but he didn't say anything about that. He was looking for a slow-acting poison this time, something that would take a few days to kill a person. And he wants it to look natural.'

'That's an interesting change of direction,' he mused. Two possibilities occurred to him at once: either the poison-man, as Nanda called him, was a killer-for-hire and had moved on to another assignment, or he was still involved in the Rostikov case. If the latter, his new target must be related in some way to Navdina's death.

'What did you tell him?'

She donned her most evil smile, an expression that always made him shiver a little. 'I gave him maricus.'

'Oh? But he might have educated himself since the last time you spoke to him. He may know what maricus is.'

Her smile became scornful. 'Naturally I told him that it was ijgaroot. When powdered, they are similar enough to fool anyone who is not an expert like myself.'

He nodded sagely and her smile turned cat-like with satisfaction. She had been clever, indeed. Ijgaroot was a poison of the type the man was looking for: when ingested by its victims it caused a sickness that lasted for three or four days. The symptoms were similar to a number of common ailments, so its use was rarely detected.

Maricus, on the other hand, was not fatal. When ingested it caused a violent rash: uncomfortable but not particularly dangerous to the victim.

Said rash was also nice and visible.

'You are perfectly amazing today,' he smiled. He was really grateful: if her mysterious customer was still involved with Navdina's case, she might have given him a strong lead.

Instead of returning his smile, Irinanda stared at him, her expression hostile. 'What do you do with your time?'

He blinked. 'What?'

She gestured at the pungent room with its crowded shelves and general lack of furniture. 'What is this for? Why do you need it if you're a gentleman of Ekamet? Why does a gentleman of Ekamet involve himself in the poison-and-herb trade? How in the world does it make sense to waste half your time going to parties and spend the other half solving murders?'

'I don't often go to parties.'

'You went to one the other night.'

28

His eyes narrowed. 'Have you been watching me?'

She lifted her chin, undaunted. 'I hear things.'

He stood up. She wasn't a short woman by any means, but he was quite a bit taller. He stepped closer, forcing her to look a long way up into his face.

'Stop hearing things,' he said quietly. 'My business is my own, and none of yours.'

She stared back at him, her pale blue eyes wintry. 'You keep things from me.'

'And why shouldn't I? Who are you to demand my secrets?'

'So you admit that you have some.'

'Answer my question.'

She drew herself up, a futile gesture in the face of his superior height. 'I'm your friend,' she said coldly. 'Unless I'm much mistaken, I am your only friend. It isn't right that you keep important things from me.'

He stepped back and gestured invitingly at the trap door. 'Thank you for your information.'

She shot him a look of hatred. 'Tell me if anything comes of it. If it isn't too much trouble.'

He inclined his head and opened the trap door, holding it while she made her way down the ladder in a few long, graceful movements and disappeared.

He closed the door again and returned to his seat on the bed. Nanda was difficult when she got hold of an idea. How far would she carry her suspicions?

Part of him wanted to tell her. She was right: he had few real friends, and there was nobody in whom he could confide about his life as the Malykant. It could be lonely.

But a larger part of him had no intention of telling her. Solving the murder was only part of his job; the other part was much worse. Would she understand, or would she despise him too? He couldn't risk it. Because without Nanda's friendship, he really would have nobody at all.

*Malykant.*

The sibilant voice whispered through his dreams, drawing him towards consciousness. He opened his eyes to complete darkness, or near complete; a hazy phantom hovered near his face, pale and faintly glowing.

'Eetapi,' he murmured. 'What's afoot?'

*Death is on the wind*, the serpent replied.

Konrad was out of bed in an instant, groping blindly for his clothes. It took him a few moments to dress and then he was down the stairs and out into the street, Eetapi gliding ahead of him and Ootapi trailing behind.

The night was cold and very, very dark; the sky was free of clouds and empty of moonglow, for the moon was in its dark phase. Stars glittered coldly above as Konrad hurried through the streets of Ekamet, fumbling with the buttons of his coat to fasten the wool closer around his chilled throat. The city was silent and empty at this hour, and his footsteps rang in the quiet.

Eetapi was leading him northwards through the city, past the centre and into the richest quarter. A premonition twisted his gut as he realised where they were headed: directly, unerringly towards Rostikov House. Had Irinanda's gambit failed? Had the poison-man succeeded after all?

*Death is within*, Eetapi whispered as they stopped outside the front door of the house. The building loomed, dark and imposing and firmly shut against the world. He slipped around to the back. Nothing stirred; all was undisturbed, as far as he could tell in the darkness.

A servants' entrance stood at the rear of the house, a sturdy wooden door with a small window and, he doubted not, strong bolts on the inside.

He brushed his fingers against the lock. The metal grew chilled under his touch and he heard the faint sound of the well-oiled lock pulling back, clicking open. Another moment, and a faint squeak of metal told him the bolt had withdrawn itself also.

Konrad opened the door just wide enough to pass through. He stepped into a small rear kitchen, a utility area that was, thankfully, empty of inhabitants.

*Eetapi*, he said in the silent way. *Lead me.*

The serpent materialised in his mind's eye, keeping its semi-corporeal form hidden. He followed her lead out of the tiny room, through the main kitchen in which a single maid snored, and through at last into the more opulent parts of the house.

Eetapi stopped at last outside the study. Its door was ajar, and a light burned within.

*Is there danger?*

He felt the serpent's negative. *No living soul is within,* she confirmed. *There is only death.*

He pushed open the door, slowly so it wouldn't creak, and stepped inside.

The corpse lay near the window. It was partially hidden behind a wing-back chair that sat near the fireplace, so Konrad couldn't see the face. But the clothes told him this was a man, and not a servant. He crossed the room in swift strides and knelt by the side of the body.

With a shock, he recognised Lord Amrav Rostikov. He lay on his back, hatless and without his cravat, waistcoat or hat: he wore only a loose shirt and trousers. His throat had been cut.

*Serpents,* he said immediately. *Bind his soul.*

They did so, weaving the scattered shreds of it together and binding it to the corpse with the strength of their Master's will. Rostikov's mouth opened and his eyes widened in shock. Or was it fear?

'Tell me what happened,' Konrad ordered, pitching his voice low. 'Quietly.'

The corpse's mouth worked but nothing emerged.

'Who killed you?' Konrad said.

Rostikov grunted, and his arms flailed.

'Who killed you?' Konrad repeated. 'Tell me quickly.'

The corpse grunted again, an inarticulate, urgent sound. He shivered and tears leaked out of his eyes.

Suddenly understanding, Konrad knelt and pried the man's lips apart.

The corpse's tongue was missing.

He sighed. *Release him,* he ordered the serpents. They obeyed, and Lord Rostikov's corpse settled back into the stillness of true death.

Konrad retrieved his knife, working quickly. He'd already been in the house for too long. He cut into the corpse's torso, opened it, and carved away the flesh that coated his ribs. He chose one of the sturdiest of the rib bones and extracted it, wrapping it in cloth and storing it in his coat.

This done, he paused to examine the room. Everything appeared to be in order; nothing was broken or upset, and the room did not

31

appear to have been robbed. He did not find the weapon that had been used to cut Rostikov's throat.

He left the room, leaving the door ajar as he'd found it. He strode back through the house, past the maid that snored, beautifully oblivious, in her place by the cold kitchen fire, and back out of the rear door. The locks and bolts slid smoothly shut again at his bidding, and silence returned to the Rostikov dwelling.

He could think of only one reason why the killer would remove Lord Rostikov's tongue after he was dead. That the culprit knew he was hunted by the Malykant was no surprise: everyone knew what the missing rib bones meant. But the specifics of his methods were not, and should not, be known.

Someone knew about his reanimation of Navdina Rostikova. Someone knew that corpses could still speak, were they encouraged by the right means. And that person had taken steps to ensure that Amrav Rostikov could not identify his killer.

What worried him most was *how*. Had the killer researched the role of Malykant and found someone who could give detailed information? He doubted that. Such details were secret, protected on pain of death. Merely to find such a person would be difficult; encouraging them to share their knowledge would be virtually impossible.

That meant that he had possibly — probably, even — been observed when he spoke with Navdina's corpse. And that in turn meant that he might have been identified.

He'd been wearing his customary wide-brimmed hat, he knew. It was cold out in the Bones at this time of year, so he had been wearing a thick coat and a scarf. His hands had been gloved. He doubted that much of his face had been visible as he had worked on Navdina's corpse, but nonetheless. He would have to be more careful.

*Eetapi,* he said in his mind. *Ootapi. Watchers. You are my eyes in the spirit lands. Was any living soul present at the binding of Navdina Rostikova?*

*We think not,* Ootapi replied.

*But it is not impossible,* Eetapi added. He understood. They had bound the spirit of Navdina and held it while he questioned her. While thus occupied, they could not simultaneously keep watch over him.

He made his way to the small park near to his house and sat down on a bench, drawing his hat down over his eyes. Dawn would not be long in coming, and sleep was out of the question for him now.

It was difficult to imagine what the consequences might be of his exposure as the Malykant. He doubted not that his ability to perform the role would be compromised; therein lay the logic in keeping the title a secret. In order to move about unobserved, he must be anonymous; and for the Malykant to be feared as was proper, his identity must be a mystery.

But if he had been identified, the killer had known who he was for days and had not yet chosen to expose him. Perhaps he was yet safe. But he had been careless at the scene of Navdina's death. He must take much greater care from now on.

Konrad returned to Rostikov House a few hours later, as soon as he judged that the alarm would have been raised. He arrived to find the house crawling with activity: policemen moving in and out of the front door, taking tools inside and removing evidence; reporters hoping to catch a word with a detective; servants fleeing the house in a panic. Konrad hung back. A day or two ago he might have gone inside with impunity, but now he was reluctant to draw attention to himself.

He waited until he saw a familiar figure emerge from the house, his dark blue overcoat closely buttoned up and his inspector's hat tall on his head. Konrad fell into step beside Nuritov as the man made his way around the side of the house.

'Savast,' Nuritov greeted him. 'I imagine you already know the identity of the victim.'

Konrad inclined his head. 'What have you learned?'

'Victim's tongue was removed,' he replied. 'No indication as to why. Throat was slit, ragged job; not a professional killing by any stretch of the imagination. Ground floor window was open. We think the killer got in that way.'

Konrad's brows went up. 'A ground floor window? In which room?'

'Parlour,' Nuritov said, with a sideways glance at him. 'Does that mean anything to you?'

Konrad said nothing. There had been no ground floor windows open a few hours ago, but he was not inclined to admit to a police inspector that he had been inside that house last night.

'Is anyone ill?' he asked instead.

Nuritov looked at him oddly. 'Ill how?'

'Suffering, say, from a variety of rash.'

'Not that I know of, but we haven't finished interviewing everyone yet. Why do you ask? Got some kind of lead?'

Konrad smiled. 'This one I cannot share, but note this: if anyone inside that house should develop any such ailment in the near future, it is significant. And you'll let me know, if it happens.'

'All right.' Konrad could hear the exasperation in the inspector's voice, but he was unconcerned. He'd done his duty in alerting the man: the details could be spared. He didn't want Irinanda's name to come up again.

'Keep an eye on it,' Konrad said. With a nod to Nuritov, he departed.

6

Two sharpened rib bones now rested in Konrad's inner coat pocket. He hoped fervently that he would not have to add a third.

He had retired to The Malykt's temple, as he often did when the leads on a mystery ran dry and he was unsure where to turn for answers. The peace in this place was soothing; it calmed the furious whirl of his thoughts and cleared his mind, the better to see the patterns that lay beneath the confused assortment of clues he had collected.

Sometimes he felt The Malykt's presence brush against his mind, as cold and merciless as winter itself. The Overlord had granted Konrad considerable privileges in exchange for his service, and he expected swift results. In his years as the Malykant, he had never yet failed his master. What the consequences of that might be he did not know, but the mere prospect was enough to set his heart beating quick and hard with fear.

Such a rush of feeling was rare for him. Emotion was an impediment to the calm clarity of mind he needed in order to carry out his duties - *all* his duties. And so, when he had become the Malykant, his new master had taken it all. Konrad had felt some core part of his soul wrenched away and scattered to the winds, and since then, where his emotions should have been he felt only emptiness, and a faint echo of the feelings he might otherwise have had.

The only exception was his reaction to the Spiritlord Himself. Determined to retain the loyal service of his chief disciple, The Malykt had left Konrad's fear of Him intact. A pleasant gift, Konrad thought as his bound soul shivered under the eye of his master.

He forced himself to take slow, deep breaths, drawing his usual calm around himself until his heartbeat slowed and his mind cleared. *Think, Konrad.* He had uncovered many pieces of this puzzle and they *would* fit together somehow.

Lord Amrav Rostikov. Konrad had been inclining towards him as a suspect; after all, he stood to gain the most from Navdina's death. But now he, too, lay dead and cold, and he had been prevented from speaking of his murder. Two Rostikovs... he discarded the idea that Navdina's fate might have been intended for another. Might Irinanda's poison-man hold some manner of grudge against the family? He knew of no particular crime the Rostikovs had committed, but perhaps something lay hidden behind their respectable facade.

If that was the case, then Rostikov's young wife might be in danger. Perhaps not; she had been in the house when her husband was killed, yet she had been spared. Did that mean she was exempted from whatever curse dogged the rest of her family, or had she been more directly involved?

Then there was the nurse, Etraya Marodeva. Perhaps she knew something of it. Her manner was not as he would expect from a woman in her position. He would speak to her again, and today. If she had any information, she *would* tell him.

His skin prickled with the awareness that he was being watched. Raising his head, he saw a dark figure sitting midway up the tiers across from him, a woman by her shape and posture. The brim of her hat shaded her face, but he could see her mouth. She was smirking at him.

'Nanda,' he said softly, knowing she would hear him. 'You are following me.'

She stood up and made her way around to his seat. 'You are paranoid,' she replied with a wicked smile. 'I came to pay my respects to His Greatness and I find you, shivering with cold and fear under the eye of The Malykt. What can it mean?'

Konrad snorted. 'If you may pay your respects to His Greatness, why mayn't I do so with equal innocence?'

'And the reason for your fear?'

'I was cold.'

'Cold? I think not.'

Konrad said nothing.

'Well,' she said, shaking her head. 'I have shopping to do.' She turned away. He might have expected her to be angry – she frequently was, with him – but her manner struck him as sad, and that bit at his heart. He watched, undecided, as she picked her way back down the tiers to the ground, and left the temple.

He went after her.

'Nanda, wait.' He didn't have to run far. She stood outside the main door of the temple, hands folded, obviously expecting him. He glowered at her in faint annoyance. She was far too good at manipulating him, for no reason he could imagine.

Now he noticed that her little gold-furred monkey travelled inside her cloak. The damned creature's expression mirrored hers: smug.

'Yes, Konrad,' said Irinanda, a small smile tugging at her lips.

'Are you just being a plague, or are you inclined to help?'

She lifted her chin. 'Help with what?'

'Solve the murder. No, I am not going to tell you why, so don't ask.'

She grinned outright at that. 'I'll help.'

'Then find the poison-man.'

She gave a little mock-bow, her hand over her heart. 'Yes, my liege. As you command.'

'This is not a game, Nanda. Take some care.'

Irinanda nodded seriously. 'I know. See you soon.' She wandered off, disappearing into the evening shadows.

Konrad watched her go, hoping he hadn't made a colossal mistake. But he had the feeling that Nanda could handle herself very well indeed.

As he finally turned to leave, movement flickered at the edges of his vision. Several figures were hurrying up the street, on their way to one of the several temples that waited here. Their movements were brisk and hurried; none of them looked at him. This was as he expected.

The movement that had caught his attention had been a stealthy one: the suggestion of a dark figure just slipping out of sight. His senses prickled. He was being watched: he would swear to it.

*Serpents*, he called silently. He relayed to them the glimpse he'd had of his pursuer and they darted away.

Unwilling to appear suspicious, he began the walk back to his home, his pace slow. It wasn't hard to appear lost in thought. Why would somebody be following him? His mind flew back to Amrav Rostikov's missing tongue. Somebody knew his methods; perhaps they had identified him as well.

That thought was a chilling one. If it was so, what was the intended purpose behind having him shadowed? Was the pursuer gathering information, with a view to exposing Konrad's identity? Or was it worse still?

The serpent-shades were back, twining their glacial spirits around his soul.

*No one is there, Malykant.*

Far from reassuring him, this news only deepened his concern. He had learned to trust his senses over the years. That somebody was following him he had no doubt, but that person was apparently adept enough to evade his serpents. That suggested two things.

One: he or she knew about Eetapi and Ootapi, too.

And two: whoever was on his tail was no amateur. Most likely a hire, then, and a professional. But a professional what? Investigator, or assassin?

A day later, and the investigation at the Rostikov house was mostly over. The crowds of reporters were gone, and Konrad passed only a single solitary policeman on his way in. That suited his purposes well.

He gave his card to the butler and waited. Analena Rostikov was in mourning for her husband, but still he thought she would agree to see him. He'd gone to considerable trouble to arrive here undetected; though he had made it home yesterday without incident, he had been awake and on edge all night, expecting some manner of confrontation or attack. None had yet come, but he remained vigilant.

The butler returned. 'Her Ladyship is at home,' he said.

'Thank you.' Konrad followed the servant upstairs and into the drawing-room. As the butler discreetly withdrew, Konrad studied the new widow.

She was sitting bolt upright on an uncomfortably hard divan. Her mourning attire was impeccable, but she looked tired and her face was drawn and white. He recognised the signs of agitation in her posture and the way her hands fidgeted restlessly with the trimmings of her gown.

He felt a stab of sympathy for the woman. She couldn't be more than twenty-five or so, he guessed; much the same age that Navdina had been. She was shocked, upset and afraid: he read that in her.

'Lady Rostikova,' he murmured, offering a bow. 'Forgive my intrusion. I wished to convey my condolences, and also to offer my services to you.'

'Your services?' She looked at him without much interest, her eyes dull with tiredness.

'If there is anything I may do for you, you have only to name it.'

She said nothing for a moment. Her gaze dropped to her lap, and she swallowed hard, blinking.

'Are you some kind of private investigator?' she enquired, fixing her cool blue eyes on him again.

'An interesting guess, my lady. Why should you suppose it?'

'I met you for the first time after Lady Navdina's death. You went looking for us deliberately, I suppose. And you were here again yesterday.'

Konrad blinked. He hadn't entered the house yesterday - at least, not after his midnight visit. Could she possibly know about that?

'I saw you from the window,' she added. 'Out there.' She gestured vaguely.

He bowed. 'I suppose I am an amateur investigator, of sorts.'

Her eyes narrowed. 'It is a strange profession for a gentleman to undertake.'

He shrugged, unwilling to be goaded. 'Even a gentleman must have something to do with his time.'

'Most gentlemen find they can occupy themselves perfectly well without surrounding themselves with murders, thefts and criminals.'

'It is an interest of mine,' Konrad replied coolly. 'And I have an aptitude for the work.'

'Very well, Mr Savast. As unusual a specimen as you may be, if you can solve this mystery I shall be profoundly grateful to you. As long as the truth remains hidden, I exist in fear of my life.'

'Then you think yourself a target?'

She lifted one elegant shoulder in a shrug. 'What else am I to think? Until recently there were but three of us bearing the Rostikov name. Now I am the only one remaining. I cannot help but imagine that I may also be at risk.'

'But you saw nothing, two nights ago? You heard nothing?'

She shook her head. 'Nothing. But I am not a light sleeper. Perhaps if I had been, then poor Amrav might not have died…'

She pursed her lips tightly together, mastering herself quickly. Konrad watched silently.

'Why was your husband in his study at that time of night? Did he retire as normal?'

'Amrav liked to read late. He was often in his study until the early hours of the morning. That night was no different. I retired before midnight, but he did not come to bed before I fell asleep.'

'Do you know of anyone who might have wanted to hurt your husband?'

She bit her lip, her eyes filling with tears as she shook her head. 'He had many friends. But he was wealthy, and he had a high position in Ekamet. Perhaps jealousy…'

Konrad leapt on that. 'Was there anyone in particular who was jealous of him?'

'No. Nobody that I know of.'

Konrad sighed, frustrated. He was out of questions, and she had given him nothing useful. 'There is one particular servant under your roof with whom I'd like to speak further. Her name is Marodeva?'

Was it his imagination, or did she stiffen at those words? Her posture was already so rigid that it was difficult to be sure.

'The nurse? Why should you be interested in her?'

'There is no reason for alarm,' Konrad replied calmly. 'She knew Navdina very well, and I believe she may be able to offer some useful information, if she was properly persuaded.'

Her ladyship lifted one delicate brow. 'Properly persuaded?'

'I believe she was suspicious of my questions when I spoke to her before. Perhaps if her employer were to encourage her to be open with me?'

Her face was very cold. She knew something about Etraya, he felt sure, but would she share it with him?

'I would be delighted to be of use,' Lady Rostikova was saying, 'but unfortunately Miss Marodeva is unwell and I do not think she should be disturbed at present.'

Konrad felt a thrill at those words. 'Unwell? I am sorry to hear it. Is her indisposition grave? Perhaps I may be able to speak with her tomorrow.'

She shook her head decisively. 'I doubt that very much. She is quite unwell and confined to her bed.'

Konrad hoped for more: some mention of her symptoms would be an enormous help to him. But her ladyship said nothing more, and he didn't wish to give himself away by probing further. He merely nodded.

'Perhaps I might be informed when she recovers,' he said.

'Certainly. And in turn you will let me know if you uncover anything relevant.' It was not a question.

'Of course,' he replied. Naturally he would not; he never shared details of a case with anybody who was involved.

She nodded and rang the bell. The butler reappeared.

'Please show Mr Savast out,' said the Lady coolly.

Konrad waited until he and the manservant had reached the hall before he asked his next question.

'I'm sorry to hear of Miss Marodeva's indisposition,' he said as the butler opened the door for him. 'May I ask the cause of her illness?'

'A fever of some kind,' the man replied. 'Most uncomfortable. A shame, for she's a good woman.'

'Uncomfortable?'

The man nodded, his face pale. 'Her skin burns red, and itches. She claws at herself.'

'My best wishes for her recovery,' Konrad said, hiding the chill he felt. As the door to the great house closed behind him, he stood for a moment in thought.

Etraya Marodeva had been the target of the poison Irinanda had given to her so-called "poison-man". And he had administered it in the belief that it would kill.

Presumably he was still expecting her to die of her affliction. The butler certainly seemed to believe that she would. But Irinanda had said that it was not fatal. Sooner or later her would-be murderer would realise that, too, and try something else.

He went straight to the police station and asked for Nuritov. The inspector was not available.

'Get this to him, please,' Konrad said, scrawling a note on a piece of paper. He folded it up and handed it across to the officer manning the desk. 'It's urgent.'

*Etraya Marodeva is the next target,* read the note. *She must be placed under guard. If possible, she should be removed from the Rostikov house.*

His own task was a difficult one. What connection did Etraya have to this case? Was she an accomplice, now being eliminated for what she knew? Or was it knowledge alone that made a target of her? He'd received the impression before that she knew more than she'd said about Navdina's death. Somebody wished to remove her, and it was intended to be the sort of death that would raise no suspicion. Perhaps that was so that she could not speak any further to people such as himself.

He would have to find a way to see her, and hope she remained lucid enough to speak with him. And that meant another midnight visit to Rostikov House.

This time, though, would be much more difficult, for the house was on its guard against intruders.

And there remained the matter of his unknown pursuer; just to make life *particularly* complicated.

Konrad sighed. There would be no sleep for him tonight, either.

# 7

Irinanda Falenia stayed in her shop until long after nightfall. The streets would be quiet; few people would be around to see her walking with her eyes half-closed, following a trail that nobody could see but her.

She'd found a reason to touch the poison-man, when he'd come to her shop before. Not much, and not for long - a mere brush of her fingers against his as she gave him the phial with the supposed ijgaroot. In doing so she had gained a glimpse of his thoughts; scant, but perhaps it would be enough.

An assortment of images had passed behind her eyes, flashing by so fast she had barely had time to draw meaning from them. She'd seen the bare trees of the forests outside of Ekamet, shrouded in mist; she'd seen a house, huddled low to the ground like a frightened animal; she'd seen a strip of braided, multi-coloured cloth with a tiny brass bell woven into the end.

She'd seen the likes of this last before. It was a spirit-braid, the sort that was hung up outside of superstitious houses to keep malevolent spirits at bay. It was the sort of protection one would need if one was going to live out in the Bones. Only Konrad scorned such things.

Konrad. His words echoed in her mind: *take some care*. When he had asked her to help him, she didn't think he had meant that she should track the man down to his own house. Perhaps she should take Konrad along, for safety.

But that would mean exposing her secrets to him, and he had not offered so much to her. If he did not trust her, she would not trust him either.

She stood in the street for a moment and closed her eyes, summoning her memories of her earlier visions. She waited, hardly breathing, as they replayed themselves in her mind's eye. Eyes still closed, she began to turn on the spot until her inner sense told her she faced true.

*This way.*

She opened her eyes, only a little; enough to see the street with both her physical and her spiritual vision. Houses and carriages and people passed by in a blur, unnoticed: she saw only the street in front of her feet and the destination.

Out through the city gate she walked, slow and sure, with the patter of Weveroth's small feet as accompaniment to her own soft tread. No lights shone in the Bone Forest, save an occasional will-o-wisp bobbing in the distance; but she knew better than to follow those. A pale moon shone fitfully overhead, brightening and fading again as clouds streamed across the skies.

She had to slow her steps further in order to make her way safely through the forest's irregular pathways. If she expanded her other senses she could be forewarned about the deep, ice-shrouded puddles that loomed out of the darkness, and about the pits and gulleys and layers of tangling branches that blocked her way. But her physical sight only confused her, burdening her mind with too many impressions. So she closed her eyes and viewed the night-time forest in her mind's eye alone: a landscape in ghost-white, shimmering in the moonlight, the water gleaming indigo and the earth as black as the grave.

She knew she passed the site of Navdina Rostikova's death: the traces of it hovered still in the air, threads of black sickness marking the aether. She gave this a wide berth. It was not very far beyond this place when she came at last to her destination: her spirit vision saw dwellings crouching, crabbed and dark, among the white trees, sensed people moving within them.

Rumour had spoken before of a community of spirit witches hidden out in the forests, but she had never yet seen it for herself. To the physical eye, these houses would be virtually indiscernible, so cleverly were they built: they blended into the crook of branch and trunk, into the soft rise and fall of the ground, perfectly camouflaged out here in the reaches of the Bones where few people came. Irinanda paused for a moment to admire. For a brief second, she wished that she had not forsaken her mother's people and moved into the city. This life, wreathed in the natural forces of the Bone Forest, might have been hers.

But she shook the thought away. This was no perfect world, no ideal society, not even for people like her. Somewhere in this settlement lived the man who had killed Navdina and left her body to rot in filth and uncleanliness, alone in the midst of the forest. The same man now plotted someone else's death. Even those who revered and promoted the natural balances of life and death were capable of these offences against The Malykt's Order.

The house she wanted would be on the edges of this little village, she sensed that instinctively. Her mind's image showed her a poorly tended, ramshackle version of the neatly assembled properties she saw around her now. This man, she realised, felt very differently from her about life out here. He resented the meanness of the dwellings, the relentless chill and damp of the marsh, the perpetual half-light under the endless, dripping fog. He saw none of the beauties, felt nothing for the elevation of spirit; he saw only privations, discomfort and obligations. He let his house fall to ruin and he consciously broke the principles of her mother's people.

He would want the life that Navdina Rostikova had so recently enjoyed, she felt sure. But then why kill the very people whose lives he coveted and admired? Perhaps she could find this out.

She drifted soundlessly around the edges of the witch village, growing nearer to the poison-man's home with every step. And then it was before her: the same narrow, crabbed, shabby house she'd seen in her mind's eye. With a swift pang of regret she let the spirit-vision slip away from her and opened her own eyes fully. It was difficult to discern the contours of the house in this barely moonlit darkness, even though she knew it was there. And the fog muffled all sound, the drip-drop of the rain and condensation all that she could hear clearly. Was the poison-man within?

Turning, she looked for Weveroth. She had forgotten him for a time, all her thoughts and senses occupied with the task of finding her way. But he had followed. He crouched behind her, fluffing out his drenched fur.

'Is it safe?' she asked him. He hopped forward, nose questing, and disappeared inside the house.

She waited, but he did not come out. That was clear enough. In she went, following the route that Weveroth had taken to find the door.

The house consisted of a single room, not spacious, its narrow confines cluttered with furniture and objects. Spirit-braids hung inside the doorway, like the ones she had seen in her visions. She ducked under them, taking care to avoid clattering the bells that hung from the ends and announcing her presence to the community. A bed was tucked into one corner, cupboards lined the walls and a table stood near the door. All were made simply from wood and braided withies; the covers on the bed were sewn from rough cloth and hides, warm and comfortable but simple indeed.

The house contained everything a person might need for reasonable comfort, but it absolutely lacked in luxuries or even beauty. Except for one thing. A willow-woven box rested on a shelf, placed in pride of position as if it contained something special. Opening the lid, she found a collection of three rings and a bracelet. All were finely worked out of precious metals and stones: gold and silver, ruby and even one small diamond.

They were as out of place here as she herself would be in the grand houses of Ekamet. That they did not belong to the owner of this dwelling was obvious enough. Had the poison-man indeed killed Navdina? Had he taken these from her body? But that didn't make sense: the newspapers had said that Lady Rostikova had not been robbed by her killer.

She had little time to consider the question further, for a squeak from Weveroth warned her of danger. Closing the box's lid, she cast about for somewhere to hide. It was hopeless, of course: the room was far too cramped to afford any hiding place, and she herself was too big to fit into any of the tiny cupboards, or underneath the low bed. Could she reach the door without being discovered?

She whirled, but too late: a tall man stood in the doorway, staring at her. It was the poison-man, she recognised him immediately: not only by his height and his features and the colours of his skin and hair and eyes, but also by the impression he left on her spiritual senses. His imprint on the aether was befouled, corrupted, shrouded with the sickness of his own soul and the filth he had inflicted upon the spirit-world by his crimes.

'I know you,' he said in a low voice. 'The apothecary.' He entered the house, letting the bells on the spirit-braids ring as he brushed past them. 'I could see you were one of us,' he continued, 'even though you've forsaken your village and your people and you live in a foreign *city*. I thought I could trust you not to betray me. Not to betray us. But you've followed me here. Why?'

She grinned at him. 'You've betrayed your own village, and far worse. You've no right to speak of betrayal. Besides, you are quick to jump to conclusions. Perhaps I simply wished to... hire you.'

He folded his arms, staring her down. 'Hire me. For what?'

'Twice now you've come to my shop, seeking lethal poisons. From that I conclude that you're open to certain assignments that many would balk at. If I wanted to have someone removed, would I be correct in speaking to you?'

His eyes narrowed suspiciously. 'I might have traded those poisons.'

'Maybe,' she shrugged. 'But I doubt it. Traders are only concerned with which poisons are the rarest and most valuable. You were looking specifically for the most virulent poisons, the ones that are always fatal to the imbiber. That tells me a great deal.'

'How do you know I used them myself?'

'I don't. But that's a fine collection of jewellery you have there, and I doubt you were given it for any innocent reason.'

His eyes flicked to the box on the shelf, then back to her face. 'You've been snooping.'

'Yep.' She grinned again. It wasn't the reaction he expected from her; no one ever did. It made blunt honesty combined with levity a useful tool for throwing people off balance.

It worked, again. He looked uncertain, then confused. 'What exactly are you looking for?'

'So you are available for hire. That tells me a lot, too.'

'Such as?' He folded his arms and glared at her. In that posture, and with his colouring and height, he reminded her a little of Konrad.

'It tells me you're an outcast here, or if not that then barely tolerated. And that's why you had to ask me for information. You're banned from the Old Knowledge, aren't you? Some of it you take anyway. But poison-craft isn't one of those things. There are no books out here, and nobody would teach you.' She stared at him hard, all traces of levity or even friendliness gone from her manner.

'And that's because you're tainted. Corrupted, probably beyond recall. You've already transgressed too greatly to redeem yourself. So you felt, why try? You became an assassin, one of the worst kind. When somebody came to you asking for a slow, painful, hideous death to be inflicted on Navdina Rostikova, you were quite willing to oblige. As long as they paid well. And they did, didn't they?' She glanced again at the box as she spoke. Its contents were extremely valuable. He'd been well paid for his newest, worst transgressions against the Order of the Worlds.

'You're not here to hire me.' He said it flatly, his manner turning menacing. But she was unmoved.

'The Malykant hunts you,' she said softly. 'Do you know that?'

He froze at her words, turning pale. His hands shook and he swallowed, hard. It took him some moments to get himself under control.

'You know this as fact?'

She shrugged. 'The newspapers said Rostikova was opened up and missing a rib. You know what that means. Didn't you read the reports?'

His lips twisted into a smirk. 'No books out here, as you said. No papers either.'

'You should have known you'd be hunted,' she said coldly. 'Deaths like hers, they stain the aether. Permanently. And the only thing that will ever clean away that taint is *your death*.'

He was shaking again, his eyes wild. 'No! That's not true. It's never happened before.'

'You've killed others, is that what you're saying? I'm not surprised, but I think you've been lucky. Or circumspect; the patterns of your crimes were thinner, flimsier, and they faded into the aether so that barely a hint of your wrongdoing was left. Not this time. The Malykant will find you.'

'With your help?' His voice had gone deathly quiet, and the way he was staring at her began to seem frightening.

Summoning her courage, she stared him down. 'Maybe,' she said in a similar tone. 'But with or without my help, he'll find you. You'd better tell me everything now, and maybe he'll have mercy on your miserable spirit.'

'Everything? Such as what?'

'Such as the name of your new target. The person the ijgaroot was intended for. Or the name of the person who hired you. It's somebody rich, from the look of the reward. Somebody from the city. Give me a name.'

His lips twisted in contempt as he looked at her. 'If you believe me to be so easily cowed, you are not so sensitive a reader as I thought. Though you're good, I'll admit. You read me back in the shop, didn't you? That's how you found me. I should have taken more care. I knew you for what you are, even though you're a foreigner.'

*Foreigner.* Nanda had heard that word many times before. Her pale colouring was close enough to that of the majority of Ekamet's residents, but her pale white-blond hair and sky-blue eyes marked her out as *other*. Her parents had been born far away, far to the north; and though she herself had been born in Ekamet she was not really one of them. It had been difficult, forging her place among them.

It was one of the things that drew her to Konrad. With his dark colouring, he too stood out in Ekamet. But he too had found a way to work himself into their society.

'I am a Reader,' she said, lifting her chin proudly. 'And a witch, though my roots are, as you say, far from here. It doesn't matter. The spirit-world is the same, and the natural Order is the same. And both reject you utterly.'

'I can't let you leave, of course,' was all he said in reply. 'Not if you found me so easily. You'll find me again, no matter where I go.'

The light in his eyes pierced her courage, and she began to tremble. She had got carried away in her indignation at his arrogance, the insolent way he bore himself and his filth, staining the aether further with every step that he took. She shouldn't have confronted him.

But it was too late to think of that now.

'Kill me, and you'll only increase your debt to the Overlord,' she said quickly. 'There'll be no mercy for you.'

'You may be right,' he agreed. 'But there are other ways to dispose of you.'

He advanced on her and she backed away. There was nowhere to go, of course; she soon found herself pressed against the back wall of the house, with the poison-man's large frame between her and the door. He began to whisper under his breath, invoking spirits to come to his aid. It was the corrupted spirits he called upon, of course; those

49

whose inner lights had been darkened long ago by their actions in aiding others like him. They, too, were outcasts, shunned by The Malykt and all who followed Him. And they flocked to this man's call.

He grinned nastily as wisps streamed out of the mist, twisted goblin-shapes that clutched at her hair and her clothes and pinched her skin. A hundred tiny hands grasped her, digging their tiny claws into her soul and tugging, hard. She fought, trying desperately to call her own spirit-guides to her aid; but the poison-man laughed and blew powder into her face and her wits scattered like seeds on the wind.

'Enjoy your precious spirit lands,' she heard him say, and then he and his shabby house faded. The white spirit-world she'd seen in her mind's eye became real as she was pulled bodily through. The landscape glowed brightly enough to half blind her mortal eyes, all fierce lightning etched on deep shadow. Shapes formed and faded around her as the wisps whirled and shrieked and drove her mad with their clutching and pulling and their insidious whispers inside her head.

Her mind had dissolved into a mess of fear, and though she grasped at conscious thought it eluded her. Her thoughts spun and her body whirled in confusion, seeking nothing but escape from the vicious presences that sought to ensnare her soul.

Screaming her fear and despair, she ran.

In the space she'd left behind, the poison-man stood, holding his breath as he dusted the powder from his hands. He didn't notice the tiny gold-furred monkey that ducked out of the house and sped away into the night.

# 8

Konrad left his house in the early hours of the morning, when the moon was high in a sky only partially covered with cloud. The glow it emitted was feeble, but it served to illuminate the streets somewhat. All the better; that would make it harder for his assailant to hide from him.

Eetapi and Ootapi were alert for danger, one sailing the winds a few feet in front of him and the other some way behind. They had camouflaged themselves to the utmost, so much so that even he couldn't see them with his mortal eyes.

He made no particular attempt to hide. He had grown tired of the nameless, shapeless threat hanging over him since his visit to his master's temple a day or two ago. If his pursuer intended harm, he would prefer to resolve the matter now.

In the end, though, his precautions availed him little. Ootapi's voice had barely begun to whisper a warning in his mind when a dark shape leaped out of the shadows before him. In moments he was down. A dark-clad figure loomed over him, a knife glinting in one hand. His other hand was fastened around Konrad's throat, squeezing hard.

So it was to be murder, then. Very well.

Konrad was by no means defenceless; his profession was a dangerous one and he knew how to fight. He did so now, avoiding the downward stroke of the knife and throwing the assassin off him. He made it on to his feet, and for a few moments he held his own, strike for strike, against his assailant.

But this was no ordinary threat. The man was a professional, and horribly strong; Konrad knew he was in trouble. The knife blade flashed again, too close, and a line of pain raced across his torso. The next one would probably kill him.

Sensing his danger, Eetapi and Ootapi rose to his assistance. He felt a flicker of hope: another instant and they would have the assassin's soul bound, and the onslaught would stop. Maybe he would avoid impalement after all.

The assassin was faster even that he'd feared. Perhaps sensing the new threat, the man redoubled his efforts, moving so fast Konrad couldn't even follow his movements. Konrad had only a moment to wonder where in the world his enemy had found this man before the knife blade found its mark. He fell once more, stabbed to the heart, pain crushing his chest.

He lay for an instant, panting with shock and agony, trying not to look at the hilt protruding from his chest. He watched with distant interest as the assassin's body stiffened and backed away; the serpents had him, then, but too late.

Gripping the knife's handle and gritting his teeth, Konrad pulled out the blade. He tried to do it fast, but it took an inordinately long time for the length of sharp metal to slide out of the ruins of his muscles, his skin, his heart. He kept his eyes fixed on his would-be killer as he did so, knowing the man would not expect *this*.

He waited, tense, for the renewed pain of enforced healing. He was not permitted to die, not as long as he served The Malykt. The wound would force itself closed, his flesh would knit together once more and he would be whole. It would hurt - badly - but he would survive.

Nothing happened.

He felt a flicker of panic. The Malykt's favour would last only as long as Konrad pleased Him. Was He pleased now? Had his primary servant performed as expected, these past few years? Konrad knew that if his master's favour had been withdrawn, he may not know about it at first; not until a stray knife-blade stabbed him through and, this time, he did not heal. Then Konrad's life would be over and a new Malykant would be chosen.

Was that happening now?

He tried to suppress his growing panic, refusing to let it show in his face. The assassin, still held in the grip of the serpent-shades,

52

would see nothing of his doubt.

A new thought occurred to him in the midst of his confusion. Were he to die, would it be such a bad thing? His life had its advantages, but no part of it was his own. His tasks were brutal and unpleasant, his master relentless. He was isolated and, he admitted it, lonely. Perhaps it was time to rest.

But then came the pain, waves of it gripping him tight as his tortured flesh mended itself. He lay, shaking, as the wound closed and his body restored itself to full health.

A cold voice pierced his dazed thoughts. *You have not earned a rest yet, My Malykant. Get on with it.*

*Yes, Master,* he thought weakly in reply. He got to his feet, his attention once more on the dark figure who had sought to take his life. He enjoyed the expression of complete horror on the man's face as his injured-to-the-death victim stood up and advanced on him.

'Good effort,' Konrad said to him. He had, after all, done a good job. It wasn't his fault that The Malykt hated training new servants.

The assassin's own knife was in Konrad's hand. He didn't waste any time. One quick movement drew the blade across the killer's throat and he dropped, eyes wide in shock. The serpents vacated his dying body in two puffs of cold wind, and the three of them watched dispassionately as the killer died.

Konrad stood a moment longer, flexing his arms and torso and neck. He was a little stiff, but otherwise in great health. His clothes were ruined, of course, slashed through and soaked in blood, but he didn't need to be well-dressed for his next task.

*Well, onward,* he said silently to his serpents. He walked on, leaving the body lying in the street.

Konrad's next night-time visit to the Rostikov House was easier, as he was familiar with the plan of the building and the habits of the servants. But it was also harder, for the inhabitants were alert to the possibility of intruders. He was forced to wait until the moon was hidden behind a significant bank of cloud, and then to take a less direct route into the house. The rear wall was composed of large blocks of old stone; he climbed it with ease, aiming for the servants' garret at the top.

He could feel the sickness that loomed in the room above him; its scent wove through the aether, acrid and sharp but not, to his relief, redolent of death. Etraya was very ill, but she would not die.

Not yet, at least.

Reaching her window, he paused to survey the room. As he had both feared and hoped, no attendant waited upon her. Either by order of their mistress or through fear of infection, the inhabitants of this house had left the nurse to suffer alone.

He eased open the window and slid inside, closing it behind him, for her room was without a fire and already cold, without the winter winds whirling through the casement. Eetapi and Ootapi were with him, wrapped around his arms like bracelets. They separated themselves from him and streamed over to the bed where Etraya lay.

She was far gone in sickness, that was clear. Her skin was wet with sweat and her breath came in shallow, feverish gasps. A livid red rash covered her face and neck and disappeared inside her nightclothes.

Poor woman.

*Eetapi. Ootapi. Bind her.*

Though she was living, the serpents could still merge themselves with her soul and help her to animate her own body. He had attempted this once before, on another witness whose consciousness was largely gone in illness. It was cumbersome, but it worked. Judging by the way Etraya twisted in her bed and moved her lips in ceaseless, soundless talk, she was delirious and beyond her own control. She would need the help.

He waited as the serpent-spirits' wavering forms vanished inside Etraya's tortured body. After a moment, her restless movements ceased and her lips closed. The serpents had control of her.

He sat down in the chair next to her bedside. 'Miss Marodeva,' he said, speaking softly. 'Etraya. Do you hear me?'

Her eyes opened and her head turned towards him, though she didn't seem to be seeing anything.

'Yes,' she croaked, her throat sore from gasping in her fever.

'I need you to tell me what's going on in this house. The Rostikovs. You know them better than anybody.'

Etraya coughed, a harsh, rasping sound that chilled him. He hadn't sensed her death approaching, but could he be mistaken?

'Calm yourself,' he murmured as she coughed harder. Not only was this bad for her already tortured throat and lungs, but soon she would wake the house.

To his relief her coughing subsided and she sank back into her pillows.

'The Rostikovs,' she said painfully. 'I... mustn't speak of them.'

'You must,' he insisted. 'I must know. For Navdina.'

'Navvy,' she repeated, and her face softened. 'Such a pretty child. Prettier than her mother. Lena hated her, but she didn't deserve it.'

Konrad frowned. Lena? He gripped her hand and leaned forward, trying to keep her attention. 'Etraya, who is Lena?'

'Lena was so jealous, so much anger in her. It was as if she knew... but she couldn't know. She didn't know.'

This, of course, was the flaw in his plan. The serpents could stabilise her, allowing her to talk, but they couldn't influence the flow of ideas in her fevered brain. She was rambling, and he couldn't tell if any of it was useful.

But at least it was something.

'Tell me more about Lena,' he said. 'Lena and Navvy.'

'Navvy was good to her but Lena wouldn't have it. She was cruel, so heartless. When the Lady sent her away, she said it was for her own good. And it was a good school. But Lena knew; we all knew. She sent her away from Navvy.'

The "Lady" in question was probably Navdina's mother, Konrad guessed. But who was Lena and why would the Rostikovs take a direct interest in her fate?'

Lena. A thought flashed into his mind, a dark thought. 'Do you mean Analena?'

'Her father called her Ana, but to all others she was Lena.'

Analena. The current Lady Rostikova, wife of the murdered Amrav, was named Analena. That couldn't be a coincidence.

'Where did Lena go?'

'She didn't like the school. She didn't like anything. She never understood why Navvy had a nurse and was taught at home but *she* had to go away and be taught with a hundred other girls. Poor girl. But what could I do? I had no money to give her.'

'Why should you have given her money?'

'Because she was my child. Her own mother's life was given over to another's growth and education, and she hated me for it. I loved Navvy more, she said. And it was true. Spirits help me, I did love her more.'

Etraya was growing agitated, but Konrad couldn't stop her, not yet. He was learning a great deal, despite the random nature of her reflections. He had to be sure he was drawing the right conclusions.

'Are you saying that Analena Rostikova was once Analena Marodeva?'

'That was her name,' she muttered. 'Hated, hated name. Not her name at all, Spirits forgive me.' Tears wet Etraya's face and she began to struggle against the binding of the serpents, her fists clenched.

'Calm yourself,' he said again, trying to soothe her, but she was unreachable.

'I should never have done it,' she wailed. 'I tried to undo it but it was too late. But how could she know? I told her at last and oh, she was not surprised. But she was a baby at the time...'

Konrad began to get a cold feeling in the pit of his stomach. 'You did something,' he prompted. 'When Lena was a baby...'

'They were born the same week,' she sobbed. 'The very same week, and they were so alike. It seemed like fate. I knew that the Rostikov child would have everything - *everything* - and my poor child would have nothing. It was a mere impulse, I should have resisted but then it was done...'

'You swapped them.' He saw it all in an instant, and his body sickened at the knowledge that a single, weak action by one woman twenty-five years ago had transformed the fate of two girls forever - and destroyed them both.

'I did,' Etraya wept. 'I had the care of them both on some days. One day I changed their clothes and swapped their cradles. When the Lord and Lady returned I gave my Lena into her ladyship's arms, and just like that she became Navdina. And Navvy that was, poor child, she became Analena Marodeva. I thought only of my poor girl's fate; not once did I think about the Rostikov girl. Not until later. But I couldn't undo it then.'

No; such a ruse would only work in the first blush of life, if the child had uninvolved, aristocratic parents who could afford to pay a nurse to do most of the child-rearing. Once they had grown enough to develop distinctive individual features, exchanging the infants would no longer be an option. Etraya would have had to simply live with her sin.

He knew enough of her character to guess that it would have plagued her sorely ever since then.

'Etraya,' he said firmly. 'Did you tell them what you had done?'

'I told Lena,' she said, and repeated the words twice more, her voice shaking.

'Not Navvy?'

'No! I couldn't... couldn't face it.'

'When did you tell Lena?'

'A year ago. I couldn't keep it from her, she was so angry. I thought she had to know. I thought if I confessed, I might be forgiven - be at ease...'

It hadn't worked out that way, he guessed. Analena, already angry at the injustices she saw in society, had become angrier still. And what then? Amrav Rostikov had been married only six months ago. Had she created this plan, hard on her false mother's revelations? She had pursued Amrav, married him, and killed her rival - or had her killed. It was yet unclear whose hand had actually taken Navdina's life.

But why then kill Amrav? Even if she wished to rid herself of him in time, it was unwise in the extreme to do so immediately after the death of her cousin-by-marriage. Some pieces of the puzzle yet remained unsolved.

'It's my fault,' whispered Etraya. 'My fault. Poor Navvy. Poor Lena.'

*Poor Etraya,* he silently added. She had committed a grave crime, but an impulsive one, and she'd paid for it with lifelong regrets and guilt. And at last she had had to watch her daughter, her real daughter, die for her mistake.

Such a high price on human weakness.

A high chittering noise interrupted his thoughts. He turned to see a small dark shape hurl itself against the glass of the window he had closed behind himself. It threw itself at the glass again and again and a dull thumping noise echoed around the room.

A monkey. And that was a flicker of gold fur illuminated by the low moonlight...

He crossed the room in two quick strides and flung the window open. Weveroth tumbled into the room, still chattering.

'Hush, hush,' he murmured, cradling the panicked creature. 'Don't wake the house.'

It subsided and stared up at him in silence, its black eyes huge in the darkness.

'Where is Nanda?' he murmured. He saw no sign of any message from Nanda secreted about the monkey's small body, and the creature's obvious alarm worried him.

Something had gone wrong, and it was *he* who had sent her after the poison-man.

'Calm yourself, Weveroth,' he murmured, thankful that Etraya was too lost in the darkness of her own dreams to attend to him.

*Eetapi. Ootapi.*

The serpents released Etraya and came to him, awaiting command.

*Does anyone guard the door?*

They were gone, and back in moments. *No, Malykant.*

Konrad shook his head, disappointed. Had Nuritov failed to receive his note? Or had he been unable - or unwilling - to act on it?

He gave brief thought to leaving Eetapi in attendance on Etraya, but dismissed the idea. He might need both his serpents before the night was over. He would find Irinanda, then return for the nurse.

And Analena Rostikova.

*Is the Lady of the house within?*

The serpents' answer came instantly. *No, Malykant.*

That made him pause. No? He had not really expected a negative. Where was Lena at this hour of the night? What mischief was she working, somewhere out in the city - or beyond? He suffered a moment's frustration at the thought; he would have liked to take up the chase immediately, find her wherever she was hiding and complete his obligation to The Malykt.

But no. Not yet. First, he must find Nanda.

Out of the window again he went, and down the side of the building. Weveroth scampered ahead of him and waited at the bottom.

'Weveroth,' he whispered to the monkey when he had regained his feet. 'Take me to your mistress.'

The monkey turned and ran, and Konrad and the serpents followed.

If Konrad had had time to think clearly about the matter, he might have expected to be taken to Irinanda's shop, or her house, or possibly to the poison-man. He did not expect to see the world dissolve around him before he had gone more than three steps, or to experience the stark contrasts of the Spirit-World searing his eyes and paralysing his brain with light and shadow and fear. Dread seized him and for a moment, his breath stopped. How had Nanda come to be here? And what would be left of her when he found her?

This last question was soon answered, for faithful Weveroth located his mistress with unerring accuracy. A dark figure rushed at him, dark yet lit with the living, vivid colour that was anathema to the spirit plane. A mortal, her bright, pale hair loose and streaming in the spirit-winds, her body in a frenzy of motion. She rushed past him, eyes wide and staring but not recognising him.

He turned and caught her. He needed all of his strength to hold her in her wild panic.

'Nanda.' He repeated her name a few times, speaking close to her ear, but she did not quiet. Her mind was far gone in fear, and perhaps more than that. Spirit-wisps dived and danced around her shivering form, pinching her, raking their claws through her soul, and as each howling sprite launched itself at her she trembled anew.

The serpents needed no orders from him. They flew at the spirit-wisps, and Konrad felt their inaudible snarls as faint shivers in his bones. Eetapi opened her mouth wide, too wide, and snapped her incorporeal jaws shut around the wriggling form of a wisp. She swallowed, and down it went. Ootapi followed her lead, and one by one the vicious spirits were consumed and dissolved by The Malykt's servants. Irinanda stood, alone except for the two snake-spirits that hovered near her face. She swayed.

*Bind her,* he said to the serpents then, and they obeyed. Nanda's body stiffened as they took control of her bones and muscles and skin, and she stood rigid in his arms. Her eyes, though; they jerked still, this way and that, still seeking escape. Her mind was unaware that help had come, that rescue was at hand.

His heart twisted in his chest, and for the first time in so long he was truly grateful for the harsh blessing that had dampened the strength of his emotions. He could steady her, aware of his dismay and his guilt and his fear for her but not touched by it. He gripped her hand with calm strength, turned and began walking back the way they had come. Nanda walked stiffly beside him.

It was not to his city house that he took her, nor even to her own home. He stepped out of the spirit lands and into the Bone Forest south of Ekamet. His own house rose out of the mist only a few steps ahead, strong winds setting it swaying on its long legs. He watched as the serpents made Irinanda climb the rope ladder,

59

wondering if the rigidity in her limbs would allow her to navigate the ladder successfully. Her ascent was not graceful, but she disappeared safely through the trapdoor and he hastened after her.

*Lie her down*, he instructed, and the serpents carried their prisoner to the bed and caused her to lay herself out upon it. Even recumbent, there was no hint of relaxation in her poor frightened body, and her eyes continued to jerk and shiver in her head.

'Weveroth,' he said. 'I need you to help me.' He was unsure how much Nanda's pet understood; more than it ought to, certainly, and he judged it best to speak freely to it.

Weveroth stopped at his feet and sat back on his haunches, waiting.

'What happened to her?'

The monkey lifted one paw, drew it back and then forward, opening its fingers as if releasing something. It waited expectantly for a moment, then repeated the motion.

'Something was thrown at her,' Konrad interpreted. 'Powder. I can think of three things that it might have been.' He went to his shelves and collected three jars. These he placed before Weveroth, removing the lid on each.

The monkey stuffed its nose into each jar in turn, then sat back again. It made no sign of recognition towards any of the three.

'None of those?' Konrad frowned, puzzled. Obviously whatever she'd inhaled had given her hallucinations, uncontrollable fear, paranoia and anxiety. It had also restricted her breathing: each breath came hard and short, though her chest heaved. He would have thought it would be one of these...

But there was another possibility, a forbidden one. Why had Nanda been so hounded by the cruellest shades of the spirit lands? They did not usually attach themselves idly, and never in such great numbers. Someone - presumably the poison-man - had set them on her.

And if he was willing to bargain with such creatures, nothing would prevent him from further such bargains, the sort for which a mortal must trade pieces of their living soul. What had the poison-man gained in return? Spirit dust. A concoction of mist and earth and shreds of lost aether from the Deathlands; the forsaken goblins and corrupted sprites of that dark spirit land took it and warped it, mixed it with their sweat and their spit and ground it to powder.

Its possession and use were banned across all mortal lands, that he knew. And why? Because its effects were permanent. Irinanda had taken this filth into herself and it had made itself part of her, corrupting her body and infecting her mind. No known way existed to reverse its effects.

He stared at Nanda, her thin body shivering still as she lay on his bed, held there only by the invasive influence of his serpents. Her mind was already gone, probably, and her body would soon follow, melting away into the mists of the Deathlands. His fault.

There was one thing only that he could try. The mere thought sent fear whispering through his thoughts, seeking to make a coward of him. He gathered his Master's coldness about himself, watching as his breath began to steam in the air. He closed his eyes, and prayed.

The cold deepened around him until he, too, began to shiver, clad though he was in his thickest clothes. Ice blossomed across the floor, creeping into the corners of his forest house, spreading over the furniture and reaching long-fingered hands up the walls to the ceiling.

*The Malykt, The Overlord comes,* whispered the serpents, and Konrad's heart began to pound hard in his chest.

*My servant calls, but he has no vengeance to offer Me.*

The voice was deep and dark and full of thunder. It ripped through Konrad's mind, threatening to split him in two. He gritted his teeth and stood his ground, his chin raised high. It did not do to cower before The Malykt.

'My Lord,' he managed to say. 'I have not yet completed the task You recently set for me, but with the help of this woman I am close.'

He felt the Spirit Lord's chilling disapproval at his words. *It is not permitted to you to seek help. No other may interfere in My doings.*

'Yes, Lord,' Konrad panted. 'I have erred, but the punishment for that must rest with me. I beg You to lift the affliction this woman has incurred on my behalf. It is not deserved. She sought only to serve You.'

Nothing happened. The silence stretched out so long that Konrad's hopes fled into the cold and he merely stood, empty of the depth of guilt and sadness that should have been his to suffer.

*I do so,* came the terrible voice again at last. *But not on your account, Malykant.*

Then on whose? Konrad wondered, but he did not dare to ask. He was only grateful. He bowed his head in relief.

'My gratitude is beyond expression, Lord Malykt.'

*I know.*

Then the cold was gone. The ice melted all at once into frigid water, and trickled away through the floor. The Malykt was gone.

'Konrad?' Irinanda's voice, sounding small and lost even in this humble space.

'I'm here.' He went to her, looking her over. Her shaking had stopped, and to his immense relief, her eyes were her own again. She looked on him with confusion, but also with recognition.

He knelt by the bed, and smoothed back the pale, sweat-dampened hair that lay in tangles around her face. 'I'm sorry,' he said. 'I should never have asked it of you.'

She just shook her head, and he guessed she was too tired to speak.

'But you must speak,' he said out loud. 'I need to hear what you've seen.'

So she told him, in short sentences forced from her exhausted body. It was enough.

'Thank you,' he said when she had finished. He layered blankets over her, tucked them in around her bone-white face and gave Weveroth to her.

'You'll be safe here,' he said. 'Rest.'

She didn't answer. She was already asleep.

Moving with quiet care, Konrad equipped himself for his next task. He collected a packet of powder from a locked chest and tucked it into his coat. He checked that the rib bones were in their accustomed place in his top inside pocket. He took up his hat, and the scarf that kept the winter chills off his neck.

Then, with a final glance at Irinanda sleeping peacefully in his bed, he slipped down the rope ladder and out into the Bones.

# 9

The forest was deathly still, with that air of expectancy that seems to wait, breathless, for some event to occur or some danger to pass before customary activity may be resumed. It was the dead of night, but even at this hour there should have been more *life*. As Konrad passed through the half-frozen, mist-drenched trees, animals hid in their burrows and birds cowered in the dormant winter branches. Even the moon refused to shine, hiding itself behind a cloak of heavy cloud.

Konrad ignored it all. He had his purpose now, and this was the part that he both anticipated and dreaded: the hunt, and at the end of it, the kill. He strode on, relentless, following Irinanda's directions in his mind as he made for the house where the treacherous poison-man resided.

He found the house, though not without difficulty. Nanda had told him to use his spirit-eyes, and so he did. He had not yet asked her how she had come to take this approach, nor how she was able to as a mere apothecary. That conversation could wait. But that Irinanda had secrets of her own was becoming quite clear to him.

He let the deep shadows of the real world fade as his physical vision gave way to his spirit-sight and the forest turned pale and gauzy. In this state, walking halfway between the planes, he could just about bear the extreme brights and darks of the spirit lands. The contrasts served him well now: the trees and earth faded to white, while figures and structures stained themselves darkest black.

The house revealed itself to him, tucked into the embrace of a hoary old tree. A slight sound reached his ears, coming from within. Someone, then, was at home.

Konrad stopped, letting the spirit-vision fade. He could see it, now that he knew where it was. The doorway was nothing but a slit in the woodwork, just wide enough for a grown man's shoulders to fit through. He took a moment to extract the powder packet from his pocket. With his other hand he drew a long, obsidian-bladed knife from the sheath on his boot.

Thus equipped, he went inside.

A man stood facing the far wall, his back to the door. This man was tall, with skin and hair of similar shades to Konrad's own. Konrad watched him for a moment in silence, blocking the doorway with his own tall frame. The man was pulling things out of a rough cabinet, rummaging in drawers and packing things into a bundle that lay beside him. He worked fast, knocking things over in his haste. He hadn't heard Konrad's arrival.

'Are we going somewhere?' Konrad asked in a low voice.

The man spun around, eyes wide. He didn't ask who Konrad was; he didn't need to. Konrad had thrown off the camouflage that protected his identity during his daily life. Everything that he was shone in his face, in the aura of menace and power that hung heavy in the air around him.

The man's lips moved soundlessly, his chest heaving with the effort of drawing in breath under the sudden paralysing fear that seized him. Konrad watched him in silence.

'She... spoke the truth.' The words emerged shakily, and sweat shone on the poison-man's forehead.

Konrad lifted a brow. 'She. That "she" whose sanity you condemned in order to save your own worthless skin. Another offence, for which you must also pay.'

'*Malykant*,' gasped the poison-man, and Konrad smiled.

And waited.

The rush of fear began to abate a little, and cunning reasserted itself in the eyes of the man who had destroyed Navdina Rostikova. Good. This one would fight for his life; he would run, and perhaps he would run to the one person he imagined could protect him.

'Shall we get on with it?' Konrad said mildly. He stood aside, leaving the door free. 'You have one chance.' As he spoke, he summoned the serpents from their place deep in his heart and they streamed free, coalescing into sudden brightness.

'Better hurry,' said Konrad.

And the poison-man ran.

Konrad followed. He didn't bother to run. His stride lengthened and ate up the ground, carrying him through the pitch-dark forest at inhuman speed. Ahead of him the poison-man stumbled and fell, picked himself up and ran on, then fell again. Each time he tumbled to the ground Konrad slowed his pace, allowing his quarry to maintain his apparent lead. But he never let himself fall far enough back to lose sight of his prey. He knew that every time the poison-man glanced back, he would see the dark shape that was Konrad still in silent, relentless pursuit, with the shivery gleaming shapes of Eetapi and Ootapi riding the winds beside him.

The only question that remained in Konrad's mind was the poison-man's probable destination. Where was he running to, in this last despairing flight? That he was going to Analena was likely, but she was not at home and Konrad guessed that the man knew that. It would be some secret meeting spot that he was aiming for. A rational man might think better of leading the Malykant to his co-conspirator, but Konrad had deliberately frightened this one. Frenzied with fear, still imagining desperately that he could escape, the poison-man did exactly as Konrad would expect of a coward.

Back into the city they went, in this mockery of a chase. The quarry charged down silent streets, gasping for breath through lungs burning with exertion, wandering frequently off course as he checked repeatedly over his shoulder. Konrad was still there, unshakeable, untiring, relentless.

But when he sensed that his quarry was nearing the end of his flight, it became time to drop back, conceal himself in the shadows and allow the poison-man to think he had shaken his pursuer. He sent the serpents after him instead, and they sailed away, dampening their spectre-glow to a mere flicker.

It was to a small, innocuous looking terraced house that the hunted man went, a narrow building with empty windows, decaying shutters and an overgrown garden. Konrad watched as the poison man went inside and the serpents, virtually indiscernible, ghosted in after him. A moment passed, and then a light went on upstairs. A figure moved past the window, and a second followed: a feminine shape.

It was time, then.

He stepped softly up to the house. The man had had the presence of mind to lock the door behind himself. Laudable instincts at a time of crisis, but little impediment to Konrad. He touched his cold fingers to the lock. The mechanisms sprang open under his icy touch and the door creaked ajar.

The house was too small to possess even an entrance hall. He walked straight into a small sitting room, devoid of furniture and very poorly kept. Paper hung off the walls in peeling strips, the carpet was rotting away and everywhere he looked he saw chipped paint. The rest of the house was no better. As he climbed the stairs, he worried that the faltering woodwork would fail to hold his weight. The steps shook as he climbed, but they held.

The sound of raised voices reached his ears and he paused, registering the source. At the end of a short, dim corridor a door stood closed, a slim bar of light shining at its base. There were his killers, neatly boxed and ready for him.

He approached on silent feet, listening.

'... don't truly believe he was the servant of The Malykt?' It was the female voice who spoke, and her tone dripped scorn. 'He is a fairy story to frighten children, nothing more.'

'Fool,' replied the poison-man. 'What of Navdina's missing ribs? What of your husband's?'

'The police do that themselves, to generate fear in the perpetrators. It makes us easier to catch, so they believe. Looking at you, it might well work. Lans, *pull yourself together.*'

There was silence for a few, long seconds.

'And the man I just met? What was he, an actor hired by the police? Your complacency will kill us both.' Lans, as it appeared he was called, could not hide the tremor in his words.

'You may depart as you choose,' Lena replied with cool indifference.

'*What?*' Lans gasped. 'You dismiss me? And so easily? What of your promises?'

'Which were they?'

'You spoke of marriage —'

'And you believed me! That is the precious part. What will you do, Lans, kill me as well? You will certainly get nothing more that way. Leave quietly and I will see that you are rewarded.'

Konrad heard the distinct sound of a man spitting. He could imagine the refined Lena's revulsion.

'I will leave,' Lans snarled. 'I don't know how he found me before. He could find me again. You'd be wise to leave too, but if you won't -— if you are too convinced of your power — I for one will not mourn your death.'

Lena laughed, the way a woman might laugh at a party when in company with a handsome gentleman. 'Charming boy. Go, then. I'm tired of you.'

But when Lans turned to leave, he found Konrad blocking the door. The Malykant watched as the horror dawned anew in his eyes and his breath stopped in his chest.

Then, to Konrad's surprise, his eyes filled with weird glee and he laughed.

'Well,' he chuckled. 'If it must be too late for me, at least we shall fall together.'

The words were clearly directed at Lena, but she made no sign of having heard them. She stared at Konrad, not with fear but with something nearer calculation. Her close gaze inspected every inch of his attire, noting the knife he held in one hand and the packet he clutched in the other.

'I knew it was you,' she said. 'When you kept appearing at my house. It was you that I saw in the Bones that night, when Navvy Marodeva spoke. I was right.'

'Yes,' he agreed.

'You should be dead,' she said then. 'How did you avoid my assassin? I sent the very best.'

'He was good,' Konrad admitted. 'But the Malykant is not so easy to kill, I'm afraid.'

Lena only sneered.

'You *knew*?' gasped Lans. 'You've known all along that the Malykant hunted us!'

Konrad gave her no time to reply. His arm moved sharply, and the knife flew. Lena gasped as the long blade buried itself in her shoulder, pinning her to the wall. She struggled like a stuck butterfly, but she remained caught.

In the same movement, his free hand dipped into the mouth of the bag he held and emerged bearing a pinch of sunbane powder. He threw this into Lans's face, and the swarthy man stopped laughing

67

abruptly. Instead, he choked as the powder flew down his pipes and into his lungs. His body went rigid and he fell.

And all movement ceased. Konrad bent over him, looking right into his eyes.

'For The Malykt,' he murmured. 'For your crimes against His Laws, the Overlord claims your soul.'

That was all. He sometimes made longer speeches, but he'd had conversation enough with this one.

Navdina's sharpened rib bone was in his hand. He dropped and buried the bone in Lans's chest, listening for the puncturing sound it made as the tip pierced the killer's heart.

'The Malykt comes for you,' he whispered. 'And the soul of Navdina Rostikova seeks vengeance upon you.' He leaned closer. 'She shall have it.'

Fear shone bright and sharp in Lans the poison-man's eyes. For a few quick seconds he continued to breathe, ragged gasping breaths around the fluid filling his lungs. Konrad felt the familiar chill descend on the poor terraced house as The Malykt arrived to tear away his soul.

'Lord,' he murmured, remaining on his knees for an instant out of respect. No answer came, but he did not expect any. His Master waited for him to complete his task.

Konrad stood, slowly. Then he turned to Lena.

She wasn't looking at him. Her wide eyes were fixed on the fresh corpse that had been her lover and accomplice only a few moments ago. Her pretty face was chalk white, her trembling lips almost as red as the blood that soaked her arm and torso. She had stopped struggling, though that may only be the paralysing effect of shock and fear.

Konrad moved until he stood directly in front of her. It was only then that she lifted her eyes to his face and met his cold gaze.

But not with contrition. In an instant, her manner changed from a shocked stupor to fiery anger.

'You've no right to judge me,' she spat.

Konrad stilled. Had she known somehow, precisely the right words to say to make him pause? Was she expecting a reprieve, some kind of weakening in him? Or was this nothing but the wild pronouncements of a mind in trauma?

He was not given to self-doubt. It was one of the qualities that made him a suitable servant to Death's Overlord. But when he did doubt, it was on these terms. He himself was no saint. He had committed offenses of his own in the past, some of them grave. That, too, rendered him a fitting Malykant, for he was no self-righteous zealot; like those he hunted, he had to atone for his past.

But he also had more understanding than was comfortable. Sometimes, he was called upon to punish the crimes of individuals whose circumstances he could relate to all too well. He could not even say for certain that he himself would have acted differently, were he placed into a similar situation. Lena's case was not one of these; she had taken her revenge not on the perpetrator of the crimes against her but against people who were uninvolved. No excuse could be made for her.

Still, he could not help but sympathise with her anger at the turn her life had taken, when she had been due so much more. It made it harder to stand here as her executioner and hear her story, knowing that the ending could not be changed.

He kept his face expressionless as he looked back at her, his doubts hidden. He made no reply to her accusation, merely waited.

Lena lifted her chin and stared at him with pure hatred. 'Well, then. Do as you must. Why do you hesitate?'

'It is no hesitation,' he replied. 'I must first hear your ... explanations.'

She sneered. 'I will not explain myself to you.'

He smiled, in a small way. 'It is not to me that you must explain yourself. The Malykt hears your words.'

She went very still at that, her eyes darting as if she might see the Overlord crouched somewhere in this pitiful room. She would not, of course. When The Malykt was near, there was no manifestation: only a presence, cold and dark and stern.

Another moment passed, and she began to feel it too. He could see it in the way her breath stopped and the fear crept back into her eyes.

'Most of your story is known to me,' Konrad said. 'One element only remains unaccounted for.'

'And what is that?' she breathed. Blood still poured from the wound he'd created in her shoulder, and she was growing pale.

'The role of your husband, Amrav Rostikov, in this tale.'

Her mouth twisted. 'I won him fairly, though it wasn't hard. It was

Navdina that introduced us, isn't that ironic?' A shiver racked her body, beginning at the bleeding shoulder still pinned to the wall. 'What?' she added when Konrad said nothing. 'What are you really asking? Did I love him?'

Konrad narrowed his eyes. 'What I am asking is, *did you kill him?* '

'Yes.' She said it simply, without inflection or any apparent feeling.

'Why?'

'Because he knew.'

He didn't have to ask what Amrav Rostikov had known. Her face told him everything. Lord Rostikov had discovered somehow that his wife had planned and ordered the killing of his cousin. Perhaps he'd also learned of her true history. Here lay the recurring, and so frustrating tragedy of crimes: one led so swiftly, so easily, to another.

So she had killed her husband in order to conceal her involvement in Navdina's death. But was it so simple? He remembered Lans's words, spoken only minutes ago. *You spoke of marriage.*

'His death was planned,' Konrad guessed. 'But not so soon, and not like that.'

'No,' she sighed. 'Something "accidental", and undramatic. But he pried into my affairs.'

Konrad recognised *that* tone. It said, "I deny responsibility for this offense; I was pushed to it by circumstances beyond my control. The victim brought it upon himself."

It never did fly with him.

'And Etraya?' he asked.

At that her cold blue eyes turned to twin chips of ice. He shivered a little at the depths of her hatred for her former nurse; for her supposed mother.

'Is she dead yet?' she said.

'No, nor will she die anytime soon. Your accomplice failed.'

Her eyebrows rose. 'I was told... ijgaroot is always fatal.'

Konrad smiled mirthlessly, thinking of Irinanda. 'He was tricked.'

Lena looked as though she would like to hunt Etraya down herself and throttle her to death with her own hands. Konrad didn't doubt that she was capable of it.

'Why didn't you stop at killing *her*?' Konrad asked. Not that he would have condoned the murder of poor, broken Etraya Marodeva any more than that of Navvy Rostikova, but it would have made more sense.

Lena shrugged, then gasped with pain as the gesture pulled her torn shoulder against the knife. 'My goal was not vengeance. My goal was to regain what's mine.'

He shook his head. 'You could have publicised the story Etraya told you. She would have vouched for her part in it, I'm sure.'

Lena shook her head vehemently. 'Not when it would have damaged Navdina. She loved her more than she ever loved me. Of course she did; Navdina was *her* child. And besides, who would believe the word of a mere nurse and her daughter? Wealth, status: these things will always win over any little matters such as truth or right.'

Konrad's lip curled involuntarily. 'And the poison? You could have given her a quick death; instead you chose a prolonged and most painful one. Was that not vengeful?'

She stared at him with hatred. 'She had my life,' Lena hissed. *'My life! And in exchange for all those years of stolen affluence I inflicted a mere ten minutes' pain upon her. I was lenient.'*

Konrad considered this information; considered her, helpless before him and facing her own death, yet still defiant and wholly unrepentant. Still capable of seeing herself as the injured party. She'd destroyed her cousin-by-marriage, despite the fact that Navdina could bear no responsibility for her mother's actions. She had further planned and carried out the murders of her husband and her former nurse in order to cover her earlier crime and secure her position as the only possible recipient of the Rostikov title and fortunes. And she had concealed her knowledge of the Malykant's hunt from her accomplice Lans, probably hoping that he would bear the brunt of The Malykt's vengeance instead of her.

All of this had been done with no apparent compunction at all.

'Thank you,' he said at last. He took the knife from her shoulder and she drew in a quick breath, a gasp of mingled pain and fear. She swayed, on the point of collapse.

'And now?' she said, with the barest hint of a tremor.

'Amrav is waiting,' Konrad replied.

Her body tensed, just for a split second. He had been waiting for that. Gathering her flagging strength, she bolted, running for the door. But he was too fast for her. He tossed a handful of the powder into her path and she ran full into it. In seconds she had fallen to the ground beside her lover, all her striving reduced to the simple effort to breathe through paralysed throat and chest.

Konrad stood looking down at her for an instant. He took no pleasure in this part of his role: if he had he would have been no true Malykant, no better in fact than she herself. But he could do it, because he must. And because the part of himself that would have screamed and wept at his actions was gone, taken by his master.

The bone was in his hand, its sharpened tip ready. Her eyes moved in her drawn face and she watched its progress as he knelt over her. What was she thinking behind those frightened, defiant eyes? Did she know that her soul would be bound to her murdered husband's until she had paid for his death? Did she guess how fierce the torment would be?

Deliberately, he put those thoughts away from his mind and raised the bone. A single gesture, and it was done; the stake was buried in her heart; her life drained away, and Analena's soul was given into the unforgiving care of The Malykt.

Konrad waited in silence while his master's work was completed. When the Overlord's presence had drained away and only the familiar, unthreatening chill of winter remained in the room, he stood. He gazed for a moment at the twin corpses of Lans the poison-man and Lena Marodeva lying side by side, the bones of their victims piercing their cold hearts.

Then he left the house, stepping out into the drifting snow that fell softly from the darkened skies.

# EPILOGUE

Irinanda was still asleep when Konrad returned to the house-on-stilts high among the trees. He swung himself up through the trapdoor with slow care, unwilling to disturb her. She didn't wake as he moved about the room, cleaning the blood from his hands and replacing his blood-spattered clothes.

But when he moved to the bedside and stood looking down at her sleeping face, she woke almost immediately. Her pale eyes opened slowly and she stared up at him, her face white and drawn within the tangled nest of her white-blonde hair.

'Are you well?' he asked after a moment. She looked healthier than she had when he left; she was at least lucid, and her breathing was regular. But she remained so white and weak.

'I should be dead,' she said flatly. 'Or worse.' She moved to sit up, but he held her down.

'Stay,' he murmured. 'You still need rest.'

'I'm fine,' she snapped. But Konrad wouldn't relax his grip. At last she sank back into the pillows with a harassed sigh.

'I should be dead,' she repeated. 'But I'm not. What did you do?'

Konrad said nothing. Nanda knew he wouldn't - couldn't - answer that question.

If she knew that, she didn't accept it. He saw contempt in her eyes at his silence, and his soul shrivelled a little further.

'Where have you been?' she said then.

He sighed and lifted his eyes to the ceiling. He couldn't answer that either; not that he needed to. She knew where he had been.

73

'Nanda,' he said seriously. 'Your help was... truly important. Thank you.'

He received nothing but a stiff nod in answer to that.

'And... I am sorry that you were endangered by it.'

Some of her frigidity softened at that. 'I was the one who insisted, as I recall.'

There were a number of possible responses he could have made to that. He didn't need to have given in to her questions and guesses. He hadn't been obliged to give her a task, and he shouldn't have sent her after a man who was obviously dangerous. But the slight thaw in her manner was pleasant and he didn't want to risk ruining it with these uncomfortable truths.

'What's next?' she said, her eyes searching his face.

She'd find no hint of a clue there, he knew, as his face was as impassive as always. 'I will take care of you, until you are well. Then I will go back to the city.'

'Back to being a gentleman,' she said with faint scorn. 'Until?'

'Well. Until next time.'

'What's it like?'

The question took him by surprise. He was still more surprised to realise that he wanted to answer it. He badly wanted to talk to someone about the strange double life he lived.

But he couldn't, not really. Not even when it was Nanda.

'It is a purpose,' he said finally.

He expected another surge of anger from her at this vague response, but if anything she looked rather sad.

'Someday you'll tell me more,' she told him. 'I am determined.'

Konrad inclined his head, permitting himself a small smile. He felt a brief flush of warmth at those words. "Someday" meant they were still friends; that she expected to remain friends for some time yet. If she wasn't already repulsed by the things he did as the Malykant, then maybe there was hope for them after all. Maybe he wouldn't lose the only friend he had.

'Maybe I will,' he replied. 'Someday.'

# THE IVANOV DIAMOND

# 1

Konrad Savast's habits might be considered odd even by the most open-minded of persons. Gentleman of the city of Ekamet he may be, and a wealthy one besides; nonetheless he found it necessary, from time to time, to shed the trappings of luxury and make his way out into the marshy Bone Forest, there to gently divest that dangerous woodland of its most virulently poisonous plants.

He also kept company with few living souls. His most regular companions were the shades of two long deceased serpents, Eetapi and Ootapi, and an apothecary as eccentric as he was.

And tonight, his other companion was a corpse.

Again.

Sitting alone in the dark in the house of a stranger, Konrad's reflections were not of a pleasant cast. Fortunately for him, the more peculiar elements of his work were hidden from the majority of Ekamet; all, in fact, save for Irinanda believed him to be no more than Mr Savast of Bakar House, a man of good looks, obscene wealth and considerable address. But that comfort only extended so far. His was a lonely life.

No man should spend so much time in conversation with corpses, he thought, as he gazed upon the dead face of the middle-aged man he'd been summoned to visit. The serpents had brought him here. His task, as always, was to uncover the identity of the killer and deliver justice. Not the civilised justice of the police and the courts, but a more primal kind: the merciless justice of The Malykt, the great spirit who presided over the process of dying. Nothing was more abhorrent to The Malykt than the unnatural death of murder, inflicted by those without soul or conscience. As the Malykant, foremost of The Malykt's servants, Konrad was obliged to be detective, judge and executioner in one.

Sometimes his task was relatively easy. And sometimes – like tonight, he suspected – his task was rather harder. The forty-something man lying before him bore no visible wounds, no signs of trauma, nor any clues as to the cause of his death. There was no tell-tale stain upon the ether to warn him of any interference in this man's demise. And, most tellingly, there was no lingering soul.

*Serpents,* Konrad said in the silent way. *One more attempt, please. Bind him for me.*

The binding involved gathering the traumatised shreds of the victim's soul and restoring them to the body, briefly reanimating the corpse. His serpents, given to him by his Master, were the agents in this unpleasant business, but tonight they had failed.

*It is as we said before,* Eetapi said after a few moments. *Nothing lingers.*

Konrad frowned, thinking. It was unheard of for the soul to depart entirely when a murder had taken place. The spirit, too agitated, indignant and distraught to pass peacefully on to the Deathlands as they should, remained – at least in part – near the site of the crime. That was one reason why the Malykant did as he did: those souls required justice before they could seek rest.

If this man had been murdered, as the serpents claimed, then some part of his soul must be here, lingering near the body he had worn in life. If there was no soul, that suggested that there had been no murder. The spirit had simply passed on.

*Why did you bring me here?* he queried his companions.

*The Malykt sent us,* Ootapi replied.

*The Master Himself?* Konrad was startled – and afraid. He had been woken in the middle of the night by the two shades, as was not uncommon, and brought to this house. Normally they uncovered these crimes themselves, through some means Konrad did not understand. It was unusual for The Malykt to interfere directly.

What was it about this particular death that had The Malykt and his shades disturbed? The man even wore the hint of a smile on his dead face, as though he had died peacefully in his sleep the way most hoped to do. How could there be foul play here?

But if The Malykt said so, then He must be correct. As a poison-master himself, Konrad could think of a number of poisons that would kill quietly and without trace – though none that offered any explanation for the absence of soul. If his Master required an investigation, then he would make one; but the lack of soul made his job much harder, for he could have no conversation with this dead man to elucidate the circumstances of his death.

He stood up from the chair he'd taken and began his usual investigations. The man appeared to be in his mid-forties, with a healthy countenance; no long, wasting illness this, then, but a short and apparently painless one. He was dressed in a working man's clothes, his hands roughened by labour. The room now inhabited by corpse and detective was situated above a small baker's shop, and Konrad felt sure that the man was the owner.

A search of the tiny house – three small rooms in all – revealed the man's name: Pietr Orlov. He was indeed the baker, making a small but sufficient living from his little shop below. No signs of other inhabitants suggested the existence of a wife or children. Nor did Konrad's search furnish any clues as to strife or difficulties in Orlov's life that might explain his death. How could such a simple man have attracted the sort of hatred or calculation that might lead to murder?

Whoever had killed him – *if* he had been killed – had gone to some trouble to ensure that his death appeared to be natural. There were always reasons for that. Perhaps Pietr had been in line to inherit something valuable; that would give a relative a reason to do away with him without wanting to attract suspicion. But given the extreme simplicity of his surroundings, that was hard to believe.

Konrad returned to the bedchamber and stood for a moment, looking down at Pietr Orlov's dead face. He could not bring himself to take a rib. Such a tool would be necessary for the completion of his task, if he were to find a killer; it was required of him by his Master. But to so violate this peacefully sleeping soul would be intolerable.

And so he left the corpse alone, his cold torso untouched. The body would be discovered in the morning and taken to the cold morgue beneath The Malykt's temple; he would have two or even three days before Pietr Orlov's remains would be burned and his spirit formally committed to the overlord's care. If he discovered any real evidence to hint at a crime, he would find the body there and carry out this unpleasant obligation.

For now, though, he simply called the serpents to his side and quietly left the house.

Puzzling though the case may be, there was one secret source of satisfaction to Konrad: the involvement of poison gave him an excuse to visit Irinanda.

He probably didn't need an excuse: she was always welcoming, in her prickly way. But the circumstances of his double life meant that Nanda was his only real friend, and that damaged his pride. It always soothed to have a reason to visit.

He found her in her apothecary shop, as usual. She lived above the shop, and hardly left the premises except to scour the Bone Forest for some of the materials she sold.

'Good morning, Nanda,' he greeted, happy to find the shop empty. She was sitting on the little chair at the back of the room, reading a book – something about herbalism or poison-craft, he had no doubt. She looked up as he entered and gave him a distracted smile.

'Just let me finish this page,' she murmured and dropped her gaze back to the book. Konrad waited, content to watch her read. Just looking at her made him feel better. It wasn't just her beauty, though she *was* beautiful to him: white-blonde hair, lily-fair skin and blue eyes looked so exotic compared to his own olive complexion and dark hair and eyes. But there was also a vitality to her that attracted him. She did nothing half-heartedly; she cared deeply about everything she did, and it showed. He found it inspiring.

A small monkey with gold fur ran along the counter towards him, tail raised in greeting. Weveroth was Nanda's most loyal companion, her friend and her assistant; his intelligence was peculiarly well developed. Konrad hadn't asked her why. She was almost as secretive as he was.

He was engaged in feeding bits of dried fruit to Weveroth when Nanda shut her book and put it away. She stood up and advanced, eyeing his clothing with displeasure. Most people fawned over him for his fine clothes and his apparent wealth, but to Nanda these things were meaningless. She liked his other identity better: the Konrad who spent hours or days out in the Bones as she did, collecting plants and poisons.

'A visit from Konrad-of-the-city,' she said, raising her brows. 'More corpses today?'

He grimaced. Nanda's manner of speech could be so... unceremonious. Blunt, even. 'One corpse,' he replied. 'Looks like a natural death.'

'But isn't?'

'Apparently not. I... have to investigate.'

To that she merely nodded. She'd learned of his life as the Malykant, or rather she had somehow guessed. On the plus side, that meant that his involvement with all the worst murder cases neither alarmed nor surprised her.

'So, what does that have to do with me?' She took over the feeding of Weveroth, taking the remaining fruit out of his hands. The monkey seemed happier with the new arrangement, so he didn't protest.

'I was hoping to consult you on the materials used.'

She shot him a narrow-eyed look. 'You don't need my help. You're at least as knowledgeable as I am.'

'Perhaps, but I'd still like your opinion. And I'd also like to employ your connections.'

'I'm listening.'

And she listened without interruption as Konrad detailed the state of Pietr Orlov's corpse.

'No signs of poisoning, then? No discolourations, contortions?'

'Nothing at all. To all appearances he died in his sleep.'

'Hmm.' Nanda considered this in silence for a moment. 'I can think of a few ways in which such a thing could be accomplished. The poison may have been ingested or inhaled, or administered through the ear. As for the substance... I can think of only one likely candidate. But you know what I am going to say.'

'Nonetheless,' Konrad smiled, 'I'd like to hear it.'

'Ceruleaf. It's fast and painless, and it begins by putting the victim into a deep sleep.'

Konrad nodded. Ceruleaf was his own guess, but it was a difficult poison to trace. 'Do you have any of that in here?'

Nanda was already out of her seat before he'd finished the sentence. She disappeared into the back room for a few seconds, then emerged carrying a small phial containing a fine, rich blue powder.

'I never keep much of it around. I haven't sold any lately, and no, this hasn't been disturbed.'

'You're becoming quite a detective,' Konrad grinned. 'So it didn't come from your shop. Would you be willing to ask around? Somebody must have sold some – or perhaps been robbed.'

'Possibly,' Nanda said. 'My last task from you was rather more exciting than I'd hoped.' But she said it with a twinkle in her marvellous eyes, despite the fact that her last adventure had been not only exciting but life-threatening.

'This one should be simple. Anyway, what are the chances of keeping you away from the case?'

'Minimal.'

'Of course. Better to give you something to do, then. I've learned that lesson.'

She grinned up at him, a smile full of mischief. 'I was useful, last time.'

'And you'll be so again, good Nanda, I've no doubt.' He removed his hat and swept her an exaggerated bow. 'You know where to find me if you learn anything interesting.'

'You're not leaving already?' Her smile dissolved into an expression of surprised dismay.

He had been, but he paused, feeling pleased. Nanda wasn't demonstrative; it was rare for her to express any direct desire for his company.

'I can stay,' he allowed, 'but only if there's tea. I am parched.'

'I am sure,' she said slowly, 'that such a substance as tea can be found somewhere on the premises.'

Konrad's next visit was to his old friend, Inspector Nuritov of the Ekamet Police. Nuritov was a mid-level officer who was frequently assigned to cases of homicide. He knew Konrad as an amateur detective; he thought him eccentric, perhaps, but he had no objection to sharing information provided he was compensated.

But there were times when Konrad's requests puzzled the inspector exceedingly, and the matter of Pietr Orlov was certainly one of those.

'The man's dead, you say?' Nuritov's eyebrows, the same sandy colour as his hair, furrowed into a frown.

'Quite dead.'

'When did he die?'

'Last night, or early this morning.'

Nuritov shook his head. 'No homicides have been reported today, Savast. Are you sure you've got it right?'

'I discovered it by accident,' Konrad said. It was more or less the truth. 'Looks like a natural death, that's the thing, but something about it bothers me.'

Nuritov had just returned to his office. He spent a moment struggling out of his coat and tossed his hat onto a chair before he replied. 'All right,' he said, sitting down at his desk. 'Tell me everything.'

Konrad told him almost everything, naturally excepting the part about his serpents. Nuritov raised his brows, but he didn't ask how Konrad came to be in Orlov's room; he'd learned not to enquire. Probably he put it down to the vast network of "contacts" he supposed Konrad to have.

'No signs of forced entry, I take it?'

Konrad shook his head. 'None, but the house is modest, to say the least. It wouldn't take much to get in without leaving a trace.' He knew; he'd done it himself.

'And no clues as to the supposed intruder's identity?'

'Not a one. The house was practically bare. The man hardly seemed to own anything.'

Nuritov sat back in his chair and surveyed Konrad with scepticism. 'And yet you're convinced there's a mystery here.'

'There may be,' Konrad sighed. 'I'm not sure, no. But Orlov had the appearance of being a strong, healthy man. Why would he suddenly expire? It's a rare thing.'

'Rare, but not unheard of. Are you sure you aren't manufacturing mysteries out of boredom?'

Konrad smiled faintly. It was true that he had enjoyed some weeks of liberty since his last case, but he had plenty to occupy him and rarely suffered from boredom. 'I don't wish for suspicious deaths purely for entertainment, no. Nor am I seeking a miracle from you. But if you could look into Pietr Orlov's background for me, I'd be grateful. His family, too.'

The inspector agreed affably enough. 'If anything turns up about this Orlov fellow, I'll let you know.'

2

Tired from his nocturnal adventures of the night before, Konrad hoped for a decent rest to follow. He was never at his best when he was sleep-deprived, and he had a feeling that the Orlov case would be tricky.

But it was not to be. After a few hours of uninterrupted slumber, Konrad was dragged out of sleep by Ootapi.

*The Malykt sends us again,* said the splintered-ice voice of the male serpent.

*Is it Orlov?* he queried.

*It is another,* Eetapi told him in her melodic tones.

Another what? Another corpse? Konrad was out of bed in an instant, quickly shaking off sleep. He dressed rapidly and made his way in silence to the rear door of his city house. As he stepped out into the night, his serpent-spectres streamed ahead of him, their translucent shapes clearly visible to his eye.

They led him out of the richer sector of Ekamet and into the merchant's quarter. Here were some fine houses, though on a more modest scale to those enjoyed by the aristocracy and the very wealthy. The serpents came to a stop outside one of these, a large terraced house four storeys high.

*Inside,* Eetapi said. *In the servants' parlour.*

Konrad eyed the building with misgiving. This was a different matter from Orlov's little house, in which he lay alone. A house this large would have at least five servants, perhaps more, plus the family. He would have to take much more care.

Making his way to the back of the house required him to walk back to the end of the street, then pass around to the rear of the row of buildings. He counted carefully: eight houses and then the ninth was the one he wanted. He walked across the rear garden, taking time and care, until he reached the back door.

The Malykt had given him a number of gifts with which to carry out his investigations, and one of these made locks and bolts little barrier to him. He touched cool fingers to the sturdy lock on the servants' door of the silent house and it opened for him. He heard bolts drawing themselves back on the inside, and then he was able to open the door. This he did with care: had anyone else heard the noise?

He stepped into a mercifully empty – and very cold – back kitchen. Moving with the silent stealth of long practice, he followed his spectres through into a short passageway, and then into a small, comfortably furnished servants' parlour. Inside, a youngish man lay on a sofa, apparently asleep.

It was the work of a moment to establish that he was not asleep, but quite dead.

*Light,* he requested, and his spectres obligingly brightened the ghostly white glow that clung to their incorporeal forms. He had shut the door behind him, but still he would work fast: he wanted no wandering, sleepless servant to notice a thin beam of light under the parlour door.

Konrad checked the body thoroughly for any wounds, obvious or subtle. Like Orlov, this man had none. And like Orlov, he appeared to be healthy and strong, with no signs of lingering illness or physical weakness. He was a handsome man, dark-haired and apparently in his thirties. That he was a servant in this house was obvious from his costume, but he was a high-grade one; if not a butler, then a front-of-house footman.

How long had he been dead? Not long, Konrad judged; his body still looked disconcertingly close to life. If he worked fast, he might have time to catch the soul before it departed.

*Bind him,* he instructed his spectres, and as one they dived towards the manservant's lifeless shell and disappeared. Konrad didn't know exactly what it was they did, but the result of these bindings was a talking corpse that could sometimes give the Malykant information about their death.

Last time, of course, it had not worked. Orlov's soul had not lingered. Would their efforts be successful tonight?

As he thought this, the serpents faded back into view.

*The soul is absent, Malykant.*

Konrad sighed. No soul, no clue. For the second time in two days – or rather, nights – he had been called to the side of a fresh corpse whose soul had apparently departed as normal. Why had he been summoned?

But the Master could not be wrong. In sending Konrad to this scene, The Malykt asserted that this man's soul had *not* passed into His care as it should have. Konrad had to trust to that, and find another explanation. But what could possibly have become of the manservant's shade? It was a rare thing for a ghost to resist the Passing, but it sometimes happened. For a ghost to resist the Passing *and* wander away from its earthly remains – or the site of its death – was highly unusual.

For *two* souls to do this in such a short space of time was unfathomable.

The circumstances surrounding these two deaths were too similar to admit of a doubt: they had not occurred naturally, and the murders must have been perpetrated by the same person. That meant there was a connection between the killings. Konrad would worry about the problem of the missing souls later: first he would find out what linked these two crimes.

Turning away from the body, he spent a few minutes in thorough examination of the scene. The parlour wasn't particularly clean. A few articles lay about the room: a ragged newspaper from two days ago, a pair of worn slippers, a box of matches. Besides these the room was bare, rather like the sparse surroundings of Pietr Orlov. Nothing struck him as out of place or unusual. Most importantly, there was no sign of any drinking vessel that might have been used by the dead man – and therefore might have contained a poison. If a venom had been taken orally, the killer had removed the evidence.

Konrad felt that he was running out of time. He had been in the parlour for more than half an hour already, and he felt his position to be precarious. A house full of servants was rarely still for more than an hour or so at a time; if he stayed much longer he was sure to be discovered. With a last regretful look at the silent form on the sofa, he left the parlour and made his way back through the house and outside. He still didn't know anything about the slain manservant, but he would find out everything he could in the morning.

Returning to that prosperous street first thing the following day, Konrad found the house in obvious disturbance. The servants' door was wide open and, as he watched, a boy in his early teens came hurtling through it and departed at a run. He judged that the body had not long since been discovered.

He sent a silent call to Eetapi and Ootapi, and they materialised before him. Their translucent bodies were all but invisible in the morning sun; he saw them only with his spirit vision.

*Go and eavesdrop,* he instructed. He didn't need to say anything further: they knew what kind of information he wanted, and how to find it out.

*Yes Malykant,* they said and drifted away.

Konrad retreated to a safe distance, stationing himself where he could see the house without being observed by its inhabitants. He waited patiently for more than half an hour, shivering a little in the cold winter air despite his thick coat and boots. The sky was leaden with snow and the dull grey light cast an air of sullen misery over the row of luxurious houses. Fitting, Konrad thought.

He sensed rather than saw the serpents' return. They settled around his neck, putting their cold faces close to his ears, and began to whisper.

*The man is Mikhail Ivan,* said Eetapi. *A trusted manservant. He had worked here for three years. The house is owned by Alexander Nureyev, a carpet merchant. He was happy with Ivan's service.*

*Ivan had no enemies within save one,* Ootapi continued. *The butler resented the goodwill his master felt towards Mikhail, and feared for his position.*

*Did the butler not give satisfaction?* Konrad enquired.

*Yes. His fears appear to have been unfounded. We do not think the merchant meant to replace him with Mikhail.*

Konrad nodded slowly. *Anything else?*

*The servants are unsettled. They say Mikhail was in fine health and fear some event must account for his death. But the merchant is calm. He does not call it suspicious.*

Two possible angles here then, Konrad thought. First, the butler. A paranoid man without scruples might well remove the younger servant he feared would replace him. But if his fears were largely

87

baseless, it seemed a particularly extreme action to take. Besides that, the obvious similarities between Ivan's death and Orlov's discouraged Konrad from relying on this theory: what possible motive could the butler have had for killing Orlov? It was hardly possible that a lowly baker could have posed any threat to him.

But what of the merchant? His coolness in the face of his servants' agitation was odd, and his refusal to consider the possibility of foul play could be suspicious. But then again, the servants would have known Mikhail in a way that his employer probably had not. It may be merely the natural conclusion of a man with no reason to believe that his footman's death was peculiar, and who preferred to maintain peace in his household.

And again, there was Orlov. Everything about the baker's case counted against the possibility of the merchant's involvement, as it did the butler's. Unless Konrad could discover some clear connection between Orlov and someone in that house, he must assume that Ivan had been removed by some outside agency.

*Thank you,* he said to his serpents, and dismissed them. He walked alone in the direction of his house, deep in thought.

Halfway there, he changed his mind and went to the police headquarters instead. Finding Nuritov out, he slipped a note under the door of his office with the name of Mikhail Ivan and a request for information. If there was a link between Orlov and Ivan, he hoped the inspector would be able to uncover it.

A reply came from Nuritov the following afternoon, in the form of a letter.

*Can't leave the office,* it began. *I've looked into Orlov and Ivan – lifestyle, past history etc – and there's nothing unusual in either case. No sign of secrets either. Definitely the two most boring people I've ever had to investigate.*

*As far as I can tell, they did not know one another and had nothing in common. Are you sure they were murdered?*

*I'll write again if anything comes up.*

*- A. N.*

Konrad folded the note with a sigh, and put it away in his desk. There *had* to be a connection and he had been sure that Nuritov would discover it. The man was a terrific inspector and he had some skilled people working for him. What if he was right to question their cause of death? What if the two men had died of natural causes, in a similar way, at around the same time? Stranger coincidences had happened.

But his Master said otherwise, and Konrad had to have faith in The Malykt. If those two souls had not passed on to the Deathlands, then something peculiar was happening whether their deaths were natural or not.

Konrad sat in his favourite armchair, stretched his long legs out onto the footstool and folded his arms behind his head. Closing his eyes, he sought for his serpent-shades.

*Remind me of the circumstances of each death,* he requested. *Beginning with Orlov.*

For the next half-hour, he revisited each of the scenes of death with the help of Eetapi and Ootapi. Nothing in either case had struck him as significant before; nothing struck him as significant now. If the two men had been killed, the crimes had been carried out by someone skilled at removing all trace of their presence.

The only possible lead Konrad could think to follow was the manner of their deaths. Irinanda was probably right about the poison: ceruleaf was quick-acting and much less violent in its effects than many others. But how had it been administered? He felt instinctively that the peaceful repose of both men had been no mere seeming: they had died in their sleep. In which case, it was unlikely that the poison had been ingested. That left two options: the poison had been inhaled or injected in some manner.

Nanda was the person to ask about that. The depth of her knowledge alarmed Konrad sometimes: she knew all manner of details about the poisons she sold, as if she had personally tested the unique properties and applications of each one. In truth she merely collected that information from customers, associates and colleagues; she was curious-minded and adept at putting herself in just the right places to pick up plenty of tidbits.

Nonetheless, she could be unnerving.

His thoughts full of muddlesome, puzzling Irinanda, Konrad jumped violently when Nanda's own voice spoke from the doorway behind him.

'Here you are,' she said, rather obviously. 'Lounging around? How very... privileged of you.'

Konrad leapt out of his chair and spun around to face her. She was wearing a blue cloak with the hood up, and the familiar, teasing smirk that she frequently adopted around him.

'Am I interrupting your interlude?'

'My *interlude?* I was thinking!' Konrad folded his arms and glared at her. He was quite a bit taller than she, and he knew himself to be intimidating when he wanted to be.

Nanda merely grinned. 'About what?'

*You,* he thought promptly, and felt his face flush in a mortifying way. 'I was thinking about this case,' he said coolly. 'No leads have turned up and I'm stumped.'

Nanda shrugged off her cloak and threw it over the back of a chair. 'May I sit down?'

'Of course, but...' Konrad frowned at the discarded cloak. 'Why didn't my man take that for you? Why *are* you here anyway?'

'He didn't, because I didn't use the front door,' Irinanda replied, settling herself in his own favourite armchair. 'And I'm here because I have information for you and I thought you might want it right away.'

'Nice try, but that doesn't fly,' Konrad said, hanging her cloak on the back of the door. 'Normally you'd send me a nice, peremptory note of summons. If you do come to see me, you go to the marsh house. You *never* come here.' Never was a strong word, but the perfect truth in this instance: Irinanda professed to hate his luxurious lifestyle and had always avoided Bakar House.

But she only shrugged. 'Maybe I was lonely.'

'*You?* Lonely?' He laughed. 'Never.'

She shot him a mischievous smile, showing a hint of a dimple in one cheek. 'Weveroth's keeping shop for me, but I shouldn't stay long.'

Konrad's eyebrows shot up. Weveroth was keeping shop? The *monkey?* He blinked at her, but she didn't elaborate.

Then again, the little gold-furred simian was oddly intelligent and peculiarly capable, so perhaps it shouldn't surprise him. He let that one pass.

'Tell me what you've found,' he said instead, snatching the footstool and carrying it over to the other chair. Nanda's blue eyes glinted at him with annoyance, but she merely tucked her legs up under her and leaned back into the softness of the chair.

'Maybe luxury has its benefits,' she murmured, closing her eyes in pleasure. 'I could do with one of these in my house.'

'I'll send you one,' he promised. 'Just as soon as you tell me what you've discovered.'

She opened her eyes and smiled at him. 'Perhaps I shouldn't have got your hopes up. I haven't found much. But I did enquire with the other poisoners.'

'And?'

'And there's a tiny shop right on the edge of the city, new place, just opened up last month. The owner's a friend. He says his supply of ceruleaf has been raided.'

Konrad sat up. 'Yes? Does he know who did it?'

Nanda shook her head. 'He didn't even notice it had happened until I asked him about his stock of that particular poison. He'd had a full jar of it – new shop, you know, and he hadn't sold any of it yet. The jar's gone.'

Konrad slumped back into his chair, dejected. 'Don't tell me. No clues left behind, no hints of any kind as to who took it.'

'Correct. You're welcome to look for yourself if you like; Danil said it would be all right. But I've checked as thoroughly as I know how and asked plenty of questions, and I came up with nothing.'

'I'm starting to hate this case,' Konrad groaned. 'Though your information isn't useless by any means: it does suggest that there *is* a ceruleaf poisoner loose in Ekamet.'

'Thank you,' Nanda said stiffly.

'Sorry,' he muttered. 'I didn't mean that it's worthless. It's just that I've never had a case with so little to go on and it is driving me crazy. Here's a question for you. What's the best way to administer ceruleaf?'

'The best way? You mean the most effective way, or the most untraceable way?'

'If there's a method that's both effective and untraceable I'd be interested to hear about it.'

'The ear,' she said promptly. 'A careful poisoner could use a syringe of some kind to apply a liquid ceruleaf-powder solution to the ear canal. If he or she did it while the victim was asleep, it would result in the sort of death-scene you described.'

'The ear,' Konrad repeated slowly. 'So we are looking for a poisoner of unknown gender, with considerable knowledge of both poisons and the weirder methods of application. And also a reason to kill a humble baker and simple manservant, on opposite sides of the city, with no money or assets of any kind and no connection to anything more nefarious than bread and silver trays.' He paused. 'Should be easy.'

Irinanda narrowed her eyes at him. 'We?'

'All right, I.'

She gave him a rare smile without any mockery in it. 'I don't mind "we".'

He smiled back. 'All right, mine ally. What do you suggest should be our next move?'

Her smile disappeared. 'No idea.'

'Excellent,' he sighed. 'Me neither.' A disturbing thought occurred to him and he frowned. 'They took the whole jar, you said?'

'If you were wondering, yes, that is enough for more than two lethal doses.'

'So there could be another target.'

'It's quite possible, yes. We'd better catch this person before they have chance to use the poison again.'

'Agreed, but how? With what? We're at a standstill here.'

'You'll think of something.' Irinanda stood up and looked around for her cloak.

Konrad didn't miss the choice of pronoun. So much for "we". 'Leaving already?' he said, retrieving her cloak for her. 'This was a short visit indeed.'

'I told you it would be.' Nanda accepted her cloak from him and swirled it over her shoulders, drawing the hood up to cover her white-blonde hair once more. She grinned up at him. 'Let me know how I can help.'

'Wait,' Konrad said, stopping her as she made for the door. 'Have dinner with me.'

She lifted her pale brows at him, her expression incredulous. He couldn't tell if she was pleased. 'I told you, I have to get back. I can't leave Weveroth to mind the shop forever.'

'But you could come back in a little while.'

She glowered up at him. 'Is this because I said I was lonely?'

He held up his hands and stepped back, a picture of innocence. 'Not in the slightest!'

She rolled her eyes. 'Actually I have another engagement. Danil invited me to dinner tonight.'

Danil? It took a moment for him to remember: she'd mentioned Danil as the man with the new poison shop. A friend of hers, she'd said.

He scowled. 'Very well, leave me.' He took another step back and out of her way, squashing the flicker of disappointment he felt. What had possessed him to ask anyway? The question had emerged before he really knew what he was going to say.

'Sometime,' Nanda said, sailing past him with her chin high, 'I might invite you to have dinner with *me*. How about that?'

That, Konrad thought, defied belief. If it was unusual for her to visit him at Bakar House, it was at least as unlikely for her to invite him – or anyone – into her house. But before he could think of a suitable reply to this small miracle, Nanda had gone.

'That would be fine,' he mumbled uselessly to the empty doorway.

Danil Dubin proved to be a quiet young man with a mild manner and more than passably good looks. Konrad went straight over to his shop, hoping to find Nanda there, but she hadn't yet arrived for her dinner engagement.

'Mr Savast,' Dubin said, stammering over the name a little. 'Iri said you might visit but I didn't really think – I mean, it's an honour, sir.'

*Iri?* Konrad's scowl deepened. 'Is it an honour? Why?'

'Oh... well, you're a prominent personage in Ekamet, sir, and, um.' Dubin floundered to a confused halt, and stared at the floor.

'For no great reason, Mr Dubin; merely for possessing great wealth. Can you name a single truly impressive thing that I've done?'

Dubin's cheeks flamed red and he didn't look up.

'I didn't think so,' Konrad sighed. Honestly. His wealth was comfortable but not nearly as considerable as people thought; the widespread belief in his princely riches had come from the Order of the Malykt, and they spread those rumours for his benefit. Doors opened to people who had wealth, they'd said; it carried considerable power with it.

Konrad couldn't deny that it had served him well on more than one occasion. He had gained access to many places that would have been closed to him otherwise; places he needed to go in order to fulfill his role as the Malykant. But his status as a city celebrity irritated him enormously.

'Miss Falenia didn't happen to mention why I'm here, did she?' he said with terrific restraint.

'M-miss Falenia? Who... oh, Iri.' Dubin risked a glance up at Konrad's grim face. 'Something about the ceruleaf?' he mumbled.

'Quite so. You aren't going to ask why I'm interested in the ceruleaf, are you, Mr Dubin?'

The young man shook his head. He looked so depressed that Konrad's annoyance faded. The kid might be foolish but he was probably harmless.

'Where do you store the ceruleaf? I would like a few minutes alone in that area, and then I shall leave.'

Dubin hastened out of the room and Konrad followed. The young poison trader had a small storage room behind the shop floor, packed with jars of powders, leaves and roots. Konrad could see at a glance that nothing was out of place: hundreds of jars sat in perfectly ordered rows, each one sporting a tightly sealed lid.

'Who has had access to this room in the past few weeks, Mr Dubin?' Konrad said, his keen eyes sweeping across each shelf in search of a clue.

'W-well, anyone, Mr Savast,' the miserable young man mumbled. 'I've only just got started, you see, and for a while I had lots of things in boxes and... well, I wasn't too careful about security. Hardly anyone knew I was here.'

And that would be why the thief had chosen this shop, Konrad thought with an inner sigh. Lots of fresh stock, an empty shop and a careless – or clueless? - owner.

'My thanks,' Konrad said shortly, and stalked out of the storeroom.

On his way out of the shop he bumped into Irinanda. She had changed her clothes and now wore a pretty red dress under a dark cloak, and a necklace of polished glass. Her hair was loose. She looked very different from the Nanda he knew, more usually attired in her thick workroom coat and with her hair bound back.

As he approached, she stopped where she stood – blocking the doorway – and gave him a cool, speculative look. 'I hope you haven't been scaring my friend, Konrad.'

He didn't like the slight emphasis she'd placed on the word "friend". What was that supposed to mean?

'Of course I have,' he growled. Lifting the brim of his hat in a salute, he waited with exaggerated politeness for her to move. He could hear Danil Dubin trotting up behind him, practically radiating awkward delight.

'Iri! You're a bit early – I mean, not that I'm – it's marvellous that you're here. You know Mr Savast, I assume? No, wait, I meant – of course you do.'

Nanda's eyes flicked to Danil. Judging from the faint surprise in her eyes, the kid wasn't usually such a bumbling idiot.

Oops, thought Konrad. He'd scared the boy more than he'd meant to.

'Do enjoy your dinner,' he said with a false smile, and as soon as Nanda moved he slipped past her and out the door. He strode away into the cold, darkening evening feeling profoundly irritated. The visit had brought him no leads and no clues: just an aggravation. Why would an independent, intelligent woman like Nanda waste her time on such an infantile youngster as Dubin?

# 3

While Irinanda spent her evening in the dubious pleasure of Danil Dubin's company, Konrad walked home alone, his mind busy with a difficult decision that he had to make.

If he was to enact vengeance for the deaths of Orlov and Ivan in the usual manner, he required some piece of their physical bodies with which to do it. Typically, he took a bone from the rib cage. The process was messy and invasive, and he wouldn't do it lightly.

Did he have enough evidence to justify the taking of a rib from each of the two men? He had to be certain that their deaths were unnatural, and he still wasn't, quite. But the ceremonial burning of Pietr Orlov's body would probably take place on the morrow, and Ivan's funeral soon afterwards. If he was going to do it, it would have to be tonight.

He had no direct evidence of murder in either case, but the implications were increasingly convincing. Firstly, there was the intervention of The Malykt. Secondly, the theft of the ceruleaf from Dubin's shop, a poison which would certainly produce death in the manner he'd observed if it was administered in the right way. And thirdly, the evidence of the victims themselves: they were both strong, young or youngish men in good health, who had no reason to expire as they had done.

And there was the little matter of the missing souls.

His decision made, Konrad directed his steps towards The Malykt's temple, turning the collar of his coat up against the cold. It was only late afternoon, but winter had shortened the days; night had settled in during the short time he had spent in Dubin's shop. Flickering gas-lights shone over the darkened streets, still busy with vehicles and pedestrians hurrying home before the freezing chill of the night set in. Konrad kept to the shadows, easily avoiding the notice of the people he passed.

Bypassing the front door of the temple, Konrad went in by a small, unobtrusive back entrance. The morgue was situated beneath the grand building and he went directly downwards, pausing only to rid himself of his coat and hat. He didn't want to get blood on either of those articles.

This facility for the dead was run by fellows in the Order of the Malykt. The organisation was small and select; its members were chosen for a variety of qualities, one of the greatest of which was discretion. Those who knew – or had guessed – Konrad's role would never reveal his identity as the Malykant: the Master saw to that. The official on duty waved Konrad through without hesitation, and he passed into the bone-chilling cold of the temple's depths.

Orlov had already been laid out for burning, which meant that his funeral was to take place first thing in the morning. Since he was a poor man, his Ceremony of Passing would probably occur alongside those of several others of similar station. Konrad stationed himself at the dead baker's side, and summoned his serpents. The two shades materialised promptly, their ghostly shapes prominent to Konrad's spirit-eye.

*Eetapi. Ootapi. See that I am unobserved.*

The serpents faded back into the aether and Konrad stood quiet, waiting. Until recently, these were precautions that Konrad had only taken when he had reason to believe himself watched. But during his last case as the Malykant, he had been observed in secret by the killer he sought, and his identity discovered. This had led to... complications, when the killer had sent an assassin after him, hoping to destroy Konrad before he could carry out his vengeance.

Luckily for him, his enemy had not known that The Malykt's protection extended to the preservation – and restoration – of his life, when necessary. He had avoided death, but the experience had been painful and unpleasant and he had no wish to repeat it.

The serpents returned.

*All is clear,* Malykant, said Eetapi. *No one is near save those loyal to the Master.*

Konrad nodded. Good. Rolling up the sleeves of his fine white shirt, he retrieved his obsidian knife from its sheath in his boot and began his work.

The incision was made skilfully. In his past life, Konrad could never have imagined himself performing such distasteful surgeries upon the bodies of fellow men and women, but as the Malykant he had learned fast. The Malykt had also done him the further service of dampening his emotions; he could pursue the more unpleasant aspects of his job without feeling more than mild revulsion in some distant part of his soul. It was true that most of the higher and finer emotions had left him along with those of a more negative persuasion, but he accepted this. It was a fair trade, given what he had to do.

He opened up the chest cavity with care, grateful for the lack of blood. Here was the first advantage to postponing this procedure: the state of the corpse eliminated most of the mess that he had to deal with when the kill was fresh. A series of quick, deft incisions bared the thickest and sturdiest of Orlov's ribs, and he efficiently carved one out. He wrapped the bone in a piece of cloth and tucked it into a pocket, ready to be cleaned and sharpened later.

He took the precaution, on this occasion, of sewing the torso shut once more. When he had finished, Orlov's torso was restored to a decent appearance, albeit with a long scar running from his neck to his abdomen.

The body of Mikhail Ivan, the manservant, had not yet been prepared for the ceremony. Konrad retrieved it from the storage units along one wall, borrowing an empty table for his own preparations. Within half an hour he had completed his grisly operation on Ivan's cold remains and returned the body to its appointed place. The manservant's bone went into his pocket alongside the baker's. Konrad wasn't concerned about mixing up the two: he had only to touch one of the bones in order to learn who it belonged to.

Konrad left the morgue to find that nearly two hours had passed; Ekamet's citizens had gone home to their dinners and the streets were quiet. Unwilling to face the cold, he wished briefly that he had taken his carriage to Dubin's shop instead of walking; then he would have the equipage to convey him home. But on second thought, he did not regret that his coachman knew nothing about his visit to The

Malykt's temple; he didn't want the man wondering about his master's activities and drawing any inconvenient conclusions.

Instead, Konrad hailed a hired carriage and suffered the jolting motion of the cheap vehicle, grateful enough to be protected from the harsh winter wind that howled through the streets of Ekamet. He was soon restored to the warmth and luxury of his own home. Over the course of the evening he would retire to the little, securely-locked workroom that he kept in his house and prepare the two rib bones for later use. Then, with his weapons ready, the only task remaining was to identify the killer of Orlov and Ivan and put the bones to their appointed use.

*Simple,* he thought sourly.

Unsure where else to turn, Konrad began his endeavours on the following day by returning to Nuritov's office. He found the inspector in residence, but on the point of leaving the station.

'I can't talk much now,' said Nuritov cheerfully. 'Big case to attend to this morning.'

'Oh? Anything I'd be interested in?'

'Hard to say. Do thefts intrigue you as much as murders?'

'Ordinarily, no,' Konrad replied. 'But it depends on the circumstances.'

'This one's likely to be sensational,' said Nuritov with more than professional enthusiasm. 'One of those big diamonds vanished last night. You know the sort: big as a chicken's egg and worth more than I am. A lot more. It belonged to Anton Ivanov. You know, the banker?' The inspector bustled about the office as he spoke, fetching all manner of useful items from his desk drawers and his cupboards and packing them into his pockets. 'I'm usually on homicide but they're bringing most of us in on this one. Huge case.'

Of course it was a huge case. Anton Ivanov was one of the richest men in Ekamet – by a long way. He had the power to make life very difficult for the police if they didn't find his diamond for him.

Konrad knew Ivanov a little, and he didn't think the man was the type to blame the police force if the diamond was lost. But they couldn't be sure of that. And even if Ivanov was gracious about it, the media would be reporting on every detail as the case progressed. The police would throw everything they had at this one.

People like Pietr Orlov and Mikhail Ivan tended to get forgotten when crimes were committed against the likes of Ivanov. It irked Konrad to think that the wealthy ran roughshod over the rights of the poor, even when it came to justice – and that he, of necessity, had been installed as a member of that elite class.

Well. If the police didn't have time for Orlov and Ivan, he did. He would make sure that their deaths were avenged.

'Good luck with that,' Konrad said, backing out of the way as Nuritov lunged for a filing cabinet that stood behind him. 'I was hoping to talk to you about the poisoning case. The baker, and the manservant?'

'Oh yes? What did you want to discuss?'

'I'm at a standstill on it. I was hoping there might be some resource you haven't already tapped, something I can use to find out more about them.'

Nuritov shook his head. 'Not that I can think of. Far as police resources can tell, there was no connection there and no motive for murder. I'm sorry I can't help you further, truly. I must be off. Drop in at Ivanov's if you feel like it – should be an interesting case.' With that, the inspector donned his hat and left the office, leaving Konrad behind alone.

Konrad wasn't disinclined to follow Nuritov's advice and look in on the Ivanov case. Such a heist could well be fascinating. But he refused to allow his own time to be drained away on such a project when the banker already had the majority of the Ekamet Police working on it. His own duty was to the two forgotten men. But where could he search next?

In the end he went home, and stripped himself of the expensive clothes and adornments that marked him out as a gentleman of wealth. He donned instead the rough, sturdy, inelegant garments that he wore for his sojourns out in the Bone Forest. Thus attired, and with Mr Konrad Savast's refined accent dropped in favour of his natural tones, he set off for Pietr Orlov's street. Somebody there must know something about the baker. Somebody must have seen something on the night that he died. Konrad resolved to interview everyone in the immediate vicinity of Orlov's bakery, and then to repeat that process at the house in which Ivan had served. He must, he *hoped*, he would turn up something he could use.

It was evening again before Konrad returned home. Late evening. He was a figure of dejection as he let himself back into his house, using the rear entrance to avoid being spotted in his unusual clothes. He had spoken to more than thirty people over the past ten or eleven hours, and learned nothing save that both men were, to all appearances, fully as plain and simple in their lives and doings as Nuritov had concluded.

Orlov had been a sociable man. In the mornings he rose early to bake the bread he would later sell in his shop; his evenings were spent at a local drinking house. He arrived at the house by eight in the evening, every evening, and left again three hours later. Despite appearances, his friends at the drinking house swore that Orlov drank only lightly. He went for the company, not the alcohol, and was usually sober when he returned home. As far as Konrad could learn, that was the pattern of his life, simple and regular and absolutely without deviation. His last visit to the drinking house had been four nights ago, and he had been exactly the same as ever: jovial, talkative, in good health and apparently untroubled.

So much for the baker. Ivan's story was even less promising. He lived at the house of his employer and most of his actions were witnessed by his fellow servants, or his boss. He engaged in no unusual activities while on the premises of his employment, and his one night off a week was always spent with a young lady who worked as a housemaid at a different house along the same street. His job had been secure, and he had been held in high esteem by servants and employers alike; even the butler, though suspicious, had not apparently held any serious grudge against him. He, too, had been in perfect health and excellent spirits immediately prior to his death.

No leads lay in any of this, that Konrad could see. When they lived such plain lives and had so few adventures or activities, how could these two men have become targets for murder? No connection had emerged in his investigations, either; not so much as a single person had been known to both men, nor had they frequented the same drinking-houses or patronised the same shops. Their lives had been wholly separate from one another.

Disgusted with himself and suffering the first twinges of despair, Konrad retired to bed. He was weary. His sleep had been twice disturbed over the past few nights, and a long day on his feet had left him feeling drained, physically and mentally. He dismissed his manservant early and, tucking himself under the deliciously warm blankets of his bed, he went to sleep.

Eetapi and Ootapi woke him up sometime later. A glance at the clock – conveniently illuminated by the shades' ghost-glow – told him that two in the morning had only just struck.

Two in the morning. He'd had four hours of sleep.

*And?* he snapped, a burgeoning headache adding to his testiness.

*More death,* Ootapi said, his splintering-ice tones sounding oddly cheerful.

Konrad shot out of bed and groped for his clothes, trying to shake the pain and fuzziness from his head. 'No need to sound quite so happy about it,' he muttered grumpily.

*You sought a lead, Malykant,* Eetapi said. If it was possible for a dead snake's ghost to grin, Konrad would've sworn she was doing just that.

*Not like this! I was supposed to catch the killer before they had chance to target anyone else.*

Neither of them bothered to answer that and Konrad finished dressing in the silence. When all necessary layers of clothing were in place, he strode to the door.

*You can't go,* said Eetapi.

*He stopped. What do you mean, I can't go?*

*There are people there.*

He scowled up at the pair of glowing ghost-lights that hung near the ceiling of his bedroom. *You waited until* after *I was dressed to tell me that?*

Ootapi's thin body rippled in an equivalent of a shrug. *Nobody told you to get dressed.*

A growl escaped Konrad's throat. *Tell me what's happened,* he ordered. *The plain truth, and no mucking about.*

Eetapi drifted down from the ceiling to hang around his neck. The gesture was vaguely affectionate, and might have been pleasant if it wasn't for the deathly cold that she carried with her. *Dead lady,* she whispered in his ear. *In a rich house. The Master sent us there.*

Ootapi wreathed himself around Konrad's waist. *She had been ill for three days. Her death was expected. Her chamber is full of mourners, so you cannot go.*

Three days. Then her illness had struck shortly before Pietr Orlov had died. But that didn't mean they were connected.

*Damnit,* he swore. *We need to go! She must be soulbound, before her spirit deteriorates past rationality and —*

*No soul,* Eetapi interrupted.

*What?*

Ootapi's tail twitched. *We looked. Her soul is missing.*

*Not just frayed beyond recognition and past speech, but absolutely gone?* Konrad prompted. He needed to be sure about this.

*Gone,* the serpents said together.

Konrad's heart beat faster. Here was his link. Three such occurrences happening within a few days of each other could not be a coincidence. And The Malykt had marked this death for investigation, just like the others.

But the manner of death wasn't the same. She had died after a few days' illness. If the same killer was behind all three, why would that person vary the method in this case?

*Did you find out who this woman was?* Konrad demanded.

*Her name is Iolanta Lyubova,* said Eetapi. *She was married to Igor Lyubov. Their house was large and there were servants.*

Konrad didn't recognise the name of Lyubov, but the serpents' description at least confirmed that they were a rich family. That, too, did not match: the only similarity between Orlov and Ivan — besides the manner of their deaths — was their poverty. If Iolanta Lyubova was a victim of the same murderer, she was certainly the odd one out.

*Who attended her death?*

*A husband,* said Eetapi.

*Hers, I suppose?* Konrad prompted.

*Yes,* Eetapi snapped.

*All right. Carry on.*

*A nurse,* said Ootapi.

*A sister,* Eetapi added. *That was all.*

Three people, two of them family. They weren't going to leave that woman's body alone tonight.

Konrad sighed, and began to undress again. *All of this being the case, I think you didn't need to wake me.*

*You said we should always wake you when we learn of such a death,* Ootapi hissed.

Konrad rolled his eyes. He had certainly said that, but he'd thought they had common sense. At least a little bit. *If I can't go there until morning then I didn't need to know about it until morning, did I?*

*Oh,* said Eetapi doubtfully. Her tail flicked, twice. *So you want us to go away?*

*Yes. Please, please go away. I can't solve a case if I can't think straight due to sleep deprivation.*

There was a disgruntled silence, and then the two corpse-lights faded away, leaving Konrad's bedchamber blissfully dark once more. He sank back into bed with a grateful sigh. Guilt, pressure and puzzlement could wait until the morning, when he had a clear enough head to deal with them all.

4

Konrad rose early the following morning and made his way directly to the house of Igor Lyubov. This death may have differed from the others in many respects, but it was still inflicted by ostensibly natural causes; he was therefore surprised to find Nuritov and two of his colleagues at the house when he arrived. The inspector grinned at him as he approached, looking far too cheerful for a homicide detective this early in the morning.

'I guessed you'd be turning up,' said Nuritov cheerfully. 'I wish more of my men – paid professionals, mind – were as dedicated as you.'

Konrad chuckled. 'I need to keep busy. The professional boredom of the man-of-leisure would probably kill me otherwise.'

Nuritov nodded. 'Can't say it'd suit me either.'

'I heard,' Konrad said carefully, 'that the victim was ill. Is that right?'

The inspector nodded. 'Violently, for the past few days.'

'Then why are you here? I thought you were tied up on the diamond case.' Nuritov shouldn't have been at the scene so early. He didn't have Konrad's unusual sources of information, so how could he have known that the death wasn't a natural one? For that matter, who had even reported this woman's death?

Nuritov lit a cigarette and took a puff. 'Well. Looks like this may be the diamond case. Or part of it.'

'Oh? What's the connection?'

'The victim,' he said with a wave of his cigarette, 'was the sister of

Madam Yulia Ivanova.'

'The banker's wife?'

Nuritov nodded. 'The very same. Think it's a coincidence that her sister falls ill and dies within days of the robbery? By all accounts the woman was in the best of health less than a week ago.'

Konrad frowned, thinking. That fit the profile of the other victims, but questions remained. Why had she been subjected to days of illness before she had died? If she had been killed by the same person as Orlov and Ivan, why hadn't the same method been used? The two earlier deaths had been quicker, simpler, more efficient; it didn't make sense.

Then he thought back to the serpents' information of the night before. Three people had been at the dead woman's bedside all night: her husband, a maid... and her sister.

'Who does the diamond belong to?' he asked Nuritov.

The inspector grinned. 'Quick on the uptake. Are you sure I can't tempt you to join my team? I could use you.'

Konrad smiled faintly. 'You have my assistance anyway.'

'True, true. The diamond was owned by Anton Ivanov, technically, but it was for his wife's use. She wore it whenever she reasonably could, and it was kept in her rooms.'

'Rooms?' Konrad prompted.

'Her bedchamber, specifically. She loved the thing and was afraid of losing it, so she kept it close.'

'Right,' Konrad murmured. 'So if someone wanted to steal it, they'd have to get past her. Or...'

'Or get her out of the way, yes.'

'But killing her wouldn't do it; it would throw the house into uproar, and would result in the diamond's being moved – probably into a bank.'

The inspector nodded enthusiastically. 'If I was planning this robbery, I'd have gone with this idea myself. She and her sister were close; when she heard that Iolanta was ill she packed up and left right away. Much as she loved the diamond, she evidently loved her sister more. I doubt she even gave the diamond a thought.'

'And she stayed here for a few days, which was ample time for the robbery to be pulled off.' Konrad paused, his brow darkening once more. 'So there's a probable connection. Any proof?'

'Nothing solid, yet.'

'Even supposing we're right, what did the baker and the manservant have to do with any of this? Neither one had any connection to Ivanov's household, that I recall.'

'I'll check it over again,' Nuritov said, 'but I can't remember anything coming up, either.'

'And they both died before the robbery was committed, so it's hard to fathom how they could have been involved.'

Nuritov puffed on his cigarette in silence for a moment. 'It's going to be a tough one, this,' he commented at last. He dropped the cigarette and stepped on the burning stub. 'I'd better get back inside.'

'I'd like a look at the body,' Konrad said quickly. 'Any chance you can arrange that for me?'

'Of course. Follow me.'


Iolanta Lyubova had been in her mid-twenties, Konrad judged. She had a pleasant face, or would have before illness and pain had forced the beauty from her features. She lay alone in the centre of a large bed, looking small and frail in the midst of an expanse of blankets.

Konrad was grateful to note that the room was empty. He leaned over the poor pale corpse, inspecting her closely without touching her. 'Supposing this was murder,' he said to Nuritov, 'have you found out how the poison was administered?'

'No. Her husband told us that she first fell ill three nights ago, but as I'm sure you know, symptoms usually take some time to manifest. I can't be sure when she was given the dose – *if* she was.'

Konrad nodded. He saw nothing on the body to guide him, but he hadn't really expected to. A few days of serious illness would be enough to remove any signs of foul play. 'There's something else that doesn't fit with our theory,' he said, looking up. 'If the purpose of this was to remove Iolanta from the crime scene, why use a lethal poison? There are plenty of compounds that could have been used to make her ill for several days, without killing her in the end.'

The inspector nodded seriously. 'That is a problem. Perhaps the killer didn't know that.'

'Hmm.' Konrad shook his head. 'This person has now chosen two different poisons for his (or her) victims, depending on the effect that he or she wished to create. There's no sign of clumsiness or experimentation. Whoever's responsible knows their poisons – or they hired someone who does. I do believe this was a deliberate choice.'

Nuritov tilted his head. 'So you're sure this was murder? And connected to the other two?'

Konrad nodded. 'I am.'

'How?'

He thought briefly about explaining his reasons to Nuritov. The man was open-minded. He might accept the idea that Konrad had a pair of dead snakes as advisors, who could detect a highly unusual lack of soul in all three victims. He might believe Konrad's explanation that none of those souls had crossed into the Deathlands as they should have. He *might* swallow all that, and still allow Konrad to work cases with him.

Or he might decide that Konrad was a dangerous lunatic and have him excluded from all future investigations. Many people in Ekamet were aware of the spirit realms and knew at least a little about the supernatural. But many others treated the Spirit Overlords as symbolic figures, and remained closed to the rest. Konrad wasn't sure where Nuritov stood in the debate.

'I can't explain,' he said at length. 'I've some information that's too shaky to share, but I'll let you know when I have more.'

Nuritov eyed him with displeasure, but he nodded. 'I can't treat this as officially linked to the Ivanov case without evidence, so it'll have to remain inconclusive for now.'

'You'll keep me informed?'

'Yes.' The inspector paused. 'Not that you deserve it.'

Konrad smiled faintly. 'I know.' He tipped his hat and left the room.

He dithered on the way down the stairs, wondering whether he should try to talk to Madam Ivanova. After a moment's reflection, he decided against the idea. Nuritov would have told him if she'd had any useful information to give, and he himself had nothing new to ask her. He walked straight out of the house and made his way home.

A note from Irinanda awaited him. She had written it in shining blue ink and drawn silver stars all over the paper. He picked up the whimsical thing and read, *Come and see me.*

Somewhat peremptory, as usual. He had nothing pressing to do for the next hour or so, however; Nuritov would run down any possible connections between the three victims much faster than he could, and he had no other leads to follow.

No other leads save the new type of poison, that is, and Nanda was the person to help him with that. So he summoned his carriage back to the door and made his way directly to her shop.

She was dealing with a customer when he arrived, and two others stood in line. He found an out-of-the-way corner and waited, trying to be unobtrusive, watching Nanda's movements. Her shop was neat as always, and well-stocked; she sold all manner of plants from mild herbal remedies to virulent poisons (though the latter required a license to purchase). She also sold compounds and concoctions of her own making, some of which were renowned across Ekamet.

She herself was a picture of casual efficiency, if such a thing was possible. She dispensed with the formal professionalism of some of her rivals, habitually appearing in her well-worn laboratory coat and with her hair loosely pinned up. Her manner was cordial but never ingratiating. Konrad knew that some of the city's wealthier – and snootier – residents scorned patronising her shop as a result, but he'd never told Irinanda that. She wouldn't care. Anyone with any discernment valued her for her pragmatism and sincerity, and her shop was the busiest in Ekamet.

Irinanda ignored him pretty thoroughly until her customers had gone away satisfied. Then she turned a big smile on him, her air of slightly detached efficiency evaporating.

Konrad waved the note at her. 'Do the stars help?'

'Enormously. Give me that.'

He handed it over and watched with mild bemusement as she proceeded to draw another scattering of stars, this time in gold ink.

'I'm in an artistic mood,' she said by way of explanation. 'But there isn't much room for creativity in herbalism.'

'That's not true. Your concoctions are thoroughly creative. It's why they're so popular.'

She flashed a grin at him. 'True, but it's not quite the same. There aren't so many wonderful *colours*.' She drew a few more stars.

He smiled briefly. 'So how did it go with Dull Dubin?'

That made her laugh. 'Oh, you think him *dull*.'

'I might have called him "feeble" instead, only I would have lost the exciting alliteration.'

'Feeble,' she repeated thoughtfully. 'Because he's shy?'

'Do you call it shy? He was barely capable of stringing two words together.'

'You know,' she replied, her eyes still on the paper, 'you might get along better with people if you stopped trying to intimidate them.'

'*Trying* to?' he protested.

'Oh, you're typically successful. That's the whole problem.'

Konrad glowered. 'I don't deliberately scare people.'

She merely cocked an eyebrow at him.

'Not *all* the time,' he amended.

'It's all right,' she said, handing the note back to him. 'I can imagine it would get to be a habit, after a while, when you're an agent of vengeance. It's sort of your job, isn't it? To send people running from you in screaming terror?'

He glanced around, alarmed. 'Don't say that in public, please.'

'We aren't in public. We're in my shop.'

'Same thing. There might be strangers around.'

She shot him a look of sparkling mischief, but didn't say anything else. Glancing down at the note he still held, Konrad discovered it to contain a glittering rainbow arching above the silver-and-gold stars and the few words she'd written. He blinked at it in disbelief, then stuffed it into his pocket. *Rainbows?*

'Maybe you're right,' Nanda said after a moment. 'Perhaps Danil would benefit from a bit more of that swaggeringly aggressive masculinity. After all, it is *so* attractive.' She mimed a swoon, her tone dripping sarcasm.

Somewhat to Konrad's own surprise, that annoyed him so much that he couldn't think of a reply. He turned away for a moment, studying the uninteresting ceiling until he felt less pained.

'Why did you want to see me?' he asked at last, turning back to face her.

The shop was empty.

'Um. Nanda?' He stepped around the counter and through the little door that led into the back. He could hear her moving around in there. She didn't look up as he followed her inside.

'Dull Dubin told me something interesting,' she said, her arms full of jars and paper packets. She thrust an armful of them at him, muttering, 'Hold these.' He ended up following her around the storeroom while she piled him higher and higher with jars, heedless of his comfort.

Well, he thought sourly. One person certainly isn't afraid of me.

Nanda waited until he'd staggered back out to the shop and set all the jars on the counter before she elaborated.

'Ceruleaf wasn't the only poison taken,' she said as she began topping up her small, elegant glass display jars from the bigger, sturdier ceramic storage vessels. 'He has hoaren root missing, too.'

Konrad nodded glumly. Hoaren root was the right type of poison: it would have produced the sorts of symptoms that Iolanta Lyubova had suffered, and in high doses it always resulted in death.

Oddly enough, hoaren root had beneficial effects as well, if taken in very small, strictly controlled doses. That was the odd thing about plants. It kept people like Nanda in business: self-medication was strongly discouraged, since it was so easy to accidentally kill oneself.

He toyed briefly with the idea that Iolanta had suffered just such an accident, but he dismissed the thought. A death of that nature would have been tragic, but normal enough. Her soul would have passed on in the usual way, and Konrad wouldn't have been called to investigate. If she had died by hoaren root, it wasn't because she had accidentally overdosed herself.

'You don't seem surprised,' Nanda commented when he still didn't say anything.

'I'm not. Did Dubin know about this when I saw him yesterday?'

She shook her head. 'He discovered it this morning.'

Konrad blinked. The clock on Nanda's wall told him that the hour was still early; it wasn't even half past ten. Dubin had made the discovery early, then. Had Nanda still been there?

'Don't look so fierce,' Nanda said, shooting him an amused look. 'Dubin would have told you if he'd known about it before.'

That wasn't why he was looking fierce, but he certainly wasn't going to explain it to her. 'I'm sure he's a model of decency. The information's too late, though. The root's already been used.'

Nanda stopped what she was doing and stared at him. 'Another body?'

'Mm. A woman this time.' He told her everything, sparing no details. Nanda had already proved that she could be trusted, and he valued her opinion. She saw things differently, and her knowledge was surprisingly wide given her relative youth.

She listened to his tale in silence, her face thoughtful.

'So the boys are certain there's a link?' she said when he'd finished.

He frowned, puzzled. 'The boys?'

'Your serpents.'

He laughed. 'Actually one of them is a girl.'

'Oh, a *lady*. I am sorry.'

'Eetapi will forgive you. Yes, they're sure. I just can't figure out what it is.'

Nanda turned back to her task and refilled several more jars, her movements slower this time. She was obviously thinking, and Konrad didn't interrupt her.

'Maybe there wasn't a connection,' she said at last.

'Then how—' Konrad began, but she held up a hand.

'Maybe there wasn't one *before* they died.'

'You mean their deaths are the connection?'

'Yes,' she said a little impatiently. 'That's obvious. But I am also wondering whether a connection might have developed, if they had lived.'

Konrad's eyes widened. 'You mean... they might have been involved in the diamond case, if they hadn't been removed first.'

'Precisely.'

'But how would anybody know that? There's no pre-existing link between those two men and the Ivanov family.'

Nanda shrugged. 'Possibly not, but that doesn't mean they couldn't have got tangled up in it.'

'A baker?'

'Why not?'

'Supposing you're right, how could anyone possibly predict that?'

Irinanda gave him a mysterious smile. 'There are those whose speciality is to read the future, Konrad.'

He lifted his brows, unable to hide his scepticism. 'You mean fortune telling? Surely that's impossible on such a scale.'

That earned him some hearty laughter. 'Impossible?' she choked. 'Coming from you that is... priceless. You're a supernatural being yourself.'

'All right, all right,' he growled. 'It's not something I've ever heard of except in very minor incidents. Is that better?'

'Yes,' Nanda said, sobering. 'But your having never heard of it doesn't mean it doesn't happen. I'm not talking about the fortune-telling your Bone Forest gypsies do. There are more powerful things in this world.'

'Such as?'

'Haven't you heard of the Oracles?'

Konrad shook his head.

'You should get out more,' she informed him, and disappeared into the back again, taking an armful of jars with her.

Konrad sighed, swept up the remaining containers and followed. Nanda could be so thrice-damned *difficult*.

'I apologise for my scepticism,' he said. 'Is that better? Will you tell me what you have in mind?'

'Are you going to dismiss it?' she asked without turning around.

'Not if it's credible.'

She snorted. 'Where I come from...' she began, then stopped and turned around. 'You do know where I come from, I assume?'

'Of course,' he said defensively. 'Marja.'

She nodded, looking faintly pleased. Or at least less annoyed. 'I was born here, but my parents are both Marjan and I've visited their home country before. Many times. Things are very different there.'

Konrad didn't know very much about the land of Marja, but he didn't want to admit it. He knew that it was a rather large country situated some way to the north of his own land, Assevan – of which Ekamet was one of the largest cities. The climate in Assevan was cold, but Marja was even colder. Its peoples typically bore Nanda's colouring: very pale skin, white-blond hair and pale eyes.

He knew that Assevan and Marja shared a spirit-world and that their Deathlands were connected. He also knew that the Marjan sections of those otherlands were very, very different from the spirit-worlds he was used to. Konrad did not go there.

'We have a tradition for reading the future,' Irinanda continued. He didn't miss her sudden use of the word "we" instead of "they". 'It isn't a precise or a reliable art, and it's hard to imagine anyone being capable of it to this degree. But I don't believe it's impossible, by any means.'

'You're saying that a Marjan Oracle committed these crimes.'

She shook her head. 'Not necessarily. But I do think a Marjan Oracle was helping the killer, at the very least. An enormously powerful one.'

'Why would such a powerful and rare person involve him-or-herself with a theft and a string of murders?' Konrad asked, frowning.

'I've no idea. Why does anybody commit thefts and murders? There are always reasons.'

That he had to concede. 'Do you know of anybody who could have done this?' he asked. 'We're talking about someone who could have predicted that Orlov and Ivan would be involved in some specific – and damaging - way, and either acted against the two themselves or given their identities to another. That makes for an alarmingly detailed glimpse of the future.'

Irinanda chewed on her lower lip. 'Off the top of my head, no. But I know who to ask. I'll work on it.'

Privately, Konrad didn't hold out much hope for this line of enquiry. It seemed too far-fetched. But Nanda was right: he couldn't say for sure that it wasn't possible, and therefore it had to be investigated. He could trust Nanda to do the job well.

'Meanwhile, I'll pay a visit to the Ivanov house,' he said thoughtfully. 'Maybe I can find out how a baker and a manservant might have come into contact with that house, or that family, around the time of the robbery.'

Irinanda beamed at him. 'Off you go, then. I'll contact you if I turn up anything interesting.'

Konrad opened his mouth to protest at this peremptory, if cheerful, dismissal, but thought better of it. In any fight with Nanda he always seemed to come off worst, somehow.

'See you soon, then,' he said mildly, and left.

Anton Ivanov wasn't exactly a friend of Konrad's, but he could be called a friendly acquaintance. In his role as the wealthy Mr Savast of Bakar House, Konrad moved in some of the same circles as the banker's family. They'd met at various parties and other functions, and Konrad had paid an occasional social call on Madam Ivanova.

Still, that wouldn't make it easy for him to just walk in and ask for all the details about the missing diamond and Yulia Ivanova's sister. He didn't advertise his interest in mysteries (Nuritov being the sole exception to this general principle). His visit would have to look like a social one.

Konrad expected to find the banker at home, despite the day and the hour. The Ivanov household had been thoroughly disrupted in the past few days, so it certainly wouldn't be business as usual for Anton.

And he was right, though the Ivanovs' butler tried to turn Konrad away at the door. If Anton himself hadn't appeared by chance and waved Konrad through, he would've been denied entrance. It was a small piece of luck, but appreciated. Konrad wasn't above hoping hard for some more.

Anton Ivanov was almost as tall as Konrad himself, though in every other respect he differed. His skin was pale and lined with encroaching age; his hair was iron grey, his eyes piercing blue. He had an air of quiet command that typically sent people hurrying to obey his orders – despite the reserved, almost subdued manner in which he delivered them. 'Anton,' Konrad said, shaking the banker's hand.

'I'm so sorry about your diamond.' He had been going to add a note about the man's sister-in-law as well, but at the last second he remembered that he had no logical reason to know about it.

Anton looked tired, but he smiled a little. 'My thanks. It's a bad business, but it hurts my wife the most. And she has enough to trouble her at present, alas.'

Konrad did a creditable job of looking mystified.

'You won't have heard,' Anton continued. 'Her sister died this morning.'

Konrad made some consolatory noises and arranged his features into an expression of regret. He didn't have to work very hard at that. He did sincerely regret that he hadn't been able to prevent Iolanta Lyubova's death.

'You'll take some tea, Savast? It's a little chaotic around here, mind; Yulia's still at her sister's house and the police are in at all hours. But I think we can find you something.'

Konrad abruptly felt guilty for adding to the mess of Ivanov's household. 'Gladly, but I can't stay long. Business of my own. I just wanted to drop in and offer my support, such as it is.'

'Good of you,' said the banker briefly, and led him through to his study. Konrad had only been into this room once before, and that had been a few years ago, but he found it unchanged. A huge desk dominated the space, full of hefty drawers for storing hefty stacks of papers. An enormous blotter covered half the surface, framed by an array of expensive pens. The whole room was given over entirely to business: Anton didn't have hobbies.

Konrad took a seat. 'Has the thief been discovered?'

'Alas, no,' Anton replied, sitting down behind his desk with a long sigh. 'The police tell me they are making progress, but as far as I can tell they haven't uncovered any real information.'

That didn't surprise Konrad much. If the two sets of crimes came from the same source, then he would be willing to bet that the police wouldn't find any substantial leads. He knew from experience how good this person was. Three murders, and they hadn't left any real clues behind.

Anton slumped in his chair and closed his eyes. It struck Konrad that he looked more than tired; he looked beaten down with weariness, the sort that took more than a few days to develop.

'Are you well, Anton?' he asked, tentative. He didn't know the man well enough to guess how he'd take a direct enquiry about his personal health.

'Oh, yes... yes,' came the reply, but it sounded uncertain. 'Troubles always come in groups, don't they say? I have had many come upon me at once, that's all. Every domestic inconvenience imaginable, and some difficulties at the bank. Then the diamond, and now a death in the family.' He shook his head.

Konrad's interest quickened and he leaned forward a little. 'What kind of inconveniences?'

Anton shot him a puzzled look. 'Oh, staff, staff. I'm sure you've encountered many such trials yourself. I wouldn't ordinarily count it as a problem, but with everything else...'

Remembering himself, Konrad sat back with a short laugh. 'Oh, yes. I've had some trouble with servants lately. My cook has threatened to leave me, and I think she's serious.'

Anton chuckled. 'No lady of the house, that's your problem. Yulia's a marvel. When old Karpa died – our butler, you might recall – she found not one but *two* replacements in short order. I've no idea how she does it.'

Konrad blinked. 'Why did you need two replacements?'

'Oh, the first one died. Can you believe it? We sent for him but word came back that he was dead.' He shivered a little. 'I don't mind admitting that I found it disturbing. Too many deaths have been happening lately.'

Konrad's mind whirled, putting pieces together at speed. 'Where did Yulia find this unfortunate?' He tried to make the question sound casual, but his persistence was obviously making Anton uncomfortable.

'Oh, I don't recall,' the banker said with a wave of his hand. 'Yulia handled everything.'

Konrad abandoned all pretence of casual interest. 'Anton. I hate to press you, and I am well aware this will seem strange, but I'd very much like to know more about this man. Do you remember his name?'

'Of course not. Why the questions, Savast? Surely my domestic affairs cannot be of any interest to you.'

'I can't explain,' Konrad said, frustrated. 'Is there anyone in your household that would know the man's name?'

Anton closed his eyes and rubbed at his forehead as if his head pained him. 'I'll ask my housekeeper,' he said at last, and the look he directed at Konrad clearly suggested that he thought him insane.

Konrad waited in silence as Anton rang the bell. A servant appeared almost instantly, and was sent to fetch the housekeeper. A minute later, a woman in her sixties came through the door, wearing a sober black dress and an efficient expression. She made her employer a curtsey and looked curiously at Konrad.

'Do ask your question, Mr Savast,' said Anton Ivanov, and he sounded weary.

'There was a new butler hired recently, who failed to arrive,' Konrad said without wasting any time. 'What was his name?'

The woman frowned and spent a few seconds in silent thought. 'I don't recall, sir,' she said, to Konrad's disappointment. 'But,' she added an instant later , 'I believe the family name was Ivan. I couldn't swear to it though, sir.'

Ivan! Mikhail Ivan. Konrad didn't doubt it. But then why hadn't he heard that the man had been about to change his employ?

Because he hadn't told anyone, most likely. Mikhail Ivan had been a footman for some years, and had applied for the more senior position of butler in the hopes of receiving a promotion and a higher salary. But he wouldn't make any noise about it; not until he had secured the job. And he'd died before he'd heard the news.

Here was the first solid link between the two cases. Konrad felt a rising excitement, which was quickly crushed again. What possible threat had Ivan posed to the scheme, that justified his removal?

Anton and the housekeeper were both staring at him, puzzled by his silence. He smiled at them both and stood up.

'I'll not take up any more of your time, Anton. Thank you for the tea.' He shook the banker's hand, aware that he'd made himself look like a lunatic but lacking the time to do anything about it.

He stopped the housekeeper on his way out of the building. 'The man who answered the door to me today. Your butler?'

'Yes, sir,' the woman said, plainly confused.

'He must be very new, then.'

'He's only just started, that's true.'

'Where did you find him?'

'Well, we was in a mess, sir, when the other one – Ivan – didn't turn up. Golovin presented himself. Said he'd heard that we had a position open and offered himself for it on the spot.'

'And he was hired?'

The housekeeper stiffened, perhaps disliking the implied reproach. 'He had excellent references.'

'No doubt,' Konrad muttered. 'Golovin, you said his name was?'

'That's right. Iosif Golovin.'

Iosif Golovin. 'I'd like to speak with him. Where can I find him?'

'He is not on the premises, sir.'

Konrad lifted his brows. 'He was here when I arrived less than half an hour ago.'

'He has since left the building, sir,' the housekeeper repeated, and her tone was stubborn. She didn't trust the drift of Konrad's questions, that was certain, but he didn't get the impression that she was lying.

If Iosif Golovin was the sort of man Konrad suspected him to be, he'd have reason to be wary.

Annoyed, Konrad offered only a curt nod in reply to the housekeeper's words, and strode out of the house. He now had two tasks to occupy him for the rest of the day. One: alert Nuritov to the new butler, if the inspector hadn't already flagged him as suspect. Golovin's appearance in that house, on this particular week, was highly suspicious and Konrad had no doubt that Ivan had been killed in order to make way for him. Golovin may merely be more corruptible than the younger manservant, whose character had appeared to be beyond reproach. In which case, his involvement with the diamond robbery might have been as simple as letting the intruders in and looking the other way while they robbed his new master. If so, Nuritov would handle him.

If he had a more direct involvement with the case, then he was something more of a professional and he had probably left the house for good. Konrad wouldn't find him — or his colleagues — by hanging around the Ivanov house.

Konrad's second task for the day was to research the Ivanov diamond. If his theories were correct, someone had taken enormous trouble to get at it. Why? It wasn't about money, that he felt sure of. Such a jewel was too recognisable to be easily sold; it would have to be broken into smaller pieces first, and that was risky in itself. Why go to so much trouble to steal this one diamond, only to destroy it and sell the pieces for money? There were simpler ways to get rich. Many of them.

In which case, the perpetrator wanted the diamond itself – whole. And that raised a few questions. Was it a collector, who wanted a prize specimen for his cabinets? If so, why choose this stone? Diamonds of that size were rare, but there were one or two others in the world that Konrad knew about. Had it been something personal? Maybe there was something in the past history of the jewel that might explain the theft. Or perhaps the stone had been taken purely to damage the Ivanov family, and it had nothing to do with the diamond at all.

Too many questions. Nuritov would already have covered the latter possibility; he and his colleagues had been working flat-out on the diamond case for the past two days. Konrad would look into the possibility that the theft *did* have something specific to do with the gem. The task would be dull, but hopefully fruitful; and by the time he'd finished, Irinanda might have something to bring him about the Oracle.

Konrad's research uncovered nothing obviously incriminating about the jewel, but it did give him plenty to think about as the clock ticked around to past midnight and still he heard nothing from Irinanda. He was about to go to bed when he heard movement in the doorway, and a long shadow crept across the floor of his study. He jumped violently, his heart beginning to pound; but then a familiar voice said, 'Good evening.'

'Nanda,' he muttered. 'Do you *have* to scare me like that?'

'Sorry,' she grinned, coming all the way into the room. She handed Weveroth to him and took a chair.

Konrad looked down at the little golden-furred monkey he'd ended up holding. 'Why do I have this?'

'He likes you.'

'I'm flattered. How did you get in?' He set the monkey gently in his lap, and the creature promptly huddled up, fluffing out his fur. Konrad realised that the fire had all but gone out some time ago, and it *was* rather cold.

'I slid under your front door. There's a gap almost half an inch wide, did you know that? It must be draughty in here.' She shivered. 'It *is* draughty in here.'

Konrad eyed her. All right, so she wasn't going to tell him how she'd got in without alerting any of his servants. 'Do you know, this is the second time you've come here, and in the same week? It is disturbingly out of character.'

Her smile widened. 'We must all make sacrifices. I have brought you some names.'

'Ah!' Konrad sat forward, relieved and eager. A clear lead, at last!

'Hold on,' Irinanda said, making restraining motions with her hands. 'I don't know how much use it will be to you.'

'Why don't you tell me what you've got, and then we'll decide.'

She nodded. 'I asked around. Three names came up in connection with a Seeing of the sort of scope we were talking about.'

'A seeing?'

'A Seeing. As in, into the future.'

'Oh.'

'It's what Oracles do.'

'All right, I get it. Who are they?'

Nanda arranged herself into a cross-legged position and sat up straight. 'Aleksi Grempel is one. He's half Marjan, half Assevan. Elderly. He lives in a hut out in the wilds of Marja and it's said he hasn't spoken to a human being in about ten years.'

Konrad nodded. 'Legends have lied before, of course.'

'Of course. The other is Kerttu Nylund. That's a she, in case you were wondering, and she's a bit younger, though nobody seemed to know much about her other than that.'

Nanda sat back with an air of having finished her recital.

'That's two,' he prompted.

She nodded wisely. 'It is two. Your skill at counting is irreproachable.'

'You did say there were three?'

'Did I? I'm fairly sure I said two.' Her ice-blue eyes glinted at him dangerously.

Konrad wasn't cowed. 'This is important, Nanda. I need to know everything you've got if we're going to solve this mystery.'

'The third name is irrelevant.'

'If this mysterious third person is capable of this kind of Seeing, then the name is not irrelevant.'

'But I know that she didn't do it.'

Konrad smiled. 'So it's a woman. Good. Keep going.'

Irinanda got up to leave, but Konrad was faster. He put himself between her and the door and backed her into her chair. 'If you're helping me, then you're honest with me,' he growled. 'Nothing less will do. I've kept nothing from you.'

Irinanda looked away, her expression full of anger and... something else. Worry, Konrad would have said, though that didn't make sense.

She mumbled something.

'A little louder,' Konrad said.

She glared up at him, eyes blazing fury. 'The third one is my mother!'

Konrad took a step back. '*Oh.*'

'Yes, OH. And it wasn't her, so don't even think it. She would never lend herself to something like this.'

Konrad backed off, hands raised. 'All right.'

There was silence for a moment.

'How well do you know your mother?' Konrad hazarded.

'Stupid question,' she spat. 'People tend to know their own parents pretty well.'

Konrad managed a twisted smile. 'I wouldn't know. I haven't seen mine for approximately thirty-two years.'

Irinanda stared at him. 'Oh,' she said at last. 'Well, I know my mother. She wasn't the Oracle who did this.'

'All right.' Konrad sat down again and made himself comfortable. 'So. Aleksi Grempel or Kerttu Nylund. I'm hoping it's the latter, or we'll be making a trip out to the wilds of Marja and it's a bit cold for my taste.'

Irinanda was still staring at him, though her manner had turned suspicious. 'That's it?'

He lifted a brow at her. 'What's it?'

'You're just going to believe me?'

He shrugged one shoulder. 'Why not?'

She slouched in her chair, eyes still fixed on his face. 'I thought you'd be difficult about it.'

'Why would you think that?'

'You're difficult about everything.'

That made him laugh. 'Coming from you, that's... well, it may be the worst insult I've ever received.'

She scowled.

'So. How do we find Mr Grempel or Madam Nylund? Any ideas?'

Irinanda's irritation melted into a smile. 'There's an obvious solution I can think of.'

'Oh?'

'If you want to find an Oracle... ask another Oracle.'

His eyebrow went up again.

'Don't worry,' she smiled. 'I happen to know one.'

'Isn't your mother in Marja?'

'Usually, yes.'

'Like I said, I was hoping to avoid a journey up there.'

'I thought you'd say that,' Nanda replied, jumping neatly out of her chair. 'So I asked her to come down instead. She'll be here tomorrow.' With a brief, sunny smile, she trotted to the door and went out.

'Er, wait... Nanda?' He followed, but when he reached the door she was gone.

And so was Weveroth.

Konrad paused, feeling faintly disturbed. How in the world did she *do* that?

And how in the world could the elder Madam Falenia make the journey from Marja to Assevan in a day? How had Nanda even got in touch with her so fast?

None of it made sense. Konrad got the uncomfortable feeling – and not for the first time – that Nanda had a lot of secrets.

Maybe even more than him.

# 6

Konrad's sleep was unquiet.

He'd retired to bed as soon as Irinanda left, and he had fallen asleep immediately. Then he dreamed. The dream began with a deathly chill that seeped into his darkened bedroom, frost blooming over his furniture and ice creeping across the floor. It was familiar, this bone-cold feeling and the gut-wrenching fear that went with it.

The Malykt had come to visit.

In his dream, Konrad lay paralysed with terror, sweating in the biting cold air. He kept his eyes shut tight – not because he was afraid to look, but because there was nothing to see. The Malykt never manifested; He was merely a Presence.

*You dally, My Malykant,* came the wintry voice, stark with disapproval. *Days have passed, and My lost souls have not returned to Me.*

It was generous of his Master, Konrad thought, to take *almost* all of his servant's more powerful emotions but leave the paralysing terror associated with His presence. It made these conversations so... unpleasant.

*I have made much progress, Master,* Konrad replied.

*Not enough. You waste time sleeping when there is yet work to be done.*

*I am only mortal, Master,* Konrad protested. *Sleep is necessary if I am to be fit to work.*

The Malykt did not deign to make any verbal reply to this defence. Konrad merely felt a flood of rejuvenating energy wash through his trembling body, banishing his tiredness. His mind sharpened beneath the fear.

*More is at stake than your career as My servant, Konrad Savast. Work harder.*

The biting cold abruptly lessened, and warmth seeped back into Konrad's limbs as consciousness gradually replaced sleep. The feeling of vitality did not fade. He sat up, watching with numb attention as blue-glowing frost melted off his floor and furniture and the room gradually returned to its normal state.

He was puzzled. It wasn't unheard of for the Master to reprimand him for slowness; the Overlords' grasp of mortal time was flimsy, Konrad had concluded before, and They didn't always understand the limitations of mortals. But The Malykt's manner had been more urgent than usual, and His approach wholly without subtlety. He had never hauled Konrad out of bed before, and he had certainly never rejuvenated him like this.

Konrad privately hoped that He never would again, either. Energy buzzed through his frame, so potent that he shook with it. His body crawled with jittering vitality and he couldn't stay still: he leapt out of bed and dressed in a feverish hurry, then began to pace circles around his room, trembling violently.

What could he do with the night? Irinanda's mother would not arrive until the morrow, and she was his only clear lead.

The morgue, he realised. He hadn't yet paid his customary visit to the third victim's corpse, and his collection of rib bones remained at two. Increasing it to three would be his first task. And then?

Then... perhaps he would test a theory that had been growing in his mind ever since the previous day, and his hours spent researching the great diamonds of history. It required a trip into the spirit-worlds, which was always to be avoided if he could; but with The Malykt's energies roaring through him, he was in a better position than usual to navigate that dangerous place safely.

Looking down at himself, he realised he had already dressed in his city clothes. He stripped everything off again and grabbed his marsh-clothes out of the concealed drawers in which he stored them when he was in Ekamet. On went his heavy trousers and thick shirt, his tall boots, his long coat, and finally his gloves, scarf and hat. All of these items were well-worn but well cared for, designed to keep him warm and dry and protected for his forays out into the cold and treacherous Bone Forest.

He paused once more to trade his snake-headed city cane for a long, stout stick of elm wood. Then he strode off into the cold, cold night, his two serpent-shades streaming out behind him like ribbons of sickly moonlight.

It had been a few weeks since Konrad had last ventured out into the Bones. In his absence, the season had deepened into true winter, and all lingering traces of softness had vanished from the vast forest that surrounded Ekamet. The ground was usually marshy, with pools of stagnant water spreading across the earth. Now all was frozen into crisp soil that crunched underfoot and stretches of treacherous ice. The bone-pale, twisted trees were dormant, their contorted branches stripped bare of life. Few animals stirred in the depths of this harsh winter night.

Konrad huddled further into the thick scarf that wound around his throat, his body already feeling the chill despite his layers of clothing. He kept one hand wrapped firmly around the stick he used to feel his way across the ice; the other rested in the pocket of his coat, gripping the small object he'd dropped in there on his way out of the house. As he walked, he loosed the control he kept over his Spirit Vision and allowed it to gradually take over from his mundane sight until he was staring directly into the spirit lands. The black darkness deepened and the trees paled to stark white; the earth and ice faded away underfoot, replaced by roiling banks of mist glowing in lightning-white, unearthly blue and sickly green. A few steps carried him out of the living world and into the spirit world.

He was instantly aware that he was no longer alone. No creature, living or otherwise, met his eyes as he strode purposefully forward, but he could feel the pressure of their attention fixated on him: a living man wandering the spirit-plane. His warmth and vibrancy was at odds with the pervasive chill of their domain, his vitality a powerful lure. This was the realm of wisps and goblins and dark fae, of wandering spirits and shades and nameless things. There was nothing remotely human about this place.

For a time, Konrad simply walked. It was unwise to show fear out here; its denizens could sense it and they were quick to take advantage of it. Fortunately for Konrad, he had little capacity to feel it, outside of the presence of The Malykt. He walked on, aware of the malevolent attention he was getting but largely untouched by it.

When he judged he had gone far enough, he stopped and drew

the tiny object out of his pocket. The diamond flashed with a stark, eye-hurting brilliance in the strange light of the spirit-world, throwing that light back out with still greater luminescence. More than that, it glowed. A softly pulsing light began to seep from the jewel, echoing the unearthly blue, purple and green shades of the roiling mist underfoot.

The avid attention of Konrad's unseen audience shifted abruptly to the gem. Konrad felt their avarice, their burning desire for the thing. With a distant feeling of trepidation, he realised he was in considerable danger.

He put the jewel back in his pocket and continued walking.

He had barely gone ten paces before he was stopped. A glowing white light materialised before him and began to convulse. It writhed and clawed its way into the grotesque shape of a twisted goblin, all leggy and beaky and staring at him with lightning-bright eyes.

'Malykant,' said the thing.

'You know me, then,' said Konrad gravely.

The goblin-thing bobbed its head with frantic enthusiasm. 'All know you. You stink of *Him*.'

Konrad could only imagine that he did, indeed, *stink* of The Malykt's influence at the current time. He probably radiated it.

Good. They were less likely to attack him if they knew he was under the protection of a Spirit Lord.

'What do you want of me?' Konrad asked the thing.

'That shiny token that you carry,' the creature said, its hissing voice becoming sly. 'Have you much use for it?'

Konrad kept his fingers curled tight around the diamond he carried. 'It is useful to me on occasion, yes.'

'I could relieve you of it,' the goblin said.

'Why should I allow you to do that?' As he spoke he could feel a hundred eyes fixed on the exchange, waiting on the outcome of this first attempt on the diamond.

'I will give you something in return,' said the shining goblin-thing.

'Something valuable?' Konrad prompted. 'This object is precious to me and I would require something equally precious in return.'

The goblin licked its insubstantial lips. 'I offer one year of my service,' it said.

Konrad lifted a sceptical brow. 'Oh? And what would your service entail, that it should be considered valuable?'

127

'I can make you stronger,' the thing said, its eagerness growing. 'I will add my strength to yours; no sickness will touch you, and no one will dare to—'

'Nonsense,' Konrad growled, cutting it off. He loomed over the goblin-thing, aware that he was *very* tall and dark and terrible in the creature's eyes. 'You are weak. Of what use would your so-called strength be to me? Begone.'

The creature gave a despairing cry and vanished.

Konrad walked on. Two steps, three... and another light appeared, thrashing and cursing and hauling itself into another crabbed, wizened goblin shape. This one was larger than the first, and he got the impression that it was female – if such things could possess a gender. The goblin's eyes shone an eerie shade of purple, glinting with greed.

'I am stronger,' she said without preamble. 'I will serve you better, Malykant.'

Konrad narrowed his eyes, and kept his tight grip on the diamond. 'Why would you possess this thing?' he demanded.

'It would give me great power.'

'Of what nature?'

The goblin stretched her ethereal lips in a malevolent smile. 'You see the way it shines, Malykant. It amplifies all that it touches. I will be greater, far greater than I am, if I have this thing. And all that great strength will be at your service for...' she paused. 'Two of your years.'

Konrad surveyed the glint in her eye and the expression of naked cunning that wreathed the grotesque creature's face. 'Perhaps so, but I see you for what you are. You would betray me the moment it suited you to do so. Begone!'

The goblin howled and vanished.

Konrad walked on, pondering the two goblins. He understood what the second had meant about the diamond's power to amplify; this was what he'd learned in his reading about the rarest and most valued of precious jewels. It was the clarity of the gems: they absorbed any surrounding energies and threw them back out again, at a brilliance of fivefold, tenfold strength. A glance at the way the diamond picked up the weird energies of the Spirit World and reflected them back had confirmed that for him.

A desirable trinket for a spirit-goblin, then, certainly. But his books had given him another clue: there was one other spiritual property associated with the diamond. One more test yet lay before him.

The third spirit to bar his path was the largest yet, a large sphere of light as wide across as his forearm. It hovered in the air before him, pulsing steadily with energy. This wisp did not bother to alter its form; it formed words through a series of echoing vibrations which Konrad felt in his bones more than heard with his ears.

'I offer you three of your mortal years in service,' said the wisp.

'Three is not enough,' Konrad replied.

'But I am stronger than those who came before. With the jewel I will be stronger than the rest of my kind.'

'And with that strength you could break any agreement between us,' Konrad said. 'Do you deny that you would?'

The wisp lost its peaceful demeanour and began to thrash, glowing brighter. 'You doubt my word, Malykant?'

Konrad sneered at it. 'I doubt the word of all such beings as you, and with good reason. Your kind are notorious for making deals, and then finding ways to twist your way out of them. Is this not the truth?'

The wisp became angry. 'Your own kind is hardly honoured for its truthfulness, *mortal man.*'

'Quite true,' Konrad said. 'And our avarice is almost the equal of yours. If I wanted your service, why should I pay for it? Why should I not just take it?' He withdrew the diamond from his pocket and thrust it at the wisp. 'You seek to own this thing, but it is not wholly avarice that motivates you. It is *fear.* Is it not? Such a thing has more power over you than you have admitted to me.'

The wisp's thrashing intensified until it became a frantic blur of light. Konrad could feel the thing's terror. 'Get it away from me,' it hissed.

'But a moment ago you begged me to give it to you.'

The wisp hissed again. 'Ownership over it will protect me from it. Malykant, *I beg you.*' Its struggles were weakening as the diamond slowly mesmerised its will.

'So you had no thought of using it to subdue others of your own kind?'

'None,' said the wisp faintly, and Konrad knew it was lying. It had grown peaceful again and now hung in the air, bobbing faintly, its attention locked on the diamond. The jewel swirled with lazy colours and shone with ghost-light, a performance that almost mesmerised Konrad too. He quickly drew his eyes away from the jewel.

'You may have it,' he said. 'As your prison.'

The wisp gave an agonised howl as the diamond brightened. A flash of light blinded Konrad for a moment, and then the wisp was gone.

Looking into the jewel, Konrad could see a new mote of light pulsing at the heart of the stone. The wisp hung there, a malevolent presence held in suspension, bound by the cruel hardness of the diamond.

He could feel that the strange power of the gem had grown. And now he had a powerful wisp at his disposal, forced to do his bidding as long as it remained bound within the gem. He considered letting it go – it hadn't been his intention to take a prisoner from the spirit-lands, only to test his theories. But he was troubled.

The diamond he held was only half an inch in diameter, if that. Nonetheless its mesmerising power had been enough to subdue the rage of a powerful wisp-spirit, and that same spirit now lay, bound and servile, at the heart of the stone. He wouldn't have been surprised to find that even this small diamond held sway over still more powerful beings.

The diamond belonging to Anton Ivanov was as large as his wife's clenched fist.

What manner of spirit could one bind with a jewel of that size?

Konrad didn't enjoy speculating on that point. In the right hands, the very greatest of the mundane spirits could be mesmerised and bound with such a tool, no doubt. Perhaps even the ruling spirits.

And where did the three missing souls fit in? Konrad had read that a good diamond could exert similar power over the human spirit as well, once the soul was severed from its mortal shell. He began to piece together the sequence of events in his mind. Pietr Orlov had been killed, and his soul trapped within a small diamond, perhaps smaller even than the one he now held. The soul of Mikhail Ivan had been likewise enslaved, either in the same jewel or in a similar stone.

Then the Ivanov diamond had been taken, and afterwards Iolanta Lyubov had died. That her soul now resided in the depths of Yulia Ivanova's prized gem, Konrad didn't doubt, though the precise mechanics of that eluded him. How had the killers taken her soul? She had been well attended when she had died.

But perhaps her living spirit had been extracted *before* her physical body had fully expired. It would have put her in a vegetative state prior to her death, but given the violence of her illness, that would not have surprised those who were close to her.

Subsequent to the taking of the third soul, the first two would have been transferred into the greater jewel. Someone now had a diamond larger than a chicken's egg, with three souls and who knew what else to power it. They'd created an artefact of appalling power over the denizens of the spirit lands.

The intention could only be to enslave one of the Great Spirits: not a Spirit Lord, like The Malykt, for they were beyond mortal interference, but the most powerful of those that inhabited the spirit plane. Such a being would make Eetapi and Ootapi look as weak as new kittens.

The Malykt was right. A great deal was at stake. The Great Spirits were necessary; their presence and their doings kept the spirit lands whole and functional. The enslavement of one would result in untold trouble and turmoil.

And besides that, what could a mortal man – or woman – do with an enslaved power of that magnitude? He didn't want to think about it.

The vicinity had gone eerily quiet after his enslavement of the third wisp. The other beings had scattered, afraid of finding themselves in a similar predicament. It was probably lucky for him that wisps and spirit-fae were cowardly creatures.

Turning his steps homeward, Konrad hastened his stride, the jewel with its prisoner flaring in his hand. He crossed back into the mundane world and allowed his Spirit Vision to fade with some feelings of relief: the stark contrasts and lightning-white light of the spirit lands were hard on his eyes.

He arrived to find that dawn had come. Shoving the diamond back into his pocket, he hurried in the direction of Irinanda's shop.

7

When Konrad knocked on the back door of Irinanda's shop, she answered straight away.

'Konrad,' she said by way of greeting, though there was little welcome in her tone.

'Morning,' he said, eyeing her warily.

She didn't smile. 'Come in.'

He did so, feeling a little alarmed. Had he done something to annoy her?

She closed the door behind him, locked it, and turned around to fix him with a cold stare.

'If you give my mother any trouble at all,' she said in a low voice, 'I'll... well, I'll do something unpleasant to you!'

'All right,' said Konrad mildly.

'I mean it!'

'I know you do.'

Nanda calmed down a little, though her hostility didn't ebb entirely. 'Good.'

Konrad frowned. 'Why do you imagine I'm going to make trouble for her?'

'Because she's an Oracle and you're professionally suspicious.'

That almost made Konrad grin, but he managed to suppress it. Professionally suspicious. Well, indeed.

He spread his hands in a gesture of innocence. 'I've no need to accuse her of anything. I just need her help.' He attempted a winning smile, but Irinanda still looked doubtful. Abandoning the effort with a sigh, he asked, 'When do you think she'll arrive?'

By way of answer, Nanda pointed a single finger up at the ceiling.

'Upstairs,' he interpreted. 'What, she's already here?'

Nanda nodded solemnly.

Konrad stared. 'Is that possible?'

A faint twinkle of humour appeared in her blue eyes. 'Apparently.'

It occurred to Konrad to wonder why Nanda was so tense and wary of him. For someone who'd called *him* professionally suspicious, she was doing a pretty good job of it herself. Was it something to do with her mother?

He got his answer a moment later. A faint sound behind him caught his attention and he turned to find a formidable-looking woman standing in the doorway.

*Formidable* being an understatement.

He couldn't say exactly what it was about her that he found so intimidating. She resembled Irinanda quite closely – or the other way around, he supposed. She was tall, fairly well-built and with the terrific posture of a supremely confident woman. Her hair was white-blonde, like her daughter's, only hers had paled still further with age. She was probably in her late fifties, he judged, with lines creasing her pale face and crow's feet around her eyes. Her hair and clothing were neat and somehow practical and beautiful at the same time.

Perhaps it was her eyes that did it. Ice-blue like Nanda's, they were sharp and fierce. He had the uncomfortable feeling that she saw everything about him with the brief, piercing glance that she directed at him.

A moment ago he might have concluded that Nanda's tension came from concern for her mother. He quickly revised that opinion. Her concern had been for *him*.

'Madam Falenia,' he said and bowed. 'It is an honour.'

Irinanda's mother said nothing. She released him from her gimlet gaze and cast a faintly questioning look at her daughter.

'Konrad Savast, mother,' said Irinanda.

The older woman's eyebrows rose, just the slightest bit, and the next look she cast at him was different. Speculative? Konrad wondered just *what* Nanda had told her about him.

Well, now he knew where Nanda had got her fiercer qualities.

'You're seeking the one who helped your killer,' said Madam Falenia. 'Yes?'

'Yes, ma'am,' Konrad said. 'If there's anything at all you can tell me—'

'Kerttu Nylund,' she said with a faint smile. Then she turned and left the room. Konrad heard a faint creak as she began the ascent back to the rooms Irinanda lived in above the shop.

Konrad blinked. 'Is that it?' he asked Nanda.

'Mhm. That's it.'

'I thought it would be more... complicated.'

Nanda chuckled. 'Mother said it is the easiest question she's been asked in some time. She didn't have to look far.'

Konrad blinked at her. 'How so?'

Nanda flopped into a chair, looking tired despite the fact that it was barely seven in the morning. 'There are only two real possibilities, aren't there? Mother agreed with that. And she'd know. One of them's a man – Aleksi Grempel – and the other, Kerttu Nylund, is a woman. Mother took a quick Look and said right away that it was a female Oracle.'

Konrad opened his mouth to ask more questions, but changed his mind. He didn't have a clue how Marjan Oracles worked and he wasn't sure he'd understand it if Nanda tried to tell him.

Moreover, he didn't need to understand it just now, nor did he have the time to try. He trusted Nanda, and she trusted her mother's skill absolutely.

'I was hoping to ask her a couple more things,' he said, gesturing vaguely in the direction of the stairs. 'Do you think...?'

'No need. We went over everything before you arrived.' She yawned hugely. 'She can't See much about the perpetrator behind all this, but she said he's male and a little younger than she. He's Assevan. And she said he is someone you know.'

Konrad stared at her, thunderstruck. 'Someone *I* know?'

Nanda nodded.

'All right. Anything else?'

'He's in Ekamet.'

'That's helpful. Does she have any idea where exactly?'

This time, Nanda shook her head.

Damn. He'd hoped that Farsight would be more precise. Especially when enacted by one of the three most powerful Oracles in the world.

That gave him a thought.

'I don't mean to question your mother's abilities,' he said carefully. 'But the other Oracle – Kerttu, apparently – gave out a lot of precise details about the planned theft of the diamond. I thought your mother would be able to give us an identity.'

Nanda shook her head again. 'It doesn't work quite that way. She will have done as my mother did for you: looked for glimpses of the event, and recorded every detail she Saw. The killer will have had to piece together the information she gave him in order to narrow down the identities of the two men.'

That made some sense. If Kerttu had been able to give a physical description of Orlov, along with some idea of his profession and a clue as to his whereabouts in the vision, it would have been possible to learn who he was. Possible, if not easy.

'Does she know where Kerttu is?'

'Why?'

'Because this other Oracle is the quickest route to our killer. She's dealt with him; she must know who he is.'

'Are we pressed for time?'

Konrad told her everything he'd learned or guessed about the diamond. The perpetrator of the theft and the murders might now be in Ekamet, but it couldn't be long before he crossed into the spirit lands to finish carrying out his plans. Konrad would prefer to get to him *before* he made that journey.

Nanda nodded at intervals, but she looked puzzled. 'Did you learn why he killed those two men?'

'I think so,' he said. He relayed to her the details he'd learned from Anton Ivanov, about the death of his butler and Ivan's application for the post. 'I am guessing that the replacement butler was much more amenable to bribery than Ivan would have been,' he finished.

'And the baker?'

Konrad smiled faintly. 'That one was harder. The only thing Pietr Orlov did each day other than run his shop was to visit his local public house. I walked that way yesterday and paced out his probable route. I found that the shortest way to reach it is currently blocked by road repairs; he would have had to circle around those and that took him close to the rear of the Ivanov house. If he'd been passing that way at the wrong time, he would've seen something inconvenient.'

Nanda nodded. 'So killing him removed that possibility and also furnished them with another soul.'

'Precisely.'

'Poor man,' she sighed. 'Well, to answer your earlier question: Mother knows where to find Kerttu. Or rather, she knows where Madam Nylund goes when she is in Ekamet.'

'Where?'

'I can't just tell you. I'll have to take you, or you'll waste most of the day looking for it.'

'Then let's go,' Konrad said.

Nanda sighed and hauled herself to her feet. She looked so tired; more so than if she'd merely skipped a night's sleep. She looked as though she'd skipped at least three. Did this have something to do with her mother's extraordinarily fast journey from Marja to Ekamet?

Konrad knew better than to ask.

'Are you all right to do this?' he asked instead.

She shot him a glare. 'Of course I am.'

Konrad backed off.

Another thought occurred to him as they left Nanda's shop. 'If you two went over all of this before I arrived, why did your mother come down?'

Irinanda smiled. It was a sideways, mocking, smug sort of smile that made him faintly nervous. 'She wanted to meet you.'

'Oh?' he said. 'Why was that?'

'Oh... all sorts of reasons.' She grinned again, more broadly. 'Maybe I'll tell you... someday.'

Nanda had been taking notes. Probably from him. 'Cruel,' he commented.

'But fair.' With that, she shut the door of her shop and led him out into the streets of Ekamet.

Konrad wasn't surprised when Nanda took him straight to the south gate of the city and out into the Bone Forest. Dawn had only just begun to lighten the skies, and it was still very dark beneath the trees. Konrad allowed his Spirit Vision to bleed into his mundane sight, just enough to turn the virtually impenetrable shadows into clearly silhouetted outlines of trees, branches and hillocks. He didn't wish to trip and fall headlong into the hard, frozen ground – as much for the sake of his dignity as for this health.

'It was interesting, meeting your mother,' he said as they walked.

'Interesting,' Nanda repeated. 'That does not sound

complimentary.'

'Well,' he said carefully, 'she is rather... impressive.'

She laughed softly. 'Impressive. Yes, that's exactly what she is. I used to be terrified of her when I was a child.'

'Only when you were a child?'

'All right. Maybe I'm still a little afraid of her.'

The problem with a woman like Nanda's mother, Konrad reflected, was that wherever she went, she would inevitably rule. He'd read that on her without any difficulty. That realisation gave him some insight into Nanda's choices; he'd always wondered a little why she lived in Ekamet instead of with her mother's people in Marja.

'I know my way around out here quite well, you know,' he offered. 'I don't have to drag you all the way out there with me; just tell me where to go.' It was only the truth. The Bones were dark and sinister and tricksy, and most of Ekamet avoided being out in the marshy forest if they could. They stuck to the carefully-maintained roads that connected Ekamet with other cities and towns in Assevan and beyond. But to him, the Bones was a refuge. He'd spent untold hours out here in the past few years, and he even kept a residence among the trees. Of sorts. It was a one-room hut raised above the forest floor on strong wooden stilts, and it was the only place in the world that truly felt like his.

'I know you do,' she said. 'But... well, why don't you have a go at directing me to your chicken-leg house from here? Don't point or anything. Pretend we're back at my shop and you've only got words to tell me where to go.'

She had a point. There weren't too many obvious landmarks out in the Bones, and there certainly weren't street names to navigate by. What would he say? Veer southish for... a while. Maybe five minutes or so, but that was according to how long it would take *him* to walk the distance, and Nanda was shorter. Then turn a little eastward, cross one of the several streams that bisected the wood... he had names for all of these places, but they were names he'd invented himself.

He dropped the argument. 'Chicken-leg house?' he protested instead.

'That's what it looks like. A giant chicken stretched up on too-long legs, trying to break through the canopy.' She paused. 'Such as it is.'

'That does not sound complimentary,' he retorted, borrowing her words of a few moments ago.

She grinned. 'But it is. It's cute.'

'Cute?'

'Cute. Konrad Savast, personal servant to the Spirit Lord of Death, lives in a cute chicken-legged house.'

'Ouch,' Konrad said faintly. 'My dignity. You've slaughtered it.'

She flashed a dimple at him. 'I like it much better than that monster you have in town.'

'So you've said before. I can't think why. I have a hot tub in there.'

'A what?'

'A big, deep tub full of hot water. For bathing.'

'Something tells me you aren't talking about the usual tin-tub-before-the-fire routine.'

He grinned. 'It's about three times that size and much deeper.'

She was silent for a moment. 'All right. I concede that offensively gargantuan wealth has its advantages.'

'You can try it sometime.'

'The wealth or the tub?'

'The tub. The wealth might be harder to arrange.'

She shook her head. 'Kind, but *no*.'

'No?' he said, surprised. 'Really? I thought you a convert in the making.'

Her tone turned withering. 'That's very kind of you, Konrad, but I am *not* going to lie naked in a tub full of hot water within twenty miles of you.'

'I wouldn't intrude,' he said, injured.

'That isn't the point.'

'Twenty miles,' he mused. 'How far is your house from mine?'

'Shut up.'

Konrad smiled.

A few minutes later, Irinanda stopped. 'Here we are.'

Konrad looked around. He saw bare white trees, widely spaced over frozen earth. The terrain was a little more solid than many other parts of the Forest, with none of the pools of water (or currently, ice) that he often had to navigate past. Dawn had arrived in full, casting plenty of light by which to discern a distinct lack of anything approaching a residence.

'We're where?'

'I thought you said you know the Bones,' Nanda said, inexplicably kneeling down on the ground.

'I do. I mean, I know where we are, but I don't see an Oracle.'

Nanda didn't answer. She knocked three times on the ground, and the noise resounded dully as though she'd struck something made of wood.

She sat back and waited. Konrad waited too, listening for approaching footsteps.

Instead, a door opened in the earth.

Nanda smiled and stood up. Evidently there were some stairs beneath the door, for she climbed steadily downwards until she disappeared from sight.

'Come on, Konrad,' she called back to him, her voice echoing oddly.

Konrad eyed the doorway. It looked small, and he was anything but.

'You'll fit,' came Nanda's voice again, now sounding distant.

She was right; he did, though he had to duck and roll his wide shoulders through the gap. Flat stone stairs led down into a packed earth tunnel that wound still further underground. Konrad trod carefully, head bowed to avoid the ceiling. He'd heard rumours before about underground dwellings out in the Bones, but he'd always thought they were probably untrue. After all, most of the forest was too wet for something like this.

The tunnel ended at another door, a taller one of stone. It was open, and he could see lights flickering inside. He stepped through to find Nanda sitting at a stone table, set into the middle of a round-walled room. It was comfortably furnished, even though most of the furniture was constructed from stone. Table, chairs, cupboards, bookcases (with books) and a small bed competed for space in the tiny chamber. He saw no other doors to suggest the presence of any further rooms.

Sitting opposite Nanda was a Marjan woman, older than the elder Madam Falenia. Her hair was nearly white, her face a map of wrinkles. She lacked the intimidating aura of Irinanda's mother, appearing much more congenial. In fact, she was so much like a kindly grandmother that Konrad was immediately suspicious.

'Oracle Nylund,' he said cautiously, taking care not to close the door all the way behind him.

'Malykant,' she replied, with a courteous dip of her aged head.

That alarmed him. 'You know me?'

She tapped one eye with a crabbed claw of a finger. 'I Saw you.'

'Saw me? When?'

'I Saw you coming to me. You carry four deaths with you.'

Konrad thought of the three rib bones nestled in the pocket of his coat. He was burdened with three deaths, yes; but four?

'Is the fourth my own?'

She smiled a little. 'Not yet. The fourth is the one who is responsible for the other three.'

Konrad nodded. 'You helped him.'

'I did, Malykant. And you are going to kill him.'

'Yes.'

She nodded slowly. 'Good.'

He frowned. 'Good? You helped him. Why should you be glad at the prospect of his death?'

The old woman sighed, and gestured to a chair. 'Sit, Malykant.'

Konrad stayed where he was, until Nanda tugged on the cuff of his sleeve. He looked down at her. Her expression was faintly pleading.

'You know her,' he realised.

'She's a friend of my mother's,' Nanda confirmed. 'Of the family, really. I've known Mother Kerttu since I was a child.'

'Why didn't you say so?'

She shrugged. 'It wasn't that important. Please, Konrad, sit down. You're too tall to stand all the way up there while we're seated.'

Smothering his misgivings, Konrad sat. 'You're telling me your mother is friends with a woman who aided a triple murder.'

Nanda's eyes flashed. 'Don't speak about her as if she wasn't here.'

'Peace, Malykant,' said Mother Kerttu. 'Sit a moment more, and I'll tell you all.'

Konrad said nothing, but he didn't move either. He watched the old woman closely.

'Imagine,' she said quietly, 'if you could look into the future. What would you See?'

'A lot of terrible things set to happen,' Konrad growled. 'Like murder.'

Unperturbed, the Oracle nodded her white head. 'A man came to me and asked me to See something for him. A crime. A theft. He wanted my help to accomplish this theft cleanly.'

'Did he tell you why he was stealing this diamond?'

She smiled faintly. 'Of course not, but I Saw that, too. I Saw what he would do with the information I gave him. And I Saw many possible outcomes.' Her eyes narrowed. 'Watching the future is no easy task, Malykant. There is no single path forward. There are hundreds of possible paths. Thousands. For every decision there are a thousand possible consequences.'

Konrad began to understand. 'What did you See for the theft?'

'I Saw a number of ways in which he could have accomplished the theft.' Her eyes bored into his. 'Most did not involve killings. You know as well as I, Malykant, that the jewel could have been powered by other means. You have recently done this yourself.'

He thought of his own small diamond, still in his pocket with a wisp of the fae trapped inside. 'Human souls—'

'Are more powerful in some respects, yes, but it is also risky to trap them. And yet I encouraged him to do precisely that.'

Konrad blinked. Perhaps he didn't understand after all. 'You *told* him to kill those people?'

'In a manner of speaking, yes.'

He stared at her, appalled. '*Why?*'

'Because of the consequences. If he had empowered his gem by other means, this crime would not have been discovered until it was too late.'

'You mean until after he had enslaved a Great Spirit.'

She nodded, and waited, her manner expectant.

Konrad rubbed at his face, feeling tired in spirit if not in body. 'But if he killed someone, then I would be sent after him.'

Her eyes gleamed. 'You are formidable, Malykant, and clever. You must prevent him from completing his crime. If he succeeds in binding a Great Spirit to his will, the eventual consequences of that will be far more severe. That I promise you.'

Konrad sat in silence, his face turned away from her. She had admitted to condemning three innocents to death, and with a calm that chilled him to the core. That was bordering on monstrous.

But, he could well imagine the damage a ruthless person could do with the Ivanov diamond and an enslaved Great Spirit. Three deaths looked negligible in comparison.

He suddenly felt heartily glad that he was the Malykant and not an Oracle. A lifetime of making those kinds of choices would send him insane. Meeting Irinanda's eyes, he could see that she felt the same. Her face was white and drawn.

He turned back to Mother Kerttu. 'Couldn't you just have told someone what he was planning to do?'

She regarded him placidly. 'Who would I have told?'

'The police, or—'

'About a crime that hadn't been committed, and with no evidence against the person I would have accused?'

Konrad stared at her helplessly. His heart protested that there must have been something she could have done to circumvent the consequences of this theft; some method that didn't involve the deaths of three innocent people. But his head told him that she was probably right. Would anyone have listened to one such as her, with such a wild tale to tell?

She returned his stare without expression. 'Do you know who it is you seek?'

He shook his head. 'I've been told it's someone I know, which does not narrow it down by much.'

Her eyes were rheumy with age, but as she looked at him – looked *through* him, really – they began to clear. 'Someone you've worked with, Malykant.'

Her use of his title just then was no coincidence, he felt sure. Someone he worked with as the Malykant meant someone of The Malykt's Order.

That ought to surprise him more than it did. As soon as he'd realised there was a soul stone involved, he'd feared it himself.

He took a deep breath. 'Do you know his name?'

Mother Kerttu nodded. Her eyes were now bright blue, and sharp.

'Then let me have it, if you please. There isn't time for guessing games.'

The Oracle nodded her head once. 'Iakov Gusin is his name.'

Iakov Gusin. Konrad shivered a little. He was a devotee of The Malykt's Order, and not a pleasant one. More than twenty years older than Konrad, Iakov held a position of considerable respect. But that was because many people believed him to be the Malykant. Konrad felt that the man went out of his way to encourage the notion.

Konrad also suspected that Gusin resented not being chosen for

142

that (theoretically) high honour. That was ironic. Konrad hadn't wanted it, but he'd had no choice but to accept the burden. Perhaps, though, that was the whole point. Konrad did what he had to because it was his duty; Gusin looked like a man who would enjoy the more violent elements of the job.

That didn't necessarily make him a murderer, though.

'You know him,' said Mother Kerttu, still staring at him with those weirdly blue eyes.

He sighed. 'Yes, and I don't like him. But I find it hard to believe that he'd do something like this. He's aggressive, yes, but he's one of the old guard. He's been The Malykt's for decades. Could he so betray the natural order?'

'There can be no doubt,' she said quietly.

'I mean you no disrespect, Mother Kerttu, but how can I simply trust your word?'

'You need not,' she said with a faint smile. 'Even now he is crossing into the spirit-realms, with his jewel and his souls and his black heart. If you place yourself in his way, you'll see that I am right.'

Konrad's heart sped up a little. 'Where is he going?'

'I think you can guess, Malykant.'

Perhaps he could. If he was right about Gusin's ambitions, then his actions made a horrible amount of sense. As the Malykant, Konrad had two shades bound to do his bidding – Eetapi and Ootapi, the serpent-spectres. They had been given to him by The Malykt. Their role was to assist him in carrying out his appointed tasks for the Master, but they occasionally served him in other ways, too. They warned him of dangers, assisted his judgements and added their strength to his when he needed it.

The fact that the Malykant had those advantages was known within The Malykt's Order, even if most of them did not know who held the position at any given time. The prospect of it would be appealing to a man like Gusin.

He was trying to give himself those powers *without* being burdened with the duties of the Malykant. But he wouldn't settle for merely equalling the advantages that the Malykant enjoyed. Eetapi and Ootapi were strong, but that strength faded into insignificance when compared to that of a Great Spirit.

'He is after Nuutanami,' said Konrad.

'That fits with everything I have Seen,' she agreed.

Konrad sighed, a headache forming behind his eyes. Nuutanami was one of the Queens of the spirit world. She didn't always take a physical form, but when she did she adopted the shape of a giant mother serpent.

'Konrad,' Nanda said softly. 'Can he capture her with the soul diamond?'

Konrad stood up. 'Possibly. He'll be empowering it with every fae being he comes into contact with on his way to Nuutanami. The souls are only part of it. I need to get in his way, immediately.'

'I?' Nanda stood up too, a challenge in her posture and her expression.

'I,' Konrad repeated firmly. 'You should stay with Mother Kerttu, Nanda.'

'Oh, I should?' She folded her arms. 'Why is that?'

'Because this will be dangerous,' he said, glowering at her. 'And... unpleasant.'

She shrugged. 'I'm going with you.'

He didn't waste time arguing with her; he didn't have the time to waste. He merely bowed his head to Mother Kerttu in brief thanks, and left.

Nanda hadn't expected that. By the time she caught up to him he was already outside once more and striding into the spirit lands. She caught at his arm, but he shook her off.

'Konrad,' she gasped. 'Don't leave me behind—'

He crossed over, ignoring her. Light and shadow blazed in stark contrast before his eyes, and the strange winds of the spirit-lands howled around him, tugging at his hair and his long coat.

Behind him he heard a curse and then footsteps, both muffled by the swirling mist that hugged the ground.

'Nanda,' he growled, whirling around. 'Already you are slowing me down. Go back.'

The winds had already dishevelled her neatly-arranged hair, whipping strands of it around her face. She stood there, out of breath and obviously afraid but nonetheless unmoved. 'No.'

'You cannot keep up with me.'

'Then I will follow at my own pace.'

Konrad cursed inwardly. He didn't have time for this. Gusin was ahead of him, well on his way to Nuutanami's nest. He really didn't want to take Nanda into that mess, but he couldn't leave her alone behind him either.

With a low snarl of frustration he grabbed her hand and began to walk once more, dragging her along behind him. As he travelled, he let the demeanour of an ordinary human melt away until his true nature as the Malykant lay starkly revealed. With it came some of the hidden powers that his Master granted to him. His body blazed with strength and energy and his stride lengthened, eating up the ground at impossible speed. He kept his grip on Irinanda's hand; without the contact she would have no chance of keeping up with him. He was now moving far faster than any human could possibly go.

He knew where Nuutanami's nest lay. Lengthening his stride still further, he walked on, inexorable, as the mist-shrouded spirit lands streamed by him.

8

Konrad knew when they were near Nuutanami's nest, because the quality of the atmosphere changed. The air cooled and the mist faded, moisture crystallising into points of ice floating incongruously some way off the ground. The wind picked up, hissing sibilantly as it shrieked past his ears, chilling him to the bone. Irinanda stumbled along behind him, frightened and fighting for breath; he sensed her discomfort but he couldn't slow down, not now.

The hazy, ethereal foliage of the spirit lands thickened around him and he had to force his way through thick, deathly-white leaves and vines, surprisingly solid in their attempts to detain him. He ignored their grasping fingers and strode on, using his body to keep Nanda sheltered behind him. The sibilance of the wind increased, voices shrieking in his ears.

He ignored it all.

All at once, the foliage melted away behind him and he broke through into open space. A low valley stretched before him, hemmed in on all sides by tall, jagged and impassable-looking hills. Trees stood in rows around the edges of the valley, taller than any he'd yet seen in these lands, so tall that he could barely see the tops.

Nuutanami's nest was wound among the branches of a cluster of those trees. Unlike the pale trees, the white hills and the spectre-pale grass of the valley, the nest was a dark mess of shadow, woven from night and dark dreams and hunger. Nuutanami wasn't evil, precisely; Konrad knew well enough that no such simple label could apply to any creature out here. But she was formidable. She was the mother of cunning; her children relied on stealth and darkness and silence to feed. She wasn't to be lightly crossed.

All of which made Konrad wonder what could have spurred Iakov Gusin into his desperate plan. Not that the odds were hopeless: the Oracle had acted as she had because there was a chance Gusin could pull it off. But the risks were enormous, too. No sane person was *that* desperate for power.

Gusin, then, probably wasn't sane.

Irinanda gasped and fell against him. 'Konrad—'

'Hush,' he murmured, silencing her with a gentle finger against her lips. He steadied her with one arm, listening. The wind had died down when they had entered the valley, and the sibilance had stopped altogether. He considered that a bad sign.

A dread voice sliced into his head, tones of howling wind and sibilance combining into a mind-splitting cacophony. *Why come you here, mortal?*

Konrad winced, blessing – not for the first time – his lack of strong emotion. Any ordinary mortal would be a useless mess of fear under the influence of that voice. He merely felt a flicker of trepidation.

*You are in danger, Nuutanami,* he replied coolly.

The Great Spirit laughed, an unpleasant sound. *What could endanger me?*

*A mortal,* he replied unperturbed.

The laughter increased.

*With a soul stone,* he continued. *Powered by many souls, both mortal and spiritkind. And he is of The Malykt's people.*

Nuutanami stopped laughing.

He waited in silence as the Mother of Serpents digested that.

*I sense nothing,* she said then.

That bothered Konrad. How could Gusin contrive to hide from Nuutanami? Had he already grown so powerful?

Or had Konrad's guess been wrong, and Gusin had gone after one of the other Great Spirits? That thought chilled him more surely than the cold of Nuutanami's valley.

*I... am sure of it,* he said, trying and failing to sound confident. *He is here somewhere.*

He felt Nuutanami's scorn. *Be gone, mortal, before I grow hungry.*

Konrad stood his ground, thoughts spinning. If Gusin wasn't

here, which spirit would he have gone after instead? None made so much sense as Nuutanami. But if even she couldn't sense him...

His thought tailed off as a shriek shot through his head, loud enough to give him an instant headache. His hands tightened reflexively on Irinanda, who squeaked in surprised protest.

Nuutanami was in pain.

'He's here,' he muttered. 'With one soul stone, nicely powered up.'

Nanda nodded. 'What do we do?'

Konrad shook his head. Gusin was making his move, that he felt sure; he'd opened up the soul stone and turned it on the Great Spirit. How in the world he'd managed to take *her* by surprise was an impossible question to answer, but somehow he had. And it had been a beautiful move, because if Nuutanami got the chance to defend herself, Gusin's plan would fail.

'Find Nuutanami,' he muttered. But how? He hoped she wasn't in her nest; he couldn't possibly climb that high.

Another piercing shriek shot through his head, full of rage and shock. The voice was weakening.

'Your ears are bleeding,' Irinanda observed.

'This way,' he said suddenly and took off, his left hand still gripping Nanda's right with bone-crushing force. That second shriek had been aimed at him, and it contained a summons – even a compulsion. It was a ploy Nuutanami used to bring trespassers to her; crueller even than hunting them down herself, she forced them to approach her ostensibly of their own will.

It was a horrible trick, but on this occasion it had its uses. Konrad followed the call like a beacon, and within a few minutes he ran into Iakov Gusin.

Konrad's fellow priest of The Malykt was an older man, his dark hair liberally streaked with grey. His skin had the sickly pale hue of someone who never saw sunlight, and his eyes were too bright. In his hands he held up the Ivanov diamond. The jewel was emitting white light so bright that it hurt to look at it.

Konrad lifted a hand to shield his eyes. Above the tableau of Gusin and the diamond writhed the pained form of Nuutanami, floating ten or twenty feet above his head. She was enormous; her body was longer than the trunks of the tall, tall trees Konrad had passed, and if she had been a being of solid substance she would have weighed more than the entirety of Konrad's large stone mansion. As it was, her body was bone-white in hue and flickered with the same ethereal lack of substance as Eetapi and Ootapi.

She was fighting Gusin with a will, her enormous form thrashing with dangerous vigour not far over their heads. But he had chosen his timing well: Nuutanami's young had left the nest and she was alone at this season. He had also taken her by surprise, and had probably set the entrapped souls to bind her while he worked to enslave her spirit.

The method was similar to Eetapi and Ootapi's ways of binding the mortal soul, he realised, and that wasn't a coincidence either.

'Gusin,' he said quietly. 'What are you doing?'

The man hadn't seen him, so focused was he on the task at hand. And with good reason, for a single mistake at this juncture would release Nuutanami. His head snapped up and he stared at Konrad.

Then, to Konrad's surprise, he grinned. 'I wouldn't have guessed it would be you, Savast, but it makes sense. Welcome!'

Konrad blinked. *Welcome?* What killer ever welcomed the Malykant?

'I wouldn't have guessed you'd have the hubris to take on a Great Spirit, either,' Konrad replied, keeping his voice even.

Gusin's eyes flared with anger – and insanity. 'Why *not?* Look at you, Savast. Young, inexperienced, weak. What business have you in taking the role of Malykant away from the likes of me? I am your senior – your *superior –* in everything.'

Konrad sighed. 'That choice is up to The Malykt, as you well know.'

Gusin shrugged. His white face paled a shade or two further as he fought to maintain his working, and beads of sweat streaked down his cheeks. 'The Master's judgement is not infallible. Obviously.'

Konrad winced. Questioning The Malykt was always a bad idea, especially over matters pertaining solely to His business. 'You'd better take that back, Gusin.'

Gusin flashed him a wild grin, gasping now with the effort of keeping Nuutanami bound. 'Here to... kill me, Malykant?'

Konrad smiled back. It was a cold smile, devoid of humour. 'You've earned it.' He held back, wary of the blazing diamond and Nuutanami's writhing form. If Gusin simply dropped the working now, Nuutanami would soon tear herself free of it – and her rage would be enormous. He wasn't sure that she'd have the precision to direct it solely at her tormentor.

He wasn't afraid for himself; The Malykt watched over him. But Irinanda was another matter.

'Here's another idea,' panted Gusin. 'Why don't you join me?'

'Join you in *what* exactly? I fail to see what you're trying to accomplish, besides enraging the Greats.'

Gusin laughed softly. '*All* the Greats, Savast?'

Konrad blinked. A moment ago he would have said yes... *all* the Great Spirits should be furious over this attack on Nuutanami. But Gusin's smugness bothered him. Was that how he'd managed to sneak up on the Serpent Queen? Had he made a pact with one of the other Greats? There was rivalry between them, that he knew, but surely it didn't go *that* far.

Gusin flashed him a grin. 'I have powerful allies, Malykant.'

Konrad stared. Was Gusin's plan to promote himself to something akin to the Malykant – or worse? Was he aiming higher still?

Irinanda suddenly appeared behind Gusin, her pale face determined. Her hand flashed out as she grabbed the diamond, snatching it from Gusin's grip.

Konrad's heart leapt into his mouth. Good god, she'd just taken the diamond and *all* of its bound workings right out of Gusin's hands. That wasn't as simple as it sounded. The entrapped souls and spirits were under compulsion through a mixture of the diamond's power and Gusin's will. With the latter dislodged, there was a chance that *all* the enraged captives would break free of the diamond prison and turn on the bearer – Irinanda.

'Nanda!' he shouted. 'Throw me the diamond!'

She shook her head, her expression one of familiar stubbornness. He could see her battling with it, striving to keep it under control. The light dimmed, and Nuutanami's struggles grew stronger as the bindings weakened.

Two things happened. Cursing and blessing Nanda's stubbornness, Konrad called for his serpents. Eetapi and Ootapi leapt to life and streamed in Nanda's direction, reinforcing her efforts with their own power. They weren't enough to tip the balance entirely in her favour, but he hoped they could buy him enough time to deal with Gusin. Then he thrust a hand into his coat pocket and drew out a pinch of the sunbane powder he used to immobilise troublesome targets.

But Gusin was a quick thinker, too. As Konrad called his serpents, the other priest drew an obsidian-bladed knife – like the one Konrad carried – and grabbed Irinanda. The blade went to her throat, scoring a thin line that quickly began to bleed. Nanda hissed in surprise and sudden fear, but she held on to the diamond.

Konrad swore. He couldn't throw the sunbane without hitting Nanda with it, too, and Gusin was using her body to shield himself from Konrad's knives.

Fighting a foe who knew his methods made things somewhat harder than usual.

'Drop the powder,' Gusin grated, his grip tightening on Irinanda. 'And the knife. And the bones.'

Konrad dropped the powder. He drew his own obsidian knife and let it fall. Then, slowly, he drew a soft cloth pouch out of his inside pocket. Three bones rattled inside the pouch. He didn't drop it right away. His gaze met Nanda's.

'Drop them,' Gusin snarled, digging the knife a little deeper into Nanda's throat. She gasped, her eyes widening in fear, and for a moment – his dampened emotions notwithstanding – Konrad felt ready to rip off the man's head.

Then Nanda moved. She took one hand off the diamond, gripping it tightly in her left. With her freed right hand, she retrieved a small knife from some hidden place and in the same movement she buried it in Gusin's arm.

He howled with sudden pain, his grip loosening enough to allow Nanda to twist away from him. Without pausing, she raised her left arm and hurled the diamond away from her, throwing her whole strength behind it. The jewel sailed through the crisp, clear air over Konrad's head, glowing like a falling star. Watching as it flew, Konrad saw Eetapi and Ootapi streak away from the thing, drawing the three human souls out of the jewel along with them.

Good. The fae spirits would fight their way out, once released of Gusin's will. All Konrad had to do was to kill him.

Gusin let out a roar of frustration, loosed his grip on Nanda and leapt after the flying diamond. Irinanda bolted in Konrad's direction, removing herself from Gusin's reach. Konrad meanwhile bent down in a swift motion and retrieved his obsidian knife.

He lifted his arm and threw. The blade flew with deadly accuracy and buried itself in Gusin's throat. His furious roar ended in a wet choking sound, and he staggered backwards, his eyes wide with shock.

Overhead, Nuutanami's furious struggles grew stronger. She let loose a furious cry, loud and piercing enough to shake mountains in their foundations.

She would pull herself free of the diamond's mesmeric power any moment now, and her fury would be loosed upon all those nearby. Konrad didn't trust to her discernment when she was in a state of shock and rage and, most uncharacteristically, fear. He had to act, *now,* and then get himself and Nanda out of there.

A quick, practiced gesture ripped open the cloth bag and three bones spilled into his right hand. Konrad leapt at Gusin, throwing the whole weight of his body against the larger, heavier older man. The two of them tumbled to the ground, Gusin still fighting to breathe around the blade in his throat.

Konrad didn't waste time. He pinned the murdering traitor with his legs and his left arm. His right rose and fell three times, and with each movement came the sickening crunch of a sharpened object puncturing flesh. He buried the rib bones in Gusin's chest, ringing the man's rotten heart. Gusin screamed as each one entered his flesh, his body bucking wildly with pain. The act bound Gusin's soul to those of his three victims, granting them some power over him once all four passed into the Deathlands. Gusin would pay his debt to Pietr Orlov, Mikhail Ivan and Iolanta Lyubova. They would make sure of it.

Nuutanami shrieked again, and this sound was full of the joy of victory. She was free. Heart hammering, Konrad leapt off Gusin and turned, looking for Irinanda.

She stood not two feet away, staring in horror at the mess of Gusin's corpse. Her gaze flicked to Konrad, took in the spray of blood across his clothes and hands and the expression of fierce satisfaction on his face. More than that, Konrad knew she would see something like joy, or close to it: it was generated not by the violence he'd engaged in, but by the pride he felt in removing yet another killer from the world, in settling the score against someone who had betrayed his own Order. But Nanda couldn't know that.

Her face was a mask of shock and horror, and all of it was directed at him.

A feeling of crawling dread began somewhere in his belly. He pushed it down.

Escape first, mend bridges afterwards, he told himself.

He broke into a run, grabbing Nanda on the way past. He kept running, all but carrying her outright, as Nuutanami's screams intensified behind him. He could imagine the scene. The Malykt had already taken Gusin's miserable soul but his body remained. Nuutanami had a target for her ire, for the time being. But when she grew tired of savaging a body who couldn't feel it, she'd go looking for something else upon which to vent her fury.

He didn't want to be around when that happened.

He ran on until the cries of the Mother of Serpents finally faded beyond his range of hearing. He kept running, his muscles screaming protest at the double weight he was carrying and his lungs burning for air. He didn't slow down until they had reached the familiar parts of the spirit lands. Then he paused to find his way back through into the mortal world, weakening with relief as the weird, harsh lights of the spirit lands faded away.

He set Irinanda on her feet. They were out in the Bones; a glance around soon familiarised him with their whereabouts, and he began to walk towards the south gate of the city and Nanda's shop.

Nanda walked beside him in total silence. Minutes passed and she didn't say a word.

'Thank you,' he hazarded at last. 'For your help.'

She didn't say anything.

He took a deep breath. 'I don't... *enjoy* it, you know. It's just... my job.'

Nanda shook her head slowly. 'It didn't look that way.'

No. He didn't suppose it did look that way, at all. He walked on, too crushed to try any further defence of himself. They passed through the gate into the city streets and on to Nanda's shop, and stopped.

He hoped she might give him some small gesture, some little sign that she didn't utterly despise him. But she moved past him and into her building without even looking at him.

The door closed behind her.

Konrad stared at it for a while, swaying with weariness. He would have given almost anything to avoid Nanda's witnessing the most brutal, violent part of his role as the Malykant — or so he'd thought.

Could he have done more to keep her away?

Perhaps. It was easy to tell himself that he'd had no time; that he'd been forced to accept her presence by circumstances beyond his control. But that wasn't really true. He could have prevented her from following him, if he'd really wanted to.

The truth was, he had *wanted* her to see it. He wanted her to know what he was, because the isolation was killing him. He wanted there to be one person in the world who knew every detail of his life – and accepted him anyway. Someone who understood the value of what he did, and forgave him for the brutality of his methods.

Well. Irinanda wasn't going to be that person.

Konrad turned and walked away from Nanda's house. He could guess her next actions. She would tend to the wound on her throat, clean herself up. Then she would go to Dubin.

Feeling sickened with everything and with himself most of all, Konrad headed back to the south gate and passed through it again. He was tired of people, weary of the pretence of civilisation. He could pass for one of them when he had to; he could cut a dash as a mannered and pleasant gentleman. But he wasn't really part of that world. He didn't deserve to be. He was a part of wilder nature, a predator. Brutal, vicious, unforgiving.

He had to be, as the Malykant, but that excuse didn't satisfy him anymore. Why had the Master chosen him for the role? Because it suited him, and he suited it. Because he could do it, and take pride in it.

Because, despite his denials, there was a part of him that enjoyed it.

No wonder Nanda couldn't stand to be around him. He was no better than Gusin.

Pulling the brim of his hat lower over his eyes, Konrad wandered out into the Bones, heading in the general direction of his workshop. The chicken-legged house, as Nanda had called it.

This was where he belonged, though it be cold and isolated and merciless. And here he would stay. Civilisation could do without him for a while; he could certainly do without it.

# MYRROLEN'S GHOST CIRCUS

# 1

Konrad Savast—poison-master, servant of the Lord of Death and gentleman of the city of Ekamet—stood surveying his wardrobe with deep distaste. His shirts were out of order again. He spotted at least four that were out of strict colour sequence, and was that a linen shirt hanging with the cotton ones? Abominable.

He *paid* his valet enough, or so he thought. Why couldn't the man keep a mere forty shirts in tolerable order? He had given time off to visit the circus, yes; but was it too much to expect that the valet see to his wardrobe first?

Sighing, Konrad sorted through the mess until he found the shirt he was looking for—a thick cotton one to ward off the late autumn chill, dark red in colour. It had a tall, striking collar, which would look well when teamed with a lace cravat. He donned these, together with a dark, well-cut coat and trousers, and stood back to survey the effect.

It did indeed look well, but the reflection gave Konrad no particular satisfaction. He frowned at the mirror and turned away.

*Master,* whispered Eetapi in his mind.

*What?* he snapped back.

*Are you well?*

Eetapi's physical form—or what passed for it—materialised in the air before him. She was a snake, or had been in life. She maintained the semblance of a serpent after death, but that was mostly an affectation. She was nothing but dust, air and consciousness.

And a dolefully melodic voice that grated intolerably on him today.

*I am perfectly well,* he replied.

*But—*

*Did you have something useful to say?* he interrupted. *A new case for me to address? Word from my Master?* He hoped that the answer to one or the other might be "yes". He would welcome the distraction.

*No,* Eetapi admitted. *We were just—*

*Just what?*

*Well—*

*Go away, Eetapi,* he sighed.

The snake faded away.

Konrad left his dressing room and marched downstairs. It had been three weeks since he'd had any real work to do, and his last few cases had been dull. A married woman had stabbed her cheating husband in his sleep; it had been pathetically easy to figure that one out. He'd had the case solved and the perpetrator dispatched within two days. There had been an inheritance battle—another one, funny how many people were willing to kill for money or property—and a crazy who'd killed a child. That one had been depressing. He needed a nice, clear-cut case, challenging but not too harrowing. A case where everyone was a villain, so he didn't have to engage in any moral dilemmas. That would be nice.

Which meant, he realised, that he was effectively hoping for someone to be murdered sometime soon. And he'd come to think of a plain old common-or-garden murder as basic work; these days it took something special to unsettle him.

That kind of detachment was necessary in his job, but it didn't make him feel any better about himself.

He marched into the spacious hallway of his mansion house, and a footman rushed to help him on with his boots. The lad sensibly kept his mouth shut, perhaps warned by the thunderous look on his master's face. Or maybe it was just habit, these days; Konrad's mood had been black for some time.

'Thank you,' he said curtly to the boy, prompted by a twinge of conscience.

The footman just nodded and scuttled away. If anything, Konrad's curt comment had alarmed rather than reassured him.

'Pah,' Konrad sighed.

He collected his hat and cane and made for the door, but before he reached it Ootapi flickered into view. Right in his face.

*Master,* Ootapi said in his mind, and Konrad winced. This one had a voice like splintering ice. If Eetapi's tones grated on him, the other serpent's words were like icicles driven into his brain.

*Yes?*

*It has been five months and seventeen days since you were last worth talking to,* Ootapi informed him.

Konrad blinked. *A most precise reckoning.*

*I have kept count,* the serpent replied gravely.

*Thank you for your diligence. Do you tell me this for any particular purpose, or merely to depress me further?*

Ootapi twitched in the air. *I hope to inspire you to some improvement.*

*An intriguing approach. It doesn't have a high chance of succeeding, does it?*

*No, indeed,* the snake agreed. *And so I would like to inform you, on behalf of Eetapi as well as myself, that our period of employment with you will terminate at the end of another thirteen days, unless some marked improvement is observed before that time.*

Konrad's eyebrows shot up. *You're handing in notice?*

*We intend to seek a post with better conditions,* Ootapi said coolly.

Konrad was speechless. Conditions? Period of employment? The snakes were envoys from Konrad's Master, The Malykt: He Who Handled Death, Passing On, Spirits and all that kind of thing. They carried messages from the Master and helped him to carry out his job—to bring murderers to justice. And they had contracts of employment? They worried about working conditions?

They could *quit?*

*Thank you,* Konrad managed after a moment. *I wish you luck with your next position.* What manner of job that might be, Konrad couldn't imagine; what else could a pair of dead snakes do with themselves?

Ootapi twitched and vanished. Konrad shrugged. Perhaps the spirit had been hoping for a different response, but what could he say? Ootapi was right: he'd been unbearable for months, and he didn't expect that to change anytime soon.

Being an outcast would do that to anybody, especially when it was deserved.

Oh, he was a popular figure in Ekamet, at least on the surface. But that was because of his wealth and style and looks; nothing that mattered, and none of the people who knew him as Mr Konrad Savast, wealthy gentleman of leisure, really knew him at all.

Those who did—those who knew what his *real* job was, how he truly spent his time—came to shun him, sooner or later. He didn't blame them. If he could shun himself, he would have by now.

Perhaps he'd get lucky sometime soon, and some indignant killer would stick a stake in him or something. Maybe his Master would actually let him die. It was probably about time for The Malykt to pick a new servant, someone younger, faster, less... jaded.

Well, Konrad could hope.

Anyway, the Festival of the Dead was in full swing across the city this week. Ordinarily it was something Konrad enjoyed. It was a strange festival, a macabre but curiously light-hearted celebration of death. People around here, they feared death as much as anyone else, and nobody looked forward to dying (well, most people didn't). But they also accepted Passing as a natural and necessary process, and the Festival of the Dead was The Malykt's time, when people honoured Him for the care he took to ensure that everyone ended up in their proper places once they died.

Konrad's identity was a secret, of course, and the role of the Malykant was controversial. Some welcomed his interference in murder cases, viewing him as a bringer of fitting justice upon those who meddled with the natural life-death cycle. Others thought him a mere brute, pointing out—rightly enough—that murder cases weren't always clear-cut and the people he slew in his Master's name sometimes had persuasive defences for their actions. Taken all together, that meant that nobody wasted time honouring the Malykant during the Festival of the Dead, but that didn't really bother him. He enjoyed the colourful clothes, the street markets and the Festival foods, and—most of all—Myrrolen's Circus. He was on his way there now.

He didn't bother with his carriage. The streets were too busy for coaches; he'd spend longer waiting to get through the queues than it would take him to walk to the field on the edge of the city where the circus was pitched. He took his time, enjoying the chill in the air—not yet the bone-chilling cold of winter that gripped the realm of Assevan for more than half the year, but a rather pleasant cold. The mornings came in draped in fog, and the mist rolled in again as soon as the sun began to set. It was late afternoon by the time he reached the acre of tents gleaming bone-white under the dying sun, and deep, thick fog was already gathering.

The circus was organised in the same way every year: an enormous tent occupied the centre of the field, within which was the grand arena. Smaller tents ringed it in widening circles, housing stalls selling seasonal food and trinkets. Konrad wandered around these for a time, sampling blood sausage and colourful sweets. He purchased a new cane for his collection, featuring a handsome silver-wrought raven atop a polished wooden stick. He was halfway down a cup of steaming tea, feeling more relaxed than he had in some time, when something furry touched his neck.

Startled, he whirled around, spilling hot tea in the process. A tiny golden-furred monkey had availed itself of his shoulder and was clinging hard to his coat. It had wrapped its long, long tail around his neck in a sort of embrace, and when he looked down, the animal rubbed its small face against his.

'Hello, Weveroth,' he said softly, stroking the creature's soft fur. He hadn't seen Weveroth in months—just as he hadn't seen the monkey's mistress. The little creature's pleasure at seeing him was obvious, and it warmed Konrad's heart just a little bit. He lifted his head to look for Irinanda. If Weveroth was here, she probably was too; but he couldn't see her.

'Where's Nanda?' he said to the monkey. He felt a bit odd doing it, but Weveroth had already proved that his powers of comprehension exceeded those of regular monkeys: there was always a chance of a useful response.

Weveroth tilted his little head, rolling up his eyes in thought. Then he lifted a paw and pointed away to Konrad's right.

Konrad blinked. This was a more direct response than he'd expected, but... he went with it. Following the monkey's pointed directions he made his way through the crowded stalls to a little market selling clothes and jewellery. Irinanda stood in front of a long mirror, making a discontented face at herself as she tried on a scarf. Her white-blonde hair was bound up as usual, and—as usual—it was doing its best to escape from its confines. She was wearing a dress Konrad hadn't seen before, red in colour and quite fetching. His heart fluttered oddly as he looked at her. She was the only person he'd thought of as a real friend in recent years, but she had disowned him after the last case they'd worked on together. She'd seen him deliver The Malykt's harsh justice, plunging a sharpened rib-bone into the heart of a particularly vile murderer.

This hadn't come as a surprise to her; she had known about his job for some time. But there was a difference between abstract knowledge, and seeing him in action. What had she seen in him that day?

Perhaps she thought he enjoyed it. Perhaps she thought he was no better than the people he pursued; that she had made friends with a crazed killer who'd merely found a way to legitimise his crimes. Either way, the experience had caused apparently irreparable damage to their friendship. She'd avoided him ever since, and he hadn't forced his presence on her.

But he had missed her.

He opened his mouth to announce himself, but hesitated. He had tried once, and only once, to visit her since their rupture; he'd thought he could explain himself somehow, talk his way out of the mess, make her approve of him again. He'd ended up fervently wishing he had not gone. Would it be like that again?

In the end, Nanda saw him first. Her cold blue eyes stared first at his face, then flicked to the little monkey sitting on his shoulder. Her expression turned wintry cold, and Konrad's heart sank like a rock.

'Weveroth,' she said coldly, 'get off there.'

The monkey didn't move.

Nanda's brows lifted. 'Mutiny,' she observed. 'Very well.' She turned away without looking at Konrad, and replaced the scarf she had been trying on. She began to walk away, and Konrad thought he would let her until some impulse sent him hurrying after her. He stood in front of her, forcing her to stop.

'How are you, Nanda?' he said mildly, trying to be pleasant.

'Quite well, thank you,' she said distantly, managing to look at him without really meeting his gaze.

Konrad waited, but she didn't ask after his health. 'Well, good,' he said awkwardly. 'I've wondered.'

Irinanda nodded. She still avoided his eye, and her feet made little shuffling steps backwards, apparently involuntarily, as if she was trying to put distance between the two of them.

With a thrill of horror Konrad realised she was afraid.

Of *him*.

Any inclination to pursue the conversation withered and died. He scooped Weveroth off his shoulder, and with a brief nod he handed the tiny monkey to his mistress. Then he walked off, feeling hot and cold all over, while some unidentifiable sensation churned in his belly.

Ah, that was it. Nausea.

He tried to put the matter out of his thoughts. After all, it wasn't unreasonable that Nanda was scared of him: everyone feared the Malykant. That was the whole point. But *Nanda?*

Dazed, he found himself standing outside the grand arena. He wandered in, his thoughts circling dizzily. Maybe he was just a crazed killer. There were some who'd argued that for years: that the Malykant was no better than his targets, except that his predations were licensed and sponsored. Was that true? In his confused state, it was hard for him to feel any conviction one way or the other.

Maybe it was true. Maybe they were all right about him, Nanda included.

A vibrant circus display was in progress inside the arena, watched by a large audience. Colours flashed before Konrad's eyes as he found a spare seat, and he gazed with numb attention at the spectacle, trusting to its novelty to distract him from his own thoughts. Exotic animals were in the ring with their handlers, going through a series of performances that didn't interest him much. Traditional stuff, this; crowd-pleasing, but not what Myrrolen's Circus was really famous for.

His attention wandered to a pair of tight-rope walkers balancing high above the arena, one small step away from probable death. That interested him more. A fair reflection of his mental state, yes: a precarious balancing act between remaining Konrad Savast, generally upstanding citizen of Ekamet, and the public perception of the Malykant as a sponsored serial killer.

*You really are miserable to be around lately,* Ootapi hissed in his thoughts. *What's the matter with you?*

*I am alone in the world and my life is full of horrors,* Konrad thought back. *Is that enough?*

He felt Ootapi twitch, a sort of mental spasm crossed with a shrug. *Of course,* said the serpent. *Maybe you wouldn't be alone if you were not so...* the snake paused to think. *Depressing,* he finished.

Konrad thought about that. The serpents were leaving him too, of course, and for precisely that reason; but it had been Nanda's loss that had begun the process. *Of course I'm depressing,* he replied, too

163

weary to snap. *I'm the Malykant. Can you think of a more depressing job?*

*You managed it better, once.*

*That was before.*

The serpent said nothing else.

Konrad went back to watching the show, keeping his mind carefully blank as the performers cycled through their colourful routines. Soon, something began to change. The bright lights in the tent slowly dimmed as lanterns were extinguished; the arena went dark. Then the lamps began to come back on, but this time they threw coloured light across the stage: ghostly shades of green and blue, a haze of purple, a sinister flash of red. Konrad sat up. Night had fallen outside, and now came the interesting part.

The previous performers had departed, taking their animals with them, and the arena stood empty. Fog rolled in, obscuring the floor, and the ghostly coloured lights drifted up into the air. They hovered there for some moments, growing fainter in the fog, and then they began to dance. Next came the eyes in the dark, hundreds of pairs of them, staring unblinking out into the audience. The show went on in similar style, a festival of light and colour shining eerily in the darkness, most of it performed well above the audience's heads.

Every year, speculation arose anew about how Myrrolen's Circus staged their night time shows. Sceptics—or the more rational denizens of Ekamet, as they thought of themselves—talked of lines and pulleys and stealthy performers dressed in dark suits. Such a thing would be impossible, Konrad thought, watching the whirl of colour before him. It would be far too complex, and everything was moving too fast for such a prosaic explanation to be plausible.

The more popular theory was that Myrrolen's Circus employed not only living performers but dead ones as well. When the light faded from the sky, the living slipped away and left the stage to the departed. Some said they were the souls of those who'd worked for the Circus when they were alive: Konrad couldn't say for sure whether that was true, but he knew that the theory was largely correct.

He knew that because he could sense them, wisps of spirit-forms concealed in the midst of the fog. Accustomed to associating with the likes of Eetapi and Ootapi, his eyes—or perhaps his mind—were sensitive to the shades of the dead, and it both thrilled and alarmed him to see them thus occupied. They puzzled and fascinated him in equal measures. Why had so many of them chosen to remain in the mortal lands, instead of passing into the Deathlands when they'd died? It was unheard of outside of the circus. He'd tried to talk with them one year, but they had ignored him, blocked him out. And so he continued to wonder.

After a time the lights faded again and the fog began to dissipate. Konrad waited, unsure what to expect next. Traditionally the lights always opened the show, but each subsequent performance was original. How would the ghosts appear next?

A shaft of light suddenly sliced through the darkness, illuminating a circular patch of the sandy arena floor. Something lay in the pool of light. Konrad leaned forward, trying to see better around the people in front of him. Whatever it was lay inert, and he waited in vain for some further action. Nothing happened.

The audience began to grow restive, and Konrad frowned, a feeling of uneasiness building in his gut. Having arrived late he was seated a long way back, so it was hard to tell... but wasn't that a human figure lying there?

The audience began to reach the same conclusion at the same time, for the whispers grew to shouting and people began to get out of their seats. Some headed for the staging area, some for the exit. Konrad stayed where he was.

Abruptly the spotlight went out, and the inert pile of humanity within it vanished from view. A second light winked into being near the front of the arena, and within it stood a dark figure, a female. She was dressed demurely in a black gown, corseted like any proper lady, but her attire was of an unusual style. The gown left her neck and shoulders mostly bare, long gloves covered her arms, and her skirts were pulled up in swags to display tall velvet boots. A miniature top-hat adorned her dark hair: the Ringmaster's hat.

Konrad blinked. This was Myrrolena herself.

'Ladies and gentlemen,' Myrrolena said, her voice somehow amplified to roll around the tent. 'Regrettably, Myrrolen's Circus will close for the rest of the night. There will be an extra performance tomorrow in recompense. We wish you a pleasant evening.' Myrrolena lifted her chin and smiled; the lights flashed as seven ravens shot into the air around her, though whether they were real or some illusion Konrad couldn't tell. Then the spotlight winked out and she was gone.

Konrad sat still until everyone around him had left the tent and the buzz of excited voices had faded. What had happened? Once the circus arrived, it didn't close for a week. It ran all day and all night; that was part of its allure. What could prompt Myrrolena to break with tradition?

He thought of the huddled figure in the middle of the arena floor and shuddered. Whoever that had been, his Malykant's instincts told him, loudly and clearly, that he or she was dead. But how, and why? And how in the world had a corpse ended up in the middle of Myrrolen's Circus?

# 2

The atmosphere of the circus was different when the great tent was empty. Without its chattering, enthusiastic audience the tent seemed barren, as if it had been abandoned for much longer than a mere few minutes. Empty space stretched ahead of him and the ceiling yawned somewhere above, its confines lost in darkness. The riotous music and applause had faded away into silence.

Concealed in the shadows, Konrad stood still, watching and listening. With the audience gone, would Myrrolena's people come out?

Nothing happened. Konrad frowned, puzzled. The audience had been removed for a reason: shouldn't there now be some reaction to the shocking appearance of the corpse? Tentatively he left his concealed position and stepped forward. If nobody was here yet, then he wanted to examine that corpse himself.

He had only just reached the vast central stage when the nearest light flickered out. He stopped, eyes wide, as all the other lights in the tent went out one by one. It happened fast: within seconds he was plunged into total darkness.

Konrad smiled. The ghosts were not gone, then.

*Eetapi,* he said silently. *Ootapi. Softly, please.*

The snakes came, but stealthily. He saw them before him in his mind's eye, but they refrained from manifesting.

*Guide me,* he requested. *To the centre. There will be a body there.*

The serpents instantly sailed away and he followed, his steps sure and unerring, for their familiar forms shone in his mind like beacons in the dark. Before long they stopped and circled, their voices chiming like funeral bells in his head.

*Look,* whispered Ootapi. *A body!* If he'd had a face, he would have been beaming all over it.

Eetapi said nothing, but he felt her glee.

He sighed inwardly. With companions like these, was it any wonder his head was a mess?

*Thanks,* he muttered. *I need a bit of light. Not too much though, please.*

Both snakes manifested, dampening their ghost-glow to a minimum. The pale, sickly light was barely enough to illuminate the motionless shape before him, and he considered requesting more; but he didn't want to advertise his presence any more than was absolutely necessary.

Kneeling beside the body, he cast a quick, professional glance over it, mentally recording the details. It was a man, of middle age— perhaps late forties—with the dark hair and pale skin that suggested a native of Assevan. His clothes were of good quality, though not so rich as to suggest any particular wealth. They were also largely nondescript. The man's features were strong and distinctive: he had a prominent nose, thick lips and bushy dark brows. His staring eyes were a common shade of blue.

Noting all of this, Konrad began to search for anything unusual about the body. He found nothing in the man's pockets, and a check of his wrists, neck and ears revealed no jewellery of any kind. Looking at him, Konrad couldn't even tell if he was likely to be an associate of the circus or not.

What he did find was a bloody wound on the back of the man's head, certainly severe enough to have caused his death. But he saw no spilled blood around the corpse except for directly beneath the head; and besides, a blow to that area ought to have pitched him face-down onto the floor, not face up.

Konrad made a note of all of that, too. Whoever this man was, he hadn't been killed here. His body had been placed here deliberately, and the location must be significant. Somebody wished to involve Myrrolena's people in the case.

He sat back, trying to calculate how long it had been since the corpse had first been revealed. The man didn't appear to have been dead for long. *Serpents,* he called silently. *Is his spirit near?*

*We can't tell,* Eetapi replied after a moment.

*Why not?*

*Because,* hissed Ootapi, *there are spirits everywhere.*

Ah.... Yes. Konrad had forgotten that. In a space swarming with ghosts, it would be hard to pick out any particular one. *You can't tell which is his?*

*Just a moment,* Ootapi whispered. *Perhaps they are wearing badges.* The serpent paused. *Hello!* he bellowed in Konrad's head. *Does anyone have a badge reading "Mine is the corpse on the circus tent floor?"*

*All right,* Konrad snapped. *No.*

*Or anything similar?* Ootapi continued. *It needn't be word for word.*

*Enough!*

Ootapi coiled himself around Konrad's neck, streaming in hazy circles that sent a cold, spinning draft over his skin. *Just trying to help,* he whispered.

Konrad swallowed his annoyance. He had learned all he could from the body alone, and the option of speaking to the man's spirit directly did not seem to be open to him. It had been a thin hope, anyway: the stress of sudden death wore quickly upon a newly separated spirit, fraying it to incoherent shreds. The man had been dead plenty long enough for that to happen.

But where could he look next for a clue? He had no idea who the man was. Perhaps someone with the circus would know—if he could find someone to speak to, living or dead.

*Eetapi,* he began—then stopped. Eetapi's presence was gone, and a moment's search confirmed that Ootapi had vanished too. He called them.

They didn't answer.

However angry they might be, they would never abandon him in the middle of a job like this. Konrad stood up carefully, looking around. Something was wrong here. His senses prickled; he felt watched from a dozen different directions. Myrrolena's ghosts had surrounded him.

Drafts picked up suddenly in the tent, cool winds tugging at his clothes and raising goose bumps on his skin. He heard a soft laugh as if from a great distance, then a deep chuckle near his ear. Incorporeal hands ran through his hair. No friendly presences, these: they distrusted him. A glow built around him, a pallid, flickering light thrown off by the ill-will that surrounded him.

'I mean no trouble,' he said calmly. 'I am here merely to—'

He stopped, flabbergasted. The corpse—undeniably solid, human and real, he would have sworn it—had disappeared. All that remained was a pool of blood, lying in eerie isolation near his feet. As he watched, that shrank and shrank until it, too, disappeared.

The horrid light faded and Konrad realised he was alone. No ghosts, no body. Where the living members of Myrrolena's Circus might be, he didn't know.

Frustrated, he rubbed briefly at his temples, sensing a headache coming on. Here was a conundrum. He had nothing to go on, not the smallest clue: no notion of the identity of the victim, no idea where the man was killed or why, or how he came to be lying in the midst of the great circus tent during the night performance. And yet, he knew The Malykt would consider it Konrad's responsibility to resolve these questions—and he certainly wouldn't accept any of these trifling obstacles as a reason not to pursue it.

A choked laugh emerged from Konrad's dry throat, startling him. He *had* wished for a case. Well, he was in luck; here was a task to keep him busy for days. Even weeks.

Possibly months.

With a sigh, Konrad turned to leave. He wouldn't risk searching the rest of the circus, not while it was still crawling with shades who definitely didn't want him there. The place to begin, he reasoned, was by investigating the circus itself. A mystery surrounded Myrrolena's travelling show, carefully maintained by Myrrolena he had no doubt; but if he dug deeply enough, perhaps he could uncover something.

A light flickered at the edge of his vision, catching his eye. He quickly turned his head, staring uselessly into the darkness. Were the ghosts returning?

Not the ghosts. The light came again, a soft pulse that illuminated a face. He caught the briefest glimpse of features in stark contrasts, pale and dark, white-painted skin with dark hair and eyes. A woman's face, her hair bound up, a small top hat balanced atop her sweeping curls.

Myrrolena's face, and she had been staring directly at him.

Without thinking, Konrad set off walking in the direction of the light. Why had she let him see her? Had it been a signal? Was he meant to follow? He would anyway: of all people, she could best answer his questions.

He forgot that he didn't have a light source, and it wasn't long before he hit the wall of the tent. He spent several long minutes groping his way around, looking for the alcove in which she'd been standing. His searching hands encountered nothing but more smooth canvas, and eventually, the exit back out into the night. Reluctantly, and with more than a little irritation, he abandoned the project. If she'd meant for him to follow her, she would have given him some further sign by now. What had her intention been? To intimidate him? Did she wish to scare him away?

If so, the clear implication was that Myrrolen's Circus had something to hide—and that only made Konrad more determined to discover what it was.

As he stepped out into the night, he felt the returning presence of his serpents.

*What happened there?* he demanded.

*We were... attacked!* said Ootapi. *Yes! By hundreds of them.*

*Thousands,* added Eetapi.

*You ran away,* Konrad said. *Admit it.*

Silence.

*I should reprimand you or something,* Konrad said with an internal sigh, *but this is me running away, too.*

*I suppose we can beat a hasty retreat together,* Ootapi said gravely.

*Thanks so much.*

Konrad spent most of the following day in the cramped office of Inspector Alexander Nuritov, his regular associate at Ekamet's police headquarters. Nuritov was easy-going about Konrad's involvement in local murder cases, putting it down to the eccentricities (and possibly boredom) of a man of leisure. And since Konrad regularly fed him information—always concealing his precise methods of discovery, of course—Nuritov was also easygoing about helping Konrad on occasion, too.

The police had received many reports of the corpse from the audience who'd been gathered the night before. They had duly sent over a few officers to look around. Even Nuritov himself had been down there that morning, Konrad had learned; but since there was no sign of a body and no real evidence of there ever having been one, there wasn't much the police could do. They wrote it off as one of the circus's weirder stunts, and went back to their regular duties.

But Nuritov listened to Konrad's account with close attention, and (to Konrad's relief) readily offered his aid. The inspector immediately dispatched two junior officers to all the local newspaper offices, with orders to search their records for any reports on Myrrolen's Circus, past or present. Following that, he'd turned Konrad loose on the police's own archives.

It made for a long day. By the middle of the afternoon, Konrad felt as though he'd personally read every piece of paper the Ekamet Police had ever filed away, and without making a great deal of progress. He was looking for any mention of Myrrolen's Circus, especially recent ones.

The Circus and all its employees were model citizens, as far as he could tell: nothing cropped up anywhere that might suggest anything questionable about the group, or give him an avenue of enquiry to follow.

Not, that is, until he began glancing through files of unsolved cases. He was bored by this time and his eyes were tired; expecting to find nothing and anxious to reach the end of his dull chore, he began flipping through, barely looking at the pages. And so when he finally stumbled over a reference to Myrrolen's Circus, he almost missed it.

It was a sketch that caught his eye, a hastily-drawn representation of a crime scene much like many others Konrad had seen: a body lying on its back on a patch of grass, eyes staring upward. It was the tent that was sketched in behind that caught Konrad's eye. It looked like a circus tent.

Frowning, he leafed through the rest of the file, rapidly reading the text. Eleven years ago—before Nuritov's time as an inspector, he judged—a suspicious death had been reported at the city show ground. An inspector had arrived quickly with a couple of officers and sketched the scene; but somehow or other the body had been left alone for a few moments, and when the inspector returned it had gone. That had instantly raised the man's suspicions; but Myrrolen's people (old Myrrolen, that was, the present Ringmistress's father) swore that the man had nothing to do with the circus. The body had never reappeared and no further evidence had come to light; in the end the case had been reluctantly abandoned.

Energised, Konrad searched the rest of the case files. The similarities between the two incidents couldn't be a coincidence: were there more? There were, he found, two more: seventeen years ago and twenty-five years ago. Two of the reported victims were male, and one female. In each case, some member of the public had reported sighting of a body, and the police had investigated—only to find that the supposed corpse had disappeared without trace.

Comparing them with yesterday's incident, Konrad found a few differences between the previous three incidents and his own case. One was the circumstances of the body, and the way it had been found: in the earlier cases the corpse had been discovered somewhere out of the way, by a wandering circus patron. None of the others had turned up in the middle of the stage during a performance. That had to be significant; Konrad noted that for future enquiry.

Secondly, none of the previous three bodies had suffered any obvious wounds. That the victims were dead was obvious enough; whether or not they had been deliberately killed was less so. This, too, could be significant, Konrad decided, remembering the head wounds on the man he'd seen last night.

Those details aside, the similarities between all four cases were eerie—and they spanned a period of twenty-five years! Who were those people, and what had become of them?

Konrad spent some time copying the pertinent details from each case into his notebook, then he carefully replaced all the files. Nuritov's junior officers ought to have returned by now, hopefully bringing several years' worth of newspaper reports with them. All the major papers reported on the Circus when it arrived, of course; none of them had much to say about it, given its mysterious nature, but the unsolved cases had raised Konrad's spirits and his hopes in equal measures. He locked up the archives room and returned to Nuritov's office.

Nuritov looked up as Konrad walked in, and grinned. 'You look like you've been stampeded over by a herd of horses.' He paused, looked more closely at Konrad, then shook his sandy head. 'No, I take it back. You *don't* look that way at all, and you should after a whole day in the archives. How do you do it?'

Konrad smiled. 'The excitement of discovery has revitalised me completely. Have you got anything for me?'

Nuritov nodded enthusiastically and gestured to a chair. 'Look,' he said, thrusting a stack of papers across the table to Konrad. 'I don't know if they'll be useful to you, but there's always a chance!'

Konrad took the papers and sorted quickly through them. They were all dated over the last few days, and all covered the arrival of

Myrrolen's Circus. Most of the articles offered the same common knowledge about the shows and printed these facts alongside similar pictures; but one had gone further, and printed an artist's representation of, apparently, much of the circus's cast. Konrad stared at it for several minutes, examining each face in turn for something he recognised.

No good. The man he'd seen was not in the picture. That didn't necessarily mean he had nothing to do with the circus; the drawing may not include all the cast members, or perhaps the dead man had been connected with the circus in some other way.

Then again, maybe the man was just a circus patron, visiting the shows and the markets like everyone else. Or maybe he'd never had anything to do with the circus at all.

Konrad frowned, disliking the uncertainty. The papers had neither ruled anything out nor offered him anything new, which was disappointing. He set them aside with a sigh, and turned back to Nuritov.

'Not much in here,' he said, 'but I found some interesting things downstairs. Look at these...'

The discoveries fascinated—and troubled—Nuritov just as much as they'd electrified Konrad, and the inspector immediately fell to thinking. 'I might be able to find more on these,' he mused, and Konrad smiled.

'Anything you can get would be terrific. Also. D'you think there's any chance of getting more newspaper reports on the circus? All the way back to the beginning?'

Nuritov nodded enthusiastically. 'Could be, could be. I'll get some men on it.'

Konrad grinned, not envying the junior officers the paperwork. 'Lucky them. But I appreciate it, thanks.'

## 3

If Konrad wanted more information about Myrrolen's Circus, what better source than Myrrolena herself? Elusive she may be, but somehow he had to find a way to speak with her.

He dispatched a note requesting an urgent meeting, but he was not surprised when no reply came. He tried posing as a newspaper reporter seeking an interview, but that elicited no response either (of course, Myrrolena was probably inundated with such requests since the unprecedented closure of the circus the day before). He tried simply turning up and asking for her, but of course nobody admitted to knowing where she was.

Having exhausted all reasonable and legal avenues of enquiry, Konrad turned (not without a certain alacrity) to somewhat stealthier methods.

*Serpents,* he whispered. *I have a task for you.*

No answer came.

*Eetapi!* He hissed. *Ootapi! I need you!*

Still nothing happened for several long moments, and Konrad began to feel the stirrings of alarm. But then Ootapi's icy voice hissed in his thoughts, *Did you forget that we have resigned? We did not.*

Konrad blinked. *Your notice has not yet been accepted by our Master. Until it has, you still work for me. Okay?*

Ootapi made a snorting sound.

*This is no game,* Konrad snapped. *A man is dead and you have a job to do, as do I. Get in here, please.*

The serpents slowly faded into view. There was something sulky about their materialisation, and Konrad scowled. 'This is unprofessional.'

Ootapi flicked his ghostly tail. *That is rather the point, Malykant.*

'Myrrolena,' Konrad said loudly, ignoring that. 'I must know more about her circus, but it is a damned mysterious business. I need to talk to her, but of course she cannot be found, and will not respond to me. I need your help in tracking her down.'

*Yes, Malykant,* said Eetapi.

Konrad waited, but Ootapi said nothing.

'And after that,' he continued, 'while I speak to her, I want you two to find out everything you can about her performers. Especially the dead ones. Yes?'

*Should we*— began Eetapi, but Konrad cut her off.

'I don't care how you do it, just get it done. And try not to be caught. Ready then? We're leaving.'

Konrad grabbed his hat and cane and strode out of the house, trusting to the idiot serpents to follow. He rode the short distance in his carriage with the blinds half drawn, blocking out the weak afternoon sunlight. At the show ground he stepped down, with a curt order to his driver to wait, and marched into the circus.

The events were in full swing once more, and he had to shoulder his way through busier crowds than ever to get inside. That was typical of people, he thought sourly: a whiff of horror or scandal and you couldn't pay them to stay away. As he worked his way towards the centre he heard the sounds of music, faint and growing louder: the performances had resumed. The day shows would still be on, but not for much longer; perhaps Myrrolena's ghosts would be somewhere nearby, awaiting their turn.

But first, to find Myrrolena herself.

*Eetapi?* he called.

To his relief she presented herself immediately, though she refrained from materialising. *Malykant?*

*It's time to hunt for Myrrolena, if you please.* He gave her a mental image of the Ringmistress, laden with everything he knew about her: her physical appearance, her air and manner, what little he knew of her life and history. It did not amount to very much, and he had a feeling that the lady may prove to be very good at concealing herself—even from his spirit-snakes.

Ah well. It was worth a try. Eetapi sailed away, Ootapi streamed

176

off behind her, and Konrad was left alone.

He had no intention of standing idle while his serpents searched. Looking about himself, he considered for a moment where the mysterious Myrrolena might be. He did not imagine she would leave the vicinity of the circus while it was in operation: she would be somewhere on its grounds. But the events spanned a large area. Where to begin?

She must have private quarters somewhere, but he wasted no time imagining he could find those. If she was there, his serpents might discover her; but he could waste all day looking for one temporary tent dwelling among many virtually identical ones.

Besides, the lady herself was unlikely to be there at this time. She should be watching over her circus, keeping an eye on the performances, ensuring that everything was running smoothly.

So that meant... she was probably somewhere nearby.

In fact, if *he* was in her shoes and he wanted to be hard to find, what better place to conceal himself than in the middle of the crowd? His gut told him he was on to something; feeling energised, he lifted his head and began scanning the circus-goers, as if expecting to see her right away. He turned a few useless circles, neck craning, before he realised how absurd he was being and stopped.

He thought for a moment. He could search in a circular pattern, starting at the main entrance and using the soaring central tent to orient himself. It wasn't a perfect plan, but without a team of people to help him it was the best he had.

He turned back towards the entrance—and stopped. Directly in front of him stood a tall woman, so close that he'd almost walked into her in his haste.

'I'm so sorry,' he muttered.

The woman smiled. 'Really, it's quite all right.' She wasn't much shorter than he was, he quickly realised. She was dressed for the cold, in a warm-looking but nonetheless elegant gown, with matching cloak and gloves. A neat hat covered her dark hair.

Konrad stared at her a little harder. She looked to be in her early twenties; her features were delicate, her skin almost as brown as his own. The only other times he'd seen her, she had been wearing white stage paint, but even so...

'Mistress Myrrolena?' he guessed.

A spark of amusement shone in her eyes. 'You were looking for

177

me, I think.'

He blinked. 'How did you know?'

'You sent me some communications to that effect.'

'You know me by sight, then.'

She inclined her head. 'Since you have also identified me by the same means, it can't be considered any very esoteric art.'

Konrad couldn't help grinning, albeit a little savagely. 'Fair point. Do I take it by this that you're willing to speak with me?'

'I may be. That depends on what you wish to ask me.'

'You can guess, I imagine.'

She smiled. 'Follow me, Mr Savast.' She turned and immediately began to walk away into the crowd, without checking to see that he was keeping up. The crowd melted away before her, somehow, but Konrad had to push his way through and he almost lost sight of her. At last they emerged into a quieter area of the circus grounds, and he followed the lady into a wide, low tent which proved to be something like an office inside. She took a seat, gesturing to a chair opposite her own.

Konrad sat down.

'So you've heard rumours,' Myrrolena said without preamble.

Konrad smiled. 'Something like that.'

'The rumours are untrue,' Myrrolena replied, with a smile matching his own. 'Of course. The supposed "body" was a misplaced prop; part of the show. Admittedly it should not have been lying in that precise spot.'

Konrad lifted his brows. 'Oh? And the reason for closing the circus?'

'We encountered a number of technical problems,' the Ringmistress said smoothly. 'Regrettable, but they are now resolved and we are fully operational.'

'Technical problems,' Konrad repeated. 'I see.' He sighed. The woman was obviously lying; he knew it, and she knew that he knew it. This was her way of telling him that she would permit no intrusions into circus business and had no intention of taking him into her confidence. There wasn't a great deal he could do about it.

But then why speak to him at all?

'I happened to have the opportunity to examine the so-called "body",' Konrad said casually. 'It looked remarkably real for a... prop.'

'Doesn't it? My craftsmen are excellent.'

'Oh, they are. What was it for?'

Another smile. 'It is the regular policy of my circus never to give away details of forthcoming shows. You understand, I am sure.'

'Perfectly,' said Konrad affably. He stood up and held out his hand to her. 'It is terribly good of you to clear all of that up. Thanks so much.'

Her eyes narrowed, but she stood up as well, took his hand and shook it. Her skin was surprisingly warm given the chill in the air.

'I'm glad we had the chance to talk, Mr Savast,' she said smoothly. 'It wouldn't do for misunderstandings to persist.'

Konrad smiled, bowed, and left. Myrrolena was of little use, then: except that her manner had told him one thing. He did not believe that the corpse had been a stage prop—not for an instant. He was too familiar with death to be mistaken in this instance. Her deliberate lies told him, plainly and clearly, that the Ringmistress was hiding something.

It might be something fairly innocent: after all, part of the success of the circus depended on its mystique. Then again, she may know exactly who the slain man was and why he had been killed. If he had anything to do with her circus, the story could reflect poorly on her business and that gave her clear motivation to try to cover it up.

It was a small, thin sort of clue, but Konrad would take it. He'd take anything he could get at this point. Damn Myrrolena and her talent for mystery!

*Serpents,* he called silently. *What progress?*

Ootapi shone in his mind's eye. If possible, the ghost-snake was grumpier than ever. *A whole lot of nothing, Malykant.*

*What do you mean, nothing?*

*I cannot find Myrrolena.*

*It's all right; she found me.* Somehow. Konrad frowned to himself. What were the chances that she would bump into him at the precise moment he was within the circus grounds, looking for her? There was something funny about that.

*And it is hard to sneakily spy on spirits that are not there,* Ootapi continued.

Not there? They must be there. He was standing in the middle of the circus, and it wouldn't be long before the ghosts were due to begin the night show. *I hate to say this, Ootapi, but... are you sure?*

*Of course I am sure,* snapped the serpent.

*Eetapi?*

*I have failed equally, Malykant,* she sang back.

*Failed?* sniffed Ootapi. *If there was nothing to find, then it is not possible to fail.*

*Hush,* Konrad said absently, his thoughts busy. If Myrrolena's ghosts weren't here, where were they? And why wouldn't they be on site, so close to show time?

And if Myrrolena had only planned to tell him lies, why had she sought him out at all? She could have continued with her plan of evasion; it was working perfectly well before. And he had definitely got the impression that she knew her lies would not work on him. What had been the real purpose behind the encounter?

He sighed as his head began to ache. So far, all he'd accomplished was digging up more questions. Some answers, he thought sourly, might be nice.

As soon as Konrad arrived home, his butler appeared and bowed.

'Inspector Nuritov visited this afternoon, sir, and left a series of papers for you. I've put them in your study.'

Konrad felt a little flicker of excitement at those words. Results already! Nuritov was a marvel. 'Thank you, Gorev. I'm famished. Could you bring me the usual?'

Gorev—king of butlers—bowed, and withdrew. Konrad gave his hat, coat and cane to his footman and went straight to his study. Nuritov's papers lay on his desk, a promising stack of them. He sat down and began reading.

His excitement soon faded. Working through the reports from most recent backwards, he found that the majority said the same things, year after year. They offered the usual general knowledge about the circus—its habit of turning up at the same time every year, the mystery as to where it went afterwards, that kind of thing—and gave a schedule of events and attractions. The ones from the last few years also carried Myrrolena's publicity images.

It wasn't until he'd gone back a ways that the nature of the reports changed. The first alteration was five years ago when Myrrolena's images vanished and a new picture appeared: a man this time, dark-haired and brown-skinned like Myrrolena. Konrad remembered his image: Myrrolen, founder of the circus and its namesake. Also, he supposed, the father of the present Ringmistress.

The next change occurred much further back. The reports suddenly became more effusive, more informational. There was even an interview with Mr Myrrolen himself in several papers, and a list of the circus's planned stops beyond Ekamet over the rest of the year.

Konrad checked the dates. The strangely communicative reports were dated twenty-five years ago; that number struck Konrad as significant somehow.

He turned over another paper. Nuritov had placed them in a particular order, he realised: for before him lay a police report that he'd already seen, of a strange incident at Myrrolen's Circus twenty-five years ago. A corpse had been found—or at least reported—and had subsequently disappeared, its existence roundly denied.

Twenty-five years. Konrad thought that over. Twenty-five years ago was the first of these strange occurrences; apparently that event marked the beginning of the mystique that surrounded Myrrolen's Circus. They had withdrawn into themselves, and stopped sharing any information at all save the strictly necessary. Something about the incident with the disappearing corpse had prompted this. Had it scared them in some way? Could Myrrolen, the dark-eyed, stern-looking man in the papers, have been afraid of something?

If so, his daughter had clearly inherited his fears, and continued to act upon them.

He read through the rest of the newspapers, finding his way through to the first appearance of Myrrolen's Circus. Those informed him that Myrrolen had been raised in a circus community and had been a performer himself for many years; his travelling show was a new interpretation on the traditional theme, which promised something special for the citizens of Ekamet.

Something special, Konrad thought wryly. Yes: Ekamet had witnessed the Ghost Circus for the very first time. He didn't need the news reports to tell him that it had been a sensation. The Circus continued to draw huge audiences precisely because it was unique.

And uniquely frustrating. But despite the lack of solid answers, he felt today that progress was being made, however slow; and his thoughts, impenetrably black for so long, were beginning to lighten accordingly. In fact, he felt better than he had in weeks. After all, there really was nothing like a fascinating, difficult—and, yes, frustrating—case to distract him from his private woes.

# 4

A note arrived from Nuritov the next morning. Gorev brought it in on a tray, interrupting Konrad's breakfast; Konrad read it and instantly sprang up. 'I shall be going out, Gorev, right away. Have the carriage brought round, would you?'

'It's already at the door, sir,' said Gorev, and a moment later the door opened to admit the first footman carrying Konrad's coat, hat and cane.

'Have you taken up mind-reading?' Konrad asked with a grin as he quickly donned his layers.

'Not exactly, sir,' said Gorev, smoothing his grey hair. 'Only the Inspector sent a boy especially, and the lad was in a tearing hurry. I imagined it might be urgent.'

Konrad chuckled. 'You're a marvel.'

'I know, sir.'

Konrad left his house at a brisk walk, and directed his coachman to hurry. There were definite perks to being the Malykant, he thought as he sat back in his plush seat, watching the streets of Ekamet sail by. He hadn't inherited wealth: on the contrary he had grown up poor. His luxurious lifestyle had been bestowed upon him as part of his job. It helped, no doubt about it: he could go anywhere, into the highest houses and the lowest as necessary. And in the meantime, the money and comfort were intended to go some way towards compensating him for the pressures of his job.

And for a long time, it had. But the perks had worn thin some time ago; were they worth the misery, anymore? Perhaps he had simply got used to them, started taking them for granted.

Or maybe he was simply getting old. Old at thirty-five. He laughed silently at that, more with misery than mirth. When had he lost the ability to enjoy life?

Ah well. The carriage drew up at the police headquarters: time to work. Konrad put these unhelpful reflections from his thoughts, and jumped out.

'Keep it handy,' he said to his coachman, who nodded and touched his hat.

Konrad swept inside and went straight through to Nuritov's office, sparing only a slight acknowledging wave for the officer on duty at the desk. They all knew him by now.

'Come in, come in,' said Nuritov as Konrad arrived. 'That was fast.'

'I have a good driver,' Konrad replied as he stepped inside. 'And a good butler.'

Nuritov was sitting behind his desk, leaning back comfortably in his chair. Opposite him sat an unfamiliar woman, huddling in a grubby-looking shawl. She appeared to be somewhere in her twenties, though it was hard to say where exactly; her face was youthful but drawn with an anxiety that made her look older. Her clothes were plain and simple, and none too clean either. She didn't come from wealth, then, not by a long shot.

'This is Galina Maslova,' Nuritov said. 'She came in a couple of hours ago. I thought you might like to hear her story.'

Konrad smiled and sat down, near to her but not too near. She looked jumpy.

Nuritov smiled reassuringly at the woman and said, 'Mr Savast is a consultant of ours. He's been looking into an unusual case recently and he may be able to help you.'

Galina Maslova nodded. 'It's Oleg,' she said. 'My husband. He's missing.'

'Is he!' Konrad said in delight.

Galina blinked at him, and Nuritov coughed.

'Er,' Konrad amended, 'I am sorry to hear that. Could you tell me about your husband?'

'He's gone,' Galina repeated.

'You mean that he left you?'

Galina shook her head vigorously. 'No! Well, I mean *yes,* but not willingly. He would not.'

'When did you last see him?'

'Three days ago,' she said, with the confidence of a woman who has been counting the hours. 'Oleg went off to that circus and he never come back.'

Ahh! Promising. 'Could you describe him for me, please?'

Galina sighed and rolled her eyes, as though she'd already gone through this several times. She probably had.

Tough.

'He's taller than me but not as tall as you,' Galina said wearily. 'Bigger'n you, too. Fair bit older than both of us, I reckon.'

Konrad sighed inwardly. 'Dark hair, pale skin, watery blue eyes, big nose? Bushy eyebrows?'

Galina stared at him. 'You've seen him! Where is he? Why hasn't he come home?'

'I'll get to that in a minute. Do you know why he went to the circus?'

She shrugged. 'He went every day. Said something about a job down there. Didn't say what though, before you ask.'

Konrad sat back, considering that. He wasn't surprised to find that this Oleg character had been connected with the circus— assuming that Oleg was his man. But it seemed probable that he was. How many other men of that description had lately visited the circus and vanished?

Finding out what kind of job the man had been doing might be tricky, but at least it was a lead.

'Is there anything else you can tell me about your husband?' Konrad tried.

The woman sighed. 'He's been wrong ever since he got involved with that circus place.'

Konrad leaned forward. 'Oh? And since when was that?'

She shrugged. 'Couple of years?'

'When the circus left, did he—did the two of you—ever go with it?'

She shook her head. 'Oleg's a clerk year-round. He just does circus work when it come in.'

A temporary contractor of some kind, called upon when the circus came into town? Interesting. Konrad wondered if Myrrolena had people like him in every city in which the circus appeared—and what they did for their money.

'When you say "wrong"...' Konrad prompted.

She shook her head. 'Don't know. Every time it come around, he gets odd. Hardly talks to me, and it's like he's worried half the time or more.'

Doing something less than legal, perhaps? Konrad smiled, thanked her, and stood up. He had no intention of breaking the news to her about her husband—that was what Nuritov got paid for. 'I'll see myself out, Inspector.'

Alone in her apothecary's shop late at night, Irinanda Falenia stood surrounded by the tools of her trade, hard at work. As the popularity of her shop had grown, so had her free time decreased. Part of her success was owing to the diligence of her research: she worked constantly to refine her elixirs, salves and potions to greater effectiveness, an ongoing project that took up a great deal of her time.

Success was nice, but if she spent more hours in her shop during the day, she was obliged to spend more hours in her workshop during the night. It all meant a lot less sleep for her.

'Bring me the inkwort, Weveroth,' she murmured, without looking up. There was a scrabble of small paws as her monkey leapt to the shelves where she kept her supplies. A moment later he leapt back and placed a small jar on the table before her. She scooped it up, dumped a quantity into her mixing bowl and slapped the top back on.

'Irid root,' she said next, and Weveroth leapt to assist while Nanda stirred and stirred the mix.

She was nearly finished with testing her newest formula when she became gradually, uncomfortably aware that she was not alone. She felt it in the prickling sensation near her neck, and the way her body stiffened unconsciously.

Looking up, she was just in time to see Weveroth's tail disappearing behind a box.

Nanda swallowed. She put down her tools, delicately dusted her hands off on her apron and then removed that article, smoothing down her dress. Lifting her chin, she said, 'Yes, Madam?'

She managed to inject a faint note of testiness into her tone. It helped, sometimes, to give the impression that she was productively employed, thereby heading off reproach.

It didn't work this time.

'Busy, are we?' said a voice that was deceptively soft, disturbingly disembodied, and unmistakeably disapproving. The words echoed out of the air, unattached to any corporeal form. Nanda could never tell where her Mistress was standing at any given time—if indeed she was in the room at all.

'Very busy, Madam, as always,' Nanda said firmly.

'So busy, in fact, that you have had no choice but to neglect a task I have specifically given to you. And for some time, it appears.'

Nanda's mouth felt dry. 'Yes, I... unfortunately that's true.'

There was a long pause. Irinanda's heart thumped harder with nerves, and she felt her calm beginning to fracture.

'I'm sorry,' she said suddenly. 'I couldn't do it anymore.'

The silence continued unbroken.

'Not after I'd seen him... at work.'

Nanda couldn't find the words to explain further. She waited nervously for a response, her mind replaying the incident that had weakened her confidence in Konrad.

She had seen him hunt down and dispatch a man who had killed, or ordered killed, a number of people in Ekamet several months ago. Konrad was good at it, of course: he had served as the Malykant for years—at least a decade, she would guess.

But it hadn't been the brisk, efficient way he had killed his target that had bothered her. It hadn't been the relentlessness of his pursuit. And it hadn't been his emotionless demeanour, because in spite of everything Konrad said about his Master's "interference" in his feelings, he *had* felt something that night. She was sure of it. Somewhere deep down, he had enjoyed what he'd done. It had shone in his dark eyes, just for an instant: a degree of deep satisfaction, even a note of joy.

The person he had killed had been a particularly revolting murderer, yes. Nanda had tried, and failed, to muster any compassion at all for him and his gristly fate. But still... did that fact alone justify Konrad's apparent pleasure in his task?

All of a sudden, Nanda had felt that she knew dangerously little about her friend. And for the first time, she had been afraid to delve any further into his character. She didn't want to know what she might find in the depths of Konrad's mind.

A cool wind brushed across her shoulders, making her shiver. 'Of course it is horrific,' said the voice. 'That is why I gave you this task.'

Nanda nodded, letting out a shaky breath.

'Someone must remain close to him. What he does is monstrous; he must be humanised, or he will become a monster. It is the eternal flaw in My Brother's approach.' The cool wind crept up over Nanda's face and ruffled her hair, like icy hands touching her cheeks. 'I have seen it happen, more than once. The role of Malykant isolates the holder; madness seizes the mind, and the Malykant becomes that which he most despises. Do you wish to see that happen again?'

Was it already too late for Konrad? Nanda hated herself for thinking it, but she couldn't help it. Somehow, she had forgotten Konrad as a person, as her friend; all she could see was the Konrad who had smiled, sharp and fierce and savage, as he had watched the life drain out of his target.

Nanda took a deep breath. 'Why did it have to be me?' she asked, hating herself for the plaintive note in her words.

'Because he trusts you.'

Nanda said nothing.

'There is no one else, Irinanda Falenia.'

Nanda opened her mouth to reply, but as suddenly as it had arrived the presence disappeared. She took in a huge gulp of air, putting her trembling hands to her face for a moment.

A scuffling sound at her feet alerted her to Weveroth's return. He rubbed his head against her leg and chittered.

Nanda sighed. 'I'm all right, Wevey.' She looked around, feeling a little disoriented. What time was it? After midnight. He would be asleep of course—she'd have to put off her visit until tomorrow.

No, that wouldn't do. Konrad didn't seem to sleep much. She had visited him before at later hours than this, and always found him still up. She couldn't use the late hour as an excuse to procrastinate.

Fetching her coat and hat, she donned both quickly and hoisted Weveroth onto her shoulder. At the door she paused, her eyes straying to the top of her powder cabinet. On it stood a glass bottle.

She crossed the floor in quick steps, fetched it down and took a long pull. The liquor stung as it went down, making her eyes water.

Coward's courage, perhaps, but if it helped...

Nanda replaced the bottle, opened her door and stepped forth into the chill, dark night.

Konrad sat in his favourite wing-back chair, his head resting wearily against the satin upholstery. It was late, and the fire had burned low, leaving his study in shadow; but the servants had already gone to bed and he couldn't summon the energy to leave the chair in order to tend to it himself. It didn't matter much; he couldn't sleep anyway, and there was little he could do on the circus case until the morning.

Supposedly he was using the night hours to think over the information he'd gained thus far and decide where to look next, but his sleepy brain had long since given up on any pretence of rational reflection. He was drifting somewhere between asleep and awake when a voice suddenly shattered the long silence, as incongruous as a dream.

'It's a little chilly in here, isn't it? But perhaps you like the cold.'

Konrad blinked and shook his head. Had he fallen asleep? But the voice sounded real—and the comment was far too prosaic for a dream. He sat up, suddenly alarmed, and looked around. The room was too dark for him to see anything beyond the immediate circle of the fireplace.

'Who's that?' he demanded. The voice was female, and for a heart-thumping second he thought it must be Irinanda. She had been known to sneak into his study before, by some means he still didn't understand. But the deep, smooth voice was unlike her light tones.

'Nobody particularly terrifying,' said the woman, clearly amused. 'This is a social call, if you like.'

'Conducted rather later at night than is usually considered appropriate,' Konrad observed. 'Also, one usually begins by introducing oneself.' He had eased himself out of his chair and stepped beyond the range of the firelight; if he wasn't to have the advantage of seeing his visitor, he didn't see why she should have the advantage of seeing him either.

There was silence for a moment, and then a figure appeared near the fireplace. He must have blinked and missed her movements, for her sudden visibility took him by surprise. The soft glow of his dying fire revealed a tall woman dressed in dark clothes, with dark hair and eyes and brown skin like his own. She wore a cool, superior smile which he found rather insulting.

'Mistress Myrrolena,' he said. 'To what do I owe the pleasure?'

Her smile broadened. Hidden in the shadows as he was, he nonetheless had the uncomfortable feeling that she was looking straight at him—and seeing him clearly. 'A social visit, as I said. You intrigue me, Mr Savast.'

'Oh?' Ordinarily he might have felt flattered at such a comment from an attractive woman, but something about her manner was making his skin crawl.

'You are very interested in my circus.'

'Not really.'

Her brows went up. 'But you have been asking so many questions.'

He wondered briefly if she was referring only to his previous meeting with her, or if she somehow knew about his other research as well. But how could she? 'My interest is in the... shall we say, suspicious circumstances surrounding certain events?'

'How vague.'

'You do not need me to be specific, Mistress Myrrolena,' he said, folding his arms. 'This is a waste of my time and yours; perhaps you could tell me why you are here.'

'My name is Estella.'

Konrad merely bowed—confirming in the process that she could see him, for her lips quirked in amusement—and waited.

'You are not with the police force, are you?' she said after a moment.

'I am not.'

'Are you an independent detective?'

'In a manner of speaking.'

'A hobby, is it?'

'Something like that.'

She nodded slowly. 'There are many things you are not telling me.'

Konrad grinned. 'You've been less than open with me, come to think of it.'

She acknowledged that with an inclination of her head and turned away. 'I will be a little more forthcoming, then, Mr Savast,' she said. 'I am looking for assistance.'

Konrad waited for more, but she ventured nothing else. 'What kind of assistance?' he prompted.

'Matters are not altogether well within my circus,' she said. 'An outsider's perspective may be useful.'

Konrad shrugged. He was getting colder standing so far away from the fire, and since hiding didn't appear to work with her he advanced back into the faint circle of warmth. He was careful to keep his distance from Myrrolena, however. 'That may well be true, but why ask me?'

She looked gravely at him. 'I don't know why you devote yourself to mysteries, but you appear to have a reputation for excellence at it.'

Oh. 'Thanks,' he said lamely.

'It wasn't a compliment.'

Fair enough. He cleared his throat. 'Why don't you tell me a bit more about this problem of yours?'

She hesitated, and he read suspicion in her eyes. 'I know that you have connections with the local police,' she said after a moment. 'There are... reasons why I would prefer for them to be kept at a distance.'

'You're asking for my discretion.'

She inclined her head.

'From the police.'

She nodded again.

He sighed. 'You must admit, Ma'am, that such a request sounds suspicious. Is there something illegal in the arrangements relating to your circus?'

'Not exactly.' Her black eyes gleamed in the light of the fire, and he couldn't read anything in them at all.

He paused to consider. Obviously she would give him nothing until he promised not to share it with Nuritov. He wasn't as bothered by this as he ought to have been. His profession left him little room to follow the precise letter of the law as it was.

Still, he felt mildly traitorous to Nuritov as he answered, 'Very well. Though I reserve the right to employ police resources as normal, should I need to.'

She hesitated, then nodded. 'May I?' she asked, gesturing to his chair.

He smirked. 'Having let yourself into my private study at this late hour, I am surprised you trouble to observe any of the niceties.' He waved her into the chair and sat down in the (regrettably less comfortable) one opposite.

She grinned back at him. 'One makes small efforts, from time to time.'

Propping himself more-or-less upright in his chair, Konrad said, 'What is it that you want?' He laced his fingers together, fixed his gaze on her face, and waited.

'The man you saw,' she said slowly, 'is named Oleg Maslov.'

Konrad nodded once. 'I know.'

She blinked. 'He was working for me on a temporary basis, a short-term contract renewed annually for the past few years.'

Konrad nodded again. 'What were his duties?'

Estella Myrrolena hesitated. 'He was an administrator, of sorts.'

'Doing what?'

'In each city we visit, we hire a local to handle recruitments for us. We are always inundated with applications after a few performances, but most of them are unsuitable. Maslov's job was two-fold: he gave us the extra help we needed to go through the applicants and determine who might suit, and he was also tasked with searching out other possible recruits as appropriate.'

'So he was a recruiter for you. Well paid?'

Myrrolena's eyes narrowed. 'Moderately, yes.'

'Was he any good at it?'

'As it happens, yes. He had the potential to be one of our best.'

'Did he give you any recruits yet this year?'

She shook her head.

'Hm.' Konrad pondered that, letting his gaze drift in the direction of his shadowed ceiling. In his experience, people who died suddenly in suspicious circumstances often—not always, but often—proved to have got themselves into deep water somehow, and usually through some illegal or dangerous activity. But Maslov's role with the circus did not seem questionable in any way. 'How did you find Maslov?' he asked.

Myrrolena's dark brows drew together. 'I can't remember,' she said after a moment's thought. 'I will try to find out for you.'

Was she being evasive? He couldn't tell: she was hard to read, with her perfect composure and self-possession.

'Why are you here, telling me this?' he asked. 'What would you like me to do for you?'

Myrrolena drew in a long breath and let it out in a sigh. 'I lied to you before, about the body,' she said.

'I knew you were lying.'

'I knew that you did. That's why I am here. It may have nothing to do with my circus, but the positioning of his corpse suggests otherwise. Someone placed it there deliberately. Were they sending us some kind of message, or were they trying to discredit us? Or is it something else entirely? And who wishes us harm? This is what I wish to know. But I have neither the skills nor the time to investigate the matter as you do.'

He grinned. 'What if I don't have time either?'

'You've been working hard on the investigation for someone with no time.'

'How do you know that?'

'I hear things.'

Konrad suppressed the urge to roll his eyes. A parade of mystery always wore him out, and he was tired enough as it was. 'Since we appear to have the same goal, I see no reason to refuse to work with you.'

'That's kind of you,' she said, and he couldn't tell whether she was being sarcastic. 'I will compensate you for your help, naturally.'

'I don't need money.'

'Everyone needs money.'

He shrugged.

'Very well; what do you need?'

'Information. I need you to tell me everything you know about Maslov. Also, if I ask you anything about your circus I need you to be open and honest with me.'

Was that a split-second hesitation before she nodded? Probably not, or why had she come to him in the first place? Tiredness was making him paranoid.

'And,' he added, 'I will need a reliable way to contact you.'

The hesitation was undeniable this time, but she smiled with apparent graciousness. 'Of course.' Standing up, she approached the fire, and the circle of firelight shone dimly on her face. She held out a small piece of paper, and bent down to offer it to him. 'The girl at this address will be able to find me. Leave a message with her and it will soon reach me.'

Konrad frowned, disliking her sudden nearness and the peculiarity of the arrangement. 'Can you not simply tell *me* how to find you?'

'It isn't that simple.' She smiled.

Konrad sighed and took the paper. His fingers brushed against hers as he did so; her skin felt burning hot. How did she manage to stay warm when he was icy with cold in this dark and echoing room? That thought made him feel irritable, and he stood up, ready to dismiss her.

He turned dizzy with the sudden motion, swaying on his feet as his vision blurred. Groping blindly behind him for the chair, he grabbed it and clung for a few moments until his sight cleared. 'Well...' he said when the feeling had passed, 'professional zeal would lead me to question you now, but I appear to be tired. Tomorrow, early?'

'I'll be at the circus at the ninth hour,' she said. 'Where we met before.'

Konrad nodded and turned away, but she blocked his path.

'There is some urgency, Mr Savast,' she said in a low voice. 'The circus leaves Ekamet soon.'

He nodded impatiently, wishing she wouldn't stand so close. 'In that case you'd better let me sleep, hadn't you?'

'Oh, I'm sorry,' came a new voice. 'I didn't realise you had company, Konrad.'

The words were apologetic but the tone was anything but. 'Nanda?' he said, spinning around so fast that he almost fell over. 'What are you doing here?'

'Hello to you too,' she said dryly. She must be standing well back from the range of the fire, for Konrad couldn't see her. Her voice came from the direction of the doorway, however.

He didn't bother asking how she'd got in.

'Charming of you to visit,' he said lightly. 'Not the best time, though.' He couldn't decide whether he was more elated that she'd come, unnerved about why she was there, dismayed about the presence of Myrrolena or just plain too exhausted to deal with any of it. Some of all of that, he decided.

'So I see. I'll come back... sometime.'

'No, wait,' Konrad said, leaping forward to try to intercept her.

At the same time, Myrrolena said, 'No need to leave on my account. I am going.'

Konrad turned back, but by the time he had completed that motion, Myrrolena had already gone. 'Er, Estella?' he said uncertainly.

No one answered.

'Estella, is it?' Nanda said, coming into the room. 'I'm so glad

194

you've been making new friends.'

He sighed. 'Something like that. Remind me to find out how that disappearing thing works.'

Nanda sprawled in the chair Myrrolena had just left, and narrowed her eyes at him. 'In my case I expect that to remain a mystery, thank you. In hers, though...'

'What?' he prompted.

'You two looked cosy there.'

He shrugged and slumped back into his own chair, passing a hand over his weary eyes. 'We weren't.'

Nanda looked tired herself, he thought; her pale skin was marred with dark circles under her blue eyes, and her white-blonde hair was mussed as if she hadn't been near a mirror in a while. 'Who was that?' she said seriously.

'A client. Sort of.'

Her eyes darkened with concern—and annoyance. 'I leave you alone for five minutes...'

Konrad's brows shot up at that. 'Five minutes? More like six months!'

She made a dismissive gesture. 'Five minutes, six months, same thing.' She glowered at him. 'Why are you working with her? It isn't a good idea.'

'I'm working with her because I am investigating her case. And I need her information. Why isn't it a good idea?'

She rolled her eyes. 'You didn't notice that she is *lamaeni*?'

He stared. 'What...?'

'*Lamaeni*. Spirit-sucking undead fiends who feed off the energies of the living?'

'I know what they are,' he said testily.

Actually, come to think of it... 'They don't drink blood?'

She sighed. 'No, Konrad, they don't drink blood.'

'How do you know she is *lamaeni*?'

'It is perfectly obvious. At least to me.' She eyed him. 'Careful she doesn't feed off you. You should never let them get too close. Feeling a bit tired, are you?'

'You are remarkably casual about my brush with death.'

'She didn't look like she wanted to kill you.'

'You reckon? The conventional wisdom on creatures like *lamaeni* is that they're deadly killers.'

195

'Conventional wisdom also says that they drink blood. It's a convenient rumour; the *lamaeni* probably started it themselves. People think that if the creature isn't hanging off their neck, they're okay.'

'Seriously, Nanda. Aren't you worried at finding me with a spirit-sucking night fiend in my study? Even just a tiny bit?'

'Not really. They don't need to kill in order to survive; they usually just draw a little life-energy from many targets, which does no worse to the individual than tiring them out. They *can* kill and sometimes they do, but that makes them no different from the rest of us, right?'

Konrad felt that as a jab at him. He looked away.

'I didn't mean anything particular by that,' Nanda said quickly.

Konrad shrugged. Not knowing what else to say, he said nothing. Nanda didn't say anything either. The silence stretched.

'So...' he said finally, still not looking at her. 'Why are you here?

'Just saying hello.'

'After six months of nothing?' He shot her a quick, narrow look.

She beamed winningly back at him. 'Yes.'

Konrad hesitated, watching her. She put on a good act; on the surface she appeared to be her old self, comfortable with him once again. For a few seconds he allowed himself to hope that all was well; but it couldn't last. He knew her too well. Underneath the cheerful demeanour, she was still wary.

And the carefully-honed suspicious part of his brain wouldn't let him relax and be happy either. Why would Nanda suddenly turn up now, after so long without a word? He knew her to be whimsical, but this was taking it too far. There had to be a reason she was here, and it wasn't a random social visit.

His head swam. He was so tired, he felt ready to pass out. Nanda's face blurred in his vision. 'I have to sleep,' he said, standing up carefully. 'It was nice of you to come by.'

There was a surprised silence as he made his way to the door, but then Nanda spoke. 'Konrad, don't meet her alone again, please. Take me along.'

'I thought you said she wasn't going to kill me.'

'Even so, the *lamaeni* are dangerous.'

He paused at the door. 'And what are you planning to do about it?'

'I'm not sure,' she admitted. 'But I seem to be more knowledgeable than you on this topic. It might help.'

He felt that he ought to be making all manner of interesting connections regarding Myrrolena's true nature, her circus, and the Maslov case, but it wasn't happening. Maybe Nanda's presence tomorrow would help; two minds being better than one and all that. 'Nine in the morning,' he said. 'I'll come for you before that.'

'You never told me who she is.'

'Estella Myrrolena.'

'Of the circus? That Myrrolena?'

'Yes, that one.'

Nanda whistled. 'That's interesting.'

'Maybe, but just at present I don't care. Can I sleep now?'

'Oh... sorry. Night, Konrad,' she said softly.

'Night.'

5

By the time Konrad and Irinanda arrived at the circus the following morning, Konrad had brought his wayward friend fully up-to-date about the case and the progress of his investigation. He had been grateful to have a clear topic of conversation at hand; it prevented any more of those awkward silences.

Somewhat uncharacteristically, Nanda reserved comment, confining herself to asking questions. She didn't push him about Myrrolena, and as a result he told her more than he might otherwise have done.

Having slept, he was feeling better. Not razor-sharp and keen-witted, precisely, but better. It now occurred to him that, as *lamaeni*, Myrrolena had placed herself perfectly. As the Ringmistress of a circus, she had not only her sizeable circus-troop to draw from (the living members, at least) but also the audiences in any city she visited. That allowed her to spread her predations across large numbers of people. Did she do that because she wished to avoid inflicting too much harm upon any one individual? Or was it more a matter of protecting herself from undue attention? He didn't know her well enough to be able to tell.

Estella Myrrolena was waiting for them when they reached her tent. There was no one else present, which surprised Konrad not at all.

'So, Maslov,' said Konrad, after only the briefest of greetings. 'What else do you know about him?'

Myrrolena looked pointedly at Irinanda.

'My associate.'

'Irinanda Falenia,' Nanda said, extending a hand. 'How nice to meet you.'

Myrrolena merely smiled, ignoring the hand. 'I know little about his personal life,' she said smoothly, turning back to Konrad. She had yet to put on her stark white stage make-up, and he approved of that: her pretty brown skin was much more attractive.

Even if she was *lamaeni*.

'He spent little time at the circus, of course, since his role was to seek elsewhere for our new members. Really, I hardly saw him.'

'What did he do when he found someone he thought was suitable?'

'He brought them to one of my regular people for assessment.'

'I'll need to speak to that person,' Konrad said.

Myrrolena's eyes flicked to Nanda, and back. 'Of course,' she said. 'I will have him come in a little later.'

Konrad shoved his hands into his pockets—he still felt cold—and surveyed her. He was keeping his distance from her today, and so was Nanda. 'How many people has he recruited for your circus to date?'

'Four,' she replied, after a moment's thought. 'As far as I know. That is a question for my associate, perhaps.'

'I'd like to speak with all of those people as well.'

She shook her head. 'Two of them are no longer with my circus, and one has... passed on—'

'You mean died,' Konrad interrupted.

'Yes.'

'And the other?'

'I will find him for you.'

Maslov had only been with the circus for a few years. Myrrolena had said that he was good at his job, and he certainly found people; but three out of four had already left again, or died? That struck Konrad as odd.

He did not bother to point that out, though: Myrrolena's behaviour was, once again, evasive. He wondered what she was hiding. 'Do you have any theories about who killed him, or why?' he asked instead.

'The placement of the corpse is the crucial part here,' she replied. 'It was done to damage us. Perhaps to destroy us.'

'In that case, why not choose some regular member of the cast for a victim? Why pick Maslov, whose connection to the circus was tenuous?'

Myrrolena shrugged. 'My people are well protected. Perhaps Maslov was the only connected individual they could reach.'

Konrad's brows rose. 'Well protected? From what?'

'Any threat that emerges,' was her smooth reply.

'Do you have enemies?' he said. 'Fierce competition perhaps?'

'We command enormous audiences,' she said with a brief smile. 'Myrrolen's Circus is the most famous, the most desirable across the realm of Assevan. Lately we have begun visiting Marja, too. When we are in town, no other circus can seriously compete, and they know it. There is much resentment.'

'Enough to motivate someone to destroy you?'

'Possibly.'

'Do you know of anyone in particular who might?'

Myrrolena shrugged one elegant shoulder. She was wearing an elaborate gown this morning, and the movement made the dark gems of her costume sparkle. 'The circus may be colourful and lively, but it is a surprisingly harsh world behind the scenes. I have often had... tense encounters with some of my fellows, and rough words exchanged. Any one of them could have done this.' She paused. 'But I do not think that is the explanation for this attack.'

'Why not?'

'There are circumstances to suggest...' she stopped, for once seeming at a loss. When she spoke again, she lowered her voice almost to a whisper. 'Mr Savast, I hired you because I fear treachery.'

He blinked, surprised. 'You think one of your own people did this?'

'Shh,' she said, gesturing for quiet. 'Yes. I don't know who to trust: that is why I chose an outsider.' The words were spoken as calmly as ever, but Konrad detected a glint of real concern in her dark eyes. Even a touch of fear. She truly believed what she'd said— and, spirit-sucking fiend or not, she was truly worried about it.

That complicated things. Konrad wasn't sure he wanted to get tangled up in that kind of mess, especially when the organisation in question was as peculiar as Myrrolena's.

On the other hand... he had been hoping for an unusual case. Something complex, to test his abilities and take his mind off things.

For once, his wish had been granted.

'Is there anything else you can tell me about Maslov, or the case?' he asked.

She shook her head. 'Nothing comes to mind. If that's everything, I will see if I can find those people you wanted.' She stood up and strode out of the tent without waiting for a reply.

Konrad looked at Nanda. 'Odd,' he murmured.

Nanda nodded. 'She's hiding a great deal, I would say. And she's wary of both of us.'

'Might just be because she's... unusual.' They hadn't told Myrrolena that they knew of her true nature, on Nanda's suggestion. It gave them an advantage, she had said, and to accuse the woman would only put her on her guard. But the Ringmistress was plainly wondering about Nanda, and ill at ease anyway.

'Maybe,' Nanda said, but she didn't sound convinced.

When Myrrolena returned, she was greeted by identical smiles from Konrad and Irinanda. She gave them a similarly insincere one in response and said: 'Unfortunately my associates are not available at the moment.'

*What a surprise,* Konrad thought. 'I think we are finished here, then,' he said, rising from his seat. 'Perhaps you'll send them over, once they turn up.'

Myrrolena nodded and smiled a little more. 'Of course. Thank you for your diligence, Mr Savast.'

Konrad suppressed a sigh as he made for the door. Nanda followed him out; but after a second or two Konrad realised she wasn't with him. He backtracked to the door to find she had cornered Myrrolena in the tent.

'It's such a pleasure to meet you,' she was saying with a winning smile. Konrad blinked. Nanda hadn't shown any sign of being a fan of the Ringmistress's before... his eyes narrowed as he realised what she was up to.

For reasons he did not understand, Nanda could sometimes catch a glimpse of a person's thoughts if she touched them. It wasn't very accurate, she had once told him: at best, she received mere flashes of disconnected images, and had to decipher them herself. But it sometimes resulted in a useful insight.

She was going for a read on Myrrolena. The Ringmistress was acting graciously, but her wariness of Nanda hadn't dissipated and she was keeping her distance. The two talked for a few minutes, Nanda obviously trying to put the other woman at her ease. It didn't work. When Nanda moved to close the conversation, holding out her hand in a friendly gesture, Myrrolena merely inclined her head and—once again—ignored it.

Nanda's eyes narrowed. Konrad saw them flash with irritation, and then, abandoning all pretence of innocence, Nanda's hand shot out and grabbed Myrrolena's. She held on for just a second, but her eyes widened.

She dropped Myrrolena's hand and backed away. 'Pleasure,' she repeated, and then she turned and trotted after Konrad.

'Interesting?' he murmured as they made their way—quite rapidly—out of the circus grounds.

'Somewhat,' she replied. 'Later.'

He nodded and didn't press. Nanda would tell him when she felt it was appropriate—and safe. They pushed their way through a market already crowded with chattering shoppers haggling and trying on wares, and neither spoke until they reached the gate.

'Konrad,' said Nanda then, her tone wary. 'I think—'

She didn't finish the sentence, because at that moment someone grabbed Konrad's arm. He gasped in surprise, partly at the sudden contact and partly because the hand burned with heat—like Myrrolena's. Looking round, Konrad found himself face-to-face with a very tall young man with a shock of unruly black hair and angry brown eyes.

'I heard you,' the man hissed. 'Talking with her.'

'*Lamaeni,*' Nanda whispered in his ear, and Konrad nodded. He was learning the signs himself by now: that searing heat was a giveaway.

'With Mistress Myrrolena?' Konrad said in an even tone. 'You were listening?'

The other man nodded impatiently. 'Of course I was listening. I'm one of *his*. Maslov's pets.'

Konrad's brows rose. 'His pets? What do you mean by that?'

'He came to me—told me—' The young man broke off as he was jostled by a passerby, and he shook his head in frustration. 'Not here. Somewhere else. Please.'

Konrad shook his head slowly, his eyes narrowing. 'Why didn't you show yourself in there? If you knew she was looking for you.

That we wanted to talk to you.'

The man bared his teeth. 'I didn't want her to find me. She would only caution me *not* to see you, not to tell you anything.'

Konrad sighed as a familiar ache began over his right eye. Intrigue. He could do with a bit less of it. 'Do you know who I am?' he asked.

The man shook his head.

'Bakar House,' Konrad said in a low voice. 'Ask anyone how to find it—someone will know. Come tonight.'

The man nodded and melted into the crowd, so quickly that it unnerved Konrad. Intrigue plus disappearing tricks and the mysterious unliving... he turned back to Nanda and lifted his brows.

Nanda lifted her own back at him, and neither of them spoke. Then her lips quirked in a quick smile, and she patted his cheek. 'Poor Konrad,' she said. 'Life is so difficult for you sometimes.'

He snorted at that and brushed her hand aside—not forgetting that she could read him as easily as she read others. He didn't really want her poking around in his thoughts just now. A thoughtful look in her eyes suggested he was too late to prevent that, however.

He turned away. 'Off we go,' he called. 'We have work to do.'

'Konrad,' Nanda called urgently, trotting after him. 'That one is *lamaeni* too,' she hissed in his ear when he stopped.

'I heard you the first time,' he said, nodding.

'So...'

'So... what?'

'So I'm beginning to wonder how many of Myrrolena's people are *lamaeni*, aren't you?'

'Mhm. That's a question for whatever-his-name-was. What did you read from Myrrolena?'

'Nothing.'

He blinked. 'Nothing at all?'

'Not a thing. Her thoughts were completely blank, as though there's nothing there. I've never come across that before.'

Konrad beamed.

'What?' Nanda said, peering at him suspiciously. 'That isn't supposed to make you smile.'

'Sorry,' he said, sobering. 'Gets more interesting, though, doesn't it?'

'I did pick up one thing from her.'

'Oh?'

Nanda nodded slowly. 'Fear, or something like it. Might have been insecurity.'

'I noticed that too, though she covers it well.'

'It's a good act, I agree, but nonetheless: she's worried about something. It hasn't been long since she took over from Myrrolen Senior, has it?'

'No; good point. Only a few years. Do you suppose she's as young as she looks?'

Nanda shrugged. 'Can be hard to tell with the unliving, but she could be.'

Konrad eyed her suspiciously. 'How do you know so much about the unliving?'

She beamed at him.

'Right,' he muttered. 'I ought to know better than to ask.' He paused, thinking. 'You know... if Myrrolen Senior was *lamaeni* too—and chances are, he was—I wonder what happened to him?'

'Mhm,' Nanda said thoughtfully. 'Good question. Why is Myrrolena the Younger in charge of the circus in the first place?'

Konrad spent much of the day investigating Myrrolena's competitors, with periodic help (and many a sarcastic comment) from Irinanda. He did so more as a matter of form than with any expectation of finding anything useful. There was Myrrolena's manner to consider: she was hard to read, but he remained convinced that she was telling the truth about her fears. It would be helpful if she would just tell him *why* she suspected one of her own people, of course, but the Myrrolen family apparently had an entrenched habit of secrecy and paranoia that its latest scion couldn't break.

Also, his own instincts suggested that Myrrolena's competitors weren't to blame. Would anyone in their right mind mess with that circus? Whether you believed the tales of ghosts and ghouls or not, there was obviously something highly unusual about it. Besides, Myrrolena's people only appeared once per year, for a single week. The other circuses, menageries and travelling shows dominated for the other fifty-one weeks of the year. Why would it be worth their while to try to destroy Myrrolena?

Still, professionalism demanded that he make at least some attempt to investigate. He had a list of four organisations that seemed to be most directly competing with Myrrolena's type of entertainment; it took Konrad most of the afternoon to establish that the name of Myrrolena was enough to provoke distaste and unease, yes, but no stronger emotions. When Myrrolen's daughter had taken over the circus, there had been some concerns that she would change things: perhaps she would run more shows in Ekamet, and steal their business. But she hadn't, and after a few years those fears had apparently faded. Konrad encountered shrugged shoulders, raised eyebrows, rolled eyes and sarcasm, but nothing much worse than that.

'I thought it seemed odd,' Nanda said afterwards, her smooth brow furrowing. They were in Konrad's carriage on their way home. He was always amused to note that her professed distaste for luxury stopped short of rejecting his pleasant, warm conveyance back to the city centre. 'No one's really doing what Myrrolena's people do— that's why it's so successful. Besides, they visit only a few cities, for a maximum of a week once per year. The scarcity of it is partly what makes it so popular. Konrad, she doesn't *have* competition.'

'Agreed,' he smiled. 'But it had to be investigated. Myrrolena may be sure of the probable source, but until I have the same information she does, I have to investigate everything. Speaking of which, I managed to persuade Eetapi and Ootapi to keep an eye on her for me while we were gone.'

'They agreed?' Nanda looked sceptical.

'I bribed them.'

'Oh?'

Konrad eyed her and hesitated. 'I'd better not tell you what I bribed them with.'

Nanda swallowed. 'Oh. I see. One of *those* things.'

'Yes, one of those.'

'One of those macabre, morbid, alarming, probably psychotic things.'

He blinked, and stared.

'I'm just joking,' she said quickly.

'Psychotic?'

'Joking!' She patted his hand. 'You aren't psychotic. Not completely, anyway.'

'Thanks.'

She smiled.

Konrad's driver brought the carriage around the back of Bakar

House, as he usually did when Konrad didn't want anyone commenting on his (frequently odd) comings and goings. As it drew to a stop, Konrad unlatched the door and let it swing open. He jumped down... but his feet never hit the floor. Something grabbed him, held tight, and squeezed.

It wasn't like hands clutching at any individual part of his body. It was like being seized everywhere at once, by some paralysing force that rendered him incapable of resistance. Whatever it was also scorched his skin with an unnatural heat, and he would've hissed with pain if his mouth would work.

He fell headlong, dragged by unseen hands. He stopped short of crashing into the ground as something grabbed him and whipped him up into the air. His straining eyes caught a glimpse of Nanda leaning out of the carriage and staring up at him with wide eyes; then he was spinning, so fast that his vision blurred.

'Allow me, Savast,' whispered a voice in his ear. Then Konrad felt hands grab his coat, though he couldn't see them, and he was hauled away.

If anyone had asked him under normal circumstances, Konrad would have said he would love to fly. The idea appealed to him enormously: soaring through the open skies, the wind on his face, a glorious view spread before him...

This was nothing like that. He hurtled through the air at terrifying speed and with no means of controlling his progress or his descent. Freezing winds howled past his face, chilling his ears and hands until they hurt. He hardly had time to take note of the lights of the buildings below him as they sailed past. A mere few minutes brought him to the depths of the Bone Forest, the dark, craggy woodlands that surrounded the city of Ekamet. It was a place that most people avoided; but he knew these woods like the back of his hand and loved them well.

He didn't really want to visit from his current vantage point, however. His mouth remained paralysed, but he was screaming in his mind as he hurtled out of the skies, narrowly missing several pale, outstretched branches on his way down.

To his surprise and relief, the landing was gentle. He was placed on his feet in a deep pile of fallen leaves, and within a few moments he realised that the paralysis had faded. He couldn't move far anyway: he was too shaken, too frozen, too wobbly from the crazy flight.

'So,' he panted, his teeth chattering, 'are you my appointment?' He looked around but saw nobody: nothing but pale, twisted trees rapidly losing their leaves, half-frozen mud and traces of frost and ice coming in with the night.

Then a pale shape faded into view before his eyes and built into the incorporeal form of a man. The ghost hovered a little above him, so Konrad had to look up to see his face.

'I didn't like your house much,' said the ghost, and his voice sounded vaguely familiar.

Konrad blinked. The features were blurred and poorly defined, as was often the case with spirits; but he was fairly sure he was looking at the same young man he and Nanda had spoken to earlier. 'You *are* my appointment!' Silently he sent a summons to his serpents, praying that they would answer this time. They had been none too willing to do so these past few days. *Serpents? I need you. Please.*

No response came from Ootapi, which did not surprise him. But as the ghost before him smiled chillingly and began to speak, Eetapi's shivering tones chimed in his mind. *Master?*

Relieved, he replied: *I need your help here. Try not to be seen or noticed, but keep an eye on this nice chap I'm talking to.*

Feeling Eetapi move to obey, he focused once more on the young man before him. '*She* has been in your house,' the man was saying in tones of deep reproach—and fear? 'I prefer this.'

Konrad nodded, his thoughts whirling. Why did this young man speak of Myrrolena that way? Why was he avoiding her? And how in the world had this ghost hauled him halfway across the city and out into the Bones like that? He'd never heard of it before. Spirits typically had limited interaction with the living world.

'It's awfully cold out here,' Konrad said mildly. 'Can we go somewhere warmer?'

The ghost jerked his head at a nearby tree. Focusing on it, Konrad saw a door there. He'd missed it in the darkness before. He pushed it and found a staircase leading down under the ground.

It wasn't the first time that he had discovered underground dwellings out in the Bones. *How many of these are there?* he thought as he gamely started down. *And can I have one?*

'So,' he said slowly as he made his way down the stairs, the ghost's cold presence close behind him. 'How did you die?' He spoke casually, but the matter worried him. Had Myrrolena learned of their brief conversation with Maslov's recruit, and tried to remove him? If so, why—and why hadn't he known about it earlier? Had the serpents sensed the death and failed to tell him?

Then again, how did death work among the lamaeni? Some said they weren't really alive in the first place.

*No, Malykant,* said Eetapi in his thoughts. *We sensed nothing.*

Konrad frowned. Did the *lamaeni* have some way of masking their activities from spirits like his? That was an appalling thought.

'I died when I met that man Maslov,' the ghost said, his voice thick with anger.

'You looked pretty alive when I saw you earlier,' Konrad replied.

The stairs ended, and Konrad stepped out into a small, low-ceilinged room. It was rough, with walls of packed dirt, straw on the floor and nothing but logs for furniture; but at least it was out of the wind. He sat down on one of the logs.

'Would you feel more comfortable if I wore the body?' the man said.

'The... body?'

'My living form, as it was once. It's not here at the moment, but I could fetch it.' He smiled, a feral expression that sat oddly on his ghostly face. 'It takes a lot of energy to maintain the link, though, so I'll skip it if you don't mind.'

'Interesting trick,' Konrad said, watching the man warily. Did he mean that he could switch between mostly alive and generally dead, at his own will? What kind of a being *was* this?

The other man nodded. 'I thought you'd say that.' The ghost sat down on a log opposite Konrad and stared at him. 'What do you know of *lamaeni*?' he asked.

'Not enough, apparently,' Konrad replied, eyeing his companion with a mixture of intrigue, suspicion and a tiny echo of fear. 'Can we do the civilised stuff first, and the creepy stuff after?' he asked. 'What's your name?'

The young man's eyes narrowed. 'The creepy stuff?' he repeated. 'Tis a joke, I suppose. Not advisable.'

Konrad sighed and leaned back. 'You dead sorts always take yourselves so seriously,' he muttered.

Ghostly eyes flashed and the man spat, 'My name is Alad Boran, and if you knew my history you would not be so flippant.'

'Given the manner of my arrival here, perhaps there's some truth to that,' Konrad agreed. 'Which I resent, by the way. As an attempt to unnerve me, well... it worked. But it doesn't help your cause to play games like that with me. What is it that you want?'

'I want you to listen!' Alad flared.

'I was listening anyway.'

Alad scowled. 'Why was *she* in your house?'

Konrad leaned forward again, rested his elbows on his knees, and stared hard at Alad. 'Because she, like you, wants something from me. You ask me what I know about *lamaeni?* So far I know that you like to manipulate, lie as a matter of course and couldn't give me a straight answer if your unlives depended on it.'

Alad scowled, a motion that made his incorporeal form flicker oddly. It occurred to Konrad for the first time to wonder where the light in this odd little room was coming from; he couldn't see any source. 'Well I wasn't always *lamaeni,* was I.'

Konrad gave a bark of laughter. 'For all I know you people lay eggs.'

Alad shook his head. 'No one is born *lamaeni.* You have to be made so, by another. It doesn't necessarily require your consent.' He said the words so bitterly that it wasn't hard for Konrad to guess what was making him so angry.

He thought for a moment, rapidly putting pieces together, then said: 'Maslov wasn't *lamaeni.* He died like a normal human, and I'm guessing a blow to the head wouldn't do a lot to people like you.'

Alad nodded confirmation of that.

Konrad continued. 'Did Myrrolena change you?'

Alad looked down, shaking his head.

'She didn't and Maslov couldn't have. So who was it?'

'Just because they did not perform the actual procedure, does not absolve them of responsibility,' Alad snarled.

'Maslov recruited you.'

Alad snorted. 'Recruited? You could put it that way. You know why he was so good at his job? He spent a lot of time with the street folk of Ekamet. He used to be on the streets himself, he *said,* and he offered help. He seemed sincere. Some of us took it.' He sighed again, and his spirit-form wavered and winked out for a moment. 'People like Maslov look for people who are *physically* capable of circus feats: that's the official line. And we do have some performers who are still human, still alive. The particularly talented ones. Most of us, though, are *lamaeni,* and that was Maslov's game.'

'He presented Myrrolena with new *lamaeni* performers every year, harvested from the streets,' Konrad said. 'But none of you began that way—he had you turned. Is that right?'

Alad nodded. '*Lamaeni* are more useful to Myrrolena, because we cover the day and the night performances. We're more flexible, there is more we can do. And she sees the circus as some kind of refuge for people like us.'

'Did she know what Maslov was doing?'

'How could she not know?'

Konrad wondered about that, but he didn't say anything. He watched Alad closely for a moment or two, thinking. 'Did you kill Maslov?' he said abruptly.

'No. I wanted to, but no.'

Konrad grinned. 'You remember that thing I said earlier, about *lamaeni* and lies?'

Alad sneered at him. 'I am not lying.'

'Then someone else killed him,' Konrad said. 'And someone other than Maslov turned you *lamaeni.* Who was it?'

'That's irrelevant now.'

'Why?'

'Because he's gone. I'm not asking you to punish the one who turned me. I'm asking you to punish the one on whose account it was done.'

'That being Myrrolena.'

'You shouldn't trust her! She is dangerous.'

Konrad smiled. 'I think you're all dangerous. Though of the two of you, I like her better so far. The worst she has done is hidden things from me; she hasn't attempted to drop me on my head from a great height.'

Alad's gleaming white eyes flicked in his direction briefly, and Konrad detected a hint of guilt. 'I was angry and worried.'

'Apology accepted.' Konrad stretched out his legs, still cramped with cold, and chafed his chilled arms. 'So you want me to punish Myrrolena for you, somehow. Can't you do it yourself?'

Alad's eyes flashed fire. 'She is stronger than I am.'

'What makes you think I can do any better?' Konrad wondered for a chilling moment whether Alad had guessed his identity. It wasn't impossible, though he hid it well. But the ghost was shaking his head.

'Not alone,' he said. 'You know the best way to kill *lamaeni*? Destroy the body while the spirit is absent.'

'So I'm your accomplice. You'll lure her away in her spirit-form while I burn the physical remains? Is that the plan?'

'You have the opportunity to get close to her.'

'So does everyone employed by the circus. Why not ask one of them?'

'It's better if it's done by an outsider.'

That set off a few of Konrad's alarms. Alad was looking for a scapegoat, was he? 'Revenge missions don't usually pay off,' he said. 'I'd let it go if I were you.'

'She's a killer. She deserves it.'

'Yes? Who has she killed?'

'Me, indirectly,' Alad snarled. 'And maybe *she* was the one who killed Maslov. Did you consider that?'

Of course he had; the Ringmistress's evasive, manipulative behaviour marked her out as an obvious suspect. But he didn't want to pander to Alad's paranoia, so he said: 'If so, it is up to the law to punish her.' No reason to give himself away just yet.

Alad laughed. 'You know as well as I do that the law can do nothing to the *lamaeni*. We must take matters into our own hands.'

Konrad stood up, wincing as his chilled muscles protested. 'I think you need to look elsewhere for your accomplice. Can I leave without further molestation?'

Moving too fast for Konrad to see, Alad darted between Konrad and the door. 'I can't let you leave until you agree to help me.'

Konrad smiled bleakly. 'You're going to kill me? Please do. You'd be doing me the most enormous favour.'

Alad's eyes narrowed. 'More jokes.'

'No, really. I'd have topped myself months ago if I could've summoned the energy to give it the proper thought. It's hard to work out the best way to do it. Should I stab myself, slice open a vein, swallow something unhealthy? Tedious stuff. If you could make it fairly painless I'd appreciate it.'

The ghost blinked. 'Um. Well, how about your nice Marjan friend? Does she want to die too?'

Konrad suffered a brief twinge of alarm at that idea: but then he thought of all the peculiar and remarkable things Nanda had done

211

since he had known her. 'She can take care of herself,' he informed Alad. 'Look, you aren't fooling me. You can't kill anyone, can you? You're nothing but bluster. That's the real reason you want an accomplice: you might hate Myrrolena, but you couldn't kill her even if she let you. And it speaks well of you. I'd run with it if I were you, and stop with the stupid threats.'

He waited, but Alad only stared at him with wide eyes and said nothing.

'Well then,' Konrad said with a tight smile. 'I'd better be off. Cases to solve, people to chase, that kind of thing. Thanks for the information.'

Alad made no reply, but after a moment he drifted aside, leaving Konrad free access to the exit. 'I'll be watching,' he said as Konrad began to climb the stairs.

'You enjoy that,' Konrad called back. He was partway up the stairs before a new thought occurred to him, and he turned. 'Alad,' he called down. 'You know why Myrrolena visited me? She's looking for the person who dumped Maslov's corpse in the middle of her circus. She asked for my help. I'd give that a bit of thought, if I were you.'

He sought for Eetapi again as he climbed back to the surface. She was there, a silent presence coiled around his own thoughts. *What did you make of that?* he asked her.

*I do not think he intends to harm you. The pattern of his thinking showed no such intent.*

*Do you have any information I couldn't have worked out for myself?*

*I could discern nothing more specific. These lamaeni guard their thoughts well.*

Typical.


Konrad was obliged to hire a cab to get home. He viewed the contraption's approach with distaste: a rickety little thing on two wheels, drawn by a single pony. The driver didn't look too keen.

But it was that or walk, and the night was rapidly turning cold. Konrad flagged the cab down, handed over some coins and sat down, hoping nothing particularly unpleasant marred the seats.

The drive home was slower than he was accustomed to. In the midst of his impatience, the absurdity of his attitude struck him rather forcibly. Once upon a time, he would have considered himself lucky indeed if he could afford the fare for a private cab to take him across half of Ekamet. Now, he felt demeaned by it.

How things had changed.

Back at home, he found Nanda sitting in his favourite chair. She had a splendid blaze going in his fireplace and she sat slumped down with her feet almost resting in the coals. A tray with still-steaming tea and some sort of cake sat at her elbow, and her face was hidden behind a large book.

Konrad cleared his throat.

'Hello,' Nanda said, peeking at him over the top of her tome. 'Welcome back!'

'I can't say this is what I expected,' Konrad said, frowning.

She sat up and put the book aside. 'What did you expect?'

'I'm not sure what reaction I expected to my abrupt kidnapping by supernatural forces, but not... this.' He took a piece of Nanda's cake and sat down opposite.

She grinned. 'I knew you could handle it.'

'Your confidence is inspiring. So, do you want to hear what happened?'

'Every last bit.' She leaned forward, adopting an expression of avid attention.

Konrad relayed everything that Alad had told him, sparing no details. When he'd finished Nanda sat back, her pale face thoughtful. 'That explains a lot,' she said.

He nodded. 'I would be willing to bet it was Mr Boran who put Maslov's corpse in the middle of the stage. He definitely has a grudge against the circus, and Myrrolena especially.'

'That makes sense, doesn't it?' Nanda said.

'Indeed. He may have killed Maslov as well, but I'm not sure.' He paused. 'What I do want to know, as soon as possible, is who Maslov's lamaeni accomplice was within the circus—and why did they consider it worthwhile to turn all of Maslov's recruits? Alad said the circus takes human performers, sometimes.'

'The other interesting thing,' Nanda said, 'was that business about his living form, such as it was. Look, I found something in here.' She handed over the book she had been reading. Checking the cover, Konrad read the title: *Lamaeni: Lore and Mythology*.

'Where did you find this?' he murmured, spreading it open at the page Nanda had marked.

'In your library.'

He looked up at her in surprise. 'My library? Really?'

213

'Apparently the Malykant house comes well equipped. Haven't you looked?'

'Yes, of course I have.'

'Much?'

He looked away, uncomfortable. 'Um, some.'

'Read,' she said, gesturing at the book.

Konrad read. The chapter detailed a range of stories that had been told about the *lamaeni* over the centuries, in different parts of the world. It did not treat any of them as credible, but Konrad noticed at least one that rang true.

The story was about a *lamaeni* who had been killed when his living form had been burned while his spirit was absent. It backed up Alad's weird plan to erase Myrrolena.

'Good, right?' Nanda said when he had finished. 'Now this bit.' She gave him another page to read, this one documenting lists of "facts" about the *lamaeni*. Several of them sounded absurd to Konrad, but one interested him: the notion that the process of turning severed the link between body and soul, leaving the two forever sundered. In order to join them once more—and maintain the semblance of life in the corporeal form—the *lamaeni* was obliged to expend large amounts of life energy. They no longer generated any themselves, and so they drew on the life energies of living people around them.

This dovetailed perfectly with everything Alad had told him. Perhaps he hadn't been lying, then—or at least, not much. 'Those other three unsolved "murder" cases relating to the circus,' he said to Nanda. 'Back over three decades. I bet that's what they were. The supposed victims weren't dead: they had just turned spirit and left their bodies behind. A body emptied of its spirit would probably look quite dead.'

Nanda smiled faintly. 'Makes you wonder how safe it is to attend the daytime performances at Myrrolena's, doesn't it? A cast full of *lamaeni* all drawing madly on the audience to keep their bodies going...'

Konrad blinked. 'Come to think of it, I always did feel a little tired after those shows. All the excitement and colour, so I thought.'

'Well, you're still here, and I think the city would have noticed if audience members kept dropping dead.'

'We need to look around that circus some more,' Konrad said, frowning. 'What did Alad mean when he said Maslov's accomplice was gone? Why's he so convinced that Myrrolena is behind all his troubles? And what in the world is going on with Myrrolena herself? She begs for help but she won't tell me anything: it makes no sense.'

Nanda jumped up. 'Then let's go right away! It's nearly eleven: there should be a show at midnight.'

'And show time is the best time for sneaking around unobserved,' Konrad said, hauling himself to his feet. 'Good thinking, Miss Falenia.'

Nanda made him an ironic bow, and held the door for him. 'No, no: after you,' she murmured.

# 6

It was counter to the usual around Ekamet, but Myrrolen's Circus hit its busiest hours between eleven at night and one or two in the morning. Konrad shepherded Nanda through the bustling crowds—ignoring her eye-rolling exasperation at his solicitude—knowing full well that the main tent would be crammed when they finally reached it.

That wouldn't matter. He was not without resources, after all.

'When did the circus come in?' Nanda hissed in his ear at one point, clutching at his coat sleeve to slow him down.

Konrad thought. 'A few days ago?'

Nanda nodded. 'Tonight could be the last night, even. We'd better hurry.'

'No wonder it's busy,' was all Konrad said. He wasn't worried: his instincts told him that he and Nanda were on the right track, and his guts didn't usually talk complete rubbish.

Not *all* the time, anyway.

Ootapi continued to ignore Konrad's summons, but he had Eetapi streaming silently through the skies above him. She was on general scouting duty, keeping her ghost-eyes alert for anyone else who might like to accost, abduct, terrorise, question or generally irritate Konrad. The experience with Alad hadn't been so awfully entertaining that he'd like to do it again anytime soon.

Konrad remained patient as they pushed and shoved their way towards the main tent, though it took some effort. He was shielding Nanda with his own body, so he took plenty of elbows in the ribs, shoves (accidental or otherwise) in tender places and far too many people's feet connecting painfully with his own. Normally he would shrug off something so incidental, but of late his frame of mind wasn't up to it. By the time they reached the central stage, he felt sure his face was fixed in a barely suppressed snarl.

He paused in one of the aisles between the rows of seats and opened his spirit-vision. He had never done it here before; it was against the spirit of the event, somehow, like peeking behind the curtain at a play. But then, never before had he *needed* to know what was going on behind the scenes.

Colours drained away in his field of vision, replaced with a kind of clear darkness through which the glowing shapes of ghost-forms shone brightly. Several soon flickered into view, most of them drifting above the crowd. They had a business-like air: probably they were checking that all was ready for the next show. Others clustered in the large, cleared space in the centre of the tent that served as the stage.

Konrad checked his watch: ten minutes to go. Was the whole cast here already? He counted only eleven visible *lamaeni*; surely more were required for a show of this magnitude.

Seeing the *lamaeni* this way proved to be something of a revelation for him. They were not the same as the spirits of those departed in the more regular way; they were similar, but an air of curious vibrancy hung about them, as if they were more alive, more vivid than the truly dead. Which made sense, he thought. Their auras were not quite clear, either: they shone faintly in his mind's eye, limned in colours. The hues were feeble and poorly defined, but they were there: red, green, blue, purple, many shades. He had seen such shades once or twice in the past, without knowing what they were.

He watched them carefully now as they flowed back and forth. Eventually he saw what he was looking for: more *lamaeni* shades began to stream into the tent, most of them coming from the same direction. Focusing his attention that way, Konrad discerned a slit in the tent's canvas that indicated a door.

Very well, then.

Moving quickly, he led Nanda that way. The seats nearest to the makeshift door were occupied, of course, like all the rest. A lady and a gentleman sat there side-by-side, obviously a couple. The latter was a banker or something, judging from his clothes, and his wife was

217

smartly, if unimaginatively, dressed. They both looked up in surprise as Konrad stopped directly in front of them.

He smiled.

Konrad could be charming, he knew that. He didn't have to try a lot of the time: the mere appearance of well-groomed, well-dressed wealth and more than passable good looks was usually enough to win him favour. Terrifying people was not his usual order of business: but as the Malykant, he was good at that too.

His was a peculiar soul these days. Protected by The Malykt, augmented in some respects and bound in others, his spirit had long since ceased to be ordinarily human. Normally he kept his guard up, suppressing the obvious signs of his unusual nature. When he let them fall, people tended to notice.

The banker and his wife noticed. They stared at Konrad, eyes widening, and he knew that they were feeling a sense of growing menace emanating from him. They would struggle to explain why, later, they had abandoned very good seats in the central tent before one of the last—and best—performances of the year, purely because a well-dressed gentleman had smiled down at them. But they did. The couple muttered excuses which Konrad did not trouble to listen to, and scurried away.

Konrad gave Nanda a real smile and handed her into her seat.

She eyed him.

'I wasn't really going to hurt them,' he whispered to her.

Her eyebrows lifted, ever so slightly.

'Honest!' he protested, feeling injured. 'Just play-acting. You know.'

'At best, that is cheating,' she whispered back. 'At worst it is depraved.'

Konrad thought about that for a moment. 'Can we go with cheating? I can live with that.'

She snorted. 'Were you trying to scare me too?'

'No, of course not.'

'Oh! Well, you did a good job of it anyway.'

Konrad sighed. 'All right, you've made your point.'

'Which point was that?'

'You dislike being near me.'

If he was hoping for a denial, he would have to live without one. Nanda might have said something, but at that moment all the lights in the tent went out and music flared from somewhere. Coloured lights bloomed on stage.

Konrad expected to see the ghostly manifestations of the *lamaeni*, like the one Alad had let him see; instead he saw a stage full of man-sized puppets. They were at once eerily lifelike and deliberately strange; staring at them, Konrad felt a vague sense of wrongness about their features and forms, like people twisted just a little bit out of shape.

The *lamaeni* used their possessed puppets to act out a popular tale, a gruesome story about children and witches in the wintery Bone Forest. There was no dialogue, only music and colour and the miming acting of the puppets. Konrad wondered, a little uneasily, what was coming up: the circus had a reputation for deliberately scaring the audience. It was part of the reason for its popularity.

Shame he wouldn't get to see the whole thing.

He and Nanda watched for perhaps twenty minutes, as the atmosphere grew steadily darker and the tale more horrifying. He had to fight to avoid becoming so absorbed in the story that he forgot what he was really doing here. Eventually, he nudged Nanda.

'Time,' he murmured in her ear.

She shot him an annoyed look: the action on stage was reaching its high point.

He shrugged and stood up. It wasn't his fault there was an unsolved murder still floating about. Nor was it his fault that the best time to explore the circus was during a show, when everyone was busy on the stage.

All the lights were focused on the puppets and the surrounding seats were plunged in darkness. This masked his and Nanda's actions as they made their way towards the slit in the canvas wall that Konrad had noticed earlier; but it also made it harder for them to see. They moved slowly and carefully, gaining the door at last just as everything went quiet on the stage. Konrad resisted the temptation to look back and see what was happening; instead he lifted the tent flap and stepped silently through. Nanda followed.

The room beyond was dark. He guessed it to be an enclosed space, because there was no wind and the air felt dead. Keeping Nanda behind him, he stepped forward carefully, arms outstretched. Silence; nothing reacted to their entrance. The room seemed to be empty.

*Eetapi?* he called silently. *Do that glow thing, please.*

He waited, but nothing happened. *Eetapi?* he repeated.

*Master,* the serpent replied, *the witch is terrific, isn't she? She has just come back on stage and she is about to—*

*Eetapi!* he snapped. *I know the show is magnificent, but I need some help here.*

A faint whisper resounded in his thoughts—a ghostly serpent sigh—and a few moments later he sensed her drift into the tent behind him. She manifested as a flickering, translucent snake, allowing a soft glow to illuminate the area.

*Thanks,* he muttered.

Eetapi's tail thrashed.

Looking around, he saw a sort of tunnel of canvas stretching out in front of him. As the three of them proceeded along it, he noticed more of the subtle, makeshift doorways leading off the tunnel walls. Pausing, he looked around for some sign that might suggest a good direction to go in.

Nothing.

'What do you reckon?' he murmured to Nanda.

She pointed unhesitatingly to a doorway on the right.

Konrad looked at her. 'Is that a random guess, or one of your witchy powers things?'

She grinned gleefully. 'Witchy?'

'Yes. You know. Mysterious, uncanny, a little disturbing—and without explanation. Witchy stuff.'

'I have a *feeling,*' she told him, her smile turning mischievous. 'Is that witchy?'

He shrugged. 'I suppose we'll see. Eetapi, if you please.' He pulled back the canvas and watched as the snake floated past him, her light dimming.

A few moments later, she called back, *Come forth, Master.*

Konrad and Nanda followed the serpent through a small tent full of props and materials. The next one looked like a living area, with collapsible chairs set in a circle and a low table strewn with cups. Eyeing them, he wondered uneasily what the *lamaeni* might have been drinking—until he remembered that the circus had living performers too, at least by report.

Eetapi floated on once more and he strode after her into yet another tent, this one tiny and, apparently, empty. The serpent streamed over to the far wall and stopped.

'A tent wall?' Konrad said, beaming. 'Why, Eetapi, I could never have found this alone.'

Her tail lashed and she hissed, a frigid, splintered-ice sound that lanced painfully through his brain. *Behind the tent wall, Wise One.*

Wincing, Konrad lifted a flap of canvas to reveal a door, a proper solid wooden one with a sturdy lock on it. He wondered briefly how the circus folk had built such a thing, before realising that it probably belonged to a building that had stood in the area before; they had simply constructed their tents around it.

The question was: were they using the building for something or was it nothing more than an obstruction?

'A locked door,' he crowed, with a real smile this time. 'I *love* locked doors.' He stepped forward to examine the lock mechanism.

'I don't see the appeal,' Nanda said, coming to stand next to him.

'People only lock doors when there is something interesting behind that they want to keep,' he explained. 'Which makes it a promising find. Assuming, of course, that it isn't just farm machinery or something.'

From somewhere over his head, Eetapi sniffed.

'Difficult to get through, though,' Nanda murmured.

Konrad flashed her a dazzling grin. He pressed his fingers against the lock, and smiled when it smoothly sprang open.

'Hear that?' he whispered. 'No creaking or squealing, which means it's been used recently.'

Nanda nudged him with an elbow. Actually, it was more like a shove. 'All right, I admit it. Your Homicidal Detective tricks do come in handy.'

'Homicidal Detective?' he repeated, frowning. 'Harsh.'

'But true.'

He ignored that, gesturing for silence as he slowly opened the door. As before, Eetapi ghosted on ahead of them.

*Ooo,* she called back.

This was promising. 'Eet has found something,' he whispered to Nanda. She started forward, but he gently pushed her out of the way and stepped through first, ignoring the little inarticulate sound of irritation she made. He wasn't trying to belittle her, but if there was anything dangerous on the other side of this door then he wanted it to see him first.

Eetapi hovered near to the low ceiling, emitting a bright glow. From this he judged that she deemed it safe. Abandoning some of his caution, he looked around.

The building consisted of only one room, with no other doors besides the one he had come through. There had been windows at one time, but they were now boarded up with planks of wood. The room was small; some kind of outhouse, he guessed, perhaps belonging to a farm at one time. But there was no farming gear left here anymore.

It was crowded full of tables, atop which lay a field of corpses set shoulder-to-shoulder.

'Um,' he said, momentarily dumbfounded. He heard a gasp from Nanda as she came in behind him.

Walking slowly between the tables, Konrad peered into each face in turn. He saw men and women of all ages, races and features; all newly dead.

'So this is where they keep the human-suits,' Nanda said from behind him.

He stared at her blankly. 'Human-suits?'

'Yes, you know. They put them back on when they're pretending not to be *lamaeni.*'

She was right, of course. Konrad's over-enthusiastic instincts had seen only dead bodies; and so they were, but only for now. Just until their owners returned from the stage.

'Human-suits,' he repeated again, his lips twitching. 'Nicely put.'

She chuckled. 'Once in a while, though, someone forgets to put their coat away, and then we get a mystery.'

He nodded, thinking of those old police reports about corpses with no visible wounds; corpses that disappeared. What if someone ever discovered this place? It hadn't been hard to find. Mind you, the lock on the door had been extremely solid.

Still, didn't they have someone guarding the place?

Feeling uneasy, he looked around. *Eetapi?* he questioned. *You're sure we are alone here?*

*As far as is possible for me, Master,* she said a little stiffly. *I am not omnipotent, as you know.*

Damn. Hastily, he let his spirit vision take over his sight and swept around the room, checking every corner for unwelcome presences.

Nothing.

He let the vision fade once more, frowning. There was no evidence of a problem here, but it made no sense and that bothered him.

'All right,' he said aloud. 'Come out.' He stood in the middle of the room, surrounded by eerie, unbreathing bodies, and waited. Nanda drew back, her expression wary.

Konrad heard a low chuckle, and then a pale form drifted out of the wall ahead of him. 'You're better than I thought,' it said.

Recognising Alad, Konrad scowled. 'Impressively stealthy of you, but why are you hiding? I thought you wanted my help.'

Alad shrugged. 'I do, which is why I didn't stop you.'

'I'm not here to kill Myrrolena for you.'

Alad folded his arms and stared down at Konrad. 'Oh? Then what are you doing here?'

'I'm looking for the person who killed Maslov. You sure it wasn't you?'

'I think I would remember.'

'And you don't know who did?'

That elicited nothing more than a scowl from Alad. Konrad shrugged and turned back to Nanda. 'He doesn't know.'

'Not much use then, is he?' she replied lightly.

'Oops,' said the spirit, and faded back into the wall.

'Oops does not sound good,' Konrad murmured.

'Only one door,' Nanda said tersely,' and they're coming through it.'

Konrad looked, and saw *lamaeni* spirits drifting into the room. The show was over, then. It was too late to hide: he and Nanda stood their ground as the *lamaeni* swarmed into the room and surrounded them. They hovered several inches above the ground, penning Konrad and Nanda in like a ring of pale, angry trees.'How did these get in?' he heard someone say, and other similar questions rustled through the assembled spirits like a cold wind.

The atmosphere was hostile, and no wonder. Here he and Nanda stood, in a room that had been guarded by one of their own and secured with a particularly solid lock. Konrad could have set fire to the building if he'd wanted to, destroying all their physical bodies in the process. He doubted that all the *lamaeni*'s corporeal forms were here: a quick count numbered only fourteen. But that would take a

223

sizeable chunk out of Myrrolena's people, if he wanted to do it.

He heard an ominous, booming clang as the door slammed shut, locking the two of them inside with a small horde of angry *lamaeni.*

Konrad was surprised that they hadn't already attacked. This omission was explained when one of them—a female, he guessed, though her features were particularly indistinct—planted herself in front of him and demanded , 'Who have you told?'

Konrad blinked. 'What?'

'You obviously know who—and *what* —we are. I need to know who else you've told.' She smiled, her aura flickering violently. 'Before I kill you.'

'No one, and we aren't here to harm you.'

She loomed a little more, radiating violence. 'The papers, is it? Which one? Or all of them?'

Konrad looked thoughtfully at her, and then at her comrades spread out behind her. They radiated violence, yes, but also fear. He held up his hands to show that they were empty. 'Myrrolena hired me,' he said, speaking distinctly. 'To investigate the Maslov case.'

'Even if that's true, you shouldn't be in *here.'*

'I needed more information,' Konrad replied. 'And you lot are extremely cagey.'

'Stop *chatting,'* someone said from behind Konrad's interrogator. 'Just kill them both.'

'Or turn them,' someone else added, and that idea seemed to garner approval for there was a buzz of agreement.

Konrad felt the situation slipping out of his control. He didn't mind the idea of death all that much; but he minded it for Nanda. And neither of them wanted to be *turned.* That wouldn't suit his ideas of a peaceful oblivion at all.

The conversation obviously over, Konrad abandoned caution and dropped his wards. His Malykant's aura blazed, and he let the full weight and power of it fall upon the *lamaeni.*

He didn't know if it would be enough. When he invoked all powers and privileges, he was tough; but there were a lot of them.

They fell back with cries of surprise—and some fear. He heard the words 'the Master' repeated a few times over, and that made him wonder. What did they know of The Malykt? These beings existed outside of the Death Lord's natural order; the two ought to have nothing to do with one another. But he detected not only fear but *respect* rolling off them now.

'The Ringmistress hired the *Malykant*?' his interrogator said in pure disbelief.

'Did I really?' came a low female voice from the doorway.

Turning his head only slightly, Konrad saw Myrrolena herself standing there. How she had opened that heavy door without making a sound, he didn't know. One more weird *lamaeni* thing, he supposed.

'Hi, Estella,' he said, giving her a friendly wave.

She stared at him, and her expression was not pleased. 'I should have known,' she said. 'I shouldn't have missed that.'

He shrugged. 'Sorry. I am good at hiding it.'

She smiled faintly. 'I suppose you have to be. Just as we do.' Her gaze flicked to her people, most of them still spirit-formed and gathered around Konrad and Irinanda. 'I did hire him, nonetheless, so I'd appreciate it if you would refrain from killing, terrorising or otherwise inconveniencing him.'

The *lamaeni* fell back instantly. Konrad watched in some amazement: their level of obedience to their Ringmistress's orders was remarkable. It gave him some insight into Alad's choice of accomplice: these people were either too awed or too scared by Myrrolena to ever dream of trying to harm her. Maybe they even liked her a little.

Or maybe they just had an ingrained habit of obedience to the Ringmaster. Konrad gave a mental shrug.

Myrrolena closed the door behind herself and locked it. She was richly dressed in a dark purple silk evening gown and a dramatic, matching mask. It was odd to think that the body that wore such a beautiful garment wasn't alive, strictly speaking: to Konrad's eyes she was a vision of health.

She had been feeding, of course.

'That doesn't mean, however, that you are welcome in *here*,' she said to Konrad. 'Nor can I see why you would need to sneak around my circus in this fashion. If you needed to know something, you could have asked me.'

Konrad grinned. 'And you would have been completely honest with me—just as you were when you hired me. You told me nothing about the true nature of your circus.'

'Secrecy is necessary.'

'Yes, but in this instance it is a crucial piece of information. You want to know who messed around with Maslov's corpse? Imagine this.' He leaned back against the nearest table, ignoring the motionless body lying on it, and shoved his hands into his pockets. '*Someone* killed Maslov. For the moment, we won't worry about who. It was one of the victim's "recruits" who found him — the only one still remaining with your circus, supposing you were telling the truth about that. Seeing his opportunity to punish you for his plight, he deposited it in the most public place he could think of.'

'Alad Boran,' Myrrolena said, her eyes narrowing.

'Why didn't he just go to the papers or something, one might ask? Well, because the story sounds crazy when you just blurt it out. But by opening up the circus to a murder investigation, he might judge that sooner or later, the police would stumble over something solid. Like this room. Unfortunately for him, you lot are much more adept at covering these things up than he thought. He is, after all, pretty new at this *lamaeni* business.'

'Why would he wish to bring down my circus?' Myrrolena said. He was interested to note that she looked genuinely troubled by the idea.

'Pure resentment. Maslov had him turned *lamaeni* without his knowledge or consent, and he hasn't exactly taken to the lifestyle. He's a walking ball of bitterness. You should have tried harder with him.'

Myrrolena's face turned icy-cold, and he could almost hear her thinking.

'No, killing him won't help either. What I'm more interested in is: who was helping Maslov, and why? And what happened to that person?' He had a pretty good idea what had happened to that person, but he wanted to hear it from Myrrolena.

She stared at him, and he smiled innocently back. After a moment she said: 'His name was Jarvi. He was my father's second-in-command.' There was a note of suppressed pain in her voice that told Konrad everything he still needed to know.

'Jarvi sounds Marjan,' he observed, with a glance at Nanda. She stood, silent and still. She hadn't participated at all thus far, but he detected that she was ready to back him up if he needed it.

'He was Marjan.'

'He betrayed your father, didn't he? He destroyed him, but he did it secretly—assuming, probably, that as second-in-command he would naturally be given control of the circus. But instead it fell to you, Myrrolen's daughter. You're so young. Jarvi made himself useful to you, did he? But behind your back he was trying to turn your people against you, preparing to wrest control away from you. Unfortunately for him, you command a lot more loyalty than he expected.'

Myrrolena said nothing. She merely watched him with her dark eyes glittering with rage.

He took that as assent.

'So he started using people like Maslov, hoping to bring in enough new *lamaeni* to challenge you and yours, in time. He didn't count on anyone's *hating* the state as much as Alad appears to, but it still more or less worked: he produced at least one new *lamaeni* who hates and wishes to kill you. Perhaps others have gone so far as to try: what *did* happen to Maslov's other recruits, anyway?' Konrad shrugged. 'This went on for a few years, until you found out what Jarvi was doing and you destroyed him. I won't ask how. After that... you killed Maslov.'

Myrrolena's lips peeled back in a snarl, and she actually growled.

He held up a hand. 'Don't get carried away. I agree, Maslov was a bastard and he had it coming. I might ask why you bashed him over the head instead of sucking the life out of him or something, but the look on your face is answer enough. You lost your temper. I completely understand why smashing him to bits with a heavy object would be more satisfying.'

That disarmed her, a little. She blinked at him. 'Picture this,' she said slowly. 'Every time my circus comes to town, people disappear. Not many people, and nobody anyone would much miss: but sooner or later, someone would notice the pattern. The police, perhaps, or an enthusiastic *hobbyist* like yourself. I cannot have suspicion falling on my circus.' She lifted her chin. 'You can imagine what they would do to us, if they were to learn the truth.'

She didn't specify who she meant by *they*, but Konrad supposed she meant everyone. If the suspicions of Ekamet were raised against her circus, the whole city could turn on them in an instant. And it wouldn't take much: a rumour or two, and someone with the ear of a newspaper man. She was right there: she couldn't afford the risk.

'That's the rational argument,' Konrad agreed. 'And it makes sense, though killing him was a little over the top. You must have had him under close control, if he was entrusted with at least some of your secrets. You could have found a more creative solution. Admit it: you lost your temper.'

'Is that it?' burst out Alad. Konrad looked up, startled. He hadn't noticed the young *lamaeni*'s return. 'That's all you cared about—your circus? What about *me?* You think I wanted to be like this?'

'Do you think any of us did?' she shot back. 'Some, perhaps. Most of us, though: we learn to live with it. You will too. And it will be by far the better for you if Myrrolen's Circus remains: a sanctuary and a home for people like you and I, who are welcomed and wanted nowhere else.'

Alad snarled, and for a moment Konrad expected him to attack Myrrolena. But the Ringmistress's aura of impregnability held: she lifted her chin and stared him down, and he backed off.

'Life—even such a half-life as ours—is full of difficulties,' she told him severely. 'You can spend the rest of your unlife burning with resentment if you wish, but I recommend taking a more... mature approach. Think it over.'

There was an offer implied somewhere in there, Konrad thought, along with a clear threat. Alad could grow up and toe the line, in which case Myrrolena would take pains to make his life—or unlife— somewhat easier; or he could go the same way as Jarvi.

Brutal, but effective. And puzzling. She was a mess of conflicting attitudes, this strange woman: on the one hand, he believed her when she spoke of her circus as a sanctuary for *lamaeni*. She actually cared. But she could threaten them with instant obliteration if they threatened the circus itself, and he believed her on that score, too.

Probably even Myrrolena herself didn't really know who she was or what she was doing. She was young, and shouldering an enormous responsibility that shouldn't have been hers for years to come. It scared her.

Course, now he had a problem. Normally he would dispatch Maslov's killer in a manner both symbolic and practical, employing a bone that had once belonged to the victim. It balanced out the debt one soul owed the other, in some way that made sense in the Deathlands but none at all here. He couldn't do that: he hadn't had a chance to collect a bone from the victim, and besides, this killer wasn't alive anyway.

Twas a problem, indeed. The more so because he didn't actually want to kill her. Maslov had been a nasty piece of work, but while

Myrrolena might be dangerous, somewhere under there was a scared young woman trying to protect her people. What was he supposed to do with that?

Unless that was an act, too, which even Nanda had fallen for. How could he possibly tell? Nothing in his experience so far had prepared him to deal with the likes of Myrrolena.

The Ringmistress's eyes turned back to Konrad, and narrowed. 'Now we come to the difficulty,' she said with a slow smile. 'We are at an impasse, I think. For you cannot carry out your regular duty in my case, is that not so, Malykant?'

He knew of a way to kill her, of course: Alad had spelled it out pretty clearly. But merely killing her wasn't the point: it had to be done in the right way, or its true purpose would fail. An eye for an eye was far too simple for The Malykt: He liked a more complex form of justice. So even if Konrad got over his qualms, he had no way of carrying out the fitting form of punishment upon her. 'Regrettably true,' he admitted, spreading his hands.

'So in this instance, you can overlook my... lapse of judgement, and be on your way.' She directed a cool look at Alad. 'And leave me to my housekeeping.'

Alad shrank back, and Konrad shook his head. 'I still have a job to do. It might be a bit less straightforward than usual, but something has to be done.'

'The two of you know far more than is reasonable about me and mine,' Myrrolena replied. 'If you're going to "do your job", Malykant, I suggest you do it immediately—for reasons of self-preservation, if nothing else.'

Konrad sucked in a breath. Okay: do something to neutralise Myrrolena, or get turned into *lamaeni*, along with Nanda. Was it possible for the Malykant to be turned? He didn't know, and didn't want to find out.

But what could he do? He had no obvious way to attack Myrrolena, and even if he did, he and Nanda were badly outnumbered.

And he didn't doubt she was completely serious in her intent to neutralise *them*, if given the chance. She would brook no threats to her circus, full stop.

'Um,' he said wittily, his brain spinning uselessly.

She nodded. 'It is regrettable, of course, but you may still perform your duties as the Malykant as a member of the *lamaeni*, no? Perhaps you will even be better at it.' She paused, looking at him speculatively. 'Then again, now that I get a proper look at you... the condition might not be unfamiliar.'

His eyes widened. 'What?'

'I think you're no more alive than I am, Malykant. We both exist beyond the pale.'

Konrad blinked. 'What?' he said again.

'You died a long time ago, didn't you? The Master's essence rolls off you in waves. Without it, you would be dead and gone.'

Even The Malykt's suppressing influence couldn't deaden the buzz of fear Konrad felt at that idea. He swallowed, heart pounding, as his mind ran back over the times—several of them—that he'd died in the line of duty and been brought back by his Master.

He had always assumed that he had been restored to life, the same type and degree of life he'd had before. What if that wasn't true? What if Myrrolena was right, and he was more of a walking puppet, a Konrad-suit powered by the Lord of Death?

His thoughts were spinning into turmoil. Desperately suppressing those horrible ideas, he backed away, trying to put himself between Nanda and the *lamaeni*. Negotiate: he could still do that. 'I hold a secret of yours, yes, but you hold an important secret of mine: so perhaps we're even. If I expose you, you can expose me.'

Myrrolena's gaze travelled to Nanda's face. 'Maybe so, but this one remains a problem.' She advanced, and the gathered *lamaeni* drifted silently out of her way. 'You tried to read me, did you not?' she said. 'What did you see?'

Nanda met the Ringmistress's cold gaze fearlessly. 'Nothing, as you well know.'

Myrrolena's eyes widened slightly. 'I didn't, in fact,' she admitted. 'Interesting.'

'I wouldn't term it interesting, myself,' Nanda mused. 'Being blank, I mean.'

The Ringmistress was far too close to Nanda for Konrad's liking. He stepped closer, trying to look menacing in a protective kind of way.

Myrrolena shot him a withering look. 'This is a negotiation, not an attack. A secret for a secret,' she said next to Irinanda. 'You've many about you, I can sense that. Give me something as surety and both of you can go.'

Konrad found this exchange interesting, despite his uneasiness. Given Myrrolena's apparent willingness to obliterate both Maslov and Jarvi when they irritated her, he'd expected more ready violence from her. Apparently she'd been telling the truth about Maslov's activities: she did not want to leave a trail of corpses behind her circus.

That didn't mean she wouldn't if she felt she had no other choice, of course.

'I've nothing to share,' Nanda said firmly, not at all to Konrad's surprise.

'Sure?' Myrrolena replied, her eyebrows lifting. 'I will have to take other measures if I can't feel certain of you.'

Nanda glanced at him, and he read a touch of fear on her. But her lips tightened, and she met Myrrolena's gaze squarely.

He took Nanda's hand and squeezed it.

'Shame,' Myrrolena said, with a trace of real regret. 'I dislike leaving a mess behind me.'

As if some silent signal had been heard, the *lamaeni* as one began to advance on Konrad and Irinanda. Grabbing her hand, he stepped rapidly backwards, almost falling over a table in the process. He was no more concerned for his own safety now than he had been earlier: but he had brought Nanda into this mess, and he doubted that his Master, The Malykt, Stone-cold Bastard of Death would consent to restore Nanda to life, just because his most faithful and put-upon servant asked it of Him.

That left him with one option.

'You,' he said, pointing at Myrrolena, 'are a pain in the neck. I was hoping *not* to have to do this.'

She blinked at him. 'What could you possibly...?'

Konrad stopped listening. He was hard at work on the delicate task of ruining his day, his week, his month... maybe even his year. Concentrating to block out the minor distractions of a homicidal Myrrolena and her army of sinister, life-sucking followers, Konrad reached out to the Far Beyond.

*Er, Master?* he called. It took some effort, mind-screaming across the sorts of distances the Master dealt in. He wouldn't be able to keep it up for long.

*Master!* he called again, hoping that today would be one of The

Malykt's generous days. Supposing He had such a thing.

There was a long silence, during which Konrad noticed Myrrolena's eyes widen and her face turn paler. 'You wouldn't...' she said.

He smiled tightly at her. 'But I am.'

'But... He never interferes! That's why He has people like *you* .'

'To do His dirty work for Him? Yes. But once in a while something comes up that I can't deal with.' He took a quick breath, sweating. 'You're exactly what He meant when He talked about *problems.'*

He called a third time, shutting his eyes to close out the sight of Myrrolena's face frozen in sudden fear. It was gratifying, but distracting. He had to get his Master here *now,* before she decided to do something desperate.

Too late. Konrad heard a cry from Nanda and her arm was torn out of his grip. He opened his eyes to see her surrounded by Myrrolena's people, rapidly disappearing within a flurry of insubstantial limbs.

'Stop the summons, Malykant!' Myrrolena shouted. 'Stop and I'll call them off!'

*Malykant,* said a bone-shattering voice in Konrad's mind, and he gasped. *I presume you disturb Me for a purpose?*

*Help!* was all that Konrad's distracted mind could manage. Then he was leaping after Nanda, using every power his Master had ever given him to ward off the *lamaeni.* He flailed around him with limbs, tables, and supernatural powers. The air around him turned ice-cold and began to rain freezing icicles. He realised it was working—the *lamaeni* were backing off—

And then everyone froze as a new presence entered the room. The Malykt might be invisible in the technical sense, but you couldn't miss it when He turned up. It was the heart-pounding, gut-wrenching terror of it that Konrad enjoyed the most.

*I was busy,* the Master's voice crashed in his mind. *I hope this is worth My time, Malykant.*

Because if it wasn't, Konrad may find himself neatly vaporised. He understood perfectly well. 'Er, Master,' he said aloud. 'You remember when you said about how I could call on You in need? If I found something I really couldn't handle?'

*As I recall, you've done so a few times,* The Malykt replied with cool displeasure.

Konrad coughed. Most of those times had been early in his career, when he'd often found himself out of his depth—and he'd scared easily, too. It had kept happening until The Malykt had simply taken most of his emotions away. Problem fixed. He hadn't felt like a real person ever since, of course, but the Master didn't care about minor details like that.

'There's the problem,' he said simply, pointing at Myrrolena. The Ringmistress looked as though she'd been trying to run, until The Malykt's paralysing entrance. She stared back at Konrad, her eyes wide with fear.

'Lamaeni,' The Malykt said aloud. Konrad tried to breathe as his limbs began to shake. He hated it when the Master used His real voice. It was like having his mind shredded.

There was a pause; Konrad knew that his Master was reading Myrrolena and all her circumstances, taking stock of the situation in a mere few seconds. She might have evaded Nanda's scrutiny, but no one could resist The Malykt.

'Abominations, all of you,' said the dry, cold, excruciating voice. 'But it is not your fault, provided you abide by the agreements made between Me and your kind.'

Myrrolena swallowed, and nodded. Konrad wondered what those agreements were, but he knew better than to ask.

'I did,' Myrrolena whispered. 'I have. But—'

'*But,*' interrupted The Malykt, 'is a very bad word, Ringmistress.'

Silenced, Myrrolena nodded.

'We will talk,' said The Malykt with awful finality, and Myrrolena began to tremble.

Then her dark eyes flashed to Konrad's face, cold as ice. 'You'll be seeing me again,' she said.

From her tone, Konrad didn't doubt it.

It was over very quickly after that. Myrrolena had time only for a brief, agonised squeak before she disappeared.

*We will discuss this, Malykant,* said The Malykt in Konrad's mind. *Soon.*

Then His presence vanished also.

Silence reigned as Konrad, Nanda and the remaining *lamaeni* concentrated on breathing. Or whatever the *lamaeni* did instead of breathing.

'Well,' Konrad said when he had caught his breath. 'It's been fun. Anyone else want to assault us?'

The assembled *lamaeni* stared back at him with collective hatred, but nobody moved.

'Excellent,' Konrad said cheerfully. 'Then it's high time I was in bed.' He took Nanda's hand and led her towards the door.

'Wait,' Alad said, and Konrad paused. 'What's going to happen to the Ringmistress?'

'I don't know,' Konrad replied.

'Will she be back?'

'I don't know that either, but I'd assume that she'll be busy for a while. So I suppose you got your wish, Alad. Now go do something productive about it.' Honestly. The boy spent years scheming to remove Myrrolena, and then all he could do was bleat about it?

'But—'

'I don't like to steal a good line,' Konrad interrupted, 'but that is a terrible word. Deal with it, can't you?' He turned without waiting for a response and led Nanda out of there.

# 7

Holding his brandy glass up to the light, Konrad swirled the dark amber-coloured liquid around admiringly. It was the finest he had, aged and perfect, and he hadn't let himself touch it in nearly a year. He took a sip, savouring the rich flavour, then set the glass down.

'You know,' Nanda said sleepily, 'I'm proud of you.'

They had, by mutual and unspoken consent, gone straight back to Konrad's study after the events at the circus, stoked up the fire as high as it would go, and collapsed into his armchairs. In her quest to warm her feet, Nanda had slouched until she was almost horizontal, her toes dangerously close to the flaming logs.

It was comfortable. He liked it.

'Why do you say that?' he asked, frowning. It wasn't at all a Nanda sort of thing to say.

'You completed a case, and you didn't kill anyone. Not a single person.'

Konrad scowled. 'You talk as though I normally kill loads of people.'

A flicker of a mocking smile curled her lips. 'I *did* think it was your default setting. That the job isn't done until you've killed someone, by some means or other.'

'Just for the fun of it, I suppose?' He scowled at her. 'Well. Sending her off with The Malykt was much worse, some would argue.'

Her brows lifted at that. 'Oh? What do you think will happen to her?'

'Who knows? She might be... vaporised.' He made a drunken gesture with one hand, a flick of the fingers meant to indicate something flying apart into little pieces.

'Vaporised,' Nanda repeated.

'Painfully.'

'Well, I take it back then. You were a sadistic bastard after all.'

He held up a finger. 'She *might* be vaporised. But it's more likely that He'll recruit her.' He waved a hand. 'You know. For something.'

She peered at him suspiciously. 'For something?'

'Master's always looking for the right sort of people. Like, sadistic bastards with a sense of responsibility. And it works best if they're in a tight spot at the time.'

'Why is that better?'

'More likely to agree. It's a creative way of punishing people, when you think about it.'

'Is that what happened with you?'

Konrad narrowed his eyes at her. 'No comment.'

Nanda smiled, and let it pass.

'Something's bothering me about that whole thing this evening,' he said after a moment, only slightly slurring his words. 'Nan. Were you... glowing?'

'When?'

'That exciting bit when you were drowning under a wave of unliving fiends.' That bit had been messy, to say the least, but he couldn't shake the partial image he had in his head: Nanda decidedly *not* faltering under that swarming attack, with a faint glow coming off her. Goldish coloured, even.

She folded her arms and glowered at him from under her lashes. 'Of course I wasn't glowing.'

'You were.'

'Wasn't.'

He shrugged. 'Then I'm not answering your question.'

'Yes, you will. Maybe not today, but sometime.'

'I don't see how it's fair that you pressure secrets out of me, but refuse to share yours.'

'I do. That's you, and this is me.'

'One rule for me and another for you? I don't see how that's reasonable.'

'You don't? How curious. Give me that.' She held out her hand towards his glass.

'S'mine.' He snatched it up and took another swallow. 'You didn't want any.'

'I changed my mind.'

'Fine.' He held it out. She grabbed it off him, took a big swallow and came up coughing. 'Nice stuff,' she said weakly, handing it back.

*Master,* said a voice near his ear. *Can we talk?*

'By all means,' he said expansively, pointing to the air in front of his face. 'Right there, please, where I can see you.'

Nanda watched him with a puzzled expression until the two serpents materialised before his face. 'Hi, snakes,' she said sleepily.

'You're in disgrace,' Konrad said, pointing at Ootapi. 'You know that, yes?'

The serpent flickered, hung its insubstantial head and muttered something about self-preservation, poor tempers and working conditions.

'Fine, I admit it. I was crap,' Konrad said. 'I'm sorry. Is that better?'

Ootapi mumbled something else.

'Job market isn't what it used to be, eh? Well, that can't be helped. I'm sure you did your very best to replace me.'

Ootapi hissed at him.

'I interviewed many candidates for the post of unreliable and disloyal ghost-servant,' Konrad said, eyeing the creature severely, 'but I wasn't able to find a suitable replacement either. Isn't that lucky?'

'Did you really?' Nanda whispered. He gestured at her: shut up, please. She grinned.

*Are you still intolerable, Master?* Ootapi ventured.

'Intolerable! Why, don't I seem like my usual self?'

*You seem drunk, Master.*

He waved that aside. 'Right well, if I'm going to be less *intolerable,* I need some peace and quiet to finish persuading this nice lady to be less of a stone cold bi—um... lady.'

Nanda choked. 'You were going to say something else there, Konrad?'

'Nope. Nothing.' He waved the serpents away. 'Off with you. We'll review your duties later.' They began to stream away. Belatedly he called after them: 'I left your usual rewards in the usual place. Eetapi, it's up to you whether or not to share!'

'Dare I ask?' Nanda said.

'Best not.'

Silence fell for a while. Konrad sipped at his brandy and eyed Nanda, trying to be surreptitious. She appeared to be too busy almost-sleeping to notice. She looked comfortable, which struck him as significant. Had he managed to redeem himself somehow? Had she stopped seeing him as someone to fear?

He plucked up his courage—aided by another dose or two of brandy—and said: 'So... are you staying this time, Nan?'

Her lips curved in a wicked smile and she gave him a smouldering look from beneath her half-closed lids. 'Why Konrad, are you asking me to stay the night?'

He blinked, coughed, and swallowed. 'Um.' Was she joking? *Stupid,* he thought. *It's Nanda. Of course she's joking.*

'Actually,' he said carefully, 'I meant just... in general. You know. Not wandering back to your life and casting me off, again.'

She crossed one ankle over the other and twitched her stocking-clad toes. 'Probably.'

'Probably? Is that supposed to be reassuring?'

'You're scary.'

'I'll try to be less scary,' he said promptly.

'Liar.'

He opened his mouth to try again, but she interrupted him. 'You didn't ask your Master about what Myrrolena said.'

'Which bit?'

'You know: the part about your being dead. Or unliving. Or whatever.'

'There wasn't time,' he said quickly.

'True, but that's not the real reason.'

Konrad was silent for a long moment, his gaze fixed on the leaping flames. He didn't like to think about what Myrrolena had said: it chilled him to the core, and he had no idea how to deal with it. The best he could do was put it out of his mind, and try to carry on. 'Would you have asked?' he said at last.

She thought about that. 'No,' she finally agreed. 'I wouldn't either.'

He smiled faintly. 'There are some things a person would rather not know, eh?'

She nodded sleepily, her lips curving in a faint smile. 'You seem

238

pretty alive to me.'

Konrad smiled back. 'That's good enough for me. Now, how about some more brandy?'

# GHOST
# SPEAKER

# 1

Konrad dived into his study and all but slammed the door behind him. What an infernal crush. At least half the gentry of the city of Ekamet were crammed into his ballroom tonight, or so it seemed; he had reached the point where he could scarcely breathe amidst the bustle and the tumult of his lamentably successful event.

To his decided dejection, he was the host of this particular piece of organised, purposeless chaos. He was obliged to hold gatherings at Bakar House once or twice a year; it kept him involved in the social whirl of the city, allowing him to maintain useful contacts among Ekamet's social elite. But he detested the obligation. He was the Malykant, chief servant of The Malykt, the spirit Overlord of death; his role was to punish murderers, not to dance with silly young women until his feet were sore.

Worse, this year something seemed to have changed. His status as a bachelor — and a most eligible one, given his apparent wealth — had always rendered him susceptible to attempts to land him as a husband. He was used to fending off such attacks, but lately they had come thick and fast; it was as though someone had declared open season upon him, and the onslaught was not to end until he was safely married. It was insufferable.

His study was blessedly dark and quiet, and he heaved a sigh of relief as he loosened his cravat. A drink of something would go down well, he thought; half an hour of peace and a stiff drink would set him up, and he could face the remainder of the evening with equanimity.

He was halfway across the room before he realised that he was not, in fact, alone. Somebody was sitting in his favourite chair. Startled, a curse fell from his lips before he could catch it, and of course, it proved to be a lady sitting there.

'This part of the house is not open to guests,' he said. What was she doing, sitting here in the dark? He lit a couple of lamps and the woman in the chair sat up, blinking in the sudden glow of light.

'I am sorry,' she said after a moment. 'Only I could not bear the crush a moment longer. All those people.'

He wondered how she had managed to find her way to one of the very few quiet rooms in the house. Trial and error? He was struck by how tired she looked; her fair skin was smudged with dark circles under her eyes, and her posture was weary, shoulders slumped as she wilted into the chair. She was in her early twenties, he guessed, and pretty, with curling blonde hair and wide blue eyes.

Seeing as she was a guest at his own ball, he ought to know her name; but he'd left all that business to Mrs. Domashev, a lady of advanced years who posed as a distant relative and handled all of his entertaining for him. Such as it was.

'Miss... um, I'm afraid I must invite you to return to the ball,' he ventured. 'Your mother will be missing you, I am sure.' He kept his voice even only with an effort; all he wanted was some peace! In his own house! Infernal socialising, it was so much more trouble than—

'My mother is dead,' said the woman, frowning. 'I cannot imagine she is missing me very much.'

Konrad cleared his throat and searched uselessly for something to say.

'My name is Dominka Popova,' she supplied.

'Ah yes — of course—I was but an instant from recalling it,' Konrad said smoothly, and bowed.

She crooked a cynical half-smile at him, and shook her head. 'You were not, sir, but I shouldn't wonder that you forgot. How can anybody be expected to remember so many names? I think that half the city is here tonight.'

She made no move to get up, Konrad noted with annoyance. Sighing, he slumped into the chair opposite. 'And I wish they would go away again,' he said candidly. 'I, too, have had enough.'

She made no reply to that, merely picking listlessly at the

embroidery adorning the front of her sumptuous blue velvet gown. She was in low spirits, he thought, and it wasn't just the ball. 'I hope you will excuse the presumption, Miss Popova, but: are you well?'

Her head came up abruptly, and a sunny smile appeared from somewhere. 'Why, of course, sir!' she said, with every appearance of good cheer. 'And I mean to dance a great deal more before the evening is over, I assure you.'

He blinked. 'You will not accomplish that by sitting here in the dark.'

'No, no,' she agreed in a brisk tone. 'A little rest was all that I required.' She smiled brilliantly at him, and it struck him with sudden force that she reminded him of Enadya. Oh, not in her physical appearance; his sister had been as dark-skinned as he was himself, with the same dark hair and eyes. But her mannerisms, and that smile... the realisation struck him to the heart, and for a moment he couldn't breathe.

Miss Popova eyed him narrowly. His discomfort must be showing, he realised, and he sought at once to conceal it behind his usual urbane facade.

She was not convinced. 'Are *you* well, sir?' she enquired — displaying in the process the same sweet solicitude Enadya had always shown him, and his heart twisted.

'Perfectly,' he assured her.

'Perhaps a dance would revive you,' she offered, and jumped to her feet. 'It would certainly revive *me*. Tell me, can I persuade you?'

'Not a chance,' he said grimly. 'I do not intend to dance again for at least the next month, if I can contrive it.'

She appeared crestfallen, and sank back into her chair. The cheer had faded from her face, leaving her the same wilting young woman he had first seen. Konrad felt like a brute.

'It is so difficult...' she began, toying restlessly with the cuff of her sleeve. 'So difficult.'

'What is difficult?' Konrad prompted, after a long pause.

'Oh, life,' she said, directing at him a swift, piercing stare. 'Do you not think?'

'It can be,' he said, cautious. 'What is it that you are finding difficult, in particular?'

'Everything,' she said, wilting a little more. 'Life and death — love, romance — family — these concerns cannot be easily managed, I think. They encroach upon one another — war for attention—' She broke off abruptly, and straightened. 'All the greatest nonsense, of course,' she said, her tone suddenly brisk once more. 'We all have our trials, do we not, sir?'

Konrad blinked, confused by her mercurial changes of mood. 'Indeed, we do,' he agreed. 'In fact—' He was obliged to stop speaking, as footsteps loudly approached in the corridor outside. Abruptly it occurred to him how questionable was his current position, alone in a room with an unmarried young lady... if anybody were to catch them in such a circumstance, the consequences could be messy. His intentions might be perfectly respectable, but gossip had a habit of believing otherwise.

The same realisation came to her, it seemed, for she leapt lightly out of her chair and crossed to the door. Once the footsteps had safely passed, she made Konrad a hasty curtsey and said softly: 'I apologise for the intrusion, sir — this is your private room, is it not? I had better return to the ball.' Konrad did not have time to reply before she was gone, the door closing softly behind her.

He sat where he was for some minutes, breathing in the blessed silence left by her departure. The door was stout, and effectively blocked out the noises of the ball; Konrad could almost fancy himself alone in the building. His thoughts turned inevitably to Enadya, and he sighed deeply.

It had been months since he had last thought of her. More than a year, even. He tried not to, as a rule. Enadya, his only sister, many years his junior — and his charge, ever since his mother had followed his father into the grave. She had been calm, quiet and sensible — everything he was not — but with a sudden smile that lit up his life. So like Dominka Popova's.

She had been gone for eight years, but it still felt like yesterday to him.

Abruptly, the turmoil in his head became intolerable; far better that he seek the distractions — even the irritations — of the ballroom. With a long sigh, he levered his tired body up out of his chair and returned to the party.

It was noon before Konrad woke the next day. He knew this from the quality of the light that filtered through the gap between his heavy bedroom curtains; he altogether refused to look at a clock.

A footman appeared moments later with a tray full of something that smelled delicious. His staff seemed to have some kind of sixth sense about these things; Konrad never had to wait long for his breakfast. He hauled himself up in bed and tucked in to the food, feeling better with every bite. Ruthlessly, he thrust all recollections of the previous night's so-called festivities out of his mind; the torment was over for the year, and he had better things to do.

He ventured downstairs half an hour later, well-groomed and immaculately dressed. His butler, Gorev appeared at once and stood in the chin-raised, hands-clasped posture that meant he had something to say, but wouldn't *dream* of imposing himself.

Konrad nodded to him. 'What is it?'

'There's been some news, sir,' said Gorev in a low voice. 'I thought you may wish to hear.'

Gorev's manner and tone suggested something rather private, which astonished Konrad. Nonetheless, he beckoned the butler into his study and quietly closed the door after him.

'Go on,' he said.

Gorev cleared his throat. He was actually looking concerned, Konrad realised, and he felt a flicker of anxiety. Was it Nanda?

'It's Miss Popova,' Gorev continued.

Konrad blinked. 'Miss Dominka Popova? She who attended the ball last night?'

'The very one, sir.' Gorev hesitated, and said nothing else.

'Well?' Konrad said, growing impatient. If it had nothing to do with Nanda, then he was relieved; but what could Miss Popova's business possibly have to do with him?

'Ah... she's dead, sir,' said Gorev.

Konrad stared. 'How?' he managed at last.

'They're saying it's suicide, sir,' said Gorev. He sounded apologetic, and there was a definite glint of concern in his eyes. That meant he knew, somehow, about the conversation Konrad had had with Miss Popova the night before. Did anyone else know?

'You're certain, Gorev?' Konrad said, hoping that the tremor in his voice wasn't noticeable.

'Fairly, sir. It's all over the city. Fell from a building, so I gather.' He paused. 'There was a note.'

Konrad sank into his favourite chair with a long sigh, mentally replaying last night's conversation over in his mind. Her spirits had seemed depressed at times — and less so, at others. Could he have anticipated her actions? No. But the sick feeling in his stomach refused to listen to reason. Perhaps... there might have been something he could have done.

'Gorev,' said Konrad. 'Why is it that you felt this news would be of interest to me?'

The butler coughed, and hesitated. 'I discovered Miss Popova in your study last night, sir, when I went in to refresh the lamps. She assured me that she required nothing, and so I let her be.'

Konrad closed his eyes, waving a hand vaguely at Gorev to dismiss him. He barely heard his butler's quiet tread as he left the room and closed the door. His heart sank a little further. What Gorev meant, of course, was that he assumed Konrad and Miss Popova had enjoyed some kind of *assignation* last night; that she had been waiting in his study by appointment. Gorev was loyal and a man of sympathy; there had been no hint of censure in his looks or his tone. But if Gorev had been aware of the girl's presence in his study, perhaps others had, too.

He could not bring himself to care overmuch for such concerns as that, however. A peculiar feeling had settled in the pit of his stomach, and his mind insisted on replaying Miss Popova's sweet, sunny smile for him over and over again — and Enadya's, too, the two faces alternating in his thoughts until he could barely tell them apart. And something was not right.

Six or seven years ago, The Malykt had judged Konrad's depth of feeling to be a hindrance in his assigned task, and had accordingly removed it. Not all of it, quite; Konrad still felt echoes of the emotions he had once been beholden to. But they did not affect him; the full force of them passed him by, leaving him cool-headed and rational at all times.

Until today. That was a stab of real pain, currently assailing his gut; and something uncomfortable and unpleasant was welling up inside him somewhere. Sadness — despair — self-disgust — grief — he had felt only the barest flicker of these things for years, and now they were returning in force. He struggled like a drowning man, barely able to breathe under the sudden onslaught. He could have saved Dominka, perhaps, had he paid her more attention — had he only *tried*. He had failed her, just as he had failed Enadya.

He was obliged to sit for some time, forcing himself to breathe deeply and trying desperately to think of pleasant things. But the sensations did not pass. They grew and grew — fed, he realised, by his own fear of them. He felt dazed and confused and increasingly alarmed. How could The Malykt's protection fail him now, when he was, perhaps, more in need of it than ever? If The Master had changed His mind, He would have informed Konrad. Surely? What could it mean? And how was he supposed to *cope*?

Fear and anxiety chased each other around Konrad's head, growing larger and more unwieldy with every rotation, until he felt desperate. Pacing frantically up and down his study made no difference, and his frightened brain could not think calmly enough to come up with a sensible course of action. His eye fell on the decanters of liquor that lived upon a handsome mahogany sideboard at the back of his room, and he lunged for them.

For the next hour, Konrad kept himself well amused with a glass of whiskey, followed by one or two more. At length his body began to relax, his pounding heartbeat slowed, and the appalling fear that gripped him faded into the background. He continued to drink and drink, barrelling past tipsy, through mellow and well into stupefied — and then he felt the summons.

It began as a wave of ice-cold terror that shot through his body, freezing him in his chair. Then came a crushing sensation in his chest, a terrifying lack of air, and a violent tremor that shook every inch of his tall frame. Worse, by some margin, than the fear he had been trying to escape — but at least this was a *familiar* terror.

This reflection did not make him feel better.

Sweat poured down his face as he croaked,' M-master?'

*I require your presence,* came The Malykt's voice. It was the barest whisper, and yet it felt to him like a piercing scream that set his nerves jangling.

'At— at once,' Konrad gasped. To his relief, The Malykt said nothing more, and the appalling terror — his Master's particular gift to His most favoured servant — subsided somewhat.

Konrad waited, gulping in air. He noted distantly that all his stupefying drunkenness had deserted him completely. He waited, scarcely breathing, for a return of those other confusing emotions, but nothing happened. They had been beaten into submission, he thought sourly, by the uniquely gut-shredding horror of The Malykt's attention. A decidedly mixed blessing.

But as he thought about it, the beginnings of fear, sadness and despair began to tease at the edges of his consciousness. They were still there, he realised with a flash of panic; waiting to descend upon him the moment he let down his guard. He swallowed, and his heart began to pound once more.

Then a new voice chimed inside his mind, interrupting this most dangerous train of thought. The voice was redolent with the mournful tones of funeral bells, and sliced through his reflections like a knife through butter. *Hello, Master!* said Eetapi. She materialised in the air before him, the hazy outline of a ghostly serpent whirling in lazy circles.

Konrad squinted at her suspiciously. 'You sound remarkably cheerful, Eetapi. Has something terrible happened?'

*Something* horrible beyond words *has happened,* she said with vast contentment. *A fine puzzle. We will be happily busy for days.*

Konrad blinked. Lords, but he was keeping appalling company these days. He sighed, and stood up. 'Lead on, spirit,' he commanded. Eetapi turned a bouncing loop in the air and streamed out of the door, fading back into the air as she did so. Konrad did not need to see her with his eyes; he sensed her presence ahead of him. Pausing only to collect his coat and hat, he followed his ghostly minion out into the street.

Outside, Eetapi guided his steps towards The Malykt's temple. Beneath the imposing, white marble building was a morgue, an area operated and accessed exclusively by the Order of the Malykt. Eetapi led him to the centre of the room, where a pale corpse lay inert upon a large table. He recognised the features of Miss Dominka Popova. Something unpleasant pierced him once more as he stared at her dead face, and he forgot, for a short while, to breathe.

The room was empty of life, but he could feel The Malykt's icy presence. Terror flooded him once more, sweeping everything else away, and for a moment he stopped, unable to move for the intensity of it.

*This soul,* said his Master without preamble. *What do you know of it, Malykant?*

'Reportedly a suicide, Master,' he said quietly.

There was a pause. *Yes,* his Master said at last. *Death was sought, and yet—*

Konrad waited, most of his attention focused on the effort to breathe. Proximity to his Master was bad enough; for The Malykt to hesitate over a soul was fractionally worse. Konrad's heart sank as he waited, tense, for the spirit lord's verdict.

*It is Unclean,* He pronounced. Konrad winced. Unclean meant unnatural; the girl had died before her time, her cycle cut short. Usually this meant murder. Suicides were a different matter altogether, and nothing to do with the Malykant at all.

'Ah...' Konrad said through dry lips. 'Is it then a suicide, or murder?'

*Both,* The Malykt replied. *And yet, neither.*

Konrad blinked. 'I don't quite —'

*To seek answers is your purpose in life, Malykant,* the Master replied, with an icy severity that turned Konrad's guts to water. *Something lies terribly amiss with this soul, but it has passed on and its secrets are closed to Me. You will discover them.*

Recognising his dismissal, Konrad hastily began: "Master, there is something I wish to ask—' But a whirl of frigid air sent a freezing gale howling through the room, and then all was still once more: The Malykt had gone. Konrad took in a shaky breath and mopped at his damp face with his handkerchief. The feeling of clenched panic subsided after a few minutes, but his tremors did not pass.

He had been entertaining a faint hope that the torment of his awakening emotions was some kind of mistake; that he need only mention it to his Master and the problem would be resolved at once. That hope faded. The Malykt did not make mistakes, and He clearly did not wish to discuss the matter.

For the time being, Konrad would just have to live with it.

He gave a long sigh, trying to ignore his deep sense of foreboding, and looked up towards the ceiling where Eetapi had taken up her circling once more. 'All right,' he muttered. 'Where is Ootapi?'

# 2

Konrad stepped back out into the street some twenty minutes later, one of Miss Popova's rib bones tucked inside his coat. He had havered for some time over whether or not to take one at all; the papers were reporting suicide, and it would cause a stir when her body was discovered to bear the tell-tale marks of the Malykant's presence. But he could not safely neglect to take the bone — not if there was any chance at all that her death had indeed been murder. He felt unusually grim as he left the morgue. Normally he conducted the simple procedure without the smallest qualm, but this time... this time was different.

The rain had begun again, he immediately discovered; the leaden sky poured cold droplets down upon him, and the chill quickly seeped into his skin. The absurd clothes gentlemen wore were largely decorative, and could offer little real protection against the elements. Konrad spared a thought for his marsh gear: layers of thick fabric, a voluminous, waxed coat and a wide-brimmed hat that could fend off even the harsh conditions of the Bone Forest. It was a pity that Mr. Konrad Savast would never be seen dead in such attire.

He had reached the end of the street before it occurred to him that he had little idea where he was going. He stopped abruptly, then stepped sideways into the mouth of a narrow alley and backed up against the wall. His ghost-serpents followed and hung expectantly in the air before him.

The problem the Master had set was a thorny one. How could a person die both voluntarily and involuntarily? If Miss Popova had been compelled by someone else to hurl herself to her death, then surely her demise would be murder, clear and simple — even if she had stepped over the edge of the building by her own will. But if she had wanted to die, how could any interference by another turn that wished-for death into murder?

He needed to learn more about Miss Popova. Everything about Miss Popova. Most importantly, had she truly been inclined to suicide? If so, why? What had been occurring in her life before she died? Her comments of last night had been vague; too vague. She had implied that she suffered some kind of troubles, but had said nothing about what they might have been.

He needed to see her family. Her mother was dead, but perhaps her father could shed some light.

*Eetapi,* he said silently. *Ootapi. Find me the Popov residence.*

The serpents paused a moment in thought and then, as one, they whirled upon the air and streamed away. Konrad followed, lengthening his stride to keep up with the eager pace they set.

The Popov house was a tall, narrow and forbidding building situated on the east side of Ekamet, not far from the city centre. It was a fine piece of property, Konrad judged, as he stood for a moment in the street looking up at it. Its location alone rendered it of high value, but it was also undeniably handsome, in spite of its dark stone exterior and gloomy atmosphere. The Popov family, he judged, were far from poor.

The knocker that graced the imposing front door was wrought from some kind of silver metal — probably not real silver, Konrad imagined, as it displayed far too bright a gleam — and worked into the shape of a crow's head. It was an unusual choice of symbol to gift with pride of place at the front of the house, and Konrad regarded it for a moment in thought, trying to gauge what it said about the residents of the house.

Nothing he could determine by standing on the doorstep, he swiftly concluded. He rapped the knocker sharply — and blinked in surprise as the door opened instantly, revealing the pale and withered visage of an elderly butler.

'Yes?' he said slowly, peering down at Konrad. And down he must look indeed, for in spite of Konrad's considerable height the butler was rather taller.

'I am here to see Mr. Popov,' said Konrad firmly, attempting with his tone and demeanour to forestall any possible objections. He handed the butler a card, and then stared at him until the old man stepped back, head bowed, and opened the door wider. Konrad followed the butler up a grand flight of stairs thickly carpeted in deep, dark green and allowed himself to be shown into the drawing-room — where, to his satisfaction, he was left alone.

The house was peculiar inside as well as out, he had swiftly to conclude. The hall was exceptionally tall and echoed mightily; the inevitable result of so much dark-and-pale marble covering the floors and bare stone walls. The windows were tall and narrow, and composed of many small panes of glass; they did little to illuminate the interior, and nobody seemed to think it necessary to compensate with additional lighting.

The drawing-room was of a similar character. The floor here, too, was marble, softened with only a single dark rug in the centre of the room. A pair of low divans upholstered in dark green velvet framed either side of it, and a low table stood between. Nothing adorned the rest of the large room save sets of heavy, dark velvet drapes shrouding the windows. It looked, Konrad reflected, as though a death in the family was a minor event for the Popovs.

He took a seat on one of the divans and waited. It was by no means certain that Popov would agree to see him; he had, after all, just lost his daughter and he was no more than a bowing acquaintance of Konrad's. Ordinarily Konrad would never intrude upon the family at such a time, but his need was pressing; he hoped Popov would accept a condolence call with good grace.

Some minutes passed; so many that Konrad began to despair of his luck. He slid down in his seat a little, feeling inexplicably tired, and stretched out his legs. His gaze drifted towards the ceiling, and what he saw explained the peculiar half-sounds he had been hearing ever since he had entered the room.

An entire flock of dark birds — crows, perhaps, or ravens — roosted near the ceiling. Perches had been hung for them, draped with foliage — real foliage, as far as Konrad could tell, and fresh, which meant it was changed regularly. Or perhaps it grew up there. The birds gathered in groups, staring beadily down at the intruder upon their solitude. The shadows were deep, and the birds were well-cloaked; but Konrad received the impression of a multitude of dark, feathered bodies huddling high above.

Konrad's gaze slid back to the floor. No droppings. Popov must have a small army of people tending to his peculiar pets, Konrad thought in amazement. What could he mean by it?

Something else tugged at his senses, and Konrad's eyes narrowed. In the blink of an eye, he allowed his spirit vision to drown his normal sight, leaving him staring into the aether. The colours of the Popovs' drawing-room grew instantly starker, fading to chilling shades of ice-white and deathly black; against this harsh backdrop, the living bodies of the birds stood out like drops of ink.

Crows they were indeed, and they were not alone. Hundreds more roosted alongside them — hundreds of tiny forms whose bodies gleamed sickly white and wavered in his vision like rippling water. *Ghosts.* They were as incorporeal — and yet, as undeniably present — as his serpents. And Popov had hundreds of them bound to this place.

Konrad's interest in the man sharpened at once. The manipulation of spirits was a rare ability; those who wielded it generally found their way to The Malykt's Order, sooner or later. But he had had no idea of Popov's skill. Did Popov himself know what it meant? And what was he doing with it? Something about these huddled little birds bothered Konrad; something was wrong, though he could not identify precisely what it was that set his teeth on edge and threatened to turn his stomach.

An untrained ghostspeaker presented an alarming prospect, whatever his doings. Konrad made a note to enquire with the Order; perhaps someone else knew of his ability. Perhaps he had even been trained at some time. But he doubted it. Something felt wrong.

Silently, he called his serpents. They came streaming through the wall almost at once, and shot instantly up to the ceiling. He felt their curiosity — and their wariness.

*Find out what you can about this,* he instructed them.

The door opened and Popov came into the room. The man looked horrific through Konrad's spirit vision: a dark, lurking presence in the doorway, his spirit roiling with shadows. The effect was nauseating, and Konrad hastily allowed his vision to return to normal.

He had forgotten how remarkably diminutive Mr. Popov was. Konrad got to his feet and tried not to tower too badly over the older man. He failed.

'My condolences for your loss,' he said gravely, with a formal half-bow.

Popov eyed him, and responded at last with a brief nod. 'It is an inconvenient time to be receiving visitors, Savast, as you may imagine. I hope you will not be offended if I don't offer you any refreshment at this time.'

It was a clear dismissal, but Konrad wavered. Common decency dictated that, having delivered his condolences, he take his leave at once; but the dictates of justice required him to stay, and find out more about Dominka's life. But how to broach the subject? He was not with the police; he had no right to question the man. Even if he did, her death had been ruled a suicide, and it was too early, yet, for news of the Malykant's investigation to have reached her father.

He glanced up at the ceiling and the silent audience above. Popov's gaze followed, but he said nothing and Konrad could hardly press him about it.

'I had the good fortune to be acquainted with your daughter, a little,' Konrad ventured. 'I am sorry that she should have suffered so from melancholy.'

Popov looked strangely at him. 'And did she indeed seem melancholy, last night? At your ball?'

'Sometimes,' Konrad replied cautiously.

Popov nodded. 'Her mother's death affected her very deeply.'

Konrad raised an eyebrow.

'A wasting sickness,' Popov expanded tonelessly.

Konrad murmured another round of condolences. 'A recent event?'

'Oh, no,' Popov murmured. 'Many years have passed.'

It did not seem very likely, then, that Dominka had been suffering severely enough over her mother's demise to take her own life. Konrad sought frantically for something else to say. Popov's manner was not forthcoming, and it was visibly a strain to him to make conversation. He badly wanted to question the man about the crows, but he could not do so in any meaningful way without revealing his own abilities. He had, perhaps, reached the end of the enquiries he could make alone, and they had not been productive.

Konrad sighed inwardly, and bowed.

'I shall intrude no longer,' he said.

Popov returned the bow, his face expressionless, and said nothing. Konrad left the house feeling mildly frustrated. His task would be so much easier if Popov could only have been expansive and eager to talk. If he had to be inscrutable and silent, well... Konrad would have to find some other way to find out about his family. Inspector Nuritov may have more luck with him, he thought, once news of the possibility of murder had spread abroad; the police would then have a reason to question Popov.

Damn it all. His masquerade as an ordinary gentleman had its advantages, but sometimes it was nothing but a hindrance.

The serpents caught up to him on the street.

*What did you learn?* he asked.

*They are like us,* Ootapi reported. *In every respect.*

*Except that they are as stupid as stumps!* Eetapi merrily added. *We could hardly speak with them at all.*

*And what did they say, when they spoke?* Konrad prompted.

*Popov is their binder,* Ootapi replied. *He has been raising crows for years and binding their souls when they die.*

*Binding them to what?*

*To the ones left alive.*

Konrad stopped where he was in the street, aghast. *He is binding dead souls to living bodies?*

*Oh, yes!* Eetapi carolled. *I imagine that is why they are so stupid. They are mere shades, really; what we would be without The Malykt's interference. And so messy! Their souls are all tangled up together; one can hardly tell where each begins and ends.*

*And they are decaying,* added Ootapi. *The oldest ones are the worst; mere shapes without substance. The newer ones are more communicative, but they are also mad.*

A sudden, horrible thought occurred to Konrad. He had not instructed his serpents to practice any stealth; the last thing he had expected to find in the Popov house was a roof full of crow-ghosts and an unregistered ghostspeaker. *Did Popov sense your presence?*

*Of course not,* replied Ootapi, in tones of deepest disgust. *Have we not been your loyal servants these eight years at least? We are the best!*

Konrad suppressed a smile, and made a sort of mental bow in his serpents' direction. *Of course. My apologies.*

He walked on, his thoughts racing. What could Popov mean by capturing the souls of hundreds of crows, and keeping them all in his

257

drawing-room? Did he know how it affected them? Konrad was a very powerful ghostspeaker, and his abilities knew no limit when it came to the spirits of the departed; Popov may or may not be the same. If he couldn't speak with his crow-slaves, perhaps he was unaware of the effect his activities were having upon them. And, presumably, he did not have the assistance of such servants as Eetapi and Ootapi.

But still. His actions were disturbing indeed, and Konrad knew not what to make of them. And what *else* might he be getting up to with such abilities?

Konrad could summon neither conclusions nor answers, just yet, but he did receive the impression that the story of Dominka Popova may be far more complicated than he had imagined.

With a sigh, he pulled the brim of his hat lower against the oncoming rain and turned his steps towards the city police headquarters. It was time to consult Nuritov.

3

Inspector Nuritov greeted Konrad with a smile of welcome, and gestured him to a seat with alacrity. Konrad blinked at the inspector in surprise. It was almost as though the man was glad to see him.

'It has been a while, Savast. I trust you've been well?'

Konrad blinked again, and cleared his throat. It *had* been a while, but he would not have expected Nuritov to notice. He had not thought their acquaintance had ever progressed to such a point.

'Social season,' he said at last, with a shrug and something resembling a smile in return. He could hardly tell Nuritov the real reasons he had been absent; the Inspector knew him only as a bored gentleman of leisure with an interest in solving mysteries, and Konrad could not confide in him about his true identity.

Nuritov grinned and flopped into his own chair on the other side of his wide desk. He looked tired, Konrad thought; his sandy hair was messier even than usual and he sported shadows beneath his greenish-grey eyes. Perhaps he had been working too much. 'Ah, the lives of the rich. I don't envy you that part, at least.'

Konrad realised this was a moment when he was supposed to grin back, and managed to do so, although he felt more like grimacing. He didn't envy himself that part, either. He spent the entire season thinking longingly of his little hut out in the Bone Forest. It was raised on stilts out of the muck and moisture of the marshes, sparsely furnished but comfortable, and equipped with everything he needed to live the simple kind of life he preferred.

And it was also *isolated*.

But it was ungrateful of him to think this way. Who wouldn't want the kind of luxury he enjoyed? And he did enjoy it, much of the time. He brushed such thoughts away, and got to business.

'I'm here about the Popov case,' he said.

Nuritov's brows rose. 'Dominka Popova? Is it a case? I thought it was suicide. Sad thing, too.'

Konrad hesitated. Here, again, he found himself on difficult ground. He could hardly tell Nuritov that The Malykt Himself had sent Konrad to investigate; but on the face of it, there was no reason at all to suspect murder. 'I'd just like to be sure,' he said at last, unable to think of a better excuse.

Nuritov nodded slowly, and favoured him with a knowing look. 'Friend of hers, were you?'

'Something like that.' He frowned, realising how that sounded, and added, 'Not exactly. I held a ball on the evening in question, and she was there. We spoke a little. She seemed unhappy, but not so much that she might...' He tailed off, and shrugged helplessly. 'I can't help thinking that maybe I could have done something to help, but truly, it never crossed my mind that she might in danger of harming herself.'

'You didn't know her at all?' Nuritov said, looking narrowly at Konrad.

'We'd never spoken until that evening,' Konrad said. 'I found her hiding in my study — the crush was bothering her, so she said. We spoke for only a few minutes before she returned to the ballroom.' He sighed deeply. 'I have no personal interests in this matter whatsoever, but still... I liked her. I wish I could have guessed, somehow, that she needed help.'

'It seems to have taken everyone by surprise,' Nuritov conceded. 'But the unfortunate truth is, suicide is far from uncommon. Perhaps especially in young people — young women — whose future is uncertain. It is difficult to imagine what you could have done to help.'

'Was her future uncertain?'

Nuritov shrugged. 'I'm not very well informed about such matters, but I heard one or two things. There was mention in one of the papers about a possible match between her and — and someone whose name I have forgotten.' He began searching among the many papers heaped upon his desk, frowning. 'But I got the impression there were complications of some kind.'

'You have no idea what kind of complications they were, I take it?'
Konrad sighed.

'No, but you are in a better position to answer that question than I
am. These people will talk to you much more readily than they will
talk to me.'

Ordinarily true, but... 'I saw Vadim Popov this morning,' Konrad
said. 'He threw me out after three minutes.'

'Well, he's a grieving father,' said Nuritov crisply. 'If you want
information, seek out the gossips. Every social circle has them. Aha!'
He withdrew a slightly crumpled newspaper from the middle of a
stack and swept it open. 'Here it is. Ruslan Kanadin.' He tossed the
newspaper to Konrad, who caught it and spread it open over his
knees. The article was short; a mere few lines indicating that a
betrothal between the deceased and Mr Kanadin had been expected
for some time.

'Good,' Konrad murmured. 'Thank you for this.' He handed back
the newspaper. 'Was there anything else useful in the papers? I
haven't had time to read them closely.'

Nuritov thought for a moment, and finally shook his head. 'The
obituaries were brief all round — just a line or two about who her
parents were, that kind of thing. Which may itself be an interesting
point.'

It might indeed. Why had nobody written a proper obituary for
Dominka? She had been young, but surely there had been more to
say about her than *that*. Then again, her mother was dead, and she
apparently had no siblings; no one but her father, and Konrad could
hardly imagine the distant and silent Vadim Popov penning a
heartfelt obituary for his daughter.

'Do you know anything about Vadim Popov?' Konrad asked.

Nuritov eyed him with interest. 'Not very much. He is not *quite* a
hermit, as I gather he is seen at the kind of social gatherings nobody
invites me to. But he has something of an odd reputation.'

Konrad nodded. He knew of it himself, though it had never
seemed significant to him before. Popov turned up at events from
time to time, but participated as little as possible; and he never invited
anyone to his home. And Konrad had certainly never heard about
those crows before.

That begged another question, which Konrad filed away at the
back of his mind. Why had he been admitted that morning — and

why in the world had the butler conducted him to the drawing-room, where he would see the crows? He felt oddly disquieted. Had Popov known — or sensed — something about him after all? Perhaps his serpents hadn't gone as undetected as they imagined; perhaps Popov had admitted Konrad in order to inspect *him*.

'Listen,' Konrad said, after a moment's thought. 'I heard a rumour. Apparently the Malykant has become involved.'

Nuritov's brows shot up. Everyone knew of the Malykant, of course, though they did not know *who* he was. Signs of his passage were obvious; the bodies of murdered souls were always plundered of a rib bone, to be used later as a weapon of justice. The papers would soon report that Dominka's death was murder, not suicide, at least according to the Malykant, and Konrad could use that.

'Are you sure?' Nuritov said.

Konrad shrugged, trying to appear casual. 'That's what I heard. If it proves to be true, perhaps someone might question Vadim Popov? The police can ask the awkward questions which I could not.'

Nuritov nodded. 'Well, of course; if the Malykant thinks it is murder, then we will have to investigate. I'll let you know if we learn anything useful.'

'Thank you,' Konrad said gratefully. Nuritov's indulgence of Mr. Savast's eccentric interest in detective work was a blessing he could ill do without. 'And now,' he continued, rising from his chair, 'I will go and pay some social calls.'

Nuritov grinned at him. 'Rather you than me.'

Kavara Halim was a woman Konrad preferred, on the whole, to avoid.

Which was a shame, for she was one of the few among Ekamet's society who shared Konrad's gypsy blood. They were a decided minority, and as such, he had hoped at one time to make an ally of her — especially since she was also clever, and witty, and could be good company when she chose.

But she was also a notorious gossip. She had arrived in the city three years ago, and had instantly set about acquainting herself with everyone else's business, with remarkable success. She had a way of uncovering even the most well-guarded secrets — no one knew how — which made her both powerful and dangerous, and Konrad chose to keep himself and his secrets well away from her.

But she could be useful on occasion. He had no need to go from house to house this morning to hear all the gossip on Dominka Popova; he need only go to Mrs. Halim's. Pausing at his own home long enough to collect a particular volume from his library, he called for his carriage and departed at once for Arbat Street.

Mrs. Halim's home was a curious mixture of luxury and rusticity: the hallway of her house was narrow, its walls and floor panelled with aged oak, and strewn with fine silk carpets and colourful pictures. The effect resembled the interior of a caravan, except that everything in it positively dripped wealth. Konrad thought she overdid it, though he could not but applaud her insistence on her own style of decorating rather than merely following the prevailing fashions.

On being shown into Mrs. Halim's drawing-room, he was not at all surprised to find a number of other visitors already present. It was rare indeed to find the lady by herself; she welcomed a continuous stream of callers to her home, for they were her source of news. The decor of her drawing-room was outright exotic; she had actually hung lengths of brightly-coloured silks over the ceiling and the walls, and the lighting was soft and mysterious. It gave her something of the air of a fortune-teller about to make some mystical pronouncement — and Konrad knew very well that all this was part of her appeal. Those who courted her favour saw her as almost prescient, such was the extent of her information.

The lady herself sat in her usual place in the far left corner of the room, from whence she could see everything that occurred around her. She wore a stunning day dress of emerald silk, and her greying black hair was elegantly swept up and hung with gold beads. Her skin was a similar rich brown to Konrad's own, and beside the pale creatures and their pale gowns who occupied her sofas and divans, she shone like a jewel. She was about the age Konrad's mother would be, he judged, had his mother lived.

As Konrad was shown into the room, Mrs. Halim's eyes gleamed in a knowing fashion he found most discomfiting. This, too, was part of her routine; she enjoyed making her visitors believe that she knew all of their secrets already. It encouraged them to talk. He knew this, and yet his natural and inevitable paranoia heightened his tension considerably under the influence of that knowing smile.

He concealed his discomfort behind a smooth bow. Mrs. Halim's guests had fallen silent and observed him with rapt attention; he was

263

so rarely seen in this particular drawing-room, he supposed his appearance held something of the appeal of sighting an exotic bird. He felt the calculation in their gazes, and flinched inwardly. They guessed that something particular must have called him to visit today, and he could almost see the furious workings of their brains as they speculated as to the probable cause.

Konrad ignored them.

'You were kind enough to express an interest in a particular book, last time I had the pleasure of your company,' he murmured, addressing his full attention to Mrs. Halim. 'I'm afraid I have taken the liberty of delivering it in person.' He crossed the room and handed it to her with a polite half-bow.

The lady accepted the book with a gracious nod, and gestured to a seat. She permitted the title of the book to show for a bare instant, satisfying the curiosity of her more alert guests, as she set it down on a side-table. It was a rare title, discussing some obscure folktales from the realms of Assevan, Marja and Kayesir. Konrad possessed some mild curiosity of his own regarding the nature of her interest in that book. She wasn't a noted scholar.

Regardless. He took the proffered seat, accepted a cup of tea and sat back to wait. He considered it unlikely that he would have to reveal his hand so far as to prod the topic of conversation around to Dominka Popova; it being by far the most dramatic thing to happen among Ekamet society in some months, he fully expected to find it the primary subject of discussion across most of the city for a day or two.

And so it proved. One of Mrs. Halim's guests, a grey-haired, stately woman whose name he had forgotten, leaned a little forward and said to him in a low voice: 'Since you are here, Mr. Savast, you must satisfy our curiosity on a very particular point.'

'I shall do my best to oblige,' Konrad murmured.

'Your ball, last night!' she gushed. 'Wonderful evening. Especially for the young people. It was immensely enjoyed by all; I hear of it everywhere.'

That made Konrad feel a little more uncomfortable. She had been at his ball, and he could not remember her name? How shocking of him. He really ought to make more of an effort.

'Now,' she said, lowering her voice still further — for no apparent reason, since she must be overheard; perhaps to heighten the sense of drama. 'I *have heard it said* that you enjoyed some private conversation with Miss Popova last evening.' She leaned back a little, lifting her brows at him. *There*, her look seemed to say. *We have found out your secret.*

'She did favour me with her attention for a short time,' he acknowledged.

'Ahh,' said the lady, in tones of great satisfaction. 'She was to be soon betrothed, you know. You did know that, I presume?'

Her intended implication was hardly subtle. Konrad allowed his lip to curl very slightly, and nodded his head. 'I have heard it mentioned.'

The insufferable woman allowed the silence to stretch, most suggestively, before she appeared to relent and turned a much more kindly look upon him. Too kindly. He was sure she would have patted his knee, even, were it within her reach. 'No matter, Mr. Savast. I only hope you are not too greatly disappointed by... well, by her...'

'Death?' Konrad supplied with a cool smile. 'Her death is a tragedy. But I must urge you, ma'am, not to get too carried away with notions of any understanding between Miss Popova and myself. Really, we were barely acquainted. I believe she sought my study in the hopes of finding it empty; she felt herself in need of a few minutes' respite from the noise and the bustle of the ballroom.'

The woman looked briefly disappointed — and then a cunning look crossed her face, and she nodded, evidently concluding that Mr. Savast's bravado was admirable but that underneath it, he was a disappointed — possibly even heartbroken — man. He sighed inwardly.

'Perhaps your condolences would be better directed to her betrothed?' Konrad suggested. 'A Mr. Kanadin, I believe?'

'Oh, my, yes!' said another woman, much younger than the first. Konrad recognised her as Miss Vadek, though her first name escaped him. She was wearing too much paint on her face, he felt; it gave her face a garish look, exacerbated, unfortunately, by the yellow hue of her gown. 'Poor Mr. Kanadin! I saw him this morning. I never saw a man look so cut up.'

'Nonsense, Ela!' said the older lady sharply. 'Why, you must know they had barely been introduced to one another. He has lost an arranged bride, that is all, and will soon find another.'

Miss Vadek looked crestfallen, though whether at the public rebuke or at the loss of a tragic love story, Konrad could not tell.

The third member of Mrs. Halim's little company, a pretty, sharp-faced woman in her thirties who Konrad knew as Mrs. Eskan, spoke up at last. 'Do not despair, Anya,' she said, directing a sparkling smile at Miss Vadek. 'An arranged marriage? Pish-posh. A mere story, no doubt, put about to conceal a raging love-affair.' She winked at Miss Vadek, who looked considerably cheered by this prospect.

Mrs. Eskan turned her satirical eye upon him. 'You are very quiet, Mr. Savast,' she observed. 'You are quite resolved against sharing any insights with us?'

'I have none to share,' Konrad replied.

'None?' she echoed. 'But after so long a conference with the lady — fully half an hour's conversation, we understand! It very well may be, indeed, that you were the last person to speak with her at all, besides the merest pleasantries.' She took a sip of tea, her manner perfectly composed, but Konrad caught the glint of malice in her eyes.

He sighed inwardly. There were some young ladies who had, at one time or another, set their heart upon marrying the wealthy and influential Mr. Savast, and took his failure to propose to them as a personal slight. Mrs. Eskan had been one such, he dimly recalled, and apparently she still held a grudge against him — in spite of the advantageous marriage she had since made.

He smiled coolly at her. 'If you believe my conversation to be sufficient to drive a woman to suicide, I wonder that you take the risk of inviting it?' he said mildly. 'You have a great many things to live for, Mrs. Eskan, I am sure.'

The wretched woman's eyes glittered balefully at him and she abruptly stood up. 'I regret I must take my leave,' she said to their hostess, who remained silent and watchful in the corner. Mrs. Halim graciously consented to release her, and Mrs. Eskan swept from the room — followed, very shortly, by Miss Vadek and the woman whose name Konrad had forgotten. Mrs. Halim's parlour appeared less gaudy with fewer occupants.

'My apologies,' Konrad said with a regretful little half-bow towards his hostess. 'It was not my intention to scare away your visitors.'

Mrs. Halim graced him with a faint smile, her black eyes alight with amusement. 'Chattering fools, all of them,' she said in her deep voice. 'You made short work of Mrs. Eskan; I must congratulate you. She is usually much more difficult to dislodge.'

'No doubt she has important business elsewhere,' Konrad said smoothly.

'No doubt,' Mrs. Halim agreed.

Konrad hesitated, thinking. What he'd heard from Mrs. Halim's visitors had been mere gossip, he knew, and likely to be unreliable; it was his hostess's knowledge that he truly sought. He had noticed before that she had a remarkable ability to find the rare truths in chatter, and to unearth information that few others knew. But she accomplished this by listening, not by talking, and she had hardly uttered a word since he had arrived. How to broach the topic — without giving away the extent of his interest?

Mrs. Halim watched him with the quiet, intent look of a cat, one of her elegant hands raised to toy with the emerald pendant that hung around her neck. Her stare was unblinking, and too knowing for Konrad's comfort. He felt caught, like a butterfly under glass.

At length, however, she spoke. 'You have an interest in Dominka Popova,' she observed.

So much for his subtleties. 'I do,' he admitted.

'Of what nature?'

Konrad considered his reply carefully. 'When I said we were barely acquainted, I spoke the truth,' he said carefully, 'but nonetheless I am unsettled. I did not require Mrs. Eskan's assistance in order to discover that I may have been the last person to converse with her.'

Mrs. Halim tilted her elegant head, her stare unrelenting. 'It is not the first time I have heard of your making such enquiries,' she said. 'You were involved in that affair with the Rostikovs, were you not? Last year. And then there was the matter of that missing diamond.'

Konrad's heart sank. Curses, the woman really did pay attention. 'I have an enquiring mind,' he replied, with his best attempt at a disarming smile.

'And Inspector Nuritov is kind enough to humour you,' she replied. Her answering smile struck him as more than a little predatory.

'He is very accommodating,' said Konrad.

'What a charming man he must be,' she murmured.

Konrad's smile widened. 'Oh, yes. Quite obliging.'

She eyed him in silence for another long moment, and then, apparently, relinquished her attack. With a soft sigh, and a faint, rueful smile she said: 'I believe it was, indeed, an arranged marriage; Mr. Kanadin sought the connection after a mere few day's acquaintance with Miss Popova.'

Konrad frowned, thrown momentarily off-balance by the swift change of topic. 'Not a love match, then?'

She spread her hands. 'Who can say for sure? But it seems unlikely, do you not think? Unless you are a believer in love at first sight.' Her lips twitched in amusement at the very idea, which Konrad found offensive — though he could not deny that she was right. Of course he did not believe in love at first sight.

'But it was Mr. Kanadin who sought her hand in marriage?'

'According to my information, yes,' said Mrs. Halim. 'Before you ask, no; I do not know why. I do know, however, that her father was reluctant. In fact, I don't believe the engagement was ever announced; it was never more than rumoured.'

Konrad frowned. 'What were Miss Popova's feelings on the matter?'

Mrs. Halim shrugged. 'That is not known to me.'

Konrad nodded slowly, digesting these titbits of news. 'Is there anything else you can tell me?' he asked.

'That is the extent of my information.' Mrs. Halim punctuated this statement by taking up a section of lace that she was tatting, and absorbing herself with the task. Seeing that her confidences were at an end, he rose to his feet and bowed, taking his leave with a few polite words.

'I would advise you to take some care, Mr. Savast,' she said, forestalling his departure. 'Enquiring minds may not always enjoy their discoveries in the end.'

A perfectly redundant warning, Konrad thought, as his mind travelled briefly back over the murders he had solved and the perpetrators he had punished. As if he had ever expected *enjoyment* to come into it — anywhere at all.

He realised, however, that her words conveyed a variety of warnings, and the rest he took to heart. He must certainly endeavour to conceal his movements better. He did not relish the thought that so much of his activities were known to Mrs. Halim. How long would it be before she understood the whole?

He worried over this as he strode away from her house, his collar turned up against the insistent rain and the seeping chill. At length, however, he dismissed the problem from his mind. Miss Popova was his priority, and Mrs. Halim had given him a credible clue. If she had wanted to marry Kanadin but her father had not favoured the match, could that perhaps have driven her to despair? Or perhaps she had been reluctant, and that was *why* her father had not consented to the engagement; there could be little other reason, for Ruslan Kanadin was very wealthy and considered to be a grand matrimonial prize. Either way, none of it seemed, to his mind, to offer explanation enough for her death.

*Master!* hissed Eetapi's funeral-bell voice from deep inside his mind. Konrad started violently, earning a puzzled look from more than one passerby.

*Yes?* he hissed back. *What is it?*

*Mrs. Halim!* carolled the dead serpent. *She has help!*

*What kind of help?*

*Not exactly sure,* mused Eetapi. *It may have been a cat, once.*

*May have been?* Konrad echoed. *When?* He began to get a sinking feeling of inevitability, and could only hope Eetapi hadn't meant what he—

*When it was alive,* Eetapi hissed, confirming his worst fears. *Of course.*

Konrad frowned down at the pavement, ignoring the pedestrians who streamed past either side of him, grumbling at the obstruction. He turned and cast a searching look at Mrs. Halim's tall, colourfully-painted dwelling.

Kavara Halim, a ghostspeaker? How could that be? And how could it be that he had encountered *two* hitherto unknown 'speakers in the space of a single day?

*How did you discover this creature?* he asked his serpent.

*It is most adept at concealing itself, Master,* hissed the snake. *But,* she added proudly, *I am better.*

*Did it see you?* he enquired urgently. If Kavara Halim knew that he, too, kept a spirit familiar, how safe were his remaining secrets?

*No!* hissed Eetapi — somewhat more vehemently than was strictly necessary, Konrad thought irritably, and shook his head to clear the ringing in his ears. *I am unparalleled when it comes to stealth.*

*You mean sneaking,* Konrad muttered.

*Stealth,* repeated Eetapi firmly.

*Very good. Keep it up.* Konrad walked on, and soon drew level with his coach, which stood idle and dripping at the side of the road. *What do you mean, it may have been a cat?* he asked belatedly.

*It is difficult to tell.*

*Why?*

*Because it is decaying.*

Konrad's brows drew together once more, and he paused in the act of stepping into his coach. *Like Popov's crows?*

*Worse,* Eetapi replied.

With a deep sigh, Konrad got into his coach — and stopped abruptly halfway to a seat. Someone else was already inside.

# 4

Nanda sat on the far side of the coach, wrapped in a dark cloak, her back to him as she stared out of the window. A dripping rain bonnet with a wide brim lay discarded on the seat beside her, allowing him to see the intricate braids that tied back her white-blonde hair. She must have heard him enter the coach, but she did not deign to turn around.

'Good morning, Miss Falenia,' he said as he slumped into a seat opposite her and hurled his sopping cloak to the floor.

That got her attention; they had long since abandoned the formal modes of address between them. Her head whipped around, and she frowned mightily at him.

'If you are expecting a curtsey, you will be sorely disappointed,' she snapped.

He grinned. 'No, you are excused — but only because you are in a coach, and there is not space.'

Nanda favoured him with a withering look, and turned her shoulder. He opened his mouth to speak again, but she forestalled him by thrusting a wicker basket at him. It bore a lid, so he could not see what was inside.

'What's this?' he said, blinking.

Nanda put the basket onto his knees and sat back. 'If you take off the lid, you may find that the contents will be revealed.'

'I suppose I might,' Konrad agreed, and whipped the lid off the basket.

Three small cakes nestled inside, coloured in pink, green and blue.

Each one bore floral decorations made from sticky-looking dried fruit; Konrad could smell honey.

He met Nanda's gaze, nonplussed. 'Cakes?'

She shrugged. 'Some people find them pleasant to eat.' She looked a little defensive, as though he had offered some manner of insult.

'Ah,' he murmured. 'Did you make these for me?' the notion was pleasing; he felt a warm glow, radiating from somewhere near his hear—

'No,' said Nanda.

The glow faded.

'Well — I did make them, but they weren't for you.'

'Oh,' said Konrad.

'I made them for Dubin.'

Konrad suppressed an urge to scowl. Dubin was a young and timid apothecary whom Nanda had been seeing altogether too much of. He could not see what they had in common, even, besides their profession.

'Why, then, are you giving them to me?' he said, and held out the basket to her.

She made no move to take it. 'He doesn't eat sugar, as it turns out.'

'Oh.' Konrad cast a doubtful eye over the basket. The colours *were* a little lurid, he couldn't help noticing, and they were somewhat misshapen besides. But Nanda had made them; if she had made them for *him*, he could only have been delighted.

He might still be delighted, he mused, given that he was apparently her second choice for cake presentation. It was not a wholly ignominious station to occupy in her life. But the wicker of the basket was not tightly woven, and the cakes looked more than a little waterlogged.

'The rain has got in upon them, I think?' he said.

Nanda glanced at her handiwork, wrinkled her nose and sighed. 'So it has.' She opened the window, threw the cakes, basket and all, into the street, and slammed the window shut again. Konrad heard a distant splintering sound as the basket was crushed by a passing carriage.

Nanda directed a dazzling smile at him, and sat back comfortably. Konrad winced, and sighed. He should have just taken them, water-soaked or not.

'So!' Nanda said briskly. 'Not a suicide, then? That Popov girl.'

'Master says no,' Konrad replied. 'And also, yes.'

Nanda blinked. 'He what?'

Konrad explained; and then, forestalling her inevitable questions, he told her everything else that he had learned as well.

Nanda nodded thoughtfully, gazing at him with rapt attention, and finally pronounced very gravely, '...hmm.'

'Exactly,' Konrad agreed.

'And so, the gentleman betrothed. I am sure he knows something,' Nanda said wisely. 'Bound to.'

'Bound to,' Konrad echoed. 'But perhaps we could talk a little less about all of that, and a little more about you.'

'Me?' said Nanda innocently.

'Yes. It's been weeks. How are you?'

'I am very well, thank you, Mr. Savast.'

Konrad blinked. 'That's formal.'

Nanda waved a hand. 'You started it. Besides, you are in your gentleman-suit today. What else am I to call you?'

'Konrad used to suffice, as I recall,' Konrad said with a faint smile.

'Konnie? How about Konnie?'

Konrad's smile faded. 'What?'

'Or Rad! Raddie?'

'Ah...' Konrad said faintly. 'Come to think of it, I don't mind Mr. Savast so much after all.'

Nanda grinned at him, and inclined her head with the condescending grace of a duchess. 'I am quite bored,' she said with a serene smile. 'To answer your question.'

'Bored?' Konrad leaned forward. 'My dear Miss Falenia. How could you possibly be bored?'

'I know,' she murmured. 'Stuck in the shop, day in, day out. Mixing up the same cough remedies six times every day, and selling the same old headache powders.'

'Riveting,' Konrad agreed. 'But what of Dubin? Is he not keeping you sufficiently entertained?'

Nanda gave an indifferent shrug and stared out of the window.

Konrad tried, and utterly failed, to suppress a smile of satisfaction.

'Oh! That news pleases you, does it?' Nanda threw something small and solid at his face. Groping after the object in surprise, he discovered it to be a damp twig. 'What kind of friend are you?'

273

'The interesting kind!' said Konrad, laughing. 'You should visit me much more often.'

'For my benefit, or for yours?'

'Both, naturally.'

Nanda squinted suspiciously at him, and shook her head. 'And what are we to do? Am I to sit drinking tea in your drawing-room while we exchange comments upon the weather? Good *heavens,* Konnie, but that is no cure for boredom.'

'Oh,' said Konrad, crestfallen. 'Well — yes, you are quite right — but my hut in the Bones! You are comfortable enough out there, I think?'

'Yes, of course,' Nanda said. 'But,' she added, eyeing him in a manner he found discomfiting, 'are you?'

'I beg your pardon?'

'Do you ever go there, anymore?'

Konrad thought about that. He loved his cramped, primitive little hut. Only out there did he feel like his true self once more, blessedly free of the ridiculous trappings of his masquerade.

But now that he came to think of it... he could not remember the last time he had visited. How could that be?

He could find nothing to say, and unable to bear the expression in her ice-blue eyes — which looked horribly like contempt — he looked instead out of the window at the rain-drenched streets. His top hat felt suddenly too heavy; he tore it off and tossed it impatiently onto the seat beside him.

'You play your role with admirable dedication, Konrad, but do you remember who you really are?' Nanda continued. 'Or *is* this the real you, now?'

Konrad sighed, and allowed his forehead to rest against the cold glass of the window. It was all desperately unfair, he thought; Nanda possessed tremendous power to discomfort him, and wielded it mercilessly if she felt he was in need of a set-down. He never had the slightest success with trying to discomfort her, however; she was impervious to all his attempts, and usually managed to make him look ridiculous into the bargain. It took him too long to come up with a response to this latest sally, and at last Nanda said briskly, 'I shall help you with your case, I think. That will be amusing. And I am intrigued by Mr. Popov and his army of mad crow spirits.'

Konrad took a deep breath, pulled himself together and turned back to Nanda. 'I would be grateful for your help,' he said coolly. 'But I am not sure what to ask of you at the moment.'

'You're seeing this Kanadin fellow, aren't you? I will go with you.' She beamed, her eyes alight with enthusiasm, in another of her mercurial changes of mood. He hadn't the heart to tell her that he couldn't take an ordinary apothecary — a mere shopkeeper — into Ekamet high society.

But Nanda, of course, grasped the problem instantly without any prompting from him. 'Now, who shall I be?' she mused, pursing her lips. 'Lady Prudence Rosewine? Yes, that sounds lovely.'

Konrad choked. 'Maybe something a little less... a little more...' He floundered.

'The Honourable Anastacia Laverna Merryweather?'

Konrad returned only a blank stare, and Nanda slumped in her seat. 'You are no fun at all,' she said sulkily.

Konrad folded his arms.

'Fine, fine. I shall be Miss Everna Ejan, your distant cousin from Marja.'

'My cousin,' said Konrad flatly. He eyed her white skin, pale blue eyes and white-blonde hair; they could not be more different from his own swarthy colouring and dark hair and eyes.

'*Distant* cousin,' she repeated. 'It's perfect! You will help me find suitable garments, of course.'

'You're being very inconsistent, Nan,' he complained. 'First you chastise me for spending so much time play-acting as a wealthy gentleman and now you want to join me.'

'Not at all,' she said serenely. 'I have no intention of play-acting as a wealthy gentleman.'

Konrad rolled his eyes. 'You know what I mean.'

She shrugged. 'There must be something extremely amusing about it all, or you would not be so wholly absorbed by it. I intend to find out what it is. Besides,' she added with a smile, 'consistency renders one *so* predictable.'

Konrad gave up. He was secretly delighted at the prospect of having her along; not only would her presence enliven the proceedings considerably, but she was also a Reader. Her occasional glimpses into the minds of others had proved useful in the past, and this case was bristling with secrets.

And besides. What she proposed sounded like it might be... well, a little bit... fun.

So he reclaimed his hat, restored it to his head, and made Nanda a small, seated bow. 'Miss Ejan,' he murmured. 'It shall be my pleasure.'

She smiled delightedly, apparently in perfect charity with him again. For a moment he toyed with the idea of confiding in her; in his account of the case so far, he had left out all reference to his sister, or the alarming ways in which his supposedly stifled feelings were intruding upon him. But as he opened his mouth to speak, a sensation of acute discomfort swallowed whatever he had been about to say, and he closed it again.

He did not, he realised, want to admit any of those things to Nanda. There lay behind it all a story he had no wish to impart to her — or, indeed, to anybody; he could not even bear to think of it himself. She thought poorly enough of him as it was, or so it seemed; he could not bear to lower himself any further in her eyes. He would maintain his usual professionalism, and hide all the difficult, uncomfortable, shameful things that were troubling him. And hope that these inconvenient surges of emotion would simply go away.

A few hours later, Nanda stood resplendent in a daring day dress of striped carmine silk with a great many petticoats. A wide-brimmed hat was perched atop her elegantly coiled locks, its crown adorned with an implausibly large, ruby-red plume. Her feet were shod in high-heeled satin boots. She had borrowed one of his canes and stood posing with it in the centre of his drawing-room, her chin high and a satisfied smile curving her lips.

'Excellent,' said Konrad, casting an eye over her attire. 'You look exactly the thing. Shall we go?'

Nanda's smile disappeared. 'Is that it?'

'Is what it?'

'You must have *something* to say about my gown.' She smoothed her skirts and fixed him with a severe look, one pale eyebrow raised.

'It is very expensive,' Konrad offered.

'And beautiful! Expensive and beautiful!'

'It is very beautiful,' Konrad agreed, though privately he felt that the strong colour and loud pattern rendered it a trifle lurid. Since Nanda still looked dissatisfied, he added, 'It, um, suits you.'

Nanda made a disgusted noise and swept past him. He could only follow after, wondering helplessly what she had expected him to say.

There followed some complications as Nanda attempted to get into the carriage. Unused to the sheer *volume* of a fashionable lady's dress, she mishandled her skirts deplorably and became wedged in the doorway. Attempting to follow her into the carriage, Konrad received a faceful of carmine silk and was obliged to spend some few minutes disentangling her. They gained the seats at last; Konrad concealed a grin as Nanda perched most carefully on the edge of hers, a picture of discomfort.

'I am not entirely sure that I like this gentry-business after all,' she said with a frown.

'You'll get used to it.' Konrad smiled, and began to laugh as she shot him a poisonous glare.

'I feel like a perambulating couch,' she muttered, and Konrad laughed even harder.

Mr. Ruslan Kanadin was at home, to Konrad's relief. If ever there was an unassailable reason to be 'not at home' to visitors, a recent bereavement would certainly qualify. But the maid who opened the door conducted them straight upstairs to Mr. Kanadin's exquisitely furnished drawing-room, and the master of the house arrived mere moments later. Kanadin was a man of moderate height and unprepossessing appearance, with light brown hair, a thin moustache and a lean frame. He was exquisitely dressed, as always, and his manner the height of civilised urbanity as he made his bow to them both.

'Mr. Savast,' said Kanadin, approaching to shake Konrad's hand. 'What a pleasure, sir. I admit I was not expecting such eminent company. I suppose you have come to convey condolences? How kind.'

Konrad murmured something in the assent, but quickly realised that Kanadin was not listening; his attention had wandered to Nanda.

'Madam,' he said with another, lower bow. 'I confess myself dazzled. Whom do I have the honour of addressing?' His eyes lingered on Nanda's gown, Konrad noted, but he could not guess what the man was thinking. Was it the boldness of the design he noticed, or the fineness of the silk? Or was he actually daring to appreciate the admittedly intriguing way in which Nanda filled it out? A scowl gathered on Konrad's brow, and he was obliged to take a deep breath to smooth it away.

'This is my cousin,' Konrad said. 'My *distant* cousin, from Marja. M-miss...' His mind went blank; he had almost said *Prudence Rosewine*. What name had she finally settled upon? Ev — Ej — something... he turned his hesitation into a mild coughing fit.

'Ejan,' Nanda said smoothly, when Konrad had spluttered his way to silence. 'Miss Everna Ejan, from Marja.' She curtseyed.

'Sorry,' Konrad croaked.

'Miss Ejan. So delighted,' said Kanadin, and carried Nanda's hand to his lips. Konrad watched this with satisfaction, until he noticed that Nan had forgotten to take off her gloves. If there was no direct physical contact, he was fairly sure her skills as a Reader would be impeded. Nanda realised this at the same moment, and a flicker of acute annoyance crossed her face, quickly replaced with a dazzling smile.

'Oh, Mr. Kanadin!' she gushed. Konrad was startled to hear a pronounced Marjan accent, which she never usually displayed. 'I really must apologise for the timing of this introduction — to impose upon you at such a time! It really is quite the rudest — but when I heard the news, you know, I *could not rest* until I had expressed my very deepest sympathies to you *in person*. Indeed, I could not; I slept not a wink, all last night, for thinking of it. And dear Konrad felt exactly as I did — did you not, Konrad dear? — for he is a sensitive fellow. You would not think it to look at him, but it is true. My dear sir, will you allow me to tell you how very, *very* sorry I am?' Nanda gave him a tremulous smile — her eyes were actually shining with unshed tears — and sighed deeply.

At some point during this speech she had managed to divest herself of one of her gloves, and she now gripped Mr. Kanadin's hand in both of her own.

Kanadin looked, Konrad thought, somewhat nonplussed at this gushing speech. 'Ah — so kind of you, truly — terrible news — awful shock — quite cut up — my poor Dominka —' He stuttered and floundered his way to a stop, and made a futile attempt to withdraw his hand. Nanda's grip grew white-knuckled, even as a single tear trickled down her cheek.

'I never had the pleasure of meeting the young lady,' Nanda continued, her lip wobbling theatrically. 'I shall, I am sure, regret it *forever*. What was she like?'

'Oh,' said Kanadin, blinking at Nanda in a dazed fashion. 'Oh, she — well — very charming young woman, of course — quite lovely — I am sorry you did not know her, Miss Ejan.'

Nanda nodded sympathetically. 'Such a terrible business,' she crooned. 'Of course, she cannot have been an especially happy young lady, can she? Considering that — well. You know.'

Konrad winced at the impropriety of Nanda's comments, even as he admired her technique. He could never have asked such questions of Kanadin himself. Nanda's beauty, splendour and apparent emotion allowed her to get away with it, however; Kanadin looked mildly displeased, but not offended, and with only a slight frown he replied: 'Indeed, there were times when she did not seem entirely —'

'Oh, tragic, tragic,' Nanda sighed. 'Had that been going on for very long? It must have been *so* hard to bear — to see someone you love suffering in that way.'

Konrad watched Kanadin's face and saw a flicker of some emotion in his eyes, soon concealed.

'Very terrible,' he agreed gravely. His composure, Konrad thought, was remarkable for a man so recently bereft of his wife-to-be. But something lay behind it, he was sure. His manner was too polished, too perfectly serene; it had to be an act, surely?

Or perhaps not. But if he had really felt nothing for Dominka, why had he sought the engagement? He needed nothing from her family; she could bring him neither money nor connections that he required. It was a puzzling business. Konrad could only hope that Nanda had glimpsed something more useful.

Kanadin's confidences appeared to be at an end; his expression had turned closed, his manner slightly wary. Nanda realised it too, for she released his hand. 'Very well, and now we must go,' she said brightly, donning her gloves once more, and stepped smartly towards the door. 'Many other calls of a similar nature to pay.'

Kanadin looked as startled as Konrad felt. Konrad had time only for a bow and brief expression of the condolences before he was obliged to follow Nanda out of the room.

'That was hasty,' he admonished once they had regained their carriage.

'Job done, no time to waste,' she said, beaming. 'And what a result! You will be amazed to know that Mr. Kanadin is in love, but *not* with Dominka Popova.'

Konrad's brows went up. 'Oh? With who, then?'

'Not sure. He just thinks of her as Ana. And I couldn't find out why he was engaged to Dominka, in that case.'

'Not money, anyway,' Konrad said. 'He's far richer than the Popovs.'

'Well, this woman. Ana. He seemed fixated upon her. Every time I spoke of Dominka, he thought of Ana instead.'

'Hm,' Konrad thought. 'Maybe this Ana is poor, or of low birth. But what should that matter? He's rich enough to marry whomever he chooses.' He frowned, turning the problem over in his mind, but could find no solution that made sense.

Nanda tapped a finger against her cheek, biting her lip, but offered nothing more decided than, 'Mm.'

'Did you pick up anything else?' Konrad enquired.

Nanda slouched down in her seat and sighed. 'This gown is so uncomfortable, Konnie,' she muttered by way of answer. 'How do people bear it, all day?'

Konrad suppressed a smile. 'You can take it off soon. What else did you see?'

Nanda bit absently at the tip of one expensive lace glove as she thought. 'Whenever Dominka's name was mentioned, he thought of Ana, and he also experienced a surge of emotions... I couldn't determine what they all were. Something unpleasant, like resentment, perhaps. Regret. Anger. Even a little fear.'

Konrad's brows rose. 'Now, why would a man consent to — and maintain — an engagement with a woman he resented? Her father isn't as wealthy as all that. And fear? Anger? What could he possibly be afraid of, or angry with, regarding Dominka Popova? She seemed harmless to me.'

Nanda eyed the hole she had created in her glove with distaste. 'We need more information about Dominka,' she decided. 'And the Popov family.' She considered. 'Is there a Mrs. Popov? A mother?'

'Died years ago.'

'Well, then, we must resort to that ever-reliable source of society news.'

'That being?'

Nanda's eyes brightened as she pronounced, 'The society papers!'

Konrad grimaced. 'Not *those*. Anything but those!'

'Now, now,' Nanda said soothingly. 'I know they are the very worst thing in the world, but they are also *quite* informative. Everything to do with anybody who is *anyone at all* in Society will be in there somewhere. Gossip galore. It's perfect. And I happen to know someone who is wild about them; collects every issue of every remotely reputable magazine, and some of the less respectable ones, too.'

'Are their reports not somewhat exaggerated?' Konrad objected. 'I can hardly imagine them to be a reliable source of news.'

'Oh, certainly. But even the wildest story often has a kernel of truth hidden somewhere inside. They may turn up something useful.'

'Very well. Good suggestion.' Konrad smiled, and hesitated. 'Ah... do they ever report about me?'

Nanda's eyes sparkled with mischief. 'Oh, yes. You are a *very* popular topic.'

'I... I am? Why?'

'Two words,' Nanda said. She had removed her gloves altogether, and now sat idly inspecting her fingernails with an air of innocence he found highly suspicious. 'Eligible. Bachelor.'

Konrad groaned, and sagged in his seat.

Nanda laughed, and threw her ruined glove at him. 'The man faces down death with nary a quiver, but show him a horde of husband-hunting Mamas and he quakes in his boots!'

'So would you,' Konrad retorted, glowering.

'Nonsense. I would be perfectly capable of handling it.'

Probably true, Konrad thought glumly. He eyed her. 'How do you know what they write about me?'

Nanda actually looked uncomfortable. 'Um, by report. Sometimes I hear of one or two things...'

Konrad folded his arms and stared her down.

'All right, all right,' she muttered. 'Everna saves all the bits about Mr. Konrad Savast for me. I asked her to.'

'Everna?'

'My name inspiration had to come from somewhere.'

Konrad eyed her, torn between confusion and pleasure. He liked the idea that she collected his press cuttings; it implied a hitherto unsuspected interest in his doings. On the other hand, he shuddered to think what kinds of nonsense — most of it untrue, or so he hoped — those papers might be reporting about his lifestyle. Perhaps *this* was why she had come to disapprove of it.

It was not a problem for today, however. He had greater issues to attend to. 'Anyway,' he said decisively. 'If you would consult the gossip, I would be grateful; do let me know what you discover, as soon as possible.'

Nanda nodded. 'What will you be doing?'

'Hmm.' Konrad thought for a moment. 'I agree with you that the Popov family's circumstances and doings may be very important. It is Mr. Popov that interests me the most. I intend to find out more about these crows of his — and what he does with them.'

Nanda's brows rose. 'Oh? But you visited him before, to no avail. How do you intend to get answers out of him now?'

'The old-fashioned detective way,' Konrad said with a faintly wicked smile. 'I shall engage in a spot of Snooping.'

'Breaking and entering?' Nanda said, beaming. 'Sneaking around in the dark? Poking into dark corners and reading other people's correspondence?'

'Possibly.'

Nanda sighed, and drooped visibly. 'That is so much more interesting than reading chatty gossip magazines.'

'I'm sorry, but there can be no question of taking you with me. It is far too dangerous.'

Nanda eyed him sourly, but made no objection. 'Someday,' she growled, 'you are going to have to make it up to me.'

'Someday, we will have a truly epic sneaking session together,' he promised. 'We will break into many houses, snoop through a great deal of correspondence and poke about in a lot of dark corners. But not today.'

Nanda sniffed, and turned to look out of the window.

*Eetapi*, Konrad said silently. *Ootapi.*

The serpents, dozing hitherto in some quiet corner of his mind, sprang to attention.

*I need Popov watched,* he instructed. *Every moment of the day and night, please, until something emerges.*

*Yes, Master.* The serpents streamed away out of the window, quickly fading from Konrad's senses.

*Watch out for the crows!* he called after them. He received, by way of reply, only a distant sense of derision from Ootapi and outright contempt from Eetapi.

Well, they were flighty. They needed reminding, sometimes.

# 5

Konrad spent the rest of the afternoon trying to devise some way of sneaking into the Popov house without being detected, either by Popov himself or by his army of crows.

He failed. Whatever the purpose of those birds might be, they served as excellent guards. It would take nothing short of an all-out assault on the house's ghost-guardians to get him inside, and that was hardly the definition of stealth.

Towards the end of the afternoon, however, he received word from Nuritov by way of a note.

*Questioned Popov,* it read. *Gained little by it, I'm afraid, save more suspicions. Popov is adamant that his daughter's death was by her own desire, and not murder — whatever the Malykant may think. Seemed a touch derisive on that point. Wouldn't say how or why he's so sure, however, and clammed up mightily when I asked him about the rest of the family — tried to throw me out, too! Suspicious, wouldn't you say? I've got a recruit doing some digging on that. Will let you know how it goes, but I don't hold out much hope.*

Konrad read the note a few times over, thinking. He'd hoped Popov might have been more forthcoming with a police inspector, though he wasn't altogether surprised to find that he had not. He had to agree with Nuritov, though: his silences were becoming more revealing than conversation might have been. Why should he be so touchy on the topic of his family? And how could he be so dismissive of the idea that his daughter's death had been murder? Perhaps he had known that she intended suicide; as a parent, though, he ought to have done everything he could to prevent it, and he had not even accompanied her to Konrad's ball. Konrad felt another flash of anger on Dominka's behalf. For an unhappy young woman to be so abandoned by her father was intolerable. Even now, after her death, Mr. Popov refused to co-operate, refused to listen, refused to assist even the police. Could this be the result of grief, Konrad wondered? Anger and denial were common enough, but he had not seen so much as a flicker of sorrow in Popov's face. If he was a grieving parent, his self-control was remarkable.

He folded up the note and tucked it away in his waistcoat. Nanda would take care of the questions regarding the Popov family; he had no doubt that she would return, in time, with a sheaf of notes on that score. The gossip papers were so reliably intrusive.

Konrad was interested in Nuritov's aside regarding the Malykant. Popov had been derisive, had he? Why? Put together with his status as a ghostspeaker, that was interesting indeed.

It was high time he found out more about Popov's secrets. He had time before the serpents were likely to return; time enough, he hoped, to pay a visit to Diana.

Diana Valentina was a baker. Renowned for the perfection of her pastries, hers was an extremely popular establishment in the heart of Ekamet. Her premises were tiny, and consequently, always crowded. She spotted Konrad as soon as he entered her shop; he could tell by the tiny, crooked smile that curved her lips as she wrapped up a quartet of tiny white cakes for her next customer. But she made him wait, damn her, until she had served every customer in the shop before turning at last to him.

'Come into the back,' she said, dusting the flour from her hands. Konrad obediently followed her into the shop's tiny back room. Equipped as it was with two stone ovens on full blast, it was suffocatingly hot, and he resisted the temptation to strip off his coat immediately.

There was a long, high wooden counter at the back, topped with granite: Diana spent many hours here, rolling pastry and mixing batter. She sat down at a high stool adjacent to it, inviting him to take the other, and slid a warm pastry towards him. It was crusted with sugar and dotted with fruit, and he accepted it gratefully, suddenly aware of his hunger. When had he last remembered to eat?

'All's well with the Order?' he said, around a mouthful of flaky pastry.

'Mhm, perfectly,' she nodded. 'This is not a catch-up call, though, I imagine. Is it the Popov matter?'

He nodded, smiling inwardly at both her forthright manner and her perceptiveness. She was not even thirty, he judged; a pretty young woman, with her dark, curly hair and rounded figure. She was surprisingly young and harmless-looking for the position she occupied, which happened to be at the head of The Malykt's Order. Even Konrad was fooled, sometimes, watching her merrily at work in her bakery; but to talk to her was to understand exactly how she had risen so far.

Konrad explained in full about Dominka Popova's death, and The Malykt's confusing judgement thereupon. Diana nodded as though she knew of it already, which she probably did.

'We've known about Popov's abilities for some time,' she said when he'd finished, 'though he is, indeed, unregistered with the Order and appears to be unaware that we know about it.' She smiled briefly. 'He fancies his activities very well-hidden and has become rather cocky, I think; very cocky, if he has indeed moved his crows into his town house.'

Konrad nodded. 'He let me see them, too, which interested me.' He showed her Nuritov's note, pointing out in particular the comment about the Malykant. 'Any idea why he might feel that way about me?'

Diana surveyed him, her eyes narrowed. 'Does he know your identity?'

'I hope not,' Konrad said, appreciatively licking the remnants of his pastry from his fingers. Diana slid him another, which he fell upon with gusto. 'I can't be sure. That's partly why I'm here.'

Diana shrugged. 'I don't know of any leak there, but I can enquire.'

Konrad smiled his thanks, and took another bite of pastry. She really was the best baker in Ekamet, he thought, his eyes closing involuntarily as his mouth filled with buttery pastry and sugar. Dangerous stuff. He opened his eyes to find Diana watching him with amusement.

'Sorry,' he said. 'It's good.'

285

Diana nodded once. 'I know.'

He grinned, and devoured the rest in two bites. 'Well, anyway. If he knows who I am, I'd like to know; especially if he's got some kind of problem with the Malykant. How far do his abilities go, do we know?'

'Not all that far,' Diana said. 'He can manipulate ghosts, but he's not all that good at it — as you may imagine, from the state of those poor birds. I don't think he can communicate clearly with them. We made some covert overtures in the past — he ought to be trained, of course — but his negative opinion of the Malykant seems to extend to the entire Order, and he was unresponsive. So, we keep him discreetly monitored.'

'He takes it very seriously, though,' Konrad observed. 'His ghosts, I mean. What I saw was probably the work of years, and who knows what else he has hidden away?'

'Not me, anyway,' Diana said. 'We keep an eye on him, but he's never been under direct surveillance.'

Konrad nodded. 'The serpents are watching him at the moment; they might uncover something.'

Diana brightened. 'And how are the dear things?'

'The serpents?' Konrad said, surprised that anybody could consider them "dear". 'They are their usual grumpy, psychotic, disturbing, creepy little selves, I believe.'

Diana grinned. 'No further threats to resign?'

Konrad blinked. 'You knew about that?'

'Oh, yes. I had Ootapi here every day for a while, threatening all manner of dire consequences if I didn't find him alternative employment.'

Konrad smiled sheepishly. 'Er. Those problems have been resolved.'

Diana's smile turned sunny. 'How marvellous.'

Konrad wondered, a trifle uneasily, how much Ootapi had told her of Konrad's state at the time. Probably everything, he thought, with some embarrassment. He felt obscurely uncomfortable to think that Diana was fully aware of the weaknesses he'd shown.

'What of Kavara Halim?' he said, suddenly remembering. 'The serpents said she's also got some spirit help.'

'She's registered,' Diana confirmed. 'Virtually inept, though. I feel terribly sorry for that poor creature she's bound to herself, but she won't be parted from it.'

'The cat?'

'So it was once. A favoured pet, and she refused to let it go. Her binding was terrible, though, and the poor thing degenerated a long way before anybody knew what she'd done. We've stabilised it as best we can, but the mind's mostly gone.'

Konrad winced. Ghosts could be disturbing enough to be around even when their minds were sound, as the serpents daily demonstrated; insane animal ghosts were something else altogether. Which made him wonder anew that Popov could bear to be surrounded by them.

There came the clatter of the shop's front door opening and shutting, and the sound of quick footsteps crossing the room. 'Baker?' a voice called.

Diana stood up, dusting off her apron. 'Was that everything?' she enquired.

Konrad nodded, and rose also. 'For now. Thank you.'

Diana nodded too, but she didn't leave at once. 'Are you all right, Konrad?' she enquired, her face and tone grave.

'Perfectly,' he said, with his best smile. If she was referring to his lapse of a few months ago, then yes; he was fully recovered. Of course. Unless she was talking about the sudden re-emergence of his long-stifled emotions; but how could she know about any of that? She could not. It was impossible. But a little flurry of anxiety leaked through to disturb his composure anyway. What if The Malykt had deliberately withdrawn His protection? What if they had all decided that Konrad was no longer fit to serve as the Malykant, and he was being herded out? Diana would know, if so, and perhaps that was the reason behind her searching questions. What would become of him, if they were displeased? He barely suppressed a shiver at these alarming thoughts, which was absurd. He had never been prone to anxiety before. Everything was assailing him at once, he thought gloomily, and of course it was all the *negative* emotions he was obliged to put up with. He couldn't have experienced a sudden surge of pure joy, or love, or excitement. That was not The Malykt's way.

Diana stared into his face for a long moment, and he felt himself under the closest — and most alarmingly perceptive — scrutiny. He waited, trying to be calm, until she nodded and abandoned her inspection. 'You've been seeing Miss Falenia?' she said.

Startled, Konrad nodded awkwardly and said: 'Nanda? I... yes, of course, but why should you ask me that?'

Diana blinked at him in surprise. 'But do you not know who she is?'

'She's my friend,' Konrad said, uncertain. 'What else are you—'

'BAKER!' called the voice from the next room, feminine and strident and most unwilling to be ignored. Diana frowned in confusion, but said nothing further; she merely nodded a courteous farewell and disappeared back into her shop. Looking down, Konrad found she had tucked a third, napkin-wrapped pastry into his hands.

Perhaps he looked as though he wasn't eating enough, he reflected, dropping the pastry into the largest pocket of his coat. He left the shop, frowning, her last words echoing in his mind. *Do you not know who she is?*

What was Nanda to Diana Valentina, head of The Malykt's Order? He had not known they were acquainted; and if they were, he would have said only as shopkeepers, with premises located not too terribly far from one another. Did Nanda have some kind of secret identity, too? Was she, like Diana, only a shopkeeper on the surface, and something else besides?

If so, what in the world might she be doing? And why hadn't she told him?

Konrad resigned himself to a sleepless night, and settled down in his darkened study with a glass of whiskey and a good fire. He could not rest while he awaited the return of his serpents, and any news they might bring; besides which, he felt too unsettled. The interlude gave him a period of quiet, within which to consider all the facts, theories and revelations of the case so far.

He had not yet gleaned sufficient information to draw any solid conclusions, but there was a great deal to interest him. His instincts told him that Vadim Popov and his unsanctioned dabbling in the spirit realms was significant, but he was not sure how. Meanwhile, there was the matter of Kanadin, who appeared remarkably unconcerned about the death of Dominka, and whose thoughts turned obsessively around a woman called Ana. Why had he sought the engagement?

And Mrs. Halim? She had behaved as though she knew something particular about the Popov matter. This wasn't unusual, as she affected the same about every event of any importance in Ekamet; but what if it was significant? Did she have some connection with Popov? The fact that they were both practising spirit-binding in barely tolerated ways could hardly be a coincidence, he thought, but then, stranger coincidences had occurred.

Konrad had reached that stage of the case where, he felt, the acquisition of one or two key pieces of information would be enough to resolve all of his questions. At the moment, though, he had no real leads to follow up himself; he must wait, patiently, upon the revelations of others.

Patience was not one of his particular talents. By the time his serpents finally returned, it was three in the morning and he had taken to pacing up and down in front of his dying fire.

Serpent, in fact, as it was only Eetapi who came streaming through the crack in his window and materialised before him. *Master!* she hissed, in tones of great excitement. *You must accompany me at once!*

Konrad needed no second invitation. Within minutes he had donned his hat and coat and yanked open his front door, heedless of the noise; but he taken no more than a single step before Eetapi interrupted him.

*No!* she hissed forcefully. *Not those silly clothes! We are going into the Bones.*

Konrad shut the door again and launched himself at the stairs, taking them two at a time.

*It is wet,* added Eetapi helpfully as she trailed after him.

*Thank you,* Konrad replied gravely as he changed his attire. Away went the "silly" tight trousers and coat, the fine shirt with its voluminous sleeves, his favourite cravat and the shiny top-boots. In their place he donned, with feelings of exquisite relief, his old, sturdy, waxed trousers and waxed leather coat, with a thick cotton shirt beneath, and a pair of enormous, solid, water-proof boots which horrified his finer sensibilities. Last of all he donned his wide-brimmed rain hat, and with a sigh of contentment he left his luxurious mansion and stepped into the rainy street. Eetapi sailed on ahead, her ghostly form flickering eerily in the dripping darkness, and Konrad followed.

The Bone Forest was so-called because of the unusual appearance of its closely-crowded trees. They were very tall, very slender and very white; their jutting branches clawed at the sky like bones, flayed of all flesh and bleached pale. When the moon shone, they glowed an unearthly white; this ghostly effect, combined with the marshy, treacherous terrain, kept most people away from the forest, but Konrad loved it. He could not even have said why, precisely, but to him, such factors as isolation, cold, wet, darkness, and ghostly eeriness were decided recommendations.

Tonight, alas, thick clouds covered the sky and hid the pale light of the moon. The Bone trees loomed above Konrad, dark and dripping, surrounding him with the scent of soaked wood and mud and fresh, damp air. He smiled as he walked. Eetapi was moving at a great speed, and he adopted the peculiar, implausible stride of his office as he followed: the ground fell away beneath his feet, each step covering the distance of some five or six, and the Bones streamed rapidly past, blurring in his vision as he walked.

Soon, Eetapi began to slow, and her voice rang in his thoughts once more. *Popov has a lair,* she explained, *like yours. And we are almost there.*

*It is not a lair,* he objected, injured. *That makes it sound thoroughly nefarious.*

*Well, isn't it?* demanded the snake. *You harvest and prepare poisons in there. Talk to — and bind — ghosts. Lurk about by yourself, thinking dark thoughts. All very suspicious.*

Konrad had no answer to make to that, since it was all perfectly true. He was obliged to content himself with a terrible scowl, which Eetapi did not see.

*There,* she added a minute or two later, her voice in his thoughts dropping to the barest whisper. *See it?*

Konrad stared. He did *not* see it, whatever it was; his straining eyes saw only more bone-white trees.

*The ladder,* Eetapi hissed in disgust.

Ah. He saw it then, a length of dark rope swaying gently in the wind. Popov's "lair", then, was high up in the trees. Brave of him, Konrad thought absently; those slender trees hardly looked able to support a single climber, let alone any kind of dwelling, and they swayed alarmingly when the wind rose. He had considered such a structure himself, and had settled on stilts as a preferable alternative.

*Is he there now?* Konrad enquired of Eetapi.

*Yes,* the serpent replied. *Ootapi is watching him. We will wait here until he leaves.*

*Yes, ma'am,* Konrad said, earning himself an irritable twitch of the tail in his general direction.

*There is no way for you to sneak up on him up there,* she snapped. *Unless you have learned to fly?*

*What is he doing up there?*

*Binding another crow,* said Eetapi, with hissing disapproval.

*Another one? Is he killing them?*

*Not exactly. He spent a while roaming the Bones until he found an injured crow. Then he brought it back here and snapped its neck, and tried to bind it. He was doing that when I came to fetch you.*

Konrad mulled that over. Popov's behaviour made no better sense now than it had before. What was the wretched man doing, roaming the Bones when he should be asleep, abducting wounded birds and mucking about with their spirits?

It occurred to him that Popov might be mad. Searching for sense or consistency in the actions of an insane person was a futile endeavour. Perhaps he was obsessed; with crows, and with his own prowess (such as it was) as a ghostspeaker. Perhaps he had no particular purpose in mind at all.

On the other hand, perhaps he did.

Konrad's back began to cramp, crouched as he was in the dark and the damp. *Any idea how long he will be?* Konrad enquired of Eetapi.

There followed a few moments' silence while she conferred, he assumed, with Ootapi. *No idea at all,* she returned helpfully.

*Excellent.* Konrad sighed, and tried to make himself more comfortable. What precisely was he waiting for, anyway? Would it be better to follow Popov, when he finally emerged, or take the opportunity to examine his treetop dwelling?

He was not given long to consider this question. Ootapi's splintered-ice voice knifed suddenly through his mind, gifting him with an instant headache. *Master! Quickly! He is trying to bind himself!*

Bind himself? To what? To the body of a living crow? Konrad's mind recoiled in horror at the idea. *But, Ootapi, he would have to be —*

*Dead, yes. He has a knife.*

Oh.

Konrad erupted from his hiding-place and made a dash for the ladder. He swarmed up it in seconds, trying to ignore the alarming way it swung under his weight. A precariously-positioned treehouse

291

of pale wooden planks came gradually into view above, with a trapdoor gaping open in its floor. Konrad hurled himself through this opening and hauled himself into the building.

Like his own, it consisted of a single room. It was at least as crowded as his own hut, too, although with altogether different things. Like the Popov house in Ekamet, it bore a significant complement of living, soul-bound crows, clustered in groups atop perches near the ceiling. It also boasted an equal number of dead, stuffed crows staring eerily down from the walls, and such an assortment of knives as Konrad had never before seen.

Vadim Popov stood nearby, a small knife clutched in one hand. The sleeve of his great-coat was rolled up and he appeared to be in the process of opening the veins in his wrist. His eyes fixed upon Konrad with a cold, baleful rage and he actually snarled, a deep, tearing animal sound.

'Stop!' Konrad shouted, and lunged. Popov jabbed with the knife; Konrad caught it and flicked it away, hoping the man had not had time to do himself any significant damage. Perhaps not, for Popov instantly whirled and caught up another knife. The room was full of them; Konrad couldn't disarm him of them all. Instead, he hurled himself at Popov's legs, bringing the man crashing down. The knife fell from his fist and clattered across the floor.

*Bind him!* Konrad called to his serpents. It was both difficult and risky to take control of a living soul, even temporarily, but if it was the only way to prevent Popov's suicide, he would have to try it. He clung grimly to his prey as Popov kicked and writhed and punched in his efforts to throw off his assailant.

*Quickly!* Konrad howled, as Popov's flailing fists bounced off his head. Suddenly he had a knife in his hand again, aimed at Konrad's head. The knife stabbed down...

...and stopped as Popov's body abruptly relaxed. Warily, Konrad loosened his grip and sat up.

Popov didn't move.

'Thank you,' Konrad said out loud. He stared at Popov's blank face, wondering. 'Speak to me,' he commanded. 'What were you doing?'

'*Binding the self,*' Popov replied, his voice faint and strained.

'What do you mean by that?'

Popov's face twisted with some kind of anguish. '*Humanity,*' he growled. '*Flawed. Weak. I seek to transcend.*'

Transcend? Konrad frowned down at Popov's inert form. He'd never before heard of anybody viewing the life of an animal as *transcendence* of the human form — more the opposite. Animals were much simpler creatures, on the whole, though there were exceptions; his serpents proved that.

'Why do you feel that way?' Konrad asked him.

'*Do we not prove it daily?*'

Not much of an answer, Konrad thought. He decided to switch tactics. 'Tell me about Dominka.'

Popov's anguish increased, and a deep shudder ran through his restrained body. '*Do not ask me,*' he begged. '*I cannot speak of her.*'

Konrad frowned. Here was a truer sign of grief than he had ever yet seen from Popov; perhaps he had loved his daughter, after all. But why had he not co-operated with the police, even if he hadn't trusted Konrad? Why had he been so secretive? He was an intelligent man; he must realise that his obstinacy obstructed the investigation, and retarded the prospect of justice. 'You must speak of her,' he said sternly. 'It is painful, but it is necessary.'

Popov opened his mouth, and Konrad grew hopeful. But long seconds ticked by in silence as Popov's shuddering increased, and at length he emitted nothing but a wordless howl of misery. His body shook so violently Konrad began to be afraid he would harm himself.

*Make him sleep,* he instructed the serpents. It took a few moments, but Popov's tortured body finally relaxed once more, and his eyes closed.

Konrad sighed with mingled relief and chagrin. Why did the man have to be so cursed difficult? Konrad didn't want to believe him capable of harming his daughter — indeed, after such a display of grief, it seemed increasingly unlikely that he would have — but in his experience, the degree of caginess, secrecy and antagonism Popov had shown usually indicated that there was something to hide. If he couldn't get him to talk, even under compulsion, how could he ever determine what it was?

Konrad turned his back on the prostrate man, and conducted a quick search of the room. He found nothing of interest save yet more knives and stuffed crows, and a couple of nests tucked away in dark corners. Until, that is, he opened a crude drawer in an equally crude desk and found a single item inside: a painting.

He lifted it out. It was a portrait in miniature, fitting easily into the palm of his hand. Depicted in oils was Dominka Popova. It had been painted several years ago, he judged, for she appeared to be perhaps fifteen or sixteen years old. He had seen no family tokens whatsoever at the Popov house in Ekamet; what was this one doing, tucked away out of sight in a rickety tree-house out in the Bones? It was as though Popov could not bear to put it out in plain sight, but nor could he bear to part with it.

Konrad stared at the image for some moments, thinking. The girl looked well, and happy, though that was not necessarily any indication of her true state of mind at the time; the painter might have taken some artistic license in its composition. Still, he was encouraged by the idea that she had once been a blooming, high-spirited young girl. What had happened to change that?

He turned back to consider the sleeping man on the floor. Popov couldn't be left here; he would have his veins opened in minutes, and whether or not he succeeded in strapping his miserable soul to the body of some poor bird, he would still be dead.

*Lift him up and bring him along,* Konrad instructed, and the serpents obeyed. Popov's body rose into the air and began to hover. As Konrad climbed back down the ladder into the Bone Forest below, the sleeping man came drifting after, and followed him all the way back to Ekamet.

Diana was asleep, of course. Konrad felt little compunction about waking her up. Somebody had to deal with Popov, and he hadn't the time.

'What is it?' Diana muttered grumpily as she arrived to answer the door upon which Konrad had been furiously pounding. Her gaze travelled from his face to the inert form of Vadim Popov hovering three feet off the floor behind him, and her eyes widened. Hurriedly she opened the door, and Konrad ducked inside. Popov drifted after, and the serpents set him down gently on Diana's wood-panelled kitchen floor.

Konrad made her a brief explanation of the circumstances, and she nodded. 'I can take him into care,' she said. 'He'll be under observation until we can... well.'

Help him, cure him, constrain him, figure him out; any of the above, Konrad thought. He nodded. 'See if you can get him to talk. I have a feeling he knows exactly what happened to his daughter, but it pains him too much to speak of it. He'll need some persuasion.'

Diana's brows rose, but she nodded again, drawing her shawl closer around herself against the night's chill. 'Very well. And you? What will you be doing?'

'I'm going to take the opportunity to look around the Popov house,' he replied. 'And in the morning, I'm hoping Nanda or Nuritov will have some news for me.'

He waited, hoping that his casual mention of Nanda's name might prompt Diana to say more about her. But Diana merely smiled with a faint irony that told him she knew exactly what he was doing. 'You'd better ask her,' she said, replying to his unspoken thoughts rather than his statements. 'Not my business.'

Much good that would do him, Nanda being the queen of secrets. He pushed the matter aside, however, and took his leave. It was almost half past four in the morning, and it wouldn't be long before people would begin to stir around the city. He'd have perhaps an hour at most to search the Popov house before the servants began to wake.

He made his way around to the back door of Popov's gloomy city mansion, and let himself in. The sturdy locks turned easily under the cold touch of his fingers; another perk to his job, although not one that he altogether enjoyed using. He thought briefly of Nanda, and smiled at the memory of her enthusiasm for *sneaking*. She only said that because she had never actually done it, of course; the allure was similar to that of pirates and highwaymen and other professions that looked exciting from the outside, and involved a great deal of danger, risk and bleeding from within.

He paused a moment while his serpents streamed ahead of him, scouting the rooms beyond. A scullery maid lay asleep before the kitchen fire; they deepened her sleep, and declared the coast clear otherwise. Konrad stepped inside, and pulled the door gently closed behind him.

Due to the shortness of time, he elected to skip the servants' quarters; he had no reason to believe that any of them were involved. It was Popov's private rooms he most wanted to see. Not the drawing-room; the crows gathered there would certainly raise the alarm, once they saw him. But Popov probably possessed a study, or a private library, or something of the sort.

The serpents found it in short order, and beckoned him over with sibilant excitement. The door was firmly locked, of course, but it, too, yielded to his touch and he slipped inside. Closing the door behind him, he located a single lamp on a table nearby and lit it, blinking in the sudden glow until his eyes adjusted to the light.

Popov's study was a typical gentleman's retreat. It resembled Konrad's in its polished, dark wooden furnishings, large desk, and pristine bookshelves. There, though, the resemblance ended, for in other respects Popov's room was the twin of his hut out in the Bones. The ceiling was crowded with living, ghost-bound crows peering down at him; the walls were decorated with yet more dead, stuffed crow corpses; and the floor was littered with droppings, feathers and one or two inert, black-feathered bodies. Konrad couldn't immediately tell whether these last were stuffed specimens which had fallen from the walls, or whether some of the living birds above had met their end upon the hard floor below.

Konrad tensed, awaiting the inevitable hue and cry from the dark birds above. Nothing happened. They remained silent, unmoving; if he didn't know better, he would take every last one of them for dead and stuffed.

It was unnerving. Their silence was utterly unnatural. What in the name of The Malykt had Popov *done* to them?

The answer came to him all at once. Their unnatural stillness mirrored Popov's, after the serpents had bound him to their will. He had welded dead spirits to living ones over and over again, stuffing them haphazardly inside living bodies and binding them there; this was bad enough, but he had not stopped at binding them to each other. He had bound them all to himself and his own will as well. Konrad's eyes widened, and he stared up at the mass of bodies in utter horror. By The Malykt. The effort it took to control a single *human* soul was enormous; he could never keep it up for long, not even with the help of his familiars. It wasn't just an issue of mental strength, either; to bind a soul in *that* way was to take a part of it into your own mind, for a little while, thereby bringing your will directly to bear upon it. No wonder Popov was showing signs of madness. His head was infested with the rapidly decaying, increasingly deranged spirits of crows, some of them long-dead, all of them desperate to be released and permitted to pass into The Malykt's care.

Had he always known how to do that, or had Konrad and the serpents unwittingly showed him the way? If he'd done this recently, the pressure upon him must be intolerable. What could he possibly mean by it? What did he hope to achieve?

Konrad stood for some time, reeling under such horrific reflections, until he finally recollected himself and shook off the sensation. Diana would be able to help Popov, and there was nothing he could do for the crows just now. But he would not permit them to suffer much longer under such an affliction; he promised himself that.

A noise from some other part of the house urged him to haste, and he began a speedy search of every table, drawer and bookshelf in the room. The books, he noted, were exclusively about the same set of topics: death, spirits and the spirit-realms, The Malykt and His Order, the Malykant (a sensational title, that, Konrad noted with disapproval; something along the lines of an unauthorised, and of course highly speculative, biography of the position) and the art of the ghostspeaker. All of the titles looked new; purchased within the last ten years, he supposed.

In a locked drawer at the bottom of Popov's desk he encountered a pair of portraits — miniatures, like the one he'd found in the Bones. He took the first one from his pocket, and laid all three side-by-side atop the desk, examining them with interest and some confusion. Matching the one from the hut was a second portrait of Dominka, painted, he judged, at around the same time. The third portrait was slightly larger than these two, and depicted a woman perhaps twenty years older. The resemblance between the two was unmistakeable; Dominka's mother, then, Vadim Popov's long-dead wife. Why had he locked them all away?

Konrad had no time to think it over. The house was rousing around him, and he had run out of time. He stuffed all three portraits into the pockets of his coat and fled the house, narrowly avoiding a housemaid on her way to light the fires. He trudged slowly home through the driving rain, too weary and confused to think clearly about his discoveries. Upon reaching Bakar House he went straight to bed, in hopes of catching a few hours of sleep before Nanda or Nuritov could be expected to report.

6

'*Konrad!*' hissed a voice soon afterwards, directly in his ear. Konrad sat bolt upright, bashing his head against that of whoever had woken him, and gave an inarticulate exclamation of pain and confusion.

'Ouch!' continued the voice.

'Nanda?' said Konrad, trying to see in the pitch dark. He could make out only a dim outline of a person standing not far away.

He had a moment's heart-pounding misgiving that it might *not* be Nanda; might, in fact, be someone altogether more threatening; but in the next instant, his deliciously warm duvet was unceremoniously ripped off him and Nanda's voice said very tartly: 'Time to get up! We have a great deal to do!'

Konrad stumbled out of bed, muttering, and lurched towards his dressing room. 'Nan, *what* are you doing in my bedroom?'

'Waking you up.' She was far too horribly wide awake for this hour, wretched woman. 'Dress quickly!' she said crisply, sailing towards the door. 'Much to discuss!'

When he stumbled down the main stairs a few minutes later, still tying his cravat, he found Nanda ensconced in his study with a roaring fire going. That part, at least, he appreciated; the air was appallingly cold in the pre-dawn hours. He went straight to the fire.

'Very well; what's so blasted important?' he grouched.

Nanda shook her head. 'You're horrible in the morning, did you know that?'

Konrad fixed her with a severe look. 'This, my dear Nanda, is *not* the morning.'

'Yes it is. It's past seven.'

Konrad sighed. 'What's the news?'

A waxed cloth bag sat near Nanda's feet. She rummaged within it, producing with a flourish a stack of papers. 'Dominka Popova had a twin sister,' she said without ceremony.

Konrad blinked. 'What? When?'

'When she was born, I imagine,' Nanda said, cocking an eyebrow at him.

Konrad rolled his eyes.

'The girls lived in each other's pockets until they were sixteen, when Ana Popova died of a sudden fever. The family was stricken with grief, and Vadim and Dominka retired from public life altogether for several years. Until recently.'

Konrad thought. 'How old was Dominka when she died?'

'Twenty-five. So, it's a nine-year-old story.'

'That still doesn't explain how all mention of Ana so effectively disappeared.' Konrad's thoughts whirled. In his mind's eye, he saw the two miniatures he'd taken from Popov's various hiding places. Two paintings of Dominka, he had thought, but no: one painting of Dominka and one of Ana. Which was which?

'Vadim Popov was said to be half-mad with grief. If anybody wrote so much as a sentence about Ana after that time, he pursued them through the courts with implacable resentment. It took only a couple of cases of *that* before the papers universally agreed to leave well alone. In fact, they stopped writing about the Popovs altogether until Dominka's re-emergence.'

'Why did she come back?'

'Well, it gets more complicated,' Nanda said. 'Before Ana died, she had been seen to dance more than once with the same gentleman, at the same ball. Showed a very marked preference for him at several events, and it was generally expected that there would be an engagement in due course.'

Konrad's heart sank with foreboding. 'Kanadin?' he guessed.

Nanda nodded. 'The very same.'

Konrad began to pace back and forth as his unease grew. 'So Ana's fiance took up with her sister instead, after many years passed. That isn't so unusual a story in itself; such a thing has happened before. But something about it feels wrong.'

'I'd guess — tentatively, of course — that Kanadin didn't really care for Dominka,' Nanda mused. 'And she probably knew it.'

'All right, but why then did he form the engagement? Was he trying to please someone else — her father, perhaps? Or was he so desperate to retain some form of contact with Ana? Was he marrying Dominka for her face?'

Nanda rustled through her papers. 'There's also the mother,' she said. 'Vadim's wife died when the twins were still children. That was the first time he withdrew from society, until the girls were old enough to be presented.'

What had Popov been doing for all those years? Almost a decade, between the death of his wife and his daughters' presentation to society; and then about the same period of time between Ana's death and Dominka's re-emergence. 'I wonder if that's when he began experimenting with his crows,' Konrad said aloud.

'I reckon so,' Nanda said. Her tone was very grave, and he looked up. 'Konrad,' she continued,' I think there is more to it — worse, much worse. These crows — in Kanadin's mind, Dominka and Ana were all mixed up together, as though they were... almost the same person. He could not think of one without thinking of the other, and the way he felt...'

'Great Spirits above,' Konrad breathed. He thought of Dominka Popova's curious behaviour the night of his ball, when she had sat in this very chair, her mood changing like lightning every few minutes; her contradictory statements, her unsettled attitude. The solution, suddenly, was obvious — and appalling beyond belief.

'Vadim Popov bound his dead daughter's soul into her living sister's body,' he said slowly.

Nanda nodded. 'If he was truly so grief-stricken, perhaps he couldn't bear to lose her.'

'The death of his wife was probably the spur,' Konrad said. 'He spent the next ten years searching for a way to preserve the spirits of the departed — and used it on Ana. But his is a highly imperfect method.' He thought about the decaying crow ghosts in their madness and shivered. 'What must that have done to their *minds*?' he said in horror. Then he sat up, abruptly, as another thought occurred to him. 'Wait — but that means that Kanadin knew?'

'Yes,' Nanda said at once. 'I think he found out, though whether that was before or after Dominka's re-emergence into society, I don't know. Perhaps Ana told him.'

'So he wasn't marrying poor Dominka at all,' Konrad said softly. 'Poor, poor girl. He was marrying her sister after all, trapped as she was in Dominka's body.'

Thinking back, Konrad remembered the strikingly different attitudes he'd observed in Dominka that night. She had vacillated between a bright, cheery outlook and a deeply disheartened demeanour. Which had been Ana and which Dominka? One of them had still hoped; the other had felt nothing but despair.

'That's why the Master couldn't decide,' Konrad sighed. 'The impulse to die came from within the living body, but on this point the twins didn't agree. One wanted to live, the other wanted to die. In the end, the latter prevailed.'

Nanda was looking very sombre. 'Is that murder? I mean, the unutterable horror of it...' she stopped speaking with a shudder.

Konrad sighed deeply, and shrugged. 'Such simplistic labels were not made for matters such as these.'

His mind wandered back to Vadim Popov. Despite the man's appalling actions with regard to his daughters, Konrad couldn't help feeling a twinge of sympathy for him. To lose his wife and one of his twin daughters was bad enough; the knowledge that the death of his only surviving child was his own fault must be so hard to bear. No wonder he had been seeking a way out. What would become of him now?

Konrad and Nanda sat for a few minutes in silence, each lost in their own thoughts. Konrad realised, with a little surprise, that the case was over, and for once he was not obliged to despatch anybody. A refreshing feeling, though he took no joy in it; the circumstances of this particular tragedy were taking their toll upon him anyway. What if Enadya's soul had been bound to his, at the time of her death? For eight years they would have been sharing the same body, trapped and desperate, both equally robbed of a full and independent life; and when the problem of someone like Kanadin was added to that scenario...

As appalling a loss as Enadya's death had been, he would never have chosen that. Neither of them would.

Nanda was eyeing him narrowly, he realised. When he raised a questioning brow at her, she shrugged. 'I think this case has affected you more than might be expected,' she said. 'I've had that feeling a few times.'

Konrad frowned, shifting uncomfortably in his chair. He had thought himself admirably composed, and adeptly hiding the turmoil in his mind. He did not like the idea that Nanda could see through him to that extent.

But she was a Reader, of course. She had probably touched him any number of times in the last few days; as he helped her down from the carriage, as she oh-so-casually handed him his hat or adjusted his cravat. These little attentions were heart-warming, so he permitted them without question. It had not occurred to him that she might have an ulterior motive. He sighed and covered his face with his hands. 'Aren't I a fool.'

He felt Nanda's hand on his knee, and removed his hands again in surprise. She was leaning forward with an expression of real concern on her face; no hint of mockery or teasing. 'Do you want to tell me about her?' she said softly.

Konrad considered that. He sometimes felt that it would be a relief to confide in someone; Enadya and her fate had lived in his mind for so long, burdening him with such a weight of regret and guilt that he could hardly bear it — could not have, perhaps, without The Malykt's assistance. Would it help to share?

But to do so would be to reveal ... too much. He trusted Nanda more than anybody else in the world, but still, their friendship had not been without its complications. He had come close to losing her before, he knew, when her horror at his job and the actions it required had almost overpowered her. If she knew that he was responsible for his own sister's death, he would lose her entirely. There could be no question of it.

So he shook his head, and mustered a smile. 'Perhaps, but not today.'

Nanda nodded and sat back, her expression unreadable.

'Thank you,' Konrad added.

Nanda merely nodded again and watched him. He hated it when she did that: he could guess none of her thoughts, and was left to imagine the worst.

He opened his mouth to say something light-hearted and diverting, thus to diffuse the tension between them; but he was prevented by the sudden appearance of Ootapi in the air above his head. The serpent was agitated, his incorporeal body thrashing and flickering with pale lightning.

*Master!*

His voice in Konrad's mind was more of a hushed scream than a whisper, oddly piercing, and Konrad resisted an urge to clutch at his head.

*The man is gone!*

'The man?' Konrad repeated aloud. 'You don't mean...'

*The man Popov! And he has taken Diana!*

Konrad shot to his feet. 'Stay here,' he ordered Nanda, and made for the door at a run.

'Not on your life!' she said indignantly, and he heard the rustle of her skirts as she came after him. 'You're going to need my help.'

He didn't have time to argue with her. They ran for the front door together, pausing only to grab hastily at coats and hats, and arrived moments later on the quiet, dark, empty street outside Bakar House.

In his mind's eye he saw Vadim Popov with the knife in his hand and the weird light in his eye, on the point of doing himself irreparable harm. In his alarm, he could not think clearly enough to imagine what Popov might want with Diana, but the man was unstable and dangerous and — clearly — capable of extremes.

There was only one place he would have taken her, Konrad surmised.

'No time for the carriage,' Konrad said, grabbing Nanda's hand. 'We're going to have to run for it.'

Nanda knew what that meant. She hung on grimly as Konrad began to run, her fingers laced through his as he squeezed her hand in a bone-creaking grip. His stride lengthened and lengthened again to inhuman proportions and they were all but flying, faster than a horse could gallop, as the ground streamed away beneath Konrad's feet. They reached the city's south gate within minutes and descended into the Bones.

This was harder; no straight, neat streets existed out here to guide Konrad's steps. It took all of his concentration to find a path through the trees that shot unnervingly out of the darkness and the fog, their twisted, bone-white branches threatening with every step to take off his head — or Nanda's. And it was hard, taking someone else along; he was dragging near double his own weight on this break-neck journey, and he could not keep it up for long.

Ootapi soared ahead, and Konrad kept his focus fixed upon the serpent as the creature twisted and dove and wove through the trees. Nanda had the sense to keep close, tucking herself into the shadow of his back, and in time they reached the site of Popov's tree house unscathed.

Konrad paused at the bottom, wishing desperately that he could see into the hut balanced so far above him. *What does Eetapi see?* he enquired of his familiar.

*She is not there,* Ootapi replied. *She is gone.*

*GONE?* Konrad stood still, thunderstruck. *What do you mean?*

*I do not know where she is,* said Ootapi, his agitation seeping into Konrad's brain. *She followed him, but something happened and I can sense nothing of her now.*

Spirits above. Konrad swallowed his burgeoning alarm, pausing only to make a brief explanation to Nanda. 'I can't forbid you to follow me,' he finished. 'You must do as you choose, but please, Nan, take some care. I couldn't live with it if you came to any harm.'

Nanda merely nodded once, and gestured ahead. 'In consideration for which, I will allow you to go first.'

Konrad leapt for the ladder, cursing his binding, inflexible city clothes; he wished, briefly, that he had taken two minutes to change them before he had gone running blindly into the street. He swarmed up it, his ears straining for the sound of voices, or anything that might give him some clue as to the scene that awaited him above. There was nothing but silence.

He emerged, panting, into the hut, distantly aware that Nanda was coming up the ladder behind him. Vadim Popov stood in the centre of the simple room. The man was in a poor state: His rumpled clothes, unwashed hair and dark-shadowed eyes all proclaimed that he had not slept in a long while, and his eyes bore a wildness that made Konrad deeply uneasy. He was wielding a knife in each hand: one long and wicked-looking, the other small and sharp. Crows, living and dead, roosted on every part of his body, swarming in ragged clusters over his shoulders and back and hips and along his arms, sticking out of his pockets, balancing atop his boots.

More of them covered the prone form of Diana Valentina. She lay on the far side of the hut, wearing what appeared to be a nightdress. He could barely see the flimsy white fabric beneath the dark-feathered bodies that crowded over every inch of her, every one of them eerily silent and still. He could see her face, though: oddly expressionless, her muscles slack. Her eyes, though, blazed with fury.

He realised abruptly what the crows were doing there. Popov had set them to bind her will to his own, in a clumsy imitation of Konrad's earlier subjugation of him. He had needed all of his hundreds of crows to do it: Konrad judged that all the birds from his town house were here as well, all trying to work in concert. Even then, the restraint upon Diana was flimsy; her mind was clearly awake, and livid, and fighting for freedom, even if her body was bound. She was strong. It would not take her long to free herself of those bonds.

'I hope you did not harm her,' Konrad said softly.

Vadim looked up in confusion, but his eyes soon cleared when he saw Konrad. 'Oh, it's you,' he said, with a touch of impatience. 'No, I did not harm her. Why would I? I need her.' He sounded calm and perfectly lucid, but the light in his eyes did not fade. He was, Konrad realised, utterly desperate.

Konrad felt an urgent tug at the hem of his coat, which he ignored. Better for Nanda to stay out of this. 'Why do you need her?' he said, his eyes on the knives in Popov's fists. Better for him to talk than... do whatever he intended to do with those.

'She's the Malykant,' Popov said. 'She can help me.'

Konrad's brows rose, and something clicked into place in his mind. Popov's drawing room, and the crows. He was looking for the Malykant; he had sensed something unusual about Konrad, perhaps, and had entertained some suspicion as to his identity. The crows had been a test — one Konrad had unwittingly passed by offering no reaction to them whatsoever.

'And what are you hoping the Malykant can do for you?' Konrad asked, puzzled. The Malykant was the stuff of nightmares, a figure who only appeared in order to avenge. Nobody ever *wanted* to see him.

Popov dropped the larger knife and caught up a crow instead, his grip on the poor creature gentle but firm. 'The Malykant is the greatest ghostspeaker living,' he said, with a touch of scorn in his voice — or was it envy? His mouth twisted with something — revulsion, despair, Konrad could not tell. 'If I join my soul with these birds, I shall not die; I shall be free. But I cannot do it alone. For all my efforts, all my attempts, I cannot find out how to do it alone...'

'Your attempts?' Konrad repeated. 'Your daughter, Ana? What

was she, an experiment?'

Popov's face dissolved into anguish, and his whole body shuddered with pain. 'She was no experiment!' he cried. 'I could not bear to lose her; not my Ana! Not after Ameline!'

Ameline was his wife, Konrad supposed. The pain Popov felt was real, but he could not muster much sympathy. Dominka's face filled his thoughts. 'So you condemned both your daughters to the most appalling fate — took both their lives from them, condemned them to eventual suicide —'

'No!' Popov shouted, his eyes blazing. 'Dominka agreed to it. She was willing. So was my Ana, I am sure.'

Konrad shook his head. He was growing angry; he could feel rage simmering near his heart, swelling to unspeakable proportions and wiping away all rational thought. 'How could she have done otherwise, grief-stricken as she undoubtedly was?' he demanded, his voice shaking with rage. 'She could not have known what it would mean — how the years would eat away at them both, sowing madness and despair and —'

He broke off as Nanda unceremoniously shoved him aside on her way through the trapdoor, and he stumbled. 'Good heavens, Konrad, you really are making a terrible mess of this,' she said crossly as she shook out her skirts. 'You had better let me deal with it.'

Konrad could only blink at her in surprise, his anger dissipating in confusion. 'What? B-but—'

'It is obvious that you are somewhat *addled* with regards to this case,' she said, casting him a look of cool contempt. 'Pray stand in the corner and keep quiet. If we need you, we will let you know.' Her gaze turned to Diana, who smiled and stood up at once, shaking the crows from her arms and legs.

'Hello, dear,' said Diana, with a warm smile for Nanda. 'Thank you for that. It's been a long while since I was last caught by any kind of binding.' Her mouth twisted with distaste, and she added, with a brief glance at Popov, 'However inept.'

Nanda smiled briefly, then turned a level gaze upon Popov. Konrad she ignored entirely. 'You are sorry now, are you not?' she said gravely.

Popov had been looking back and forth between Konrad, Nanda and Diana, his face registering all the confusion that Konrad felt. 'What's going on?' he demanded. 'Who are you? And who is *he*, and how is she awake?'

'Ah, well, introductions will take but a moment,' Nanda said with a charming smile. 'That nice lady you kidnapped is Diana Valentina, head of the Order of The Malykt. The raging gentleman is Konrad Savast, the Malykant. And I am —'

'The *Malykant?*' Popov interrupted. His gaze travelled from Diana to Konrad and back again in obvious frustration, but then his face cleared. 'One of you will assist me. You must.'

'They cannot,' Nanda said gently. 'What you ask is a violation of the natural order of things, you see. You must realise that. They cannot, in obedience to their Master's edicts, permit it.'

Popov lunged at her, knife in hand; but if his goal was to compel obedience by threatening Nanda, he was to be disappointed. Nanda dodged his attack with the greatest of ease; her hand shot out; she gripped his neck hard, and the man's body began to shake so violently that he dropped both the crow and the knife. He hung in her grip, helpless and afraid. Konrad could only stare. What manner of Nanda was this?

'That was unfriendly,' Nan chided him. 'And unnecessary. I can now see that you *are* sorry, and remorseful, and absolutely petrified. Am I not right?'

Popov shook in silence for several moments, his face a mask of stubborn resentment and rage. Gradually, though, his expression turned to sorrow and then stark terror, and tears ran down his face. 'It was not meant to be that way,' he sobbed. 'I thought it was better than death...'

Diana had sidled around the room unnoticed, collecting up all of Popov's knives. She deposited them now in the corner of the room behind Konrad, and gave him a brief, grim nod. 'Guard those,' she instructed, 'and don't interfere.'

'But—' Konrad began.

'Just be quiet.'

'They asked you to undo it, did they not?' Nanda said, her tone gentle but firm.

Popov moaned something inaudible, and Nanda shook him. 'Answer me properly, there's a good man,' she said sternly.

'They asked me,' Popov said, shuddering. 'Dominka started going to balls again — I begged her not to, but she insisted. She said it was like waking up after a long sleep, or an illness. She wanted to marry

Kanadin, and—'

'*Dominka* wanted to marry Kanadin?' Nanda repeated.

'Yes,' Popov said sombrely. 'She believed that he loved her. But it was only Ana he wanted, and I couldn't allow it.' Popov's voice was growing hoarse and strained under the force of Nanda's grip, but she did not release the pressure of her fingers.

'When did she find out?' Nanda demanded.

'A month ago,' Popov whispered.

Konrad sighed. Kanadin had sought an engagement with Dominka because he knew she carried Ana within her, but Dominka had thought he courted her for her own sake. Had the sisters quarrelled? Had Dominka grown to despise her passenger? And what of Ana? Had she been aware that Kanadin knew, and hidden it from her sister? Konrad wanted to ask, but between Diana's terse commands and Nanda's quelling stares, he dared not interfere.

'Was it you who told Mr. Kanadin?' Nanda was saying. 'About Ana?'

Popov gasped an assent. 'He was heart-broken,' he whispered. 'Years later, it had not faded. I thought to comfort him.'

Nanda shook her head. 'It is remarkable how much damage a single man may do,' she mused.

'I meant no harm!' Popov gasped.

'I know,' Nanda said coolly. 'And yet, you destroyed three lives.'

Popov's sobs grew uncontrollable, and he hung there in Nanda's grip like a discarded puppet, his face red and swollen and awash with tears. Konrad looked away.

'Do not let me die,' he begged. 'The Malykt! Do you know what He will do to me?!'

'I can imagine,' said Nan, without a trace of sympathy in her tone. 'Perhaps you deserve such a fate.'

Popov shuddered violently. 'No, no, no,' he begged. 'Please. You must let me finish my work. One of these people must help me. You must—'

'I must do nothing of the kind,' Nan said sharply. 'They will not be helping you, but I might be able to.' She smiled suddenly. 'If you are a good soul and do not anger me too much.'

Popov twisted in her grip until he could look into her face. His tears continued to flow unheeded, but his voice was steady as he said: 'Who *are* you?'

Nanda smiled. 'That's true: you interrupted me before I had chance to introduce myself. I am Irinanda Falenia, Third Servant of the Shandrigal.'

Konrad gaped. The *Shandrigal?* Nanda served the Shandrigal? He opened his mouth to spurt out a dozen questions at once, but Nanda glared at him and he subsided.

The Shandrigal. High Spirit of... well, a number of things. Some called it "life", which was simplistic in the extreme but as good a term as any. The Shandrigal was to the living what The Malykt was to the dead. Somehow, Konrad felt, he ought to have realised that Nanda counted herself among that being's followers. How could he have been so dense? Or Nan so secretive?

He struggled to bring his wayward mind back to the matter at hand. Popov was begging again. 'Please,' he said, 'if you will intercede on my behalf...'

'I know you are sorry,' Nanda said sternly, 'as I can feel it in you. I am a Reader, you know. But you must admit it to yourself. Say it aloud.'

It took Popov a long time to muster the necessary courage, but he did so at last. 'I should never have done it,' he said slowly. 'To my poor Ana — my poor Dominka. I sought to save them both, from death and grief and misery, but instead I condemned them to all three.' He took a deep, shuddering breath. 'I sought to share their fate, as fitting punishment, and thus to avoid the wrath of The Malykt as well.'

Nanda surveyed him thoughtfully, her manner eerily calm. 'We will see what my Mistress has to say,' she decided.

There was no warning at all. The next instant, the tiny hut above the Bones was full to bursting with a *Presence*. It was not like The Malykt, at all; Konrad was spared the gut-clenching, icy terror that he felt in the presence of his own Master. But nor was it pleasant. He felt an intense, almost unbearable pressure upon him, as though his every waking thought and every one of his actions were suddenly laid bare to inspection — and judgement. He could barely breathe, and he began to sweat profusely.

*An interesting case,* said The Shandrigal, and that voice went through Konrad's insides like a knife.

'Madam,' Nanda said, and curtseyed, heedless of Popov's limp body dangling from her upraised arm.

*Does this man have your approval?* the Shandrigal questioned.

Nanda thought for a moment, her gaze upon Popov grave. 'He does,' she said at last.

There was silence for some time. Konrad fought an urgent desire to escape; to fall down the ladder to the floor, if necessary, and run far away, before The Shandrigal's weighty attention could be turned upon him. At length, the Great Spirit spoke again.

*I accept him as one of my own. He has dabbled freely in death; I shall now expect the opposite. Once he has saved ten times as many lives as he destroyed, I shall consider his penance paid.*

Konrad's eyes were fixed upon Nanda throughout this speech. He noticed a tiny, almost imperceptible easing of the tension in her face and shoulders at her Mistress's pronouncement. She had not been as confident as she had appeared, then; interesting.

'B-but, The Malykt,' babbled Popov.

*The Malykt will not interfere,* said The Shandrigal sternly.

Popov merely quivered.

*You may release him, Shandral,* the voice added.

Nanda did so, and Popov collapsed into a boneless heap upon the floor. Then he disappeared, and all his crows vanished along with him.

No one spoke for some moments. Konrad's mind was whirling too fast for him to form any coherent sentence, and Nanda looked tired. Diana went to her and gripped her hand with unspoken solicitude; she earned herself a grateful smile.

'Excuse me,' Nanda said softly. 'I'll be needed at the temple. Popov will require some help with settling in.'

Konrad moved away from the ladder. He could think of nothing to say, and merely watched as his best friend descended through the trapdoor and disappeared from sight. She did not catch his eye.

'Well,' said Diana with a sigh. 'That was dramatic.' She looked at Konrad, her head tilted curiously. 'You truly didn't know?'

Konrad shrugged. 'She never told me.'

'Hmm.' Diana smiled at him. 'I daresay there's a reason for that. You should ask her.'

Konrad nodded mutely. Whatever he might have said next was lost forever as a ghostly presence suddenly materialised before his eyes and whirled in seven rapid circles around his head, making him dizzy.

*Master!* screamed Eetapi joyfully. *I am freeeee.*

*Eetapi!* he replied in relief. *What became of you?*

*Those crows!* she hissed in great indignation. *They mobbed me! All of them! And they stuffed me into a teapot! AND they made me stay there!*

*A... a teapot?* Konrad looked around, and at last located a crude clay teapot lying under the table in the corner.

*A teapot!* Eetapi repeated. *Who puts a snake in a teapot, I ask you? It is intolerably rude. Utterly insufferable. I shall never speak to a crow again, as long as I live.*

*You are not living,* Konrad reminded her. *I do not know whether that will make it a very short, or an extremely long, ban.*

Eetapi flicked her tail in patent disgust, and soared out of the window. Ootapi followed, and since Diana made her farewells moments later and departed as well, he was left alone in Popov's treehouse.

It looked empty and stark without its complement of crows; as bleak as Konrad felt. Nanda had been right: the case had been hard on him, and in the wake of it he was left feeling... tired. Old. Disheartened.

He would come back here just once more, he decided, to place the miniatures of Popov's family back where they belonged. If Vadim Popov ever chose to return, he would find them waiting for him.

Konrad pulled back the long sleeves of his coat and shirt and stared sadly at the locket that dangled from a golden chain around his wrist. He opened it, with some difficulty; the hinges had grown stiff with disuse. The face inside stared back at him, a smile on her pretty, swarthy face, her black hair cheerfully disordered and her dark eyes sparkling. If only, he thought, it were possible to reverse some of the great injustices of the world. If only Dominka could be brought back; if only Ana's poor soul had not been chained to hers; if only Enadya had not died.

With a sigh, he closed the locket on Ena's beloved face and hid it once more inside his sleeves. He took the ladder slowly, feeling unaccountably weary as he eased his way back down to the forest floor.

He could not return to Bakar House just yet, he felt. He required a period of quiet, and rest, and reflection before he could return to that social world.

Rain poured from the skies as he turned his steps in the direction of his hut-on-stilts. He had no hat, and his coat was barely waterproof, but the cold water seeping through his clothes felt fitting as he trudged, alone, into the Bones.

# EPILOGUE

Konrad had been lying on the cold floor of his Bone Forest hut for some hours before he heard the first sounds of approach. Someone was coming up the ladder below.

It could be anybody, he distantly realised; his hut was perfectly visible, and perhaps he might have been followed by somebody who intended him harm. He hoped it was Nanda, but could by no means be certain of it.

He did nothing in response to these unpromising prospects save to ensure that his legs were not covering the trapdoor.

A few moments later the door swung open and Nanda's head appeared, clad in an oiled rain hat. She stared in surprise at Konrad's unexpectedly prone form splayed across the floor in front of her.

'Konrad?' she enquired. 'I do hope you are still breathing.'

Konrad made no reply save to draw a large lungful of air into his chest, trusting that she would notice the rise and fall of his torso.

'Hmm,' she said as she climbed the rest of the way into the room and shut the trapdoor. She had put aside the neat, fine gowns she wore in the city and had donned instead layers of thick cotton and wool in dark colours. A large waxed coat covered much of it, though this she soon discarded onto the floor, along with her hat. She stood looking down at him for a moment, her hands on her hips.

Konrad closed his eyes.

He opened them again soon afterwards as he felt some small creature crawling up his leg. It was the little golden-haired monkey. Weveroth made his slow way up Konrad's chest, over his throat and

313

finally sat upon his head, his tail dangling into Konrad's face. He paused there and began, very casually, to lick his paws.

Konrad couldn't help smiling, just a little bit. 'Hello, Wevey,' he said.

'That's very fine,' returned Nanda tartly. 'A greeting for the beastie, but none for me? I like that.'

Konrad's smile widened. 'Hello, Nan,' he added dutifully.

Nanda smiled down upon him. Instead of hauling him to his feet, as he might have expected, she joined him on the floor, laid herself prone alongside him and dragged him ruthlessly into a crushing embrace. Weveroth bore this adjustment in Konrad's posture with fortitude, merely moving to recline upon the back of his head.

'Right, then. Out with it,' Nanda said sternly.

Konrad groaned. 'I have nothing to share, I assure you.'

Nan made a disgusted noise. 'It is cold down here,' she said, 'and I do not intend to have to lie here all night waiting for you to get on with it.'

Konrad said nothing.

'Secrets are dangerous things, you know,' she said softly. 'They'll eat you up, if you let them.'

'Coming from you, that is a piece of the grossest hypocrisy,' Konrad replied.

He felt her grin. 'I was planning to tell you,' she said with perfect serenity.

'When?'

'Someday. But you will talk to me today.'

'Perhaps you already know the story, Miss Shandral.'

'Which story is that?'

'How... how I became the Malykant.'

'Your exploits are not so famous as all that,' Nan replied severely, but she squished him a little harder as she said it.

Konrad sighed. It took him a long time to summon the words, but at last he managed to say, very quietly: 'I killed someone.'

Nanda nodded. 'That is the usual way of it, I believe.'

Konrad blinked. 'What? Really?'

'Never mind; carry on.'

Another long sigh followed, and Konrad managed to add: 'Two people, in fact.'

'Who were they?'

'I have no idea,' Konrad said bleakly. 'I never knew their names.'

Nanda said nothing else, only waited.

'I had a sister once,' Konrad said, at length. 'Enadya. Almost ten years my junior, and our mother died when she was but five years old. Our father died long before, so it fell to me to raise her. I was only a boy myself at that time, and I wasn't... well, but. She grew into a stout girl, and then into a fine young woman.'

'You must have been proud of her,' Nanda murmured.

Konrad nodded, hesitating. The next part was the hardest to relate, and the words threatened to stick around the lump in his throat. But he tangled his fingers in Nanda's hair, took a deep breath, and continued. 'We were honest, for the most part. We took work wherever I could find it, anything anyone would give us; mending, sewing, cleaning, building. But sometimes... if it came down to thieve or starve, then of course we thieved. We had to move around a lot.'

Nanda hazarded no comment, but she nodded coolly enough: no condemnation yet, then.

'We were careful, of course, but one day I... went too far. I stole a bolt of cloth from the market. Ena hadn't had a new dress in so long, you see; I'd tried for months to save enough for it but there was always something else that had to be paid for.' The lump in his throat grew bigger, and he couldn't swallow it down. 'Ena was not pleased, though I could tell that she liked the cloth. She wanted me to take it back, but of course I could not. I'd had a difficult enough time getting out of the market without being caught; one of the traders saw me, you see, and I was pursued. I thought I had got away cleanly, but... well, the next day I received a job which took me away from Ena for some hours. They had found out who I was, I suppose, and discovered our home. When I returned that evening...'

His voice trailed off, and he needed all the comfort Nanda could offer to go on. 'I don't know, to this day, exactly what happened,' he said hoarsely. 'I think, probably, they did not mean to kill her; only she was a very pretty woman, and alone...' His mind recalled, in horrific clarity, everything he had seen when he had arrived home that night: their little one-room house in a state of chaos, and Ena's poor inert body lying near the wall, her skirts ripped and livid bruises darkening her face and her throat. Why could he never *forget*, he thought savagely. He forgot so many things every day; inconsequential things, sometimes important things, but never *this*.

He could not describe those scenes to Nanda; his throat closed at the merest attempt. 'I found them very quickly,' he said. 'Perhaps if they had not been so well-known in the town; if I hadn't remembered their faces from the market... but I did, and when I came upon them I was at least half mad with grief. They were dead before I was even aware of my intent, and I fled.' He sighed. 'I went home, and sat with Ena's body until the Malykant found me. It did not take her very long, either.'

Nanda blinked at that. 'Her?' she said with interest.

The faintest of smiles crossed Konrad's face, and he nodded. 'The one before me was female. Does that interest you?'

'A bit,' Nanda said, with an answering smile. 'But carry on.'

'There isn't much more to be said,' Konrad replied. 'I was given a choice: I could accept the Malykt's justice on the spot, or I could take on the role of Malykant myself. She was ready to retire, you see, and had been looking for a suitable replacement for some time.' His mouth twisted with distaste. 'I suppose I had proved myself ideal: I was capable of killing, but not in cold blood, and only under extreme provocation. And what I had done, I suppose, was an unsanctioned, ill-advised, vigilante-style version of The Malykt's justice anyway.'

'And you accepted?' Nanda said with some surprise.

'It did not seem like much of a choice at the time,' Konrad said faintly. 'Besides, I-I was appalled by what I had done, and everything that had happened... I felt that I owed something, and that I was owed something as well. Perhaps everything would someday be settled, if I became the Malykant.'

'How long ago was this?'

'Eight years.' Konrad was silent for some time. 'And no, nothing has been settled. Nor will it ever be, I am now certain.'

Nanda sighed, and rested her head on his shoulder. 'You're not responsible, you know. For Ena.'

Konrad's mouth tightened on an angry retort, his stomach twisting with an echo of agony. 'I am,' he managed to say calmly. 'It was my unnecessary thieving that brought such a fate upon her, and if I had not left her alone!'

'You were trying to provide for her,' Nanda said mildly. 'Ineptly, I admit, but it was well meant. You did not kill her.'

'But I did kill her murderers,' he reminded her.

Nanda said nothing.

316

'If I had turned out to be a capable killer, I thought I might as well do something productive with it,' Konrad said bitterly.

Nanda sighed softly, and said nothing; but nor did she recoil from him. She remained relaxed in his arms, and he began to feel a little soothed by her warmth. Weveroth, having apparently completed his ablutions, curled up in the curve of Konrad's neck and shoulder; Konrad appreciated that little warm presence, too.

'The Shandrigal sent me to you,' Nanda said at last.

Konrad blinked. 'What... what do you mean?'

'The Malykant is an unusual role,' Nanda said with a faint smile against his neck. 'Nobody takes it on entirely willingly, and there is always some manner of tragedy behind it. So said my Mistress, at any rate; you're the only one I have ever known. She said that for the Malykant to become isolated is the easiest thing in the world, and also the most dangerous; and it is something The Malykt never thinks of. So she sent me to you, and has kept me by your side these past few years.'

Konrad digested that. 'So we did not meet by accident?' he said at last.

Nanda shook her head.

'And... and when you almost abandoned me, you came back because?'

'Because I was made to. Yes.' Nanda said nothing for a while, giving Konrad plenty of time to appreciate the new hollow feeling in his stomach. 'But I would have come back anyway,' she said at last, 'in the end.'

'You're sure about that, are you?' Konrad muttered.

She smiled. 'Yes. My faith was shaken a little, I admit, but I know you too well to allow that to wholly overcome me. You aren't a killer, Konrad; not really. You take no real pleasure in the terrible business of meting out justice; only in granting a succession of vile murderers their just reward. And I think that, every time you do it, you're striking another blow for Ena. Aren't you?'

Konrad's eyes filled with tears, and he could only nod once in reply.

Nanda tightened her arms around him. 'I shan't leave you again,' she said softly. 'And I'll keep no more secrets from you, if you'll keep none from me.'

The tears spilled over, and Konrad managed only an inelegant sniff in response. He was rewarded with a soft laugh, and Nanda called him a number of unflattering names as she wiped his face clean with the edge of her shawl. She said them all affectionately, though, so it was all right.

'Do you mind very much?' Nanda said at last.

Konrad thought about that. 'A little,' he admitted. 'But not very much. If The Shandrigal is the reason why I am blessed with you, then I should be sending Her a profuse note of thanks, together with a great many offerings.'

Nanda laughed. 'I hope you will,' she said. 'The Mistress was a mite displeased with me for neglecting you; you might restore my credit a little.'

Konrad smiled too. 'Then I shall,' he promised. After a while, he added, 'Shall we get up? I suppose it is a little draughty down here.'

'No,' Nanda said firmly. 'I've since realised that it's actually very comfortable.'

'And it would be rude indeed to disturb Wevey,' he added.

'Oh, quite,' Nanda agreed with a smile. 'Let him sleep.'

There was silence for a time — peaceful, restful silence, and Konrad began, at last, to relax.

'I've been... feeling,' he said abruptly.

Nanda nodded. 'I know.'

She was seeing it now, he supposed, though her contact with him; she must be fully aware of the tumult going on in his body and mind.

'The Shandrigal never approved of what The Malykt had done to you,' she said softly. 'My Mistress did not think it right — or helpful. She believed that you must learn to live with, and manage your emotions; not just lock them away. They would grow all the more powerful, unbearable and unstoppable for it.'

Konrad merely nodded. The way he felt at this moment proved every word to be true. 'So... The Shandrigal did this?'

'I don't know,' Nanda admitted. 'But I think it possible.'

Konrad thought about that for a while. 'Do you think The Malykt will undo it again?'

'I think He should not,' Nan said decisively. 'My Mistress is right.'

'But...' Konrad whispered. 'It *hurts*.'

'Yes. But you can bear it.'

Konrad closed his eyes, and tightened his lips on a number of possible responses.

'I'll help you,' Nanda added. 'I'll be here.'

Konrad clutched her a little closer by way of reply, unable to speak. She seemed to require no particular response, however, and lay contentedly for some time.

At length, Nanda spoke again.

'Konrad,' she murmured.

'Mm.'

'Who was the previous Malykant?'

Konrad laughed aloud at this sudden attack. 'I can't tell you that, Nan.'

'Please?'

'No.'

# Also by Charlotte E. English:

## The Malykant Mysteries:
Death's Detective (Volume 1)
Death's Avenger (Volume 2)

## Modern Magick:
The Road to Farringale
Toil and Trouble
The Striding Spire
The Fifth Britain
Royalty and Ruin
Music and Misadventure
The Wonders of Vale
The Heart of Hyndorin

## The Wonder Tales:
Faerie Fruit
Gloaming
Sands and Starlight

Made in the USA
Middletown, DE
05 February 2020